Secret Betrayal

by

C. B. Clark

Secret Betrayal

Cover Art by *Debbie Taylor*

The Wild Rose Press, Inc.
PO Box 708
Adams Basin, NY 14410-0708
Visit us at www.thewildrosepress.com

Publishing History
First Crimson Rose Edition, 2019
Print ISBN 978-1-5092-2621-4
Digital ISBN 978-1-5092-2622-1

Published in the United States of America

Something was wrong. Something was very wrong.

Faint wisps of light seeped around the edges of the window curtains. The distant sound of traffic echoed through the glass. A lamp imbued the room with a soft, rosy glow, revealing a king-size bed. The cover on the bed was a glossy, garish pink, the pillows covered in the same lurid color, their edges trimmed with frilly, black lace.

She rubbed the back of her neck and closed her eyes, but when she opened them again she was still in the unfamiliar room. A battered desk with a large, flat-screen television on top faced the bed. The flickering images of a naked, full-breasted woman being entertained by two equally naked men played across the screen.

A wingback chair covered in faded black leatherette sat in the far corner where a door was ajar, revealing the yellowed linoleum floor of a bathroom and the edge of a chipped porcelain sink. A framed diagram of a fire escape route was posted on the back of the other door.

Was she in a hotel room? She dug her fingers into her temples. Why couldn't she remember?

Dedication

To my mother, Joan Guldner—
a Friday girl in a Monday world. Miss you, Mom.

Chapter 1

The floor heaved, and faded blue carpeting undulated like ocean swells beneath Marissa Reynold's cheek. Waves of nausea surged through her. She squeezed her eyes shut. *Breathe, Marissa. In through the nose, out through the mouth.* But breathing hurt. Her throat was raw like she'd swallowed a gallon of sand, and a brackish chemical taste furred her tongue. Her mouth was dry, her lips cracked and sore.

She opened her eyes again. Her vision wavered, and her temples pounded, but she managed to lift her head a few inches. The notion she'd somehow shipwrecked on a desert island faded against the reality of her surroundings. She was lying on the floor in a dimly lit room. It was a bedroom, maybe, but not her own. She wrinkled her nose at the musty reek oozing from the worn carpet.

She pushed to her hands and knees. The pounding in her brain mushroomed into a full-blown, jackhammer assault. With a moan, she sank onto her bottom and grabbed her head in a fruitless effort to keep her brain from exploding. Despite the pain, she needed to get up. Something was wrong. Something was very wrong.

Faint wisps of light seeped around the edges of the window curtains. The distant sound of traffic echoed through the glass. A lamp imbued the room with a soft, rosy glow, revealing a king-size bed. The cover on the bed was a glossy, garish pink, the pillows covered in the same lurid color, their edges trimmed with frilly, black lace.

She rubbed the back of her neck and closed her eyes, but when she opened them again she was still in the unfamiliar room. A battered desk with a large, flat-screen television on top faced the bed. The flickering images of a naked, full-breasted woman being entertained by two equally naked men played across the screen.

A wingback chair covered in faded black leatherette sat in the far corner where a door was ajar, revealing the yellowed linoleum floor of a bathroom and the edge of a chipped porcelain sink. A framed diagram of a fire escape route was posted on the back of the other door.

Was she in a hotel room? She dug her fingers into her temples. Why couldn't she remember?

Fake moans of pleasure emanated from the television, adding to her sense of unreality. The last thing she remembered was putting on her coat and saying good night to Joseph, the library's night security guard, and walking toward her car in the faculty parking lot.

Wisps of memories swirled through her aching brain...a horn honking, a distant siren, the swish of tires on wet roads, the beaded drops on the hoods of the parked cars, the earthy, sweet smell, the wet plops of heavy raindrops...rough hands grabbing, hurting, the overpowering stench of garlic and strong tobacco, disabling fear...Her heart hammered in her chest, and the disturbing images vanished.

She inhaled a ragged breath and pushed to her feet.

Something terrible had happened. But what? Was she still in Brunswick? Still in Oregon?

The door swung open, and a tall, lean man wearing a red baseball cap and dark sunglasses stood framed in the doorway, a white plastic hotel room key card in his hand. A deep furrow formed between his brows, and he scowled. "What are you doing in my room? Where's McGregor?" Stepping into the room, he slammed the door. He removed his sunglasses and stuffed them in his coat pocket. His navy eyes blazed.

Her heart stuttered, and the remaining moisture in her mouth evaporated. She opened her mouth to speak, but her tongue was too thick.

He strode toward her. "I asked you a question, lady. What are you doing here?"

She blinked and moistened her lips. "I…I…"

His lip curled. "Ah, forget it. I don't care what sorry story they told you. Just get the hell out."

The room spun, black spots filled her vision, her legs wobbled, and she folded, falling.

"What the heck?" He sprang forward and scooped her in his arms, lifting her as if she weighed nothing, and carried her to the bed.

She leaned her head against his broad chest, inhaling the scents of soap and fresh, damp air. His heart thudded beneath her ear, the strong, steady beat comforting.

He laid her on the bed, and she shivered, missing his body's warmth. She stared at him. Short, dark-blond hair, strong cheekbones, square jaw, and those unusual navy-blue eyes framed by long, dark eyelashes. He looked familiar. "Do…do I know you?" Had she met him somewhere before? A frisson of unease climbed her spine. Had he kidnapped her and dragged her to his room? Was she in danger? She fought the fog numbing her brain. "What's going on? Why am I here?"

His lips curled in a semblance of a smile, transforming him from good-looking to all-out gorgeous. "I don't know what drugs you're on, lady, but you should quit." He studied his wristwatch. "Look, I'm expecting someone any minute, and you can't be here. If you're feeling better, I'd like you to leave."

"But—"

"Okay, okay. I get it. You're a working girl." He fished in the front pocket of his faded jeans and dug out a leather wallet. "How much did they promise to pay you?" He tossed several bills on the bed. "That should cover it." Raking her with a scathing gaze, he shook his head. "No offense, lady, but if you wanted this little seduction to work, you could have worn something sexier."

She struggled to rise, but the sagging mattress held her like she was mired in quicksand. "You've got the wrong idea. I...I..." The room wavered as once again her vision faded in and out. She collapsed back on the bed, her world narrowing to swirling blackness.

****

Scott Bannister studied the woman lying on the bed.

Her long, dark hair fanned around her pale face, a stark contrast to the pink pillow. The dark circles beneath her eyes resembled bruises. His gut pinged, and he peered closer. He'd seen her before. But where? Not at work. His office didn't handle prosecuting prostitutes.

He scrubbed his hand over his chin, the rasp of

stubble loud in the oppressive silence of the small room, broken by the heavy breathing and moaning coming from the porn flick showing on the television. The shabby furniture, dim lighting, TV tuned to a porn channel, and oversized bed indicated the room rented by the hour for the sole purpose of illicit sex.

She wasn't the usual prostitute who paraded her wares on the street outside this dingy little hotel. Her clothes were too modest, and she was too pretty. The navy-blue wool skirt brushed her knees, and her white silk blouse was buttoned to the top, exposing not even a hint of cleavage. Her face was bare of makeup. She looked like a schoolteacher, not a lady of the night.

He rolled up the sleeve of her blouse. No needle tracks. He checked the other arm. No marks there, either. But she was on something. That was for sure. The brief glimpse he'd gotten of her eyes before she passed out revealed pupils the size of quarters.

He studied the rise and fall of her chest beneath the prim, white blouse. *Nice breasts. Very nice breasts.* He squashed the thought. *Not the time, buddy. Definitely not the time.*

Her breathing appeared normal, yet she'd passed out. What if she needed medical attention? What if she OD'd? He should call an ambulance.

He tightened his jaw. If he called for help, the paramedics would arrive, followed by a pack of voracious reporters vying with each other for the front-page photo of the city's new Assistant District Attorney, Scott Bannister, caught in flagrante delicto with a hooker in a sleaze-bag hotel.

He glared at the unconscious woman. Time was ticking. What should he do about her? He couldn't toss her out on the street in the condition she was in. But he couldn't leave her here, either. He checked his watch and ground his back molars. McGregor was late. Very late. His gut tightened. This was a setup. He should have known. Everything—McGregor's desperate plea for a secret, late-night meeting in this fleabag hotel, the drugged girl—all carefully planned.

When his assistant, Jonas, had informed him Flinty McGregor was on the phone, the hairs on the back of Scott's neck had prickled a warning. But like a dupe, he hadn't been able to resist the possibility his gut instinct was wrong, and he'd taken the call.

Scott and his team of investigators had tried for six months to find damning evidence of the alleged illegal dealings of the DeGrazzi mob. The gang members were too smart, their bonds of loyalty too tight, or their fear of Old Man DeGrazzi too real. Whatever the reason, he hadn't been able to crack the wall of silence surrounding DeGrazzi.

Until now.

Until McGregor, a longtime member of the Degrazzi organization, had called Scott's office, insisting on meeting with him and only him. McGregor had insider information on the DeGrazzi mob, and he wanted to talk.

Arranging a clandestine meeting with a career criminal was against department policy. If anyone found out, Scott would be canned. But McGregor refused to come to the office, and the covert meeting was worth the risk. If Flinty gave up the goods on DeGrazzi, no one would care Scott had bent the rules. He'd come out of this smelling like a rose.

Tugging the cap off his head, he sent it sailing

across the room where it landed on a chair in the corner. He scrubbed his fingers through his hair. McGregor wasn't coming. He should have known. No two-bit hood would spill mob secrets to the District Attorney's office. Doing so guaranteed a death sentence. But instead of listening to his gut, Scott had agreed to meet McGregor.

He hadn't even balked when the thug suggested they meet at the Condor Hotel, an out-of-the-way dive on the east side of town. As far as he knew, only bedbugs, cockroaches, and hookers frequented the shabby hotel.

But Scott was desperate. He'd do anything to take down DeGrazzi. Anything. Besides, this was his chance to prove himself, to show the people who'd voted for him he deserved the title of Assistant District Attorney for the city of Brunswick, Oregon.

He knew full well the reason he'd won the election was because a week before the vote, the other candidate had been charged with assault and battery after he'd beaten the crap out of a guy in a bad case of road rage.

Scott was determined to show everyone he could make a difference. Being caught in a sleaze-bag motel with an unconscious, hopped-up hooker wouldn't help his career goals. The people of Brunswick held their elected officials to a higher standard. Consorting with prostitutes didn't fit that mold.

Julio DeGrazzi had set the trap, baited it with the irresistible morsel of insider intel, and Scott had marched right in like a sucker. The old man must be laughing in his beard. Scott checked his watch again. DeGrazzi had to know he'd sprung the trap. More trouble was on the way.

The girl on the bed moaned and thrashed as if in the throes of a nightmare. Her restless movements shortened her skirt, and as the dark blue fabric rose, he caught an enticing glimpse of pale, slim thighs.

He gulped. He'd better get the hell out of there before he did something even more stupid than entering the room. But he couldn't just leave her. He dug in his jeans pocket, tugged out his cell phone, and punched in his assistant's number.

"Who are you? What do you want with me?"

Scott jerked his head up at the sound of the husky, feminine voice. He ended the call before it rang through.

The woman's eyes were open, her pupils unnaturally large. Sitting up, she grimaced as if in pain and swiped a lock of silky-looking dark hair off her forehead. She tugged down her skirt and drew her knees to her chest. "Don't...don't hurt me, please." Fear dulled her eyes, turning them a smoky gray.

He frowned. Why was she so frightened? Was she hallucinating in her drug-induced high? "Time to go, Sleeping Beauty." He waved his hand at the pink-covered bed. "I don't know what they told you, but I didn't request your services, and I'm not interested in what you're selling." Well, part of what he said was true. He certainly hadn't called her.

She cowered and covered her head with her arms. "Please, don't hurt me."

Another twinge of unease rippled low in his belly. "Come on, lady. Don't play games. You had your little *nap*"—he nodded at the dollar bills on the bed—"and I've paid you for your time, so you might as well call it a night and leave."

She didn't budge. "What's going on? Why am I here? Why won't you tell me?"

Why wouldn't the damn woman take her money and scram? What was she waiting for? More money? He yanked out his wallet again and fished inside for more cash. Good thing he'd stopped at the ATM on his way here. He'd thought he might have to pay McGregor for his secrets.

"I don't want your money." She swung her feet off the bed and stood. Her face paled, and she wobbled.

He lunged and grabbed her forearms, holding her upright. "Hey, take it easy." Her velvety-soft skin was warm beneath his grip.

She yanked her arms free as if she'd been scalded and backed away. "Don't touch me!"

The headache that had threatened earlier bloomed into a steady throb right behind his left eye. What the hell was with her?

Then it clicked.

Her little seduction had fallen flat, so she'd switched her game plan to an even more devious one. She'd tell the reporters how he'd lured her to his hotel room and forced himself on her. He shuddered. Rape had a bad stink, one that would destroy his career and stick with him the rest of his life.

He tightened his hands into fists so he didn't throttle her elegant neck. "Look, lady, this damsel-in-distress act you're trying to pull won't work. Not with me." He stormed across the room, flung open the door, and held it wide. "Go on. Get out. Tell your pal DeGrazzi his plan failed."

Two patches of red blossomed on her pale cheeks. "DeGrazzi?" For a moment she looked startled, but then her silver eyes sparked with fire. She planted her hands on her slim hips. "Look, I don't know who you are or what you want with me, but I want some answers, and I want them now."

Her slight body bristled, and her eyes shot daggers. She grabbed a handful of loose bills from the bed and tossed them at him. They bounced off his chest and fluttered to the carpet. "And I'm not a prostitute, so keep your damn money."

"Okay. I was wrong. You're not a hooker, but you work for DeGrazzi, don't you?" He jammed his hands in the front pockets of his jeans. "I hope he pays you well, because, lady, you've sold your soul to the Devil."

She glared at him, the force of her outrage staggering. "I do *not* work for Julio DeGrazzi."

"Yeah, right." He motioned toward the doorway. "Okay. We're done here. Off you go. Time to leave."

She ignored his demand and remained standing by the bed. "Where's my purse?"

He blew out a breath. "Oh, come on. You're not going there, are you? Your seduction scheme didn't work, the sexual assault act didn't pan out, so now you're accusing me of theft?"

He threaded his fingers through his hair, suddenly too exhausted to confront her anymore. All he wanted was to get the hell out of there, go home, and drain a pint of ice-cold beer. He heaved a deep breath. "Look, it's been a long day. I'm beat. Why don't we call it a standoff? You walk out of here and go home, and I won't press charges."

"You didn't take my purse?" Tears shimmered in her eyes, turning the irises dove gray.

He softened his voice. "No, I don't have your

purse."

"This is your hotel room?"

He held up the key card.

She staggered back a step, and her legs bumped against the bed. "And you've never seen me before."

"Nope." The second the denial was out of his mouth, he wondered if he was right. He studied her beautiful face, the creamy skin, glossy dark hair rippling down her back. She looked familiar, but from where? He peeked at his watch and blew out a frustrated breath. No time to stand around. He had to get rid of her if he hoped to make it out of this mess unscathed.

She held up her hands, palms out. "Please. I beg of you. Tell me. Where are we? How did I get here? What happened to me?"

"Don't you know?"

Her eyes flooded with tears. "No, but someone has to know what happened. If you don't, then who does?"

His disquiet grew. Had he misjudged her? Was she as much a victim of this setup as he was? As soon as the thought popped into his brain, he dismissed it. Her being in the room that night of all nights was too much of a coincidence, plus there was that nagging certainty he knew her.

"Look"—he swiped the back of his hand over his brow—"I don't know what happened to you, I don't know why you're in this room, and I sure as hell don't know where your purse is, but I do know you have to leave. If you think the situation's bad now, things are only going to get a hell of a lot worse. Whoever arranged our little get-together isn't through toying with us yet."

A single tear slipped down her cheek and trembled on her chin. "I don't know where I am, or how I got here." She gestured at the room. "I woke up on the floor just before you arrived and…" Her voice trailed off, her words lost in a sob. Tears flowed down her cheeks and dripped on her blouse.

Damn. A woman's tears were his kryptonite. He turned to mush and gathered her in his arms and held her close. Muttering soothing, meaningless words, he caressed her fall of silky black hair. Her scent—something floral and earthy like spring rain in the morning—surrounded him.

The elevator pinged down the hall, and a babble of loud voices filled the narrow corridor.

He froze as four uniformed cops, followed by a half-dozen reporters, raced down the hall toward him. At the same instant, his brain connected the dots.

He knew who she was.

His heart stuttered. Damn. He was in a far deeper pile of shit than he'd thought.

A camera flashed, blinding him.

Chapter 2

"Come on, Ms. Reynolds, it's time you came clean." The detective's cold, dark gaze bore into hers.

Marissa shifted, trying in vain to find a comfortable spot on the hard chair. After three long, exhausting hours, there wasn't one. "Detective Sandhu, I've told you what I know." She blew out a shaky breath. "Why won't you believe me?"

The pounding in her head had taken on monstrous proportions. The bright fluorescent lights seared into her pupils. Her left arm ached from where the doctor the police had called to examine her had taken several vials of blood.

"I've never met Assistant District Attorney Bannister before. I've read about him in the papers, of course, but I didn't know he was the man in the hotel room. He never told me his name." Another exasperated sigh leaked out. "I thought he'd kidnapped me."

The detective stared at her, his expression unchanging, his eyes unblinking.

A digital clock on the wall ticked off the intolerable seconds, one slow beat after another.

How much longer would she have to sit in that tiny, airless room answering the same questions again and again? "I've already told you what happened. I woke up in that hotel room lying on the floor. I have no idea how I got there. I didn't even know where I was until one of your officers told me." Her voice caught in her throat, and she bit back a sob.

The neat bristle of mustache above his thin upper lip twitched as he scowled. He toyed with his tie, running his fine-boned fingers up and down the smooth silk. "How do you explain your presence in that room? Where's your car? Did you walk to the hotel, or were you driven?"

"I don't know." She gritted her teeth and bit back her frustration. How many times did she have to tell him?

The door to the interrogation room swung open, and Detective Barbour stepped into the room. He carried a steaming foam cup in one hand and a sheet of paper in his other. He set the cup on the table in front of her. The smell of the bitter, dark coffee filled the tiny room, masking the reek of stale sweat.

He handed the paper to the older detective. Crossing his arms over his chest, Detective Barbour drilled her with a hard look. "We have the results back from your blood tests." He pointed at the paper he'd handed Detective Sandhu.

She sucked in a breath and leaned forward, her heart pounding.

"The tissue samples we scraped from under your fingernails match our homicide victim's blood type," Detective Barbour said.

"Wait a minute." She held up her hands and stared at the pale, blue-veined skin. "Are you saying there was *blood* under my nails?" Her hands shook like she had palsy. The world spun, and she gripped the edge of the scarred wooden table as an even worse reality hit home.

"Someone…someone was murdered?"

"Come on, Ms. Reynolds." Detective Sandhu laid his palms flat on the table, his face inches from hers. The sweet, cloying scent of sandalwood cologne settled between them. "You expect us to believe your hands were covered in Flinty McGregor's blood, and you don't remember how it got there?"

"Blood? I had blood on my hands?" Her fingernails scored deep into the table. The more she repeated the shocking words, the less they made sense. How could she have a man's blood on her hands? She hated the sight of blood. Even a bleeding nose made her woozy. She stared at her hands but couldn't see any blood.

"Ms. Reynolds?"

A dead man's blood under her fingernails! She met Detective Sandhu's probing gaze. "I…I don't remember anything. You have to believe me. I *don't* remember."

The younger detective, his hair a riot of gelled red spikes, tapped his partner on the shoulder. A trail of light-brown freckles sprinkled across the bridge of his snub nose. If it weren't for the steely look in his cold, blue eyes, he'd resemble the kid who delivered her pizza from the local Italian restaurant. "She may be telling the truth, at least about the not remembering."

Detective Sandhu frowned at his partner. "What are you talking about?"

The red-haired detective pointed at the paper he'd handed Detective Sandhu and used his index finger to underline a paragraph at the bottom of the page.

Once again silence hung in the room while the older detective read.

She rubbed her damp palms on the gray flannel

fabric of the sweat pants they'd given her after they took her clothes to the lab to be analyzed. The baggy sweats, along with the voluminous orange sweatshirt, were hardly a fashion statement, but they were warm.

Detective Sandhu looked up. "It looks like you were telling the truth about your memory loss."

Relief washed over her. Finally. They believed her. "I told you."

"The blood sample the doctor took from you indicates you have residual amounts of flunitrazepam in your system."

"What's that?"

"Have you heard of the date-rape drug? Rohypnol, roofies, R-2? It used to be all over the news. Young men and women partying in night clubs had their drinks doctored with Rohypnol and later couldn't remember what happened. Most of them were sexually assaulted." He scratched the dark shadow of beard on his chin. "We don't see much of the drug these days. Too many other designer drugs to choose from."

Her brain was too sluggish to think, and her heart raced in uneven spurts. "I don't understand. Are you saying someone gave me this date-rape drug?" Her eyes widened, and a fresh wave of nausea assailed her. "My God. Was *I* raped?"

The younger detective shook his head. "The doctor who examined you didn't find evidence of recent sexual activity."

Her breath whooshed out, and she sagged back on the chair. Another thought, almost as disturbing, occurred, and she lurched forward. "I don't understand. How did I ingest the drug? Who gave it to me?"

Detective Sandhu dragged out a hard-backed, metal

chair from the table, sat down, and shoved the sleeves of his shirt up to his elbows, exposing a sprinkling of fine dark hairs on his arms. "Why don't you tell us again the last thing you remember before you woke up in that hotel room?"

She grabbed the foam cup and brought it to her lips, wincing at the bitter smell of burned coffee. Her hands shook, and hot liquid slopped over the rim onto the table. "I've already told you. The last thing I remember is leaving work and walking across the parking lot to my car. I...I think it was raining." She sniffed back tears. "I...I probably went to the coffee shop. I...I always stop for a cappuccino after work, at Joe's Beanery."

"That could be where you were slipped the roofie." His eyes narrowed. "Was the coffee shop crowded? Was there a lid on your coffee cup? Did you leave your cup unattended?" He fired questions, one after the other, like staccato bursts from a machine gun.

"I don't know. I can't remember." The silence in the tiny, airless room dragged on thick and heavy. "If...if I was drugged, that explains why I can't remember, doesn't it? I've heard about Rohypnol. People can't remember anything after taking it. I'm right, aren't I?"

The staredown continued. Did he ever blink?

A sharp rap on the door sounded, and it blasted open.

The detective tore his gaze from hers and swung to the door. "Scott? What are you doing here? I thought you were holding a press conference."

The lanky, blond-haired man from the hotel stormed into the interrogation room. "All finished." His mouth twisted as if he'd eaten something sour. "Those damn reporters were after blood. I was lucky to escape with my skin."

He rubbed the back of his neck. "They received the same anonymous tip as the cops. Someone called the *Daily News* and informed them the ADA was having a lover's tryst in a hotel room with a woman whose identity would guarantee them front page headlines." His gaze zeroed in on her. "Has she come clean? Has she told you the truth?"

Marissa squirmed under his intense scrutiny. What was he doing here? Why hadn't he been arrested or at least interrogated?

Detective Sandhu shook his head. "She's sticking with the same story. Says she doesn't remember anything."

"It's the truth." The words burst out. "I don't remember because I was drugged."

Scott Bannister's gaze never shifted. "I heard someone slipped you a roofie."

"Well, then you believe me. Right?"

His eyes narrowed to piercing slits. "Did you tell the detectives you're Julio DeGrazzi's niece?"

****

The color left her face, and she sagged back in her chair as if the wind had been knocked out of her.

Scott nodded in satisfaction. Good. He'd rattled her. "Isn't that right, Ms. Reynolds? You're DeGrazzi's niece."

She blinked several times, her long, dark eyelashes framing her dove-gray eyes. But then she straightened, and her eyes turned stormy. "I don't see how that's relevant."

"You don't see how being related to this city's most notorious criminal is *relevant*?" He wheeled around to the senior detective. "Tell me, Detective Sandhu, you're an experienced homicide investigator, what do you think? Is her relationship to Julio DeGrazzi important? The media sure thought so. Her presence at the hotel is all over the news."

The detective scowled. "The murder victim was a known associate of DeGrazzi."

"Exactly." Scott placed his palms on the table, looming over her, crowding her personal space, making her squirm. "What do you know of Flinty McGregor's murder? Did you kill him? Or did your uncle have one of his henchmen do the job?"

"I don't know anything. I told you. I was drugged."

"Your hands bore traces of the victim's blood." He pinned her with a hard gaze. "And your purse was found on the ground beside his body."

"How many times do I have to tell you? I don't know." Tears brimmed in her luminous eyes. "Wait." Her eyes widened. "You found my purse?"

"And your cell phone." He'd sat in on the interrogation of plenty of suspects over the past six months, and he was pretty good at determining if they were lying. Her surprise looked genuine. Either that, or she was a damn fine actress.

A flash of unexpected guilt washed over him. Her face was pale, her eyes shot with streaks of red. She looked exhausted. No wonder. She'd been in the interrogation hot box for hours, and if the blood tests were correct, she'd been drugged. She could well be telling the truth, and here he was giving her the third degree like she was a common felon. But…and it was a huge but...she was DeGrazzi's niece. "What's your relationship with your uncle? Are you two close?"

She shook her head. "Hardly. I haven't spoken to him in five years." She swallowed again. "We...we had a falling out."

"When's the last time you saw him?"

"I told you, it's been five years."

"Not even at Christmas? Your birthday? Nothing?"

"Nothing." Her mouth tightened, her expression mulish.

Was she telling the truth? Hard to tell, but his gut told him she was on the level. So why was she in that hotel room? Tonight of all nights. "What do you do for a living, Ms. Reynolds?"

She blinked as if startled by his question. "I'm the head librarian at Brunswick City College. Why?"

Okay. He was wrong. She wasn't a hooker.

The situation grew more bizarre by the minute. The next thing she'd tell him was she donated her paycheck to the homeless and fed the needy. No matter what she said, he couldn't forget the bottom line—she was DeGrazzi's niece, and she was in that hotel room. Was she involved in the setup? That was the six-million-dollar question. "Who slipped you the drug?"

"I have no idea."

Detective Sandhu cut in. "She says she goes to a coffee shop every day after work. We're checking to see if anyone saw her tonight."

Scott narrowed his eyes and scalded her with his famous piercing glare, the one guaranteed to convince hardened criminals to spill their guts, or at the very least, soil their pants. "The last thing you remember is buying this *so-called* cup of coffee?"

"No. I don't know. Maybe. You can check my debit card receipt. Sergio, the young guy behind the counter, will vouch for me. He'll remember if I was there. I always leave a tip."

Of course she did. He slanted a look at Detective Sandhu.

The detective shrugged. "Her wallet wasn't in her purse. We didn't find a receipt."

Scott turned back to her and leaned closer. "*If* you were drugged, how did you get to that hotel room? Who took you there?"

"I *was* drugged." Her gray eyes sparked as anger rose to the surface. She pointed at the medical report. "It says so right there. I was given a date-rape drug. Why don't you believe me?"

Detective Barbour cleared his throat. "We found her car in the faculty lot at Brunswick City College. Her keys were on the ground beside the car."

"See? That proves I'm innocent. Someone abducted me from the parking lot and took me to the hotel." She pressed two fingers against her temples as if she had a headache. "But why? It doesn't make any sense."

Scott's guilt amped up a notch. Maybe she was a stooge like him.

Nah. No way.

She was DeGrazzi's niece. The old crook wouldn't set up his own flesh and blood. Would he?

"The videotapes from the hotel show Ms. Reynolds entered the lobby with a man," Detective Sandhu said. "The two of them were all over each other. The front desk clerk told us he was afraid they'd go at it right in the lobby."

Marissa's gasp filled the room. "What? That's not true. It can't be."

Detective Barbour cleared his throat. "The hotel's a piece of shit. The security cameras date from the late nineties, but from what we can tell by watching the grainy black and white surveillance tapes, he was a big guy, tall and muscular."

"At least we have a tape." Scott rubbed his hands together. "Have you run any facial recognition software? Do you have a name? Let's hear it. I'll issue an arrest warrant and have this guy behind bars by morning."

Detective Barbour shook his head. "He knew enough not to look at the cameras, and he wore a cap with the brim pulled over his face, and a pair of dark sunglasses."

"What?" The detective opened his mouth to repeat what he'd said, but Scott held up his hand stopping him. "Never mind, I heard you. Are you telling me Ms. Reynolds entered the hotel lobby with a guy wearing a cap and sunglasses?"

The red-haired detective nodded. "We found a red cap in the hotel room. We've sent it to the lab for DNA testing."

Scott's shoulders tightened. "Don't bother. The hat's mine."

The two detectives stared openmouthed.

"The hat's yours?" Detective Sandhu's thick eyebrows brushed his hairline.

Scott fished in his coat pocket and pulled out the sunglasses he'd worn as part of his disguise. The last thing he'd wanted was to be recognized sneaking into that cheesy hotel during the late hours of the night. But someone was on to him. They'd seen him wearing the hat and sunglasses and copied his disguise. His headache skyrocketed into the red zone.

"*You're* the guy on the video? You and Ms. Reynolds checked in together?" The furrow between Sandhu's dark brows deepened. "Why didn't you tell us this before?"

Scott shook his head. "That wasn't me. The man in the video was someone disguised to look like me. DeGrazzi's smart. He set the whole thing up, so suspicion would be directed at me."

"We didn't see anyone else enter or leave the hotel on any of the videos."

"You won't." He heaved a resigned sigh as the full magnitude of the elaborate trap rushed at him. "I came in through the back entrance where there aren't any surveillance cameras. My meeting with McGregor was supposed be top secret. I didn't even tell my staff.

"McGregor told me he'd make sure the back door to the hotel was propped open, and he'd leave the key card to the room behind a fake plant on a table on the second-floor hallway." His anger at his gullibility knotted his gut, and he stomped across the small room, his steps jerky and stiff. The urge to slam his fist into the wall was strong, but he kept both hands jammed in his pockets. Venting his fury in front of the two sharp-eyed detectives would only make the situation worse.

The detectives nodded, but doubt was blatant in their eyes. Their body language had switched from one colleague discussing a case with another, to cops versus a potential suspect.

Scott didn't blame them. He wouldn't believe him either. His story was full of holes. The only reason he wasn't being interrogated was because of his position. They couldn't haul the ADA in for questioning with the scattered bits and pieces of circumstantial evidence they had. But if he didn't do something, and do it damn quick, he'd be sitting behind bars, dressed in an orange jumpsuit, his career in ruins, his reputation in the toilet.

"You. You did all this," Marissa Reynolds shouted. She jumped to her feet and glared at him, her eyes spitting fire. "I saw you. You were wearing a red ball cap, and you had on sunglasses like the man in the surveillance video." She pointed a long, slim finger at him. "You took me from the college, drugged me, and carried me to that room. You murdered that poor man."

She darted around the table and grasped the front of his leather jacket and yanked hard, dragging his face down to hers. "You wanted the police to think I killed him. Why? Why are you doing this?"

Warm spittle spattered his face. He stumbled but braced his feet and faced the full brunt of her fury. "I didn't drug you, Ms. Reynolds." He placed his hands over hers, easing her death-like grip on his leather jacket. "Someone certainly did, but it wasn't me."

"If it wasn't you, then who?"

It was on the tip of his tongue to tell her to ask her uncle, but the fear and confusion dulling her gray eyes shook him. "I don't know, but I promise you I'll find out."

She searched his eyes. After an interminable minute, she blew out a breath and stepped back a step. "You'd better." She stumbled to her seat and sank down and buried her face in her hands.

Scott fought the urge to wipe his damp brow. Sweat prickled under his arms. *Couldn't the police department afford a decent air-conditioning system?* He straightened and turned to the detectives. "How did this guy pay for the hotel room? I can't imagine he was stupid enough to use a credit card."

Detective Sandhu shook his head. "Paid cash. Booked the room for one night. According to the desk clerk, the guy didn't say much. I gather the Condor's not the sort of hotel where the staff asks questions."

Scott rubbed the tightening knot in the back of his neck. He understood DeGrazzi setting him up to discredit him. That made sense. He and the crime kingpin had been combatants since Scott took office, and Scott made it his goal to stop DeGrazzi and his gang of thugs. But why would DeGrazzi drag his own niece into this mess—his librarian-niece, for God's sakes? Even if they'd had a falling out, blood still counted.

But what if he was wrong and DeGrazzi wasn't behind this craziness? What if someone else wanted to discredit Scott? The Russian's face rose before him, but he shook off the thought. Naw. The Russian had been out of the picture for years. Besides, this nightmare had Julio DeGrazzi written all over it.

"We checked the hotel register." Detective Sandhu's musical South Asian lilt broke into Scott's thoughts.

Of course. The register. Why hadn't he thought of that? Though it wasn't as if this guy was going to register using his own name. "Whose name did he use? Donald Trump? Clark Kent? Elvis Presley?"

Sandhu shook his head. "Scott Bannister."

Scott rocked back on his heels. "My name? The creep signed in under *my* name?" The air in the room suddenly got a little thicker. DeGrazzi must be having hysterics over how he'd snapped the trap.

At Scott's expense.

Chapter 3

Marissa awoke to raucous cawing outside her bedroom window. A breeze fluttered the curtains covering the open window, and pale morning light leaked into the room. The clock on the bedside table showed six o'clock. She moaned and dragged the covers over her head, hoping to smother the hoarse, grating racket.

The squawking swelled to an ear-piercing crescendo.

She threw back the covers and sat up, swiping loose strands of tangled hair off her face. *Those damn birds!* Every morning for the past week, three large black crows perched on the roof above her bedroom window and awakened her with loud, irritating calls.

She rubbed her gritty eyes, trying to erase the thick sleep fog. When she'd been released from the police station, a uniformed officer drove her home in a marked police cruiser. She'd been warned not to leave town. Even though Detective Sandhu hadn't used the dreaded word, she was a suspect. No question.

Her stomach flipped over. She—Marissa Dawn Reynolds, Brunswick City College head librarian—was a suspect in a homicide investigation. The shocking truth was like a plot from a TV murder mystery.

The first thing she'd done after she arrived home was toss the police-issue clothing in the laundry and stand under a scalding shower and scrub every inch of her body with soap and a scrub brush. She may not have been raped, but she'd been violated in every other sense of the word. The water had run cold before she finished.

Staggering into her bedroom, she'd collapsed, naked and exhausted, on her soft, queen-size bed and dragged the blankets to her chin. She thought she'd fall right to sleep, but when she dozed off, nightmare images filled with swirls of confusing colors, echoing voices, and nausea-inducing smells plagued her. She jerked awake, heart pounding, tears dampening her pillow.

The doctor at the police station who'd examined her told her that the drug she'd been given wouldn't remain long in her system, and she'd suffer few side effects from her ordeal. But all night long her stomach roiled, and her head pounded. No matter how many glasses of water she guzzled, she couldn't erase the brackish taste in her mouth.

The incessant, harsh cawing rose in volume, countered by raspy kah-hah screeches.

"Okay, okay." She tossed back the blankets, climbed out of bed, stumbled over to the closet, and grabbed her robe. Shivering in the early morning chill, she shrugged into the thick, baby blue, velour garment, cinching it at her waist with the matching sash. She shuffled down the short hall to the kitchen. After the previous night's unsettling events, she needed coffee—the stronger the better.

She still couldn't wrap her brain around what happened. A dozen questions thundered through her. Who drugged her and took her against her will to that hotel room? And why? Did her connection to her uncle play a part like the police suspected? Even worse, how did she get that poor man's blood on her hands? She shuddered and rubbed her hands, wiping away invisible blood.

She massaged her throbbing temples. As if her situation hadn't been frightening enough, that man—the Assistant District Attorney, for Pete's sake—had opened the hotel room door, and all hell broke loose. Soon after, the police, along with a pack of reporters with cameras flashing, arrived. She'd been escorted to the police station in the back of a police cruiser, her body poked and probed, every inch of her examined, followed by hours sweating in that tiny, airless room as the two homicide detectives grilled her.

When Scott Bannister strode into the interrogation room, his larger-than-life presence had sucked the oxygen out of the room. His striking blue eyes flashed when he'd revealed Julio DeGrazzi was her uncle, and the situation shifted from bad to worse. The detectives' distrust ramped up, and they eyed her with cold suspicion. It didn't matter she hadn't seen her uncle in five years. She was a DeGrazzi. Enough said.

She blinked back the sting of tears. Nothing ever changed. No matter how far she distanced herself from Julio and his poisonous lifestyle, she was branded guilty by blood. She sniffed and wiped her damp eyes with a tissue she tugged from the pocket of her robe. At least she hadn't been charged with a crime. The evidence against her was circumstantial. Her blood tests proved she'd been drugged, and the police had let her go home.

For the time being.

A soft thud emanated from her bedroom.

She froze. The crows?

Another thump.

The hairs on the back of her neck prickled. Someone was in the apartment! She should call 911, but the police had her cell phone, and she didn't have a landline. If she screamed for help, the neighbors would hear and call the police. She grimaced. But what if she was overreacting and the noise was the crows pecking on the roof? The last thing she wanted was more dealings with the police.

She tiptoed to the front hall closet and hefted the wooden baseball bat she kept for protection. Gripping the weapon with both hands, she inched toward the bedroom.

There was another soft thunk and the squeak of a floorboard.

Her heart pounded. She raised the bat high and edged around the doorframe and into the dim room.

And froze.

As if conjured by her thoughts, Scott Bannister, the all-too-handsome Assistant District Attorney for Brunswick, Oregon, stood in her bedroom, a sheepish grin on his face.

She released the breath she'd been holding and lowered the bat, but held it at her side, ready if needed. "What are you doing here?"

He shrugged his broad shoulders. "You shouldn't leave your window open, especially not a window above a fire escape. Anyone could drop in. Your next uninvited guest might not be as trustworthy." He dusted off the knees of his faded jeans, brushed his hands together, and looked around the room. "Nice digs."

A flood of heat washed over her as he stared at her unmade bed with the wild tangle of sheets and blankets.

"I like the quilt. Not something I'd figure a librarian would go for, but there you have it." He grinned.

She reeled. The dazzling teeth, the matching dimples in his lean cheeks, the golden lights sparkling in his dark-blue eyes. For a heartbeat she forgot he was the enemy, forgot the nightmare of last night, forgot everything but the weaken-your-knees power of that boyish grin.

The heat searing her face amped up, scorching through her veins. "My...my mother bought me that blanket years ago, before...before she..." She bit her lip to stop the flood of words. None of his damn business why she had a quilt dotted with pictures of winged ponies with pastel-colored manes and tails prancing across the well-worn pink, fuzzy fabric. "I asked you a question. What are you doing here?" A spurt of anger unfurled, and she glared. "Why did you climb through my bedroom window? I'm calling the police." But then she remembered...no phone.

"I believe the police are holding your cell phone as evidence." He dug in his pants pocket and tugged out a cell phone. "Would you like to borrow mine?" A smug smile played about his well-sculpted lips.

What game was he playing? She backed away. "I'll scream."

His gaze raked her in a slow perusal from her head to her toes and back again.

Her hand trembled as she tightened the neckline of her robe, remembering she was naked under the thin material.

"I'm not here for what you think, Ms. Reynolds, so you can drop your weapon. Your virtue's safe."

A twinge of something alarmingly like disappointment flashed through her, but she shook off the ridiculous thought. "My...my weapon?"

He nodded at the bat gripped in her hand.

Tightening her grasp, she held on to the weapon. She didn't trust him. He'd been in the hotel room last night, and now he was in her bedroom. "What do you want? Why did you break in? Why didn't you come to the front door like a normal person?"

"You wouldn't have let me in."

She nodded, conceding his point. If she'd spotted him outside her door, she wouldn't have answered his knock.

He massaged his eye sockets with his thumb and middle finger. "Look, I just want to talk. I think you can help."

She gaped at him, stunned by his gall. "Are you serious? You want *me* to help you? As far as I know you slipped me a date rape drug, dragged me to that hotel room against my will, murdered a man, and then..." Her words faded at the unperturbed expression on his face.

"Go on. What other crimes have I committed? Did I rob a bank? Mug an old lady? Steal from the church charity box?"

She bit down on her bottom lip to stop the threatening smile.

"See? Even you can hear how crazy your accusations sound."

"Maybe *you're* crazy."

He smoothed the palm of his hand over his short,

32

dark-blond hair. "You don't believe that. You know I didn't commit any of those crimes."

"I don't know any such thing."

"Oh, you believe me all right." A smug smile settled on his rugged face.

"How are you so certain?" Her irritation inched up a notch.

His smile grew. "Because you're standing here. If you were as terrified of me as you say, and you thought I was a dangerous murderer, you'd run out your front door and scream for the police."

His arrogance was too much. She wanted to do just what he suggested, but she remained where she was, even as she bristled with anger. The most annoying part was he was right. She believed him. He hadn't drugged her or committed any other heinous crimes. Something about him...maybe his direct, guile-free gaze, or his shock when the detectives revealed how the man in the hotel surveillance tapes had signed in under his name...whatever it was, she was convinced he wasn't the enemy.

She blew out a long breath, set the bat on the dresser, spun around, and strode out of the bedroom.

"Where are you going?" he called after her.

"I'm making coffee. I don't know about you, but I need caffeine."

His chuckles followed her down the hallway and into the tiny kitchen.

A thousand questions tumbled through her as she filled the coffee pot with water and ground coffee beans. Why was he there? What was so important he'd risk someone passing on the street below noticing the well-known Assistant District Attorney scaling the rusty, old fire-escape ladder and climbing through her bedroom window?

He wasn't there to arrest her. If that were the case, he'd have been accompanied by a couple of uniformed police officers, and he certainly wouldn't have sneaked through her bedroom window like a thief in the night.

He was good with the gab. That was for certain. After her police escort dropped her off, she'd flipped on the television and caught the tail end of his taped press conference. A scrum of excited reporters had surrounded him, microphones shoved in his face.

He'd seemed unperturbed as he issued his statement. He was quick on his feet. No doubt about that. Somehow he'd spun the facts so the reporters were led to believe he'd received a tip a murder had occurred at the hotel, and he'd attended the crime scene in an official capacity.

If she didn't know the truth, she'd have believed him. When one of the reporters asked about the dark-haired woman with him in the hotel room, he'd skated over the awkward question with a politician's slickness and implied she was an investigator with the District Attorney's office. He'd bamboozled them with a stream of smooth talk and didn't mention he'd found her drugged and dazed, or that she was related to Julio DeGrazzi.

She'd been able to slip out of the hotel room unnoticed and made it to the lobby where a uniformed officer stopped her and informed her she had to accompany him to the precinct to answer a few questions.

At least the press hadn't discovered her true identity. They knew Julio DeGrazzi's niece was somehow involved, but they didn't know what she looked like.

Her identity was safe...for now.

The second he walked into the kitchen, the back of her neck prickled, and the air in the room altered, as if the molecules shifted and rearranged into a different form. She focused on pouring coffee into two mugs. "Take anything?"

"Nope."

She whirled at the sound of his deep voice. Inches separated them...too few inches.

He reached around her and lifted a mug from the counter. The faint scent of something woodsy and masculine wafted in the air. Her chin met his shoulder, and she had to crane her head to see his face. He'd shaved. His cheeks were smooth, and the thin white line of an old scar crossed his square chin. Tiny creases bracketed his mouth.

"Do I pass muster?"

She tore her gaze from his mouth.

His midnight-blue eyes glittered.

"No...I...I..."

The mouth she'd been studying so intently twitched, and he grinned a rakish grin. A matching set of dimples popped out on his lean cheeks.

A wave of heat engulfed her, and she grabbed her cup of coffee, brushed past him, stumbled to the table, and sank on a chair. Seizing the sugar dish from the middle of the table, she spooned three heaping teaspoons of sugar into her mug.

Shrugging out of his worn, black leather jacket, he draped his coat across the back of a chair and sprawled on the facing chair. Stretching his long legs in front, he crossed his booted feet at the ankles. "Thanks for the coffee."

She gulped a swig of coffee. An immediate surge of energy zinged through her veins as the sugar-and-caffeine bomb exploded through her system. She set her cup on the table with a decisive clunk. "Okay. Time you tell me why you're here."

"I told you. We need to talk."

"And I told you and your detective friends everything last night."

"No new memories?"

She shook her head. "I've tried to remember, but last night's a blur. Maybe I recall rough hands shoving me, a smell..." She shrugged. "I don't know."

"I'm not surprised. I researched Rohypnol. Victims of the drug rarely remember the events while they're under the drug's influence. The memory loss is permanent." His mouth tightened. "Which in most cases is a blessing. Not many people want to live with the terrifying memories of a sexual assault."

She shuddered and clasped her mug in a futile effort to warm her icy hands. "I was lucky, I guess, that I wasn't raped."

"That wasn't his plan."

"Plan? Whose plan?" She sat up. "What do you know about all this?"

His navy eyes focused on her face, but rather than answer, he said, "I want you to go with me to visit your uncle."

She jerked, and coffee slopped over the edge of her mug onto the table. "My *uncle*?"

He nodded and crossed his arms over his chest. "Uncle Julio."

"I told you, I haven't seen or spoken to him in five years."

"A family reunion's about due, don't you think?"

"No. No way. There's a reason Julio and I don't speak."

"He's a crook, and you're not."

She stared at him, flabbergasted. "He's much more than a simple crook. You know that." She narrowed her eyes. "Why do you want to talk to him? You've made no secret you want to put him in jail."

He leaned forward and clasped her hand in his large, warm, masculine one. His fingers were long, his palm rough and callused. "Because I think he's the key to what happened last night."

Her immediate reaction was to snatch her hand back, but he must have read her intent in her eyes because he tightened his grip. Short of making a scene, she was stuck with him holding her hand.

"Look, Marissa, the police consider you a prime suspect in a homicide."

She sucked in a breath.

"I'm sorry, but it's the truth. Your phone and purse were found beside the victim, you had traces of the victim's blood under your fingernails, and your family connections are"—he shrugged—"questionable, to say the least."

She opened her mouth to protest, but he shook his head. "Let me finish. When I walked into that hotel room and saw you, I figured you were a prostitute, and you were part of a setup designed to destroy my reputation. You know, a headline like 'ADA Bannister caught with his pants down in the arms of a whore'."

Once again, she opened her mouth, but again, he

shook his head.

"I was wrong. You aren't a hooker." His mouth twisted. "You're a librarian at the college, and someone slipped you a roofie. The blood tests prove you were drugged." He released her hand. "Someone went to a lot of trouble to place you and me together in that hotel room."

Her hand tingled, and she resisted the temptation to examine her skin to see if any marks showed from his scorching touch. "You think my uncle's responsible?"

"No."

"How can you be so certain? If this guy McGregor was going to snitch to the police, Julio would do anything to shut him up."

"Agreed."

"Looks to me like my uncle killed two birds with one stone. He ordered one of his men to murder McGregor, silencing him and sending a message to anyone in his organization about the consequences of speaking to the cops. He arranged the crime scene so suspicion would fall on you, therefore removing an annoying ADA from the picture."

Scott sat back and clasped his hands behind his neck. The muscles in his biceps bulged. "At first I thought he was responsible too, but there's a flaw in your thinking."

"What are you talking about?"

"Not what. Who?"

She gulped another swallow of coffee. Did he always speak in riddles? Couldn't he come out and say what he meant? It had been a long night. She ached to go back to bed and sleep until this whole nightmare was a distant memory.

"I'm talking about you."

Her head jolted up. "Me?"

He nodded.

"I don't understand."

"Why, out of all the women in this city, did this creep choose you to drug and leave in that hotel room? If you didn't murder McGregor—"

She slammed her cup on the table. "I didn't—"

He held up both hands, palms out, cutting off her outburst. "Look, I know you didn't murder him, but someone went to a lot of trouble to make it look like you did." He lowered his hands. "Why were your handbag and cell phone found beside the dead man? Why was the victim's DNA under your fingernails?"

She rubbed her tired eyes. "Maybe it's just a coincidence. I was an easy target. The people behind this were in the coffee shop waiting for a single woman to come in and leave her coffee unattended for a few seconds. I happened to be that woman."

He stared at her, his eyes dark and penetrating. "You're forgetting one detail."

"What?"

"You never made it to the coffee shop. Your car and your car keys were found at the college."

Her stomach plummeted. "Then how did I ingest the drug?"

"Unless you remember what happened, we may never know."

Struggling to push the numbing fear away, she lunged to her feet. "My involvement could be a coincidence. The faculty parking lot's dark at night. A lone woman would be an easy target."

He gave her a derisive once-over. "Come on. You

don't believe that. You were chosen because of who you are, who you're related to."

She opened her mouth to tell him that other than DNA, she had no connection with her uncle. Hadn't for a very long time. But he was already speaking, laying out his theory in a calm, reasonable voice he must use to sway juries.

"Your uncle wouldn't involve his niece. No matter what disagreements the two of you have had, you're still his flesh and blood. He'd never set you up to take the fall for a murder rap. Someone else is responsible."

She gnawed on the inside of her cheek. What he said made sense. The same thought had occurred to her the previous night while she'd tossed and turned in bed. Julio DeGrazzi was capable of many vile and illegal acts, but he wouldn't harm his younger sister's daughter. "Okay, if not my uncle, who?"

His eyes hooded as he averted his gaze. "I don't want to say anything yet. It's just a hunch."

Before she could probe further, he jumped to his feet, grabbed his leather jacket from the back of the chair, and shrugged into it. "Let's go."

She clutched the neck of her robe. "Go where?"

"To visit Uncle Julio. Let's hear what he has to say."

"No way." The last thing she wanted was to visit Julio. A memory of the consequences of the last time she'd seen her uncle flashed before her. Her stomach tightened, and she squelched the disturbing image.

The tap dripped, the coffee machine gurgled and spat, and the apartment creaked under the heat of the rising sun. A distant cawing filtered through the kitchen window glass. The homey scent of brewing coffee filled the air.

He arched his eyebrows. "You don't care a man was murdered?"

"Of course I care." Her throat tightened, and she struggled to swallow. A man was murdered, and his blood was under her fingernails. Her stomach heaved at the thought of how that blood had gotten there, but how would confronting her uncle help? If he were involved, he'd never admit his guilt. He'd go to his grave before he'd confess anything to the authorities.

"But?"

"But Julio and I"—she chewed on her bottom lip and inhaled a shaky breath—"he won't be happy to see me."

"You're his only living relative."

She shook her head. "I...I can't."

"I can't make you go, but I would have thought you'd want to find out who drugged you."

"Even if Julio knows something, he won't tell us. He doesn't speak to the police."

"He might if he's concerned about you."

"Why don't you take a couple of police officers and confront him? Why do you need me?"

For the first time since he'd broken into her apartment, uncertainty shadowed his eyes. "This isn't an official visit. I'm off the book."

"Off the book?" He was the ADA and the legal official for Brunswick. How could his appearance at her apartment not be official? "What do you mean?"

He strode to the counter, leaned his hips against the hard granite, and jammed his hands in his front pockets. "You aren't the only suspect."

"What? Are you telling me *you're* a suspect?" She

laughed, but her laughter died at the expression on his face. "You're a suspect."

He nodded.

"You're a suspect." Repeating the words didn't make them any less shocking. The devastated look in his eyes spoke volumes. "Why do the police think you're involved?"

"They haven't said so exactly. It's a feeling I'm getting. That's why I need your help."

She tore her gaze from his beseeching eyes. He was right. She wanted to know who'd slipped her the drug and set her up to look like she'd murdered that man. A seed of anger unfurled in her gut. She was tired of being a victim. "Okay."

"Okay?"

"I'll go with you."

A smile broke out on his rugged face, and those devastating dimples flashed. "Attagirl."

The beat of her heart ramped up. It wasn't fair. No man should be that good-looking. She unlocked her frozen knees. "I guess I'd better get dressed."

"Can I ask you a question?" His voice was a throaty husk.

She nodded.

"Are you wearing anything under that robe?"

She sucked in a sharp breath.

An infernal smug grin plastered on his face. "That's what I figured."

Clutching the neck of her robe, she scuttled out of the suddenly way-too-small kitchen and ran down the hall to her bedroom. Slamming the door, she leaned against the cool wood, her knees rubbery, her body thrumming.

Chapter 4

Hands clasped behind his back, Scott paced across the kitchen. He needed to move, to burn up the bursts of adrenaline firing through his twitching muscles, anything to erase the image of a nude Marissa Reynolds.

Every second of every minute they'd been in the kitchen, he'd been far too aware she was bare-assed naked beneath the plush velour of her robe. The dressing gown covered her from the top of her neck to the tips of her toes, but he'd filled in the blanks. The soft sway of her breasts, the swell of her hips... He lengthened his stride, covering the distance from stove to kitchen table in two strides instead of three.

Climbing through her bedroom window was crazy, but he was pretty sure she wouldn't let him in if he knocked at her door. She'd been angry with him the previous night at the police station, and it was obvious she didn't trust him.

Who could blame her? When he showed up in the hotel room, she'd been confused and frightened, reeling from the effects of the roofie. At first he figured the situation was a setup, and she was a willing participant. But then the pieces clicked into place, and he realized who she was. He had a two-inch thick file on his desk on Julio DeGrazzi. A dated photograph of the old crook's niece was in the file.

His head was still spinning after the cops and reporters left. It wasn't until hours later, in the privacy of his condo that his cerebral cortex shut down, and his reptilian brain took over, and he realized he could use her presence at the murder scene to his advantage. If he could get her on his side, convince her they were in this trouble together, she'd take him to her uncle.

Once he breached DeGrazzi's tight security, Scott would play on the old man's protective instincts. Family was all-important to the crime kingpin. In spite of their five-year separation, Julio DeGrazzi cared for his only living relative. If he thought his precious niece was in jeopardy, he'd do anything to save her. And that recklessness would cause him to make mistakes. One slipup, one crack in his armor, and Scott would swoop in and arrest the bastard.

His plan boiled down to manipulating Marissa Reynolds, a woman whose sole crime was her blood connection to a hardened criminal. He suppressed his misgivings. He'd waited too many years, fought too hard to destroy DeGrazzi and his criminal empire. The man would pay for what he'd done, even if Scott had to use an innocent woman to make that happen.

The bedroom door opened, and footsteps echoed down the hall, growing louder as she approached the kitchen doorway.

Her perfume, something floral and fresh, filled the air, and he sucked in a breath and stopped his manic pacing.

Snug-fitting, dark-blue jeans encased her long, slim legs. She'd topped the pants with a simple white T-shirt and a rose-colored sweater. Sneakers covered her feet. She'd run a comb through her long, dark hair and smoothed out the sleep tangles he'd found so appealing.

Once again she was fully covered, and once again his testosterone kicked into overdrive. What sort of lingerie was under that outfit? Sexy, black, barely there lace? Or sensible panties and a white cotton bra?

He ground his back molars until his jaw ached and reined in his lust. This wasn't a date. She was his ticket to the most notorious crime lord in the city. That's all she was, and all she'd ever be.

Focus on the endgame.

She wasn't involved in the previous night's disaster. No matter what the police thought, he was certain of her innocence. She was even more of a victim than he was. But he needed her. No way would DeGrazzi meet with the ADA without a phalanx of lawyers present.

Bad enough those bloody newshounds showed up at the hotel. Luckily, he'd been able to keep Marissa's identity a secret. He'd managed to convince the reporters he was at the hotel in an official capacity investigating Flinty McGregor's murder, and she was his assistant. They knew DeGrazzi's niece was somehow involved, but they didn't know any details.

For the moment.

Fingers crossed it stayed that way. The press finding out who she was didn't mesh with his plan.

"Ready?"

Her soft voice drew him out of his thoughts. He crossed to her apartment door and held it open.

She stood unmoving.

He motioned toward the outside landing. "Come on. Let's go."

"Don't you want to use the bedroom window?

Aren't you afraid someone will see you with me?" Her full lips curved in a smile.

Heat flushed up his neck and settled on his face. "I'll risk it." He focused on his watch so he didn't have to see the teasing glint in her beautiful eyes. "It's early. Your neighbors are probably asleep. Besides, I have a disguise." Reaching in his jacket pocket, he pulled out the mirrored sunglasses he'd worn the night before. He tugged a black cap out of his back pocket and set it on his head, lowering the brim over his eyes. "All set."

With slow, reluctant steps, she plodded out of her apartment, closed the door, and locked the deadbolt with a key. "Good thing Mike, my neighbor across the hall, had an extra key to my place, or I wouldn't have been able to get in last night."

As if on cue, the door across from her apartment opened, and an older man with military-style, buzzed white hair stepped into the hall. "Hey, Marissa." His clear blue eyes swept Scott, and the lines bracketing his mouth deepened. "You're up early. Everything okay?"

Marissa nodded. "Hey, Mike. I'm fine. Thanks."

The white-haired man eyed Scott. He bristled with disapproval. "You sure?"

Scott plastered his best politician's smile on his face and held out his hand to the nosey neighbor. "Nice to meet you...er...Mike, is it?"

Mike's eyes narrowed, and he stared at Scott's hand as if it were a viper. He might as well be wearing a uniform. Cop oozed from every pore. "I know you. You're that new upstart Assistant District Attorney."

Scott's heart sank, and his smile faded. *So much for his disguise.* "We should get going, Marissa."

"I didn't vote for you." Mike crossed his arms over

his chest. "Know why?"

Scott heaved a sigh. "No, but I'm sure you're dying to tell me."

"Damn right I am. You're too young. You don't have any experience. What makes you think you can do the job?" Mike's upper lip curled. "Just because you have a law degree from some fancy university, you young upstarts think you know everything." His chest puffed out. "When I was on the force—"

Marissa cut off his tirade. "Sorry, Mike, but we have to go. I'll talk to you later." She scooted down the hall toward the fire exit.

Scott hurried after her.

A loud harrumph followed them. "Be careful, Marissa. You hear me?"

"Thanks, Mike." She waved her hand in Mike's direction. "See you later."

Scott's back itched as Mike's penetrating gaze followed them. The old cop hadn't hidden the fact he didn't like Scott or lawyers in general, but he wasn't the first cop who'd expressed that point of view. Some cops blamed the District Attorney's office for conviction failures. They didn't think the DA supported the cops on the frontline.

The police worked hard to catch felons, but more often than not, before they finished the paperwork, the criminal was back on the street. They thought it was politics. They weren't far off. Scott's boss, District Attorney Johnson, was up for reelection. The man had been in power for ten years, and he'd do pretty well anything to guarantee he'd win another term.

Scott heaved a sigh of relief when they went through the fire doors and descended the stairs to the apartment lobby. They crossed the small lobby to the glass doors, and he grasped Marissa's arm and pulled her to a stop. "Mike's pretty protective."

A soft smile lit her face. "Mike's like an uncle. He watches out for me."

"Like an *uncle*? Really?" He couldn't resist the jab. "The same way DeGrazzi's your uncle?"

Her smile vanished.

Way to go buddy. Rain on her picnic. "Look, I'm sorry. I—"

"Forget it." Face tight, she cut off his apology and pushed open the door to the street and stepped onto the sidewalk.

He hurried after her.

The day was early, but pedestrians crowded the sidewalk, heading to work. Traffic built as the morning rush hour began. The full-throttled roar of a motorcycle blasted the air as the bike sped past in a blur.

He studied the parked cars along the street, but nothing raised his suspicions. No one loitered in doorways. No cars idled with men sitting inside watching Marissa's building. No glint of a reporter's camera lens. He blew out a relieved breath.

The night before, he'd used his gift of gab and schmoozed his way through the questions flung at him by the demanding media hounds. They'd bought his bullshit. So far. But how long before an eager-beaver reporter uncovered the real reason he was at the hotel?

With a last, quick survey of the street, he gestured for her to follow as he led her down the block. He turned into the narrow alley behind her building. Digging out his car keys, he clicked the unlock button on the key fob. The shiny, chrome-encased headlights of a glossy red, low-slung sports car parked behind a dumpster, flashed.

"*That's* your car?"

A familiar flicker of pride filled him as he brushed a fleck of dust off the gleaming front fender. The car needed a wash and a good wax. He'd planned to do that after work that night, like he did every Thursday like clockwork. But tending to his precious car wasn't in the cards. Not that day and not until this mess was settled once and for all.

She planted her hands on her hips. "Are you kidding me? Scott Bannister, our fair city's up-and-coming Assistant District Attorney, a man who built his career on integrity, drives a flashy, high-end, foreign sports car?"

What was her point? He liked fast cars. He *really* liked this one. He'd saved for years to buy this particular model. The car was his gift to himself after he won the ADA election. It was everyman's wet dream. The powerful engine under the gleaming hood could take the car from zero to sixty in under six seconds. Not that he'd ever drive that fast, of course, not in the city, anyway.

She threw her head back and chuckled. "Man, you must have some serious inadequacy issues"—her gaze focused meaningfully on his crotch—"if you need a car like this to impress women." Her laughter rang over the distant rumble of traffic.

He stretched around her and yanked open the passenger door. "If you're finished having fun, get in. We need to talk to Degrazzi before this trouble we're in piles any deeper."

Her laughter stilled, and she climbed into the car

and settled in the front passenger seat.

He closed the door with care and strode around the car's glossy, front metal grill to the driver's side, already regretting his snide remark. She had a wonderful laugh, one that rose from deep within and burst free in a peal of pure joy. And he'd silenced her. *Well done, Scott. What's next? Are you going to tell her you're using her? Are you going to tell her the truth?*

Setting his jaw, he climbed behind the wheel. He took some satisfaction in the smooth, powerful rumble of the motor as the well-lubed pistons kicked into gear. He clicked on the surround-sound stereo system, and the funky beat of rap music filled the car. Cranking the volume, he let the tweeters and subwoofers do their jobs.

To piss her off for making fun of his car, he sang the misogynistic lyrics along with Bo Diddy Pop's deep baritone voice. He slid her a glance.

Her lips pursed as if she'd eaten something sour, but she didn't complain.

Twenty minutes later he pulled to the curb and parked in front of a towering high-rise. DeGrazzi Tower was thirty stories of the highest-priced real estate in the city. The richest and most influential movers and shakers in Brunswick made the luxury building their home. The monthly rent for a one-bedroom apartment cost more than Scott made in a year.

Julio DeGrazzi occupied the top two floors. His office was on one floor, and he resided in the penthouse like a king overseeing his kingdom. Security was tight. DeGrazzi's armed henchmen guarded the front entrance like they protected the national mint. No one entered without the express permission of one of the tenants.

Hence his need for Marissa. He shot her a glance.

Her face was pale, her hands clenched in her lap, the knuckles white.

A spurt of sympathy flashed through him. She said she'd severed ties with her uncle five years ago and hadn't seen or heard from him since. He could only imagine what crime DeGrazzi had committed to cause the rift. Now Scott was asking her to reconnect with good old Uncle Julio. "You okay?"

She shifted on her seat. "Would it make a difference if I wasn't?"

He opened his mouth to disagree but stopped. "You're right. I need you. I could probably get a warrant for one reason or another to gain access to DeGrazzi, but that's not the route I want to go. The fewer people who know about this meeting, the better. Seeing your uncle again is probably hard for you, but he'll be more willing to cooperate if you're with me."

She stared at him, her gray eyes probing. "You have no idea how difficult this is. You don't know me at all."

Her words stung, and he struggled to defend himself, but the moisture in his mouth had dried, and his tongue wouldn't work. Maybe it was just as well. What could he say? She was right. He didn't know her. Hell, he wasn't even sure he trusted her. But he needed her.

She wrenched open the door and jumped out of the car and onto the sidewalk, slamming the car door behind her with a loud, decisive clunk.

Wincing as the expensive car shuddered under the impact, he fumbled with his seatbelt. "Marissa, wait." He climbed out of the car and hurried around the hood.

She ignored him and continued her determined march across the street.

He spun at the furious roar of an engine and the squeal of tires.

A black SUV, the windows tinted dark, peeled from the curb a half-block away and sped toward Marissa.

The bottom dropped out of his stomach. "Look out!" His shout was lost in the high-pitched bellow of the SUV's screaming motor.

She turned and looked at the vehicle. Instead of racing for the safety of the sidewalk, she froze like a deer in the headlights.

Reacting to instinct, he sprinted toward her, each foot of road taking an eon to cross. Five yards…ten. His feet flew over the ground. Keeping his gaze fixed on her, he prayed he'd reach her in time.

Her eyes widened, and her mouth opened in a perfect O. Her slight body braced for impact.

A few more yards.

The acrid stench of burning rubber filled the air as the SUV's oversized tires gripped the pavement.

He lunged, throwing his body against hers, praying the impetus of his lineman's tackle was enough to throw them both out of the path of the charging SUV.

She screamed as he struck her.

He wrapped his arms around her and held tight as he rolled, fighting to put his body on the bottom, so when they hit the unforgiving pavement, he'd cushion the blow.

The car was on top of them, the front grill like a monster's vicious maw. The massive vehicle exploded past in a blast of hot air and exhaust.

Her long hair whipped across his face, blinding him.

They landed with a bone-wracking jolt and skidded a foot across the rough pavement, shredding the back of his leather jacket.

The second they hit the ground, he grabbed her arm and surged to his feet, half carrying, half dragging her the final few yards to the sidewalk. Panting, fighting for air, he released her and searched the street.

The big black vehicle had vanished.

He blew out a ragged breath and swiped his damp brow with the back of his shaking hand. *Damn. That was close.* Adrenaline surging through his veins, he wheeled toward her.

Her chest heaved, and her eyes were wild.

"Are you okay?" As soon as the words were out of his mouth, he cursed his stupidity. Of course she wasn't okay. How could she be when someone had just tried to run her down?

Her palms were scraped and raw, and one knee of her jeans was torn. Dirt streaked her cheek, and a trickle of blood leaked from the corner of her mouth.

"You're bleeding!"

She looked at him blankly. "What? No, I'm okay. I…I bit my lip when we hit the ground, but I'm fine."

He wished he were the kind of guy who carried a fancy cloth handkerchief in his pocket, but he wasn't, so he leaned close and used his thumb to gently wipe the small trickle of blood from the corner of her mouth.

Her lower lip trembled. Tears spilled from her eyes and streamed down her cheeks.

He folded her in his arms. "It's okay. You're safe." He released another shaky breath. "We're both safe."

She burrowed into his warmth.

The world disappeared, and he lost himself in her feminine scent, her soft curves, the rapid beat of her heart.

"Hey, are you two all right?"

His arms fell away, and he stepped back.

A bald, muscled hulk with a tattoo of a coiled cobra rising up his thick neck stood on the sidewalk. "Want I should call an ambulance?"

Before Scott could answer, the man's eyes widened, his waxed, handlebar mustache twitched, and he stared at Marissa. "Holy shit." He slapped his palm over his mouth. "Excuse my French, Miss Reynolds, but the boss is gonna have a fit when he hears this."

She grimaced and rubbed her shoulder. "Hello, Tiny."

He fished in the back pocket of his tight black jeans and pulled out a cell phone, punched numbers with one thick finger, and held the phone to his ear. Never taking his gaze off Marissa, he spoke into the phone. "Yeah. It's me, Tiny. Tell the boss we have a situation."

Chapter 5

In minutes, four large, overdeveloped, rough-looking goons with steroid-ravaged faces hurtled through the doors of the high rise and raced toward them. Guns were strapped in holsters across their broad chests, and their eyes were cold and hard. Shoving Scott aside, they formed a wall around Marissa and hustled her across the sidewalk.

As they passed through the glass door into the lobby, she spotted a surveillance camera mounted overhead. Another camera was positioned near the elevators, and still another was in the far corner. Every move was monitored.

The men's massive bodies blocked her view of Scott. "Wait." Her voice vanished amidst the mountain of male muscle.

Two guards broke off from the group and stationed themselves in front of the entrance, guns drawn, glaring out at the street.

Tiny grasped her arm above the elbow and marched her across the black-and-white marble-floored lobby to the bank of elevators.

"Tiny, stop." She struggled to free her arm. "Let me go."

Tightening his grip, he ignored her protests and jabbed the button for the elevator.

Enough! She stomped on his foot, wishing she'd

worn boots instead of soft-soled sneakers. When he didn't react, she twisted and rammed her knee into his crotch, thankful she'd taken that self-defense course the college offered faculty and students the previous year.

Tiny expelled a burst of air and hunched over, one massive hand clutching his family jewels. "Why'd ya go and do that?"

She backed away from his furious outrage. "I don't like to be manhandled. You should remember that." The last time she'd been in this apartment building, Tiny, acting on her uncle's orders, had tried to prevent her from leaving. She'd fought him, punching and kicking like a banshee. And won.

The elevator dinged, and the burnished metal doors slid open.

The second man placed his hand on her back and urged her into the elevator.

She resisted and held firm. "I'm not going anywhere without my friend." She looked across the expansive lobby, past the two, armed guards, and through the glass doors.

Scott stood on the street, his leather coat in tatters, both knees of his jeans torn. Dirt smudged his face.

Tiny shook his head. "No way. He's with the cops."

"He saved my life just now." She crossed her arms over her chest to hide her shaking hands. "If he doesn't come with me, I'm leaving. You explain *that* to your boss."

A dark-green minivan passed on the street outside. A couple, arm in arm, walked down the sidewalk. Another car, followed by a delivery van, cruised down the street. And still Scott waited on the sidewalk.

Tiny's nostrils flared like a bull getting ready to charge, but he blew out a breath and nodded at the dark-haired behemoth. "Go get him."

"You sure, Tiny? You know who he is, right? The boss won't like this."

"You heard her. She ain't goin' nowhere without him."

"Your funeral." With a shrug, the man lumbered across the lobby. He shoved open the door and beckoned to Scott.

Scott entered the lobby and limped past the armed men to Marissa's side. He arched a brow. "How'd you convince them to let me in?"

"I refused to go with them unless they did."

He studied the glowering ring of muscle-bound guards. The corners of his mouth twitched. "And they listened?"

She shrugged. Warmth at his admiration replaced her nervousness. "I don't like to be pushed around."

The twitch transformed into a grin. "I'll keep that in mind."

"Scan him, Joe." Tiny's deep baritone broke into their conversation.

Another guard, a clone of the others, moved toward Scott, holding a metal wand.

"What's going on?" she asked.

"Before he talks to Mr. DeGrazzi, we have to make sure he's not wired," said Tiny.

Scott stood motionless while the bodyguard scanned him for radio signals.

The guard nodded. "He's clean."

"Let's move. We're too exposed here." Tiny edged around her, keeping his distance, but herding her and

Scott into the open elevator. He didn't join them.

"Aren't you coming?" she asked.

He shook his head, his bald dome gleaming under the lobby lights. "We gotta find that SUV. Mr. DeGrazzi's waiting for you in the penthouse. Elevator's already programmed."

The doors slid closed, and the elevator began its silent ascent. The soothing scent of lavender filtered through the vents over their heads. Soft music played through the speakers.

Her heart pounded faster with each floor. She wiped her damp palms on her stained and torn pants, wincing as sweat stung the abrasions. The last time she'd seen Julio, her life was in tatters, her world a mess. She'd vowed never to talk to him again. And yet, here she was, but if anyone knew who was responsible for what happened the night before, Julio did.

She slid a glance at Scott. Hands fisted at his sides, he stared at the flashing numbers. She could almost smell his tension. Was he right? Was someone using her to get back at Julio?

The elevator stopped, and the doors swished open onto a large, open-beamed room. Sunshine streamed in through a wall of floor-to-ceiling windows and gleamed on acres of polished hardwood floor.

Blinking against the glare, she stumbled out of the elevator. The vast viewing room had undergone a transformation since the last time she'd been there. Gone were the cloth-covered, workbenches and tools of the team of carpenters hired to renovate the penthouse. They'd been replaced by expensive, minimalistic furniture artfully arranged about the open space. Two white leather padded benches faced the windows with a million-dollar view. The walls were paneled in polished, dark mahogany. A massive metal abstract sculpture consisting of gleaming copper and aluminum, crafted in such a way the strips of copper flowed across the surface in an intricate wave pattern, dominated one wall.

She nudged Scott and pointed at the metal artwork. "That's an original Jacob Varst." She blew out a breath in a low whistle. "A single panel sells for hundreds of thousands of dollars. That's if you can find one for sale."

His lip curled. "Your uncle's business isn't suffering. Looks like crime does pay."

Any moisture in her mouth dried, and her breathing kicked up a notch. For a moment, she'd forgotten why they were there and whom they were meeting. She glanced up at the high, open-beamed ceiling. More changes were evident. Several security cameras were mounted on the beams, stark proof that being a crime king had its downside. Her uncle had enemies…many enemies…and he never stopped looking over his shoulder. Somewhere, someone had a bullet with his name on it.

"Come here. You gotta see this view." Scott beckoned her over to the window.

Even though she'd stood in this same spot five years ago and looked through these windows, the incredible vista took her breath away. Downtown Brunswick stretched far below like a child's model of a city. The hub of high-rise apartment buildings was built around Mersten Park. Acres of wooded forest were interspersed with a network of walking and biking trails. The colorful blur of vehicles as they passed on the streets below looked like a French Impressionist painting.

Farther out, smoke belched from stacks at the airplane parts manufacturing plant. To the left were the familiar landscaped grounds of City College. A corner of the green, copper-plated dome of the library building where she worked was visible. In the distance, the brilliant, blue-green waters of Lake Chewiston sparkled.

"How lovely to see you, my dear, but I regret it's under these dire circumstances. Tiny informed me of the incident on the street."

At the sound of the all-too-familiar, oily tones, she spun from the mesmerizing view.

A short, wiry, middle-aged man stood in the middle of the large room.

"Julio." His name escaped on a breath of air. She hadn't seen him in five years, but he hadn't changed. A few more lines were carved across his forehead and bracketed his wide mouth. Gray streaked his short black hair and carefully trimmed beard, but his gunmetal-gray eyes held the same predatory gleam.

He held out his arms. "Aren't you going to give your Uncle Julio a hug?" His smile faded when she held her ground. He lowered his arms and swiveled to Scott. His eyes narrowed to slits. "Bannister. I must say, I'm surprised to see you here."

Scott nodded. "DeGrazzi."

Julio's lip curled in a sneer. "Am I to assume you're here on official business?" He tutted. "Your fascination with me and my affairs is edging on harassment." He tapped the toe of his handmade Italian loafer on the gleaming hardwood floor. "I assume you have a warrant."

Scott's hands tightened at his sides. "This isn't official."

"Really? Then we have nothing to say to each other." Julio jerked out a cell phone from his suit coat pocket. "I'll have my men see you out."

Marissa's stomach tightened at the venom on her uncle's bearded face.

Scott edged beside her, his broad shoulder brushing hers.

The nearness of his body and the whiff of his spicy aftershave shored up her tattered nerves. "Scott saved my life. Just now, on the street outside this building, someone tried to run me down." Her voice hitched. "If it hadn't been for Scott, I'd be dead."

Julio's expression turned thunderous. "My men informed me of your close call." He nodded at her torn pants and scraped palms. "I see you're injured. Do you need medical attention? Should I call a doctor?"

She shook her head.

"Are you sure? Your knees and palms look sore. Can I get you some bandages or antibiotic ointment?"

Again she shook her head. The last thing she wanted was his help. Being here, in this posh penthouse and in her uncle's presence, brought back too many uncomfortable memories. The sooner they got this over with, the better. She'd treat her wounds later at home.

The cell phone in his hand chirped. Never taking his gaze from her, he listened, then spoke into the phone. "That's not good enough." His expression turned furious. "Find the bastard." He severed connection and stuffed the phone back in his pocket. "There's no sign of the SUV, but don't worry, I'll find who's responsible. I have cameras posted at several vantage points outside this building. One of them will have caught the vehicle on video."

She shuddered at the menace in his eyes. As much as she wanted the driver of the vehicle punished, she didn't wish Julio's rage on anyone.

"Your cameras won't help," Scott said.

Julio's eyebrows arched. "And why is that?"

"The SUV's windows were tinted. I couldn't see the driver, and I was right there."

"We'll get the license plate number."

Scott shook his head. "There wasn't one."

"I see." Julio stroked his beard, his brow furrowed.

"We need to talk, DeGrazzi." Scott rubbed his right shoulder and winced, obviously in discomfort.

No wonder. He'd taken the brunt of the force of their crash. Her body ached in a dozen places. If he hadn't been there, if he hadn't reached her in time... She shuddered.

"Is this about saving my niece's life?" Julio's sharp voice broke into her turmoil. "Do you want my gratitude, Bannister? Well, you have it. Now get the hell out of here."

Scott didn't budge.

"Oh, I get it. You want a reward, an indication of my appreciation. No problem. I'll have my accountant write you a check. Name the amount."

"I don't want your money or your gratitude." Scott strained the words through clenched teeth. "Go ahead. Call your goons. They can toss me out of here, but it won't change the fact someone's using your niece to take you down."

Julio's face darkened, and the muscles in his small,

whipcord-lean body tensed.

She held her breath, waiting for the impending explosion.

Instead of lashing out at Scott, Julio spun around and strode across the vast, sunlit room. "Follow me."

Scott glanced at her.

She shrugged. "We may as well see what he has to say." She was used to her uncle's mercurial moods.

He nodded.

They followed Julio out of the large viewing room and down a short hallway to a smaller, cozier room. A burgundy leather couch and two matching armchairs were set before a white marble fireplace. A cheery fire crackled on the grate.

First edition, leather-bound books were arranged on glassed-in shelves along one wall. A large oil painting of horses and hounds on the hunt, an original artwork by a well-known eighteenth-century artist, filled another wall. Crystal decanters containing a variety of liquors were laid out on a gleaming walnut table set beside the large, floor-to-ceiling picture window.

Julio settled in an armchair beside the fire and crossed one leg over the other.

She perched on the couch, and Scott sat on the facing chair.

A tall, intricately carved, mahogany grandfather clock ticked the passing minutes, one sonorous tick-tock at a time. Faint sounds of the late-morning rush-hour traffic from far below filtered through the window's thick glass.

Julio tapped his fingers on the arms of his chair. His foot swung in a matching staccato rhythm belying his relaxed demeanor. "Get to the point, Bannister. I'm a busy man. Why are you here?"

"I'll bet you're busy." Scott smirked. "Graft and corruption are hard work."

Julio's thick, dark brows arrowed in a deep vee over his aquiline nose. The tapping ceased, and he gripped the armrests, his manicured nails gouging the soft leather.

Scott's hands lay flat, palms on his thighs, and he looked relaxed, but sparks shot from his blue eyes.

The tension in the room coiled and writhed like a living, breathing beast.

She spoke before the two men tore at each other's throat. "He's right to be concerned, Julio. You should listen."

The clock chimed the quarter hour. The fire hissed, and a log shifted with a shower of sparks.

Julio huffed out a breath and relaxed his grip on the armrests. "Go ahead. I'm listening." He gestured at Scott. "Talk."

"Someone's trying to destroy you and your little criminal empire."

Julio's mouth twisted in a frigid smile. "Someone other than you?" He brushed a fleck of lint off his tailored slacks. "Many have tried, but"—he waved his hand at the luxurious surroundings—"as you can see, no one has succeeded." He gave Scott a scornful once-over. "You'll be no different, I assure you."

Scott's hands balled into fists. "You're going down, DeGrazzi. Make no mistake, and it will be my absolute pleasure to be the man to put you in jail."

The two men glared at each other, nostrils flaring.

"Julio, Scott, please. This isn't helping." She

tensed, half expecting them to lock horns and battle to the end.

With a visible effort, Scott unclenched his fists and sat back on his chair. The fierce challenge in his blue eyes was evident, but he no longer vibrated on the edge of his seat, his body tense and bristling. "Yesterday I received a phone call from one of your men."

Julio's eyes widened. "One of *my* men called you? Why?"

"Flinty McGregor wanted to talk. Said he had something to tell me, something about your organization. We arranged to meet."

"I don't believe you." Something dark and primitive lurked beneath the surface of Julio's even-toned voice. "Flinty's been with me for years. He'd never betray me."

"I guess you haven't heard," Scott said.

"Heard what?"

"McGregor's dead."

Julio blinked. "What the hell are you talking about?"

"And here I thought you had cops on your payroll." Scott gave a mirthless laugh. "Guess I was wrong. Score one for the good guys."

"You'd better tell me what's going on, Bannister. I read about a murder at the Condor Hotel last night in this morning's paper, but the victim's name wasn't given. Are you telling me that was Flinty?"

She shivered at the ice in Julio's voice, but remained silent. Both men seemed to have forgotten her. She was a spectator in this match of wills.

Scott cleared his throat. "McGregor arranged a meeting with me at the Condor Hotel last night. When I arrived in the room he'd booked, Marissa was there."

Julio's feet hit the floor with a thud. "What?" He exploded to his feet and glowered at Scott. "You're lying. My niece would never go in a rathole like the Condor."

"It's true." Her voice cracked. "I was drugged and abducted from the college parking lot. When I woke up, I was lying on the floor in that hotel room. The blood sample the police took revealed I'd been given a roofie. You know, the date-rape drug." She scrubbed her hands on her thighs but winced at the sudden sharp pain of her scraped skin. Maybe she should have taken Julio up on his offer of bandages.

Julio threaded his fingers through his hair. "Are you telling me someone slipped you a drug and took you against your will to that hotel room?"

She nodded, the lump in her throat too thick to speak.

"At first, I assumed she was a plant put there at your behest," Scott said.

The frown lines on Julio's face deepened.

"I figured she was a drugged-out hooker, and you'd set me up and called the press so they'd arrive and catch me in a compromising situation." He held up his hand, stopping Julio's outburst. "Not that I had sex with her...I'd never...I mean, look at her...it isn't that she's not attractive. Any man would want to sleep with her, but..." His face reddened, and he fidgeted in his chair as if the seat was hot.

She didn't know whether to be insulted or flattered, but she took solace in his obvious discomfort.

Scott wiped his gleaming brow with the sleeve of his torn leather jacket. "Believe me, this gets worse."

He inhaled a deep breath. "Traces of McGregor's blood were found under Marissa's fingernails."

"What the hell?" A vein in Julio's forehead throbbed.

"Someone killed McGregor in the alley behind the hotel and left Marissa's purse and cell phone beside the body. That same someone tipped off the police and the press that there'd been a murder, and Julio DeGrazzi's niece and the ADA were at the scene."

The ticking of the clock was deafening in the heavy silence that fell over the room.

Julio exhaled a loud breath. "Is that everything?"

Scott nodded. "Other than the near miss by the SUV this morning."

Julio paced across the room, his hands clasped behind his back. Fury radiated off his tightly strung body like a nimbus waiting to explode.

She shot Scott a glance, but he was focused on Julio. A thread of anger slithered through her belly. The two men discussed her as if she weren't in the room. She cleared her throat. "Excuse me. I'm right here."

Julio stopped his frantic pacing and glanced at her, but in the next breath he returned his attention to Scott. "You think someone wants to take both of us down, and they're using Marissa to do it."

Scott nodded. "Exactly."

Frustrated at their continued exclusion, she leaped up and slammed her hands on her hips. "Stop talking about me as if I'm a child." She scowled. "This nightmare is happening to *me*. *I* was drugged. *I* was abducted and placed in that hotel room. Someone tried to run *me* down."

Scott shook his head. "I know you're frightened,

Marissa, but—"

Her anger exploded at his patronizing tone. She swung to her uncle. "This is your fault." She pointed her finger at him. "You're the reason I'm a suspect in a murder investigation." She wanted to scream, to yell at the heavens, to hit something… someone…him.

Julio clasped her arm, but she shook him off. "Don't touch me. Don't you dare." She blew out a ragged breath and thrust her fingers through her hair. "This is why I severed contact with you. Why I didn't want to come here today." Her chest heaved, and her breath panted in and out in loud bursts, but she didn't stop, couldn't stop. "I didn't want anything to do with you. Not after—" She blinked back the sting of tears and ignored the warning flashing in his silver eyes. Her fury was too hot, too visceral. "You remember, don't you, *Uncle* Julio? You remember what you did."

His face blanched, but he held his ground against her onslaught. "Of course I remember." He shriveled before her eyes, his voice ragged, thick with emotion. "How could I forget when I never see you, never talk to you? I miss you every day."

His distress deflated her anger like a popped balloon. Her shoulders slumped, and she swayed, too exhausted to stand.

Scott cleared his throat.

She'd forgotten he was there, a witness to her outburst. Thank God Julio stopped her before she said too much. But maybe it was time the truth came out. Maybe her long-held secret needed to be revealed. And then she could move on with her life.

Julio strode to the bar. "I need a drink." He poured amber liquid into a crystal glass. Holding his drink to the light streaming in through the window, he swirled the glass and studied the amber contents. "This is fifteen-year-old, prime scotch whiskey." He sipped the drink and closed his eyes. "Nectar of the gods."

Scott muttered a curse. "We're wasting time, DeGrazzi."

"Don't worry. I'll find the culprit." A smug smile played across his lips.

Scott shook his head. "Stop bullshitting me. You know who's behind this."

"What are you talking about?" Julio's brow furrowed. "I have many enemies. This could be an act of any number of them."

"True, but this particular enemy isn't just threatening your niece, he wants to take me down as well." Scott rubbed his chin. "And he's using Marissa to ensure that happens. He's proven he'll stop at nothing to destroy us…even murder."

Julio's eyes shot sparks. "No one"—he clenched his hand into a fist—"no one threatens my family."

Scott's brisk voice cut through the thick wall of suppressed rage surrounding Julio. "When was the last time you saw Slavadad Marischenko?"

****

Julio's face flushed red. The air in the room thickened as if all the oxygen had been sucked out. "What the hell are you talking about? I don't know anyone with that name."

Scott stuffed his balled fists in his pockets. He hadn't expected DeGrazzi to admit to knowing Marischenko, but he'd got what he wanted. The old man's face had turned apoplectic when Scott brought up the Russian's name. "Whatever you say."

DeGrazzi swigged whiskey. "Why are you here, Bannister? For the past six months you've done your damnedest to put me away." His lip curled in a sneer. "And now you expect me to believe you're here to help me and be what...my friend?"

"I'm here because last night someone tried to destroy *my* career. Whoever he is, he wants to destroy you, too." Scott's mouth twisted. "Not that I mind. Hell, he deserves a medal as far as I'm concerned, but I refuse to sit back and let this jerk toy with me."

He rubbed the knot in the back of his neck. He'd thought of this meeting all night and had gone over his words again and again to get them right. Convincing DeGrazzi to help him ferret out the culprit behind the past night's debacle wouldn't be easy. If his plan played out as he envisioned, they'd find the person behind the murder, and as a bonus, Scott would take down DeGrazzi once and for all.

"Go on." DeGrazzi made a rolling motion with his hand. "I'm listening."

Now to bait the hook. "The police believe Marissa's a prime suspect in McGregor's murder. His blood was on her hands, her purse and cell phone were found at the murder scene, and she's your niece. They're going to do everything in their power to prove she's guilty."

DeGrazzi's mouth thinned. "What do you want from me?"

And to set the hook. "Your help."

DeGrazzi barked out a laugh. "Why the hell should I help you?"

"Think about it. We find the guy responsible, I clear my name, Marissa's no longer in danger, and with any luck, I arrest you and put you in jail where you belong." He held his breath. Had he gone too far? Been too obvious? He could see the wheels turning behind DeGrazzi's closed face. He opened his mouth to say more but thought better of it. He'd said enough.

"Okay." DeGrazzi nodded. "You provide me with inside information on the police's investigation into the case, and I'll ask around and see if I can track down this jerk."

Scott jammed his clenched hand into his front pants pocket to stop from fist pumping the air. *Careful. You're not there yet, buddy.* "And I'll sign a warrant for your arrest."

For the first time since they'd stepped into the luxury penthouse apartment, DeGrazzi smiled. "You can try."

Scott blew out a breath. "Look, we both want this guy, but I won't let you take the law into your own hands. Vigilante justice isn't on the table. Once we find the person responsible, I'll arrest him."

Julio's laugh was bitter. "And then what? He walks due to a technicality? My way's better. He won't walk away from me. I guarantee you."

Scott shook his head. "No way. We find him. I handle it from there. That's the only way this will work. Agreed?"

They glared at each other, an unspoken challenge issued and accepted.

DeGrazzi held out his hand. "It's a Devil's deal, but let's shake on it, *partner*."

The last thing Scott wanted was to shake hands with the old crook, but if he wanted his help, he didn't have a choice. He met the other's man's handshake with a firm grip.

DeGrazzi's hand was soft and smooth like a woman's, his palm damp.

Scott freed his hand and resisted the urge to scrub his palm on his pants. He sank back on his chair. "What's our first move?"

DeGrazzi strolled over to the window and stared outside.

Scott risked a glance at Marissa.

Her face was pale, but her body thrummed with nervous energy, and she tapped her foot in a frantic beat on the floor much like DeGrazzi had.

His gut twisted. He couldn't allow himself to be swayed by her beauty and forget who her uncle was.

DeGrazzi sipped his drink. "Let me do some nosing around and see if I can find anything on this Marischenko character."

"If you find him, you promised you'd turn him over to me. Remember?" The last thing he wanted was DeGrazzi hunting down the person behind this mess and disposing of him before Scott had a chance to interrogate him. His plan didn't involve murder.

"Don't worry, *Mr. ADA*, I'll let you know as soon as I learn anything."

Scott's stomach rolled at the obvious false tone. This deal was a mistake. He'd been wrong to include the old man, but he needed him, needed his access to the criminal underworld. DeGrazzi could lean on people and go where the authorities, bound by a host of legalities and restrictions, couldn't. He could find Slavadad Marischenko.

The Russian gangster had been a ghost for years, impossible to track down, no matter how hard Scott searched. But, he didn't want a corpse. He needed the man alive so he could interrogate him and find out the truth once and for all. He surged to his feet. "This isn't a witch hunt, DeGrazzi. I won't let you take this guy out. When we find him, I promise you I'll prosecute him within the legal system. He'll go to jail."

Julio stared at him with narrowed eyes. "Jail?"

"If you want me to share police intel, that's the deal." He held his breath. He wasn't bluffing. As much as he wanted to catch the bastard behind the setup, he wouldn't condone vigilante antics.

DeGrazzi threw back his head and guffawed.

Scott did a slow burn. He wheeled toward the door. "Okay. That's it. I'm outta here."

"Wait."

He kept walking.

"Okay, okay. I agree. When I find this guy, I'll let you deal with him."

Stopping, he slowly turned back. The lie was clear as day in the older man's shadowy gray eyes, but Scott pretended to believe him. He had to. He needed DeGrazzi. "All right. I'll be in touch."

DeGrazzi nodded and fumbled in the pocket of his suit jacket and tugged out a small, cream-colored card and a pen. Leaning over the table, he wrote on the card and handed it to Scott. "This is my private cell number. Keep it safe. Only a very few trusted confidants know my number. Call me any time, day or night." He smiled like a shark. "Don't worry. I know how to reach you." He rattled off a series of all-too-familiar numbers.

Scott fought not to show his surprise. No one except his grandmother, his landlord, and his assistant knew his personal cell number. Suddenly the situation was all too real. DeGrazzi probably had a whole dossier on Scott. Just like the thick file Scott had on him.

He stared at the card and bit back a smile. And now he had DeGrazzi's private number. Something he hadn't had before. His plan was already bearing fruit. He looked at Marissa. "Shall we go?"

"She's staying here." DeGrazzi's firm order brooked no disagreement.

She shot to her feet. "No, I'm not."

"Marissa, listen to me." DeGrazzi's gruff voice turned pleading. "That vehicle that tried to run you down wasn't an accident. Someone's out to hurt you. I have a full security team. I can keep you safe." He waved his arm at the room. "This place is huge. You'll have your privacy. You won't even see me, unless you want to."

Her mouth set in a stubborn line. "My apartment's perfectly safe. Besides, I have my job. It's the start of term and I have a ton of work to do." She marched to the door. "I don't need you or your muscle-bound goons to keep an eye on me, *Uncle* Julio."

"But, Marissa—"

"Haven't you heard? It's the twenty-first century. There are no damsels in distress. I can look after myself." Tossing back her long, dark hair, she stormed out of the study and down the hall. The furious pounding of her sneaker-clad feet was loud on the hardwood floors.

Scott met DeGrazzi's chagrinned expression. He spread his arms wide, shrugged, and hurried after her.

Chapter 6

Traffic was heavy as Scott steered the powerful sports car through the streets away from DeGrazzi's building. He gripped the leather-covered steering wheel, his knuckles white. His rugged face was pale, and the whites of his eyes were bloodshot. He looked exhausted.

Marissa mulled over the events of the previous hour. The tense interaction between her uncle and Scott was like watching a tennis match as they flung insults at each other. Neither man was telling the truth. Of that she was certain. Each had a hidden agenda.

She understood what her uncle gained by joining forces with Scott. He'd have access to all the evidence and information the police investigators uncovered. But how would Scott benefit? He was under suspicion for murder, his entire career at risk. And now he'd agreed to work with the notorious Julio DeGrazzi to find whoever was behind the previous night's events.

She rubbed a twinge in her left shoulder. Her whole body ached from crashing onto the pavement, but at least she was alive. Were Scott and Julio right? Had the SUV tried to run her down, or was the near miss an accident? But if so, why hadn't the driver stopped? Why had he sped off? He had to know he'd almost hit them.

Had she fallen through the rabbit hole? Things like

this weren't supposed to happen. Not to her. She'd worked hard the past five years to achieve a certain level of mediocrity, to stay under the radar, to remain anonymous. And now her carefully constructed life was in shambles, and she was back in Julio's sphere of influence.

"Are you sure you're okay staying at your apartment? As much as I hate to admit, you'd probably be safer at your uncle's. He has excellent security. Tiny and his team of goons are pretty intimidating."

She blinked, startled out of her thoughts, surprised to find they were parked on the street outside her apartment building. "I'll be fine."

He undid the clasp on his seatbelt and shifted on the butter-soft leather seat so he faced her. "Look, Marissa, I'd really appreciate it if you didn't tell anyone of our meeting with your uncle." He smoothed a hand over his short, fair hair. "People wouldn't understand."

"I'm not sure I understand." She lowered her voice to match the intimate pitch of his. "Why would a man in your position agree to work with a criminal? Julio isn't behind what happened. You saw that. He didn't even know about the murder. What do you hope to gain by joining forces with him?"

His gaze slid away. "I have my reasons."

"You can't trust Julio. You know that, right?"

He laid his hand over hers where it rested on her lap. "Just promise me you won't say anything."

The warmth of his touch rattled her. His palm was broad and slightly rough against her skin. A sprinkling of fine blond hairs covered the back of his hand. "Okay, but if the police ask, I have to tell the truth. I won't lie. Not for anyone."

He squeezed her hand and released her. "I wouldn't expect you to."

Her skin tingled, and she curled her hand in her lap, already missing his comforting warmth. "I'm not stupid, Scott. I know you're not telling me everything."

He jerked like she'd struck him. "What are you talking about? You can trust me."

She snorted. "Wasn't that one of your campaign promises?" The snick of the release of her seatbelt was loud in the close confines of the tiny car. "I hope you know what you're doing. Julio's like a rabid dog. He'll turn on you in a heartbeat and rip your throat out." She pushed down on the door handle and shoved open the door.

"What happened between you and your uncle? Why haven't you spoken to him in five years?" His penetrating gaze fixed on her, imploring her to reveal her secret.

"That's none of your business."

"Maybe. Maybe not, but I want you to know I'm here if you want someone to talk to." The corners of his mouth twitched. "In spite of recent evidence to the contrary, I'm a pretty good listener."

"Nothing will change the past." The urge to reveal her deepest, darkest secret bubbled up. It would be a relief to tell him, to ease the pressure inside, to know someone understood. But with the liberation from guilt would come consequences. Dire consequences. Ramifications she wasn't prepared to face any more now than she had been five years ago. She jumped out of the car before she weakened.

His voice followed her. "Lock your windows and deadbolt your door. Don't let anyone you don't know into your apartment."

"Too late for that."

Her barb hit home, and he winced. "Call me if you see anything the slightest bit suspicious. Better yet, call 911."

She slammed the door hard, taking childish pleasure when the sleek car shuddered. Marching across the sidewalk, she used her key to unlock the lobby door, and sailed through the entrance, and across the lobby to the stairs.

The distant rumble of a finely tuned engine echoed in the small lobby.

She glanced over her shoulder. Scott's shiny red sports car swerved away from the curb and into the stream of traffic.

Taking the steps two at a time, she ran up the stairs. Bursting through the exit door, breathing hard, she hurried down the narrow hallway to her apartment. She slipped the key in the lock and unlocked the door.

The door across the hall opened. Mike Mathewson stood framed in his doorway. A wide smile broke out on his lined face. "Marissa, you're home."

"Hey, Mike. How's it going?"

His sharp-eyed gaze studied her. "I should be asking you. Look at your hands. And your pants are torn. What the hell happened?"

She shook her head. "Nothing. I...I fell." She swallowed, remembering her promise to Scott not to tell anyone of their meeting with DeGrazzi. "I'm fine."

"You don't look fine." His eyes narrowed to slits. "I heard about what happened at the Condor Hotel last night. Are you okay?"

She wasn't surprised he knew. He played poker

once a week with men from his old precinct and bowled in a police league. A murder involving the ADA and Julio DeGrazzi's niece would have definitely made the circles. Not for the first time, she was glad her last name was different from her infamous uncle's. She was pretty sure Mike didn't know Julio DeGrazzi was her uncle. If he did, he wouldn't be so concerned. "I'm okay now, thanks."

He smoothed his swollen, arthritic fingers over his shorn white hair. "I'm worried about you. They said someone slipped you a roofie."

"You don't have to worry, Mike. I'm fine. Really I am." His concern caused the sting of tears, but she blinked them back, determined to be strong.

His mouth tightened. He didn't buy her lie.

She wasn't surprised. He'd been a street cop and wore a uniform for thirty years until three years past, when he retired from the Brunswick Police Force.

He opened his apartment door wider. "Come on in. The coffeepot's on. You look like you could do with a good cup of joe, and you can tell me why the ADA was here this morning and why you look like you went a round with a wildcat."

She was tempted. He was a good listener, and it would be a relief to tell someone about the previous night and all the frightening events that had happened. Her near miss with the SUV had shaken her. To say nothing of seeing her uncle for the first time in five years. She stared into Mike's open and honest eyes, and her heart sank. She couldn't involve him in this mess. The less he knew about Julio DeGrazzi and her ties to him, the better.

Forcing a yawn, she stretched and rubbed the small

of her back. "Sorry, Mike. I'm beat. I just want to soak in a hot bath and zone out on old movies this afternoon."

His face drooped in disappointment. "Sure, Marissa."

She wilted like a limp noodle in the face of his disappointment. "How about I drop by later? We'll order pizza, and you can ply me with some of your high-test coffee."

His face lit like a beacon, and he chuckled. Mike's coffee was their standing joke. He added a tablespoon of butter to every pot he brewed and tossed in a handful of salt. The first sip was enough to strip tar off the side of an oil tanker, but the coffee didn't taste that bad. And it sure had a kick.

"That would be great." He beamed. "I'll see you around five?"

"Sure, Mike." She opened her apartment door and slipped inside. "See you later."

"Hey, wait a minute. I almost forgot." He smoothed his palm over his hair. "I'm getting to be a forgetful old man." He wheeled around and hurried into his apartment. Returning in less than a minute, he held out a padded brown envelope. Her name was scrawled across the front in large block letters.

"What's this?"

"I was on my way back from my walk—you know how I like my morning stroll." He patted his flat stomach. "Anyway, a delivery guy was waiting at the lobby door. He had a package for you. I told him I was your neighbor, and I'd take the envelope up and give it to you."

She stared at the package. Her stomach flip-flopped as a wave of unease swamped her.

"That was okay, wasn't it? I knew you weren't home. I saw you leave with Bannister, and I thought I'd save you the trouble of having to go to the depot to pick up the package."

"What delivery company?"

He stared at her, his blue-eyed gaze sharp and probing. "I don't know. Why? What's wrong? Is there a problem?"

She forced a smile. "I just wondered why the guy gave you the parcel. That's not the usual process. I mean, what if you stole my package?"

"No worries." He chuckled. "I showed him my badge." Rummaging in his pants pocket, he tugged out a slim, black wallet, and flashed it before her with practiced ease. A tarnished gold badge was on one side of the wallet and his official police identification on the other. "I shouldn't carry this around now that I'm retired, but it's been in my pocket for so many years, I feel naked without it."

A wistful smile curled his lips. "Anyway, the delivery guy didn't notice the badge has expired. He had me sign on the dotted line, pocketed my tip, and hightailed it on his bike." His smile faded. "That was all right, wasn't it?"

She gripped the padded package, feeling the thick rectangular shapes inside. Her unease grew. "That's great. No problem. Thanks for signing."

His eyes narrowed. "You're sure?"

She nodded and edged through her open doorway, anxious to rip open the package and confirm her suspicions.

He pointed at the package. "What's in there

anyway?"

Her laugh was forced, and she knew by the tightening of the lines bracketing his generous mouth she hadn't fooled him. She held up the envelope. "Oh, just something I ordered over the Internet. You know me. I love online shopping." With a wave of her hand, she started to close the door. "See you later, Mike."

He nodded, but his probing gaze held steady. "Don't forget about dinner."

The second she closed the door, her smile faded, and her disquiet ramped up. Shrugging off her sweater, she let it fall to the floor and hurried over to the couch. Her fingers trembled as she tore at the envelope, ripping open the package. Tipping the envelope upside down, she dumped a rectangular leather wallet and a cell phone onto her lap.

Her heart thudded as she stared at the all-too-familiar, black leather clutch. She ran her tongue over her dry lips. Detective Sandhu had told her the police investigators found her purse on the ground beside the murdered man, but her wallet was missing. And now, here it was. Delivered to her door. By a bike messenger. Scott told her the police had her cell phone. How did it get in the envelope with her wallet?

She shook the envelope and peered inside. No note or explanation. Should she call the police? And tell them what? That she'd found her wallet? They'd think she'd removed it from her purse before she dropped her handbag at the crime scene.

And what about her phone? If Scott told the truth and the police had her cell, how did it end up in this envelope? She punched the power-on button, and the phone glowed to life. No new text messages or calls.

Retrieving her wallet, she unsnapped the clasp and opened the wallet. Her credit cards were all present. Even her bankcard, driver's license, medical insurance card, and transit pass were still inside their leather slots.

She opened the billfold and counted the bills. Nothing was missing. Not a single dollar. Whoever found the wallet had returned it to her without taking anything. What were the odds? In this city? Her ID alone was worth hundreds of dollars on the black market.

Maybe when she was under the influence of the roofie, she'd dropped her wallet, and a Good Samaritan found it and returned it using the identification inside. Maybe the world was a better place. But that didn't explain the appearance of her phone. She should be thrilled her wallet and phone had been returned, and she didn't have to go through the tiresome process of obtaining new credit cards, applying for new identification, and buying a new phone.

Pushing back her unease, she rose to her feet and headed to the bathroom. It was time for a long soak in the tub. She made it as far as the hall outside the bathroom before she stopped, about-faced, and returned to the couch. The hair on her arms prickled as goose bumps riddled her flesh.

She picked up the wallet and unzipped the bulging change pouch. Her heart pounded like a college marching band inhabited her chest. A silver chain lay amidst the jumble of coins. Clapping her hand over her mouth, she stifled a keening wail. The strength fled her legs, and she collapsed on the couch, dropping the wallet on the floor.

A nickel and two quarters spilled out and rolled

under a chair. A length of heavy silver chain slipped out and lay on the floor like a coiled snake. The polished, heart-shaped medallion gleamed in the late-morning light.

She buried her face in her hands. Impossible. The necklace wasn't the same one. How could it be? It had been five years.

Inhaling a deep, steadying breath, she picked up the chain. Her hand shook so much she dropped the necklace twice before she managed to set it on her lap. She bit hard on her bottom lip to stop the trembling. The thick silver links gleamed as if the metal had been recently polished. She lifted the medallion and read the inscription.

Together Forever.

A sob hitched in her throat. Even though she already knew what would be engraved on the back, she turned over the silver pendant. The letters *SJC & MJR* were inscribed inside a small, stylized heart.

The world stilled. Even the beating of her heart seemed to stop. She couldn't breathe, couldn't think through the maelstrom rioting inside her head.

The persistent ringing of her cell phone pierced her distress, knifing into her skull. Grabbing the receiver, she snapped, "What?"

"Having a bad day, Miss Reynolds?" The deep, heavily accented voice chuckled, the sound chilling.

She checked the caller ID. *Unknown.* "Who is this?" Something in the man's voice stopped her from ending the call.

"I see you received my package."

Ice slid through her veins, congealing her blood. "How"—she moistened her dry lips—"the necklace…"

Unable to put into words her shock at seeing the necklace after so many years, her voice trailed off. "What...what do you want?"

"Ask your uncle. I understand the two of you have reconciled." He severed the connection, and a jarring silence filled her ear.

Ask your uncle.

How did he know she'd talked to Julio? Was she being watched? And why had he sent her a dead man's necklace? Sobs tore at her throat, and her shoulders heaved as the caller's ominous words ricocheted through her.

Chapter 7

Scott steered his car into the underground parking garage at Number One Police Plaza and parked in his assigned slot. He slipped off his sunglasses and stuffed them in his pocket. Grabbing the takeout cup of coffee from the cup holder, he undid his seatbelt, opened the door, and climbed out of the car.

Easing the door closed, he adjusted his tie and buttoned his suit coat. After the early morning meeting with DeGrazzi, he'd gone home to his condo and removed his torn and dirty clothes and stood under a searing shower until the water ran cold. But no amount of soap or scrubbing erased the stench of the backhanded deal he'd made with the notorious crime lord.

What the hell had he been thinking?

That's just it. He wasn't thinking. He never did, not clearly, not where DeGrazzi was concerned. For as long as he remembered, he'd wanted to destroy the man. The main reason he ran for the ADA position was to take down DeGrazzi. Scott was willing to do anything to achieve his goal. *Anything.* Even if it meant other people got hurt.

A vision of shaking hands with Julio DeGrazzi flashed before him, and he shuddered. If one person who'd elected him had witnessed that handshake, he'd be tarred and feathered and run out of town, his reputation in tatters.

But the deal was done. His plan was in play, and he had to do everything in his power to make damn sure his scheme worked. If not— No, he refused to think of failure. His ploy would work. Everything he cared about depended on success.

"Morning, Boss. You okay? You look like you're off in another world." Jonas Welbourne studied him through the smudged lenses of his tortoiseshell glasses. "Mind you, can't say I blame you. Last night was a disaster. Those reporters were foaming at the mouth for information. I wonder who tipped them off."

Scott grimaced. He wasn't in the mood for his garrulous assistant's endless rehashing of the previous night's events. He hadn't slept in more than twenty-four hours, and the headache that started the second he walked into that hotel room hadn't let up.

He slurped coffee and winced as the hot liquid seared his tongue. Cursing under his breath, he interrupted Jonas's endless prattling with a snarl. "Look, Jonas, I don't want to talk about this right now."

Jonas's face fell, his eager, puppy-dog grin fading. "Sorry, Scott." He bounced on his toes, fumbled with his lapel, smoothed his tie, fussed with his over-gelled hair, and wiped invisible lint from the shoulder of his natty, navy wool suit.

Once again Scott swore under his breath. Just because he was in a bad mood didn't mean he had to take his disgruntlement out on Jonas. The guy was an excellent assistant, and nobody could ask for better. Scott had hired him right out of law school. The young man was thrilled to work with the ADA. He was the first person to arrive at the office in the morning and the last to leave at night. "Sorry, Jonas. I'm beat. It was a long night."

"Well then, you're not going to be happy to hear District Attorney Johnson is waiting in your office."

Scott scowled at the unwelcome news.

Jonas held his hands up in front of him, palms out. "Hey, don't shoot the messenger. He sent me down here to see if your car was in the parking garage." His mouth twisted. "He thinks you're avoiding him."

Scott grunted. *Great idea. Why hadn't he thought of that?* Gulping more hot coffee, he strode toward the elevator.

Jonas trotted behind, continuing his endless babbling about upcoming court cases, pending investigations, new administrative directives, and the list of reporters who'd called the office wanting an official statement on the past night's homicide.

Scott half listened. He shouldn't be surprised the DA wanted to talk to him. Of course he'd want to discuss the recent events. He'd have read the report regarding the murder and probably watched Scott's statement to the press. Johnson would have questions all right. Lots of questions.

The elevator jolted to a stop, and the doors opened onto the busy front office of the District Attorney of Brunswick. A hum of energy buzzed in the air as paralegals, uniformed police officers, legal assistants, prosecuting lawyers, potential witnesses, and legal clerks bustled through the open space, going about the business of enforcing the law.

Usually Scott loved the frenetic energy, the sense that the work he did there was important, that he made a difference. But not that day. Not when he reeked of something rotten from his clandestine meeting with DeGrazzi.

He nodded good morning and forced a series of smiles at the people he passed as he marched down the wide, carpeted hall to his private office.

Before he could grab the handle, Jonas leaped in front of him and placed his hand on the doorknob and pushed open the door. He bowed and motioned for Scott to enter the office.

In spite of the strain he was under, Scott couldn't suppress a grin. He and Jonas played this game every morning, and every morning, the agile assistant beat Scott to the door. It had become a joke between them.

Jonas grinned back, his eyes bright behind the thick lenses.

Scott's smile collapsed when he saw DA Redford Johnson reclining in the leather, padded chair in front of Scott's battered and scarred partner's desk, a grim look on his handsome, patrician face. "Morning, sir, I understand you wanted to see me."

The DA studied him with the steely-eyed, steady gaze that had helped him win the last four elections. "You look like hell, Scott. Didn't sleep well?"

Scott's laugh was mirthless. "You know I didn't."

Johnson tugged back the French cuff of his designer shirt and made a show of studying his gleaming gold watch. "You're keeping banker's hours these days." His mouth twisted in a moue of disapproval. "I don't imagine the taxpayers would approve."

Scott bit back a sharp retort. Johnson wasn't the enemy. He was just playing the political game. His ADA had been caught in a messy situation, and he was worried how it would reflect on him in the upcoming election.

Scott set his cardboard coffee cup on his desk. "Can I get you some coffee, sir?"

Johnson shook his head.

Scott's heart sank. So that was the way the meeting would be. No time for pleasantries; straight to business. He inhaled a deep breath. "I assume you read the police report about the homicide at the Condor Hotel."

Johnson folded his arms in front of his broad chest. "Do you mind telling me what the hell my ADA was doing in a shit box like that? At that time of night? I'm dying to hear. I'm sure it's a doozy of a story." His spray-tanned forehead furrowed. "And don't waste my time with the bullshit you dished out to the reporters. I want the truth."

Sweat popped out on Scott's forehead. "I arranged to meet Flinty McGregor at the Condor Hotel. He was one of Julio DeGrazzi's thugs, and he said he had some information on his boss I'd be interested in."

Johnson's carefully trimmed eyebrows lowered, and he stared at Scott with narrowed eyes.

Scott swallowed the sour taste in his mouth. "I know. I shouldn't have met with him on my own out of the office. It's against department protocol, but—" He stopped. No point defending his actions. He sucked in a breath and prepared for the dressing-down he was about to face.

The DA's mouth tightened, and a pulse ticked in his square jaw, but he remained stonily silent.

"Anyway"—Scott swallowed over the thick lump blocking his throat—"the meeting didn't play out the way I anticipated."

"No kidding." Johnson expelled a long-suffering breath. "Look, I read the police report. I know the basics. What I don't understand is how a smart guy like you was so easily duped." He reached beside him, pulled out a folded newspaper, and slapped it down on the desk.

The headline on the front page screamed out at Scott, and his knees sagged. He gripped the edge of the desk. "ADA Caught In Amorous Clench With Mystery Woman." An accompanying color photo showed Scott locked in an embrace with a dark-haired woman. The picture was blurry, but part of Marissa's face was exposed. Anyone who knew her would know it was her.

"This newspaper's a rag, a gutter press. No one reads it." His voice squeaked. *Damn. Damn. Damn.* He should have known that would happen. The reporters who showed up outside that hotel room had their cameras flashing. He was lucky only the *Brunswick Scoop* had run the grainy photo.

"*I* read this paper." The DA tapped the photograph with a buffed and manicured fingernail. "Isn't she Julio DeGrazzi's niece?" His lips squeezed together in obvious disapproval. "It looks like the two of you are pretty friendly."

Heat flared up Scott's neck and burned his cheeks. "It wasn't like that. Not at all. She was crying and..." His vehement defense of his actions trailed off at the closed expression on Johnson's face.

"I don't have to tell you this doesn't look good, Scott. Not good at all."

"I'll fix it. Give me some time and I'll"—he waved his hands at the damning newspaper photo and headline—"make this go away." How in the hell would he accomplish that herculean feat?

Johnson harrumphed and called his bluff. "And just how are you planning to do that?"

"I don't know." The unceasing pounding in his head intensified. "But I'll get to the bottom of this, believe me. McGregor's murder won't be unsolved for long. I have a lead. Once we have the perp in custody, no one will care about a blurry photograph of a so-called *mystery* woman."

"I'll care." The DA shook his head, and the silver streaks in his full head of dark hair shimmered under the bright office lights. "I can't condone my Assistant District Attorney acting like a lone wolf. I need a team player at my side, not someone who thinks nothing of going against department regulations." He expelled a breath. "I'm afraid I can't allow you to continue with your investigation. You're too involved in this case, possibly even a suspect, from what I understand."

He held up his hand, stopping Scott's protest. "You can't investigate this case. Your involvement would be a direct conflict of interest." He clasped his hands in front of him and rested them on his prominent belly. "I've arranged for a temporary ADA to fill in while you sit this one out."

Jonas's gasp filled the office.

Scott had forgotten his assistant was in the room, a silent observer to the DA's dressing-down. He spun to his assistant and barked, "Leave us, Jonas."

Jonas opened his mouth and looked as if he was about to argue, but Scott glared him down, and the younger man scuttled out of the room.

Scott schooled his expression so as not to reveal how shocked he was at the DA's decision. "Are you serious? You're pulling me off the case?"

"Look, I'm sorry, Scott, but you have to understand how this looks. You're involved, whether you like it or not. I can't"—his mouth tightened—"*I won't* let you taint this case with even a hint of impropriety. It's too close to the election."

Scott blew out a breath. He sank onto his chair and sipped coffee, pleased his hand didn't shake. "So I'm off the case?" No matter how many times he said the damning words, they boomed through his head like a death knell.

"You're off every case."

His jaw dropped as he stared at his boss. "You're firing me?"

"Of course not. You're too good of an ADA." Johnson pursed his lips. "You're going to sit out these next few weeks until we clear this matter up and catch the perpetrator."

"I'm on desk duty?"

Johnson shook his head. "Better if you don't come into the office."

"Better for whom? You? Because sitting on my ass at home and twiddling my thumbs sure as hell won't help me. Think how this'll look. People will assume I had something to do with the murder. They'll think I'm guilty."

Scott breathed in through his mouth and exhaled slowly through his nose, forcing down his rising anger. "Look, Redford, we're friends, or at least I thought we were." He lurched to his feet. "Don't you see? Someone's screwing with me." He waved his hands around and gave up all pretense of calm. "Last night was about discrediting me. You're playing right into this asshole's plan."

Johnson stood and smoothed his yellow silk power tie. "I'm sorry, Scott, but I've made my decision." He buttoned his jacket over his bulging stomach. "Think of this as a holiday. Go somewhere warm. Get a tan. Get some rest. Judging by the sacks under your eyes, you could use some."

Scott fumed as his boss strode across the room and out the door. He was still stewing when the door opened a few minutes later and Jonas slipped in.

A frown marred the assistant's angular face. "You okay, Boss? Anything I can get you?"

Scott didn't bother to respond. His entire world was shaken. He'd been put on forced leave. Now what the hell was he going to do? *Go somewhere warm.* The DA's words thundered through him in a taunting refrain. He couldn't be off the case. It was too damn important.

If he was on leave, his judicial right to investigate the case was severed. He lost access to information the police uncovered in the course of their investigation. He'd be persona non grata. An outsider. No cop would speak to him once word leaked he was off the case. Worse, DeGrazzi would cut him loose, and any hope he had of finding Slavadad Marischenko and making DeGrazzi pay would be dead in the water.

"Boss?"

He focused on Jonas. "Get Detective Sandhu on the phone."

Jonas hesitated. "But didn't"—his throat worked, his Adam's apple bobbing—"didn't the DA place you on mandatory leave?"

Irritation flashed through Scott. He'd always

suspected Jonas listened at his office door. Now he knew. Unless news of his *holiday* was already office gossip. His heart raced. If so, he was too late.

No. He refused to think that. There might still be time to salvage something out of this train wreck. "Call the detective and tell him I'm on my way." He instilled as much authority as he could muster into his order. "I need to see him right away."

Jonas nodded, turned, and hurried out of the room.

Scott shoved his chair back and stormed across the office. He had to reach Detective Sandhu before the lead detective learned Scott was off the case. The police precinct was a twenty-minute walk from the DA's office. He'd get there in less than half that time if he took his car.

As he hurried down the hall to the stairs, he prayed he'd reach the precinct before the blue wall of silence came crashing down, and he was left on the outside staring in, his dick flapping in the breeze.

Chapter 8

Keeping his hand jammed on the horn and ignoring a half-dozen traffic laws, Scott squealed around the corner and screeched to a stop in a no-parking zone in front of the precinct. Leaping out of the car, he sprinted up the wide stone steps into the old, two-story, red brick building.

He dodged past uniformed cops and plain-clothed detectives, ignoring their curious looks as he rushed through the crowded main floor, down a long, dark hallway to a room in the back of the building.

The overcrowded office housed the Brunswick Police Force Homicide Detective Division and was responsible for investigating murders committed in Brunswick and the surrounding county. Twenty full-time detectives worked out of this dingy, cramped office. Today, like every other day, the bullpen was a beehive of feverish activity. The steady cacophony of ringing phones, raised voices, and the clang of the out-of-date air-conditioning system deafened.

He wove through the forest of metal desks to a small, glass-fronted office.

Detective Sandhu looked up when Scott rapped on the door and gestured for him to enter.

Scott pushed open the door and stepped inside. He sucked in a calming breath and affected a casual manner. "Hey, Ardash. How's it going?"

"Morning, Scott. I was surprised when your Boy Friday called and said you were coming over. I guess the old adage is wrong—the mountain can come to Muhammad." He chuckled and nodded at one of the two visitor chairs in the room. "What can I do you for?"

A wave of relief washed over Scott. Ardash's open, friendly manner indicated he hadn't heard Scott was off the case. "How's the family? Is little Jasinder still kicking butt on the soccer pitch?" Ardash was extremely proud of his son and loved to regale Scott on the kid's winning exploits.

But not this day.

Ardash's face paled, and he ignored Scott's friendly inquiry. "What do you want, Scott? I'm a busy man. In case you've forgotten, I have a murderer to catch."

Scott frowned at the detective's unusual sharpness. Now that he looked closer, he saw the bags under his soulful dark eyes and the sallow tone of his usually swarthy skin. "Everything okay?"

"Of course. Why wouldn't it be? I'm just under the gun on this McGregor homicide." He scrubbed a hand over his eyes. "The DA's riding my ass. He wants this solved yesterday."

Scott sat on a visitor chair and crossed one leg over the other, feigning a casual air. "That's why I'm here. I thought I'd stop by and get the update."

"I tell you, this case is a gong show." Sandhu shook his head. "We're still wading through the evidence. I can't think of another case where we've found so many clues, all pointing at one suspect."

"Tell me what you have so far."

Sandhu opened a thick file on his desk. "The lab

reports indicate the blood at the scene—and there was a hell of a lot of it—came from the victim. Not a surprise. Poor sap was stabbed twenty times in the chest, abdomen, and neck."

"Was the murder weapon found?"

"Investigators found a butcher knife covered in the vic's blood tossed in a dumpster."

"Fingerprints?"

"One full set, no smudges."

Scott's eyes widened. Most criminals knew to wipe their fingerprints from a murder weapon, or they wore gloves. It was rare to find any prints, let alone a complete set. "Are the prints in AFIS?" The national fingerprint database kept a digital record of fingerprint and DNA evidence from convicted criminals. Military personnel and anyone else who'd ever been fingerprinted were also in the system.

"No, but we had them on file." The detective sat back. "Someone handed us a present all wrapped up and tied in a neat bow. If I didn't know better, I'd think it was Christmas."

"Whose prints were on the weapon? One of DeGrazzi's goons?"

"Nope."

"Then whose?"

"Detective Barbour's interrogating the suspect now."

Scott's heart thumped, and he lurched forward on his chair. "You have the suspect here?"

Sandhu picked up a pencil and twirled it. "We picked up Marissa Reynolds an hour ago."

Scott fell back in the chair as if he'd been shoved. "What?"

"I had the same reaction. I mean, I know the lady was there last night, and she had the victim's blood under her fingernails, but I sure didn't figure her for the murderer."

"Are you telling me her fingerprints were on the murder weapon?"

Sandhu nodded.

Scott's mind whirled as he tried to take in this stunning development. "Was the knife buried under the trash in the dumpster?"

"Sitting right on top. We lifted the lid and there it was, just waiting for us."

"Seems a bit too pat."

Sandhu's mouth twisted in a wry smile. "You think?" He twirled the pencil, flipping it from one finger to the other. "I've worked homicide for over ten years, and in all that time, I've never seen such a clearcut case." He tossed the pencil on his desk and held up a finger. "First, we receive an anonymous tip informing us a man's been murdered. The tipster gives us the name of the hotel and tells us exactly where we can find the body. He even tells us where the murderer is hiding, and he informs us Julio DeGrazzi's niece is at the scene. He also calls the press and gives them the same information."

Another finger shot up. "Second, when we find the body, a woman's purse is lying beside it, and inside the purse is a cell phone registered to our suspect."

Another finger joined the first two. "The suspect has the victim's blood under her fingernails, and"—a fourth finger rose—"her prints are all over the murder weapon. Add in the fact she's Julio DeGrazzi's niece, and"—he slapped his palm on the desk—"you have a slam dunk."

"A setup."

"Of the first order. Someone's playing us big time. The only thing missing is the suspect's confession."

"And you have her in an interrogation room?"

"Look, there's no way she committed the murder, but we have to question her. Maybe she knows something that will lead us to the perp." He used two fingers to smooth his neat mustache. "Mind you, I could be wrong, Ms. Reynolds could be the dumbest criminal to walk the face of this earth and she's guilty as hell."

Scott shot to his feet. "I'd like to talk to her."

Sandhu stood and moved from behind his desk and headed for the door. "I'll take you."

****

The interrogation room was small and stuffy. Heat blasted out of the overhead vents, alternating with frigid gusts of air. At the moment, cold air pelted down on her. Marissa shivered and rubbed the goose bumps on her arms, wishing she'd worn something warmer than a thin cotton T-shirt, but when the two police officers arrived at her door, they hadn't given her time to change before they led her out of her apartment to their marked cruiser on the street below.

Detective Barbour lounged in a chair, his blue eyes filled with suspicion. "Tell me one more time about your relationship with Flinty McGregor."

She heaved a deep breath, striving for patience. "I've already told you, Detective, I didn't have a relationship with Mr. McGregor. I didn't know him."

His upper lip curled in a sneer. "So how do you explain his blood under your fingernails?"

"I can't. I've already told you that I—"

The door opened, and Scott Bannister burst into the room, Detective Sandhu at his side.

She sat up with a start.

Detective Sandhu fixed Detective Barbour with a hard look. "Has she confessed to killing McGregor?"

She sucked in a sharp breath and erupted out of her chair. "I've already told you. I didn't kill that man. You can't believe I'm a suspect." Her voice rose several octaves. "This is ridiculous."

Detective Barbour ignored her outburst. "She's sticking to her story. Someone drugged her, and she has no idea what happened until she woke up in that hotel room."

"It's not a story. Your own tests prove I was drugged." How many times did she have to repeat the same thing? Why wouldn't they believe her? They'd questioned her for hours the previous night and again that day. No matter how many times they asked the questions, the answers would be the same. She was innocent.

The red-haired detective's thin lips curled. "Apparently the wallet missing from her purse was delivered to her apartment this morning."

Scott raised his eyebrows. "Really? That's interesting."

Detective Barbour nodded. "The officer I sent to her apartment confirmed a package was delivered this morning. Her neighbor signed for it. We're trying to track down the delivery company."

Marissa wiped her damp palms on her pants, hoping the sharp-eyed detectives didn't discern her subterfuge. She hadn't mentioned that her cell phone was in the same package as her wallet, or of finding the chain in the coin pouch, or the man with the accent who'd called. The police already considered her a prime suspect; if they knew everything, she'd look even guiltier.

She plastered an outraged expression on her face. "This is starting to feel like harassment. I've told you what I know. Should I call a lawyer?"

"Not a bad idea. With all the evidence we have pointing at you, you're going to need some heavy-duty legal counsel if you hope to avoid a long prison sentence," Detective Barbour said.

The anger and frustration drained from her, leaving her emotions battered and bruised. She couldn't go to prison. She hadn't committed a crime. Innocent people didn't end up in jail. Scott was right. This was all because of her uncle. Someone was attacking him and using her to do the damage.

"I'd like a few minutes alone with the suspect." Scott's deep voice broke through her stunned disbelief.

She flinched at the word suspect.

"Now?" A deep furrow grooved between Detective Sandhu's dark brows. "We're in the middle of questioning her."

"Now." Scott's voice was filled with quiet authority.

The furnace kicked in, and a blast of hot air swept over her. The rancid stink of sour sweat and burnt dust filled the stuffy room.

"You have ten minutes." Detective Sandhu strode out of the room followed by Detective Barbour.

Scott waited for the door to close before he pulled out a chair, swung it around, and straddled the seat. He rested his arms on the chair back. "We don't have much time."

She blinked at the urgency in his voice. "What's going on?"

"Did they tell you they found the murder weapon?"

She shook her head.

"The police located a knife in a dumpster in the alley near where the body was found."

Her throat tightened as a sense of impending doom washed over her.

"Your fingerprints were on the knife."

"What? That's not possible." But what if she was wrong? A flood of nausea enveloped her, and she gagged, barely managing to sallow back her gorge. Had she murdered that man? Had she been so drugged, she'd stabbed a man to death? She'd heard of people sleepwalking or eating elaborate meals while under a drug's influence, but murder? She jumped to her feet, her legs rubbery.

"Easy." Scott grasped her elbow, holding her steady. "Sit down before you fall down."

She collapsed on the chair as if she were boneless.

"Wait here." He disappeared out the door, but was back in seconds carrying a small, plastic water bottle. "Drink this." He handed her the bottle.

Her hands shook so much she couldn't open the lid.

He took the bottle, and with a single twist, removed the cap. Rather than set the water on the table, he held the mouth of the bottle to her lips.

Her gaze met his, and in spite of the stark surroundings and the air of desolation, a flash of awareness arced between them.

She opened her mouth, and he dribbled water over her lips. She swallowed and sipped again. The water slid down her raw throat like silk, easing the tightness. "Thank you."

He grasped her hand and brushed his thumb against the sensitive skin on the inside of her wrist. "I know this is tough, but you have to be strong. Someone's doing their damnedest to make you look guilty."

"I didn't—"

He cut her off her protest. "I know. You didn't kill that man."

Her lower lip trembled. "I wish the police felt the same. They think I did it."

"No, they don't."

"Then why—"

The door opened with a bang, and Detective Sandhu strode into the room.

Scott snatched his hand back and surged to his feet.

Sparks blasted from the detective's dark eyes as he glared at Scott. "You're off the case." His voice was rife with accusation.

A look of chagrin settled on Scott's handsome face. "You know."

"The DA's office called."

"I figured Johnson wouldn't waste any time."

"You lied to me."

"No, but I'll admit I didn't disclose everything." Scott heaved a sigh. "I hope I didn't get you in trouble with the DA."

Detective Sandhu stared at Scott for a long, drawn-out minute. "I didn't tell him you were here."

Scott's eyes widened. "I appreciate that."

"I don't know what you're up to, but I hope you

know what you're doing. The DA was pretty adamant you're off the case."

"I hope I do too, Ardash."

Detective Sandhu's face was grim. "Go on. Get out of here."

Scott grabbed her hand and tugged her out of the chair. "You're not charging Ms. Reynolds, so she's coming with me."

She tensed, waiting for the detective to protest, but he stepped aside, and she and Scott walked past.

Scott paused. "Thanks, Adarsh. I won't forget this."

The detective's face remained impassive, his eyes shuttered. "I wish you would."

Scott led her down the hall, through the chaos of the crowded homicide division, and out of the building.

Once they were on the street, she dug in her heels and pulled to a stop. "What was all that? What was Detective Sandhu talking about? Are you off the case?"

A flush of red stained his rugged cheeks. "You heard him. The DA placed me on mandatory leave."

"What? Why?"

"Apparently, I'm a suspect."

"You? But you're the ADA. Why are you a suspect?"

"Because of those damn hotel surveillance tapes. I'm not sure the investigators believe I wasn't the guy who drugged you and took you to the hotel."

"But you explained that. Someone copied your disguise. Besides, why would you kidnap me? What would you gain?" She put her hand over her mouth, halting further words. Scott made no secret he'd stop at nothing to take down her uncle. What better way to destroy his enemy than to point the finger of blame in a homicide at DeGrazzi's niece? She stared into his clear, navy eyes. A chill settled through her. Was he capable of something so nefarious? Was he using her to achieve his goals?

He seemed oblivious to the maelstrom rioting through her. "My boss thinks it would be a conflict of interest if I were to continue to work on the investigation." He spoke in an emotionless voice, but his face was pale, and his body strung tight as a fiddle.

An unexpected spurt of sympathy burst to life. The shocking events of the past two days didn't just affect her. He was also caught in the middle of this nightmare.

He tugged her hand. "Come on. Let's get out of here before they change their minds and arrest you."

"Where are we going?"

"To find answers."

"Answers?"

He ushered her into his car before she could question him further. The car rumbled to life, and tires squealing, he roared onto the street.

Chapter 9

Marissa clutched the sides of the supple leather seat, hanging on as the car sped through the city, passing other cars in a blur of color.

Scott's mouth was set in a determined line as, with a blare of the horn, he blew through another red light. Shifting gears with skill and confidence, he maneuvered the sleek sports car through the mid-day congestion, weaving in and out of traffic.

"Where…where are we going?" Those were the first words she'd managed to push through her clenched teeth since they'd sped away from police headquarters. She squeezed her eyes shut as they careened around a corner and crossed two lanes of traffic amidst a blast of angry honking from the drivers he cut off. "Are you trying to get us killed? Slow down."

He shot her a quick glance before resuming his focus on the road. "I'm trying to lose the car that's following us."

She shivered at the grim determination in his navy eyes. "Following us? Who would bother to follow us?"

He shrugged. "Could be any number of people…your uncle's men, reporters, the police, whoever's behind this disaster. Maybe all of them."

One word jumped out. "Reporters?" She twisted around and peered out the rear window. The traffic was heavy, and she couldn't tell if any of the dozens of vehicles were following them. Detective Barbour had shown her the photo of her and Scott locked in each other's arms that appeared on the front page of this morning's newspaper. She'd shuddered at the lurid headline. If any reporters were on their tail, she hoped Scott lost them. The last thing she wanted was more publicity. If the media discovered who she was, she wouldn't be able to do her laundry without being recognized as Julio DeGrazzi's infamous niece.

When they reached the highway, he jammed his foot on the gas pedal, and the car purred down the road like a jaguar, overtaking long-haul trucks and passenger vehicles in a blast of wind.

She peered at the speedometer and shuddered as the car's speed surged into the triple digits. "Are they still behind us?"

In answer, he jerked the steering wheel to the right, and the car swerved off the paved highway onto an unpaved secondary road. The rear end fishtailed until the tires gripped the road, and they raced into the orange glow of the setting sun. The little car bounced and skidded on the gravel. The engine pinged and something rattled under the hood. The fancy foreign sports car wasn't built for off-pavement driving.

"Did you lose him?"

"I think so. I haven't seen a vehicle behind us for a few miles." He slowed the car and they bounced off the gravel road onto a narrow, dirt lane. A few minutes later, the glow from the headlights outlined a tiny rustic cottage. He cut the engine.

Dust settled around them, and the motor ticked and pinged as it cooled in the sudden silence.

She blew out a shaky breath, relaxed her death grip

on the seat, and stared through the passenger window. The small patch of lawn was mainly scrub, the shrubs overgrown, the front flowerbeds thick with weeds. Last autumn's dried leaves lay scattered in piles on the cracked cement steps leading to the covered front porch. The red paint on the door was faded and peeling. Gaps showed where pieces of white, cedar siding were missing from the outer walls of the bungalow. An old garage with a sagging roof loomed behind the dilapidated house set amongst an old orchard of gnarled, scabbed, apple trees.

"Where are we?"

He pocketed the car keys. "Gramm's house."

"Gramm?"

"My grandmother's house." He unbuckled his seatbelt, eased open his door, and climbed out of the car. "Let's go inside."

Why were they stopping at his grandmother's house? Were they picking up some homemade, chocolate chip cookies? She studied the house and shuddered. *Not likely.* She patted the lump in the front pocket of her jeans. When the police showed up at her door, she'd pocketed the silver chain, not wanting to leave the incriminating piece of jewelry lying on her coffee table. Good thing too. From what Detective Sandhu said, the police had obtained a search warrant and searched her apartment.

"Marissa?" Scott had opened her door and held out his hand, waiting. "Come on."

She swallowed. How long had he been watching her? Had he noticed the bulge of the chain? In spite of her misgivings, she placed her hand in his and allowed him to help her from the low-slung car.

He led her up the crumbling cement steps to the front door. Releasing her hand, he crouched and lifted a ceramic pot containing the dried husk of a long-dead plant stuck in a hard clump of dirt and removed a key from the tray under the pot.

"Your grandmother leaves her house key under a plant?"

The corners of his mouth twitched. "She's an old-fashioned gal." He turned the key in the lock and opened the door. Reaching inside, he flicked on a light. A warm, yellow glow spilled onto the porch, and he gestured for her to enter the narrow hall.

Marissa stepped inside, wrinkling her nose at the musty smells of boiled cabbage, lemon furniture polish, and damp rot. *No home-baked cookies here.* "Your grandmother won't mind?"

"Gramm's on a cruise ship somewhere in the Caribbean. Ever since Granddad passed three years ago, she's been cruising. She loves the ocean."

She followed him down a narrow hallway to a small, tidy living room.

He moved about the room switching on lamps.

The furniture was worn but looked comfortable. The floor was covered in outdated, deep-piled, dark-brown shag carpet, the beige walls lined with framed family photographs.

She moved closer to a photo of a beaming, towheaded boy of about eight holding a large blue ribbon. The dark-blue eyes and stubborn tilt of the boy's chin were familiar. "Is this you?"

Even in the dim light, the flush on his rugged cheeks glowed. "I won first place in the county spelling bee that year." He grinned a sheepish grin. "What can I say? I peaked early. Can't spell worth a damn now."

She moved on to the next photo.

It was the same boy, a little older, but with the same gap-toothed grin, same intense blue eyes, same mop of blond curls. All the photographs were of Scott. They followed him through life, celebrating his many accomplishments—chess club, speech contests, debating team, yearbook editor, key club, student council president, computer club, and a slew of academic awards.

She eyed the tall, broad shouldered, athletic-looking man. "You didn't participate in sports?" He looked like the sort of guy who played tennis on a regular basis or worked out at the gym.

The red patches on his cheeks engulfed his ears. "I was a late bloomer. When I was a kid, I was skinny and had long gangly legs and arms. Couldn't kick or throw a ball worth a damn, picked last for every team." He shuffled his feet. "I guess I was better at the non-physical stuff."

She spotted a small, framed photo on the mantel. Scott's adolescent face was all angles and sharp points. The gleam of braces covered his teeth and pimples dotted his pointy chin. He wore white, baggy pants and a matching tunic top. A yellow sash was tied around his narrow waist. "You were into martial arts?"

His ears blazed red. "Yeah. I took up tae kwon do when I was thirteen. Gramm thought it would help me gain confidence."

"Did it?"

He shrugged. "After I learned a few moves, the bullies left me alone."

Her heart bled for the young boy he was—raised

by his grandparents, intelligent, geeky, skinny, picked on by other kids—a difficult childhood by any standard. She studied the wall of photographs. "Your grandmother loves you very much."

"I'm her only grandchild. She and granddad raised me after my folks died."

She sucked in a breath. "I'm so sorry. Losing your parents isn't easy. My mother passed away from cancer when I was ten. My...my dad had a heart attack two years later. My uncle raised me." Familiar tears stung her eyes. How well she remembered the aching loneliness of life without her parents. Placing her hand on his arm in what she hoped was a comforting gesture, she asked, "What happened to your parents?"

He jerked his arm as if she'd slapped him. His eyes shuttered, the brief moment of intimacy over. Turning, he headed out of the room. "Are you coming?"

"Where are we going?"

"We have work to do."

"What are you talking about?"

He crooked a finger. "Come on, I'll show you."

She followed him out of the living room and up a set of creaky stairs to the second floor. They walked down a narrow, dark hallway and stopped before a closed door.

He opened the door, stepped into the room, and flicked on the overhead light.

She blinked in the sudden brightness.

A narrow bed covered by a superhero quilt was set beneath a window draped in matching superhero curtains. A large, flat-screen computer monitor, state-of-the-art keyboard, and high-powered computer tower sat atop a scarred wooden desk set against the back wall. A set of high-tech speakers and a laser printer were on the two-drawer, metal filing cabinet beside the desk.

Dog-eared comic books and clunky video game cartridges were stacked on a shelf beside the closet. Another, older desktop computer sat on the floor in the corner. Faded posters from old superhero and space opera movies lined the walls. Musky smells of sweaty socks, stale pizza, and adolescent hormones lingered in the room.

"Welcome to my lair." He swept his hands around the room.

"This is your bedroom?"

"It was. Gramm hasn't changed a thing since I was a kid." He shrugged, a sheepish glint in his blue eyes. "I was a geek. Still am, I guess."

"There's a lot of stuff crammed in here."

"Stuff? You mean the electronics?" The corners of his eyes crinkled. He pointed to the computer on the desk. "I installed the new system last year, and added high speed Internet, so when I visit Gramm I can keep in touch with the outside world."

"Play computer games, you mean." A smile tugged at the corners of her mouth.

An embarrassed grin lit his face. "Guilty as charged. Do you play?"

"I like books. *Real* books. Ones you hold in your hands and smell the paper, binding glue, and ink."

"You're a Luddite. Why am I not surprised?"

Her lips stretched in an answering smile. "I guess that's why I'm a librarian." She pointed at a shelf piled high with computer software. "But this doesn't explain why you're an Assistant District Attorney."

And just like that, the warmth left his face, and the gleam in his eyes dulled. "Let's get to work."

Another off-limits topic.

It seemed the handsome, mysterious ADA had a few secrets of his own. She shook off her unease. "What are you planning?"

He patted the computer console. "This baby's cutting edge. It's three times faster than the computer I have at the office. With the wireless Internet I installed, we're good to go." His eyes shone.

"Go where?"

"You'll see." He pulled up an old, hard-backed chair and indicated she should sit. Dragging a tall, rolling desk chair from across the room, he placed the chair before the computer and sat down. He switched on the machine.

The computer whirred, clicked, and hummed as it booted up. When a home screen flickered to life on the monitor, he started typing on the keyboard. His tanned, long fingers flew over the keys. The screen switched from one site to another in a confusing blur.

After several minutes of silence, she asked, "What are you looking for?"

"I'm trying to access the police database." He swore under his breath. "Damn! My password's been disabled. They've blocked me." He threaded his fingers through his hair. "I don't understand why they'd do that. I wasn't fired. I'm still on the payroll. I'm just on a leave of absence. Now we can't find any new information on McGregor's murder."

"Maybe I can help."

"You? I thought you didn't know anything about computers."

"I don't *like* computers. I never said I didn't know how to use them. A large part of my job is helping students with their research. You'd be surprised at some of the arcane subjects they come up with."

He studied her for several minutes as the computer hummed. "Okay. Go ahead. Give it a shot." His tone of voice made clear what he thought of her chances of succeeding. He fished in his pants pocket and drew out a crumpled piece of paper. Smoothing the torn scrap, he placed it before her on the desk and nudged the keyboard closer. "Here's the case number."

She read the series of numbers and letters and typed them into the computer.

****

As her slim fingers flew over the keyboard, a look of intense concentration shone on her face. She chewed on her full bottom lip.

He couldn't look away. What would it be like to kiss those lips? Were they as soft and sweet as they looked? Would she moan when he pressed his mouth to hers? Would she—*Stop! This isn't the time, and she's not the woman. Don't let her fresh-faced beauty fool you. She's Julio DeGrazzi's niece. That's all that matters.* He sucked in a steadying breath and refocused on the monitor, but his body hummed with aching awareness.

A series of numbers and symbols floated across the monitor as she typed, moving from site to site with dazzling speed and confidence.

He scrubbed his chin, chagrinned. And he thought he knew computers. She was obviously an expert at navigating the intricacies of the World Wide Web. "What are you doing?"

She focused on the flickering screen. "I'm trying to break through the firewall."

"The police firewall?"

She nodded.

"But that's illegal."

She slid him a glance. "And your point?"

His gut churned. He didn't like this. He never contravened the rules. Even in grade school when his friends skipped class, snuck candies from the corner store, or cheated on tests, he never did. Gramm had done her level best to instill respect for authority and the law in her grandson. That was one of the reasons he became a lawyer—to uphold the law. And why he'd run for the position of ADA. At least that's what was written in his official bio.

He jumped to his feet and paced across the small, cluttered room. The previous day he'd been a law-abiding, model citizen. Now he was a suspect in a criminal investigation. He'd committed even more infractions by consorting with a known criminal, speeding, driving through red lights, and now he was standing by while Marissa attempted to breach the police security codes. He should stop her. Really he should. Before it was too late. Before he was in too deep, and he couldn't go back.

"Got it."

He jerked around. "You're in?" *Too late.*

"I'm in."

He hustled over and peered at the screen. The police crime scene reports filed by the investigating officers on the McGregor homicide flashed across the monitor. Using the wireless mouse, he scrolled through the files. "The police have been busy. It looks like they've found new evidence." He scrubbed his day's growth of whiskers.

She leaned closer to the screen, and their shoulders grazed. A strand of silky black hair brushed his cheek, and the enticing scent of lilacs after a spring rain wafted in the air.

He breathed deeply as ripples of awareness shot along his nerve endings. His fingers froze on the mouse, the screen in front of him blurring.

"Look here." She pointed at the monitor. "What's this?"

He looked where she indicated and forgot all about lilacs, the warmth of her body, and her soft, feminine curves.

The photograph of a cell phone was on the screen.

"The caption under the photo states this is my cell phone." Her brow furrowed. "How is that possible? The police don't have my phone. Not anymore. My phone was delivered this morning in the package along with my wallet." She rummaged in the back pocket of her jeans and tugged out a small phone. "I have it here."

"What? You didn't say anything about your cell phone during your interrogation. You just said your wallet was returned." He narrowed his eyes. "You lied to the police?"

Her face flushed red. "No...I didn't—" She twined her hands together. "Maybe...I don't know...I...I forgot to mention my phone. I...I was under so much pressure, and Detective Barbour was so intimidating, so certain I was guilty, I couldn't think straight."

"Forgot?" He snorted. The distinctive signs of a lie played across her face. "I doubt that." No way she forgot the unexpected return of her cell phone. His stomach tightened. What else wasn't she telling him?

"Okay, so I didn't tell the detectives everything." She avoided his gaze but had the grace to flush. "Or you." She chewed on her bottom lip. "The important thing is someone removed my phone from the police station and sent it to me." Her gaze returned to his. "If the police found my phone at the crime scene, how could the man who sent me the package have it? Is he a policeman?"

How indeed?

He swung back to the computer and read the report. "As we know, the police found your phone inside your purse at the murder scene." Digital evidence like cell phones and computers collected at a crime scene were photographed and videotaped in situ, packaged in isolation bags, tagged, and recorded in the crime-scene-inventory log. Once that was completed, they stored the electronic devices in a locked evidence locker. The system was designed to be foolproof.

But not this time.

Somehow, from the time Marissa's cell phone was bagged and tagged, someone had broken the chain of custody and removed the phone from the evidence storage locker. The pain in his head throbbed as he struggled with the only scenario that made sense. Someone in authority—a cop, or one of the crime-scene technicians—was involved in the setup.

"Scott? Are you listening? How did my phone end up in the package with my wallet?"

The pain in his head flamed to a fireball. "Give me your phone."

"Why? What's going on?"

He held out his hand. "Come on."

Her hand shook as she handed him the phone. "I don't understand."

He powered on the phone and studied the apps on the home screen. His heart sank. Damn. How could he be so stupid? He should have asked her if she had a cell phone before they arrived at Gramm's.

Jerking open the top drawer of the desk, he rummaged through the jumble of copper wires, memory sticks, pens, sticky notes, and tech tools, and grabbed a small screwdriver. He unscrewed the screws at the bottom of the phone beside the charging port, slid out the back plate, removed the screws holding the battery bracket, and pried up the connector with the tip of the screwdriver. Next, he lifted out the battery and tossed it on the desk.

Her face was pale, her eyes wide. "What are you doing?"

"There's a reason your phone was stolen from the police evidence locker and later returned to you. Whoever took it installed a tracking app." He tossed her deactivated phone on the bed. "With the battery removed, the people behind this can't locate you."

"What if it's too late? What if they've tracked us here?" She jumped up and ran to the window, drew aside the curtains, and peered into the darkness. "What if they're waiting out there?"

"You haven't used your phone, so we should be okay." *Should* being the operative word. There were dozens of ways to ping the location of a cell phone. He hoped the people after them didn't have cutting-edge technology.

"What about your phone? Are they tracking you too?"

"I've installed specialty software on my phone, and the geo-location features are disabled." Sinking back on the chair before the computer, he studied the screen. *What the hell?* The burning pain in his neck flared to a four-alarm blaze.

Under Crime Scene Evidence, the report described a boot print found at the murder scene beside the victim's body. A chill rippled through him. Ardash hadn't mentioned anything about a boot print. Why was this the first he'd heard of it? He clicked the link, and a grainy color photograph of a boot print outlined in what looked like blood appeared.

A clear plastic, metric ruler set beside the boot print provided an indication of the size. The boot print was large and broad, with a marked ridge pattern on the heel and toe of the outsole. Probably made by a man's boot.

"What are you looking at?" Her warm breath brushed his cheek.

"This report says an impression of a boot print was located on the pavement beside the body." He pointed at the screen. "Look at the photograph. Whoever left that print walked through the victim's blood while it was still wet."

"It has to be the killer's."

He nodded. The footwear impression was a key piece of evidence. A pulse throbbed behind his right eye. Why would the murderer be so careless? First, the murder weapon found in the dumpster with a clear set of Marissa's fingerprints, and now this.

He lurched to his feet, sending the wheeled chair rolling across the room and crashing into a stack of boxes. Digging in the front pocket of his jeans, he tugged out his cell phone and punched numbers.

"Who are you calling?"

"My assistant. Something's off. Maybe Jonas can find more information about the print and determine why it wasn't in the initial crime scene report."

The phone rang two times and then three.

He checked his watch. Where was he? Jonas was always at the office, always attached to his phone. After six rings, he severed the connection before the call went to voicemail. He didn't want to leave a digital trail on Jonas's phone.

The cell phone chirped. The screen indicated a private number. Still frowning, he answered, his voice tentative, "Hello?"

"Boss, it's me."

"Jonas? What's going on? I just called you."

"I couldn't answer. I was in DA Johnson's office." Jonas's voice was a whisper. "He's on the warpath." His whisper became more hushed. "Look, if he finds out I'm talking to you, he'll can me. Whatever the hell you've done, you're in the dead zone. Johnson sent out a directive warning anyone against talking to you."

Scott rubbed the tight muscles in the back of his neck. "I don't understand. I thought I was on *holiday* leave."

"Word on the street is you're a suspect in Flinty McGregor's murder, and you're aiding and abetting the other prime suspect—Marissa Reynolds."

"What?"

"That's the scuttlebutt around here."

"Oh, come on, Jonas, you don't believe that."

"Of course not, but the police do. Apparently your boot print was found at the scene of the crime."

"*My* boot print?" The knot in his neck tightened. "Why do they think it's mine?"

"I don't know, but that's what they're saying." Jonas sucked in a sharp breath. "Look, Boss, I gotta go. Johnson's calling me."

"Wait, Jonas—"

Jonas cut him off. "Be careful, Scott. I don't know where you are, and I don't want to know, but the DA just issued an arrest warrant for you and the Reynolds woman." Distant voices filtered down the line.

"What?" The air whooshed out of Scott's lungs. He staggered across the floor and collapsed on his chair. "Jonas—"

The line was dead.

"What's going on, Scott? What did he say?"

He blinked and blinked again to clear his vision.

Marissa stood over him, her face pale.

"An arrest warrant's been issued. For both of us."

Her brow furrowed. "What?"

"The DA issued arrest warrants for you and me." Even as he spoke the words aloud, they didn't make sense. How was this possible? He didn't break the law...ever. And now he was wanted for murder. "The bloody boot print's mine."

Chapter 10

She gasped. "Yours? How's that possible?" She thought back to the night she woke up from a drugged haze in that sleazy hotel room. Her memories were distorted from the drug she'd been given, but she had a clear recollection of Scott when he'd stormed into the hotel room. Aside from the red cap and the mirrored sunglasses, he'd worn faded jeans and a navy shirt under his black leather jacket.

She closed her eyes and pictured him, but she couldn't remember what shoes he'd worn. Boots? Her breath hitched in her throat. Bloody boots?

"It isn't my print." He scooted his chair closer to the computer and clicked keys. "Let's have another look at that photo."

The photograph of the bloody footwear impression filled the screen. He clicked again, and the photo enlarged.

She studied his feet clad in black leather, lace-up brogues, and glanced at the screen. "What size are your shoes?"

"Twelve."

Her heart skipped a beat. The typed note at the bottom of the photograph indicated the print was made by a man's size-twelve boot. She leaned closer and studied the photo. A trademark design was incised on the heel. The pattern looked familiar. A cat's paw?

"And before you ask. I own a pair of Cougar Cross boots."

She digested this news, and pinned him with a steady look. "Just so we're clear. You own a pair of size twelve, Cougar Cross boots?"

He bobbed his head.

"What shoes were you wearing two nights ago?"

"Not my Cougar Cross boots." He rubbed the back of his neck as if easing a pain. His cell phone rang, but he ignored the piercing peal.

The ringing stopped.

And started again.

Expelling a gust of air, he picked up the phone. His jaw tightened as he listened to the caller. "Thanks, Sam." He ended the call. His shoulders hunched forward, and his body sagged.

"Who was that?"

He didn't respond.

She placed her hand on his thigh. "What's going on, Scott? Tell me, please." The hard muscle beneath her hand tensed.

He looked up, his eyes raw. "That was my landlord. The police were at my condo. They had a search warrant."

She gasped.

He laughed, but it was a hard, bitter laugh and didn't reach his desolated eyes. "It gets better." He winced and kneaded the back of his neck. "Sam says they confiscated a pair of my boots."

A chill trickled along her spine.

Their eyes met and held as the shocking reality of his news hit home. The police had confiscated his boots as evidence. They thought they were the same boots the killer wore when he walked in McGregor's blood after he stabbed him.

He rubbed his neck again. "How the hell could this have happened?"

"They can't be your boots." *Could they?* A shiver rippled through her. Of course they couldn't. He said he wasn't wearing the Cougar Cross boots at the hotel. So why did the police raid his apartment and take the boots as evidence?

"Look, I know what you're thinking."

She started to deny his claim, but he held his hand up, and the words died on her tongue.

"I see the doubt in your eyes." He heaved a breath and suddenly looked exhausted. "I haven't worn those boots for months. I don't know how these guys knew I had a pair."

"Will"—she swallowed—"the police find blood on the soles?"

"I don't know. Whoever's behind this setup is damn good. They've gone to a lot of work to frame us for the murder. I wouldn't be shocked if they somehow took my boots, used them to stage that bloody boot impression at the crime scene, and then returned them to my apartment." He slumped in the chair, and his body seemed to deflate. "God, when will this nightmare end?"

Tears stung her eyes at the desolation and despair in his voice, but what could she do? The same sense of hopelessness swamped her. A few days ago, her life had been so simple. Work, home, sleep, work, home, sleep, and repeat. And now…she bit her bottom lip hard to stop a sob escaping.

He winced and rubbed the back of his neck again.

"You're hurting." Before she considered the consequences, she moved behind his chair. "Let me help." The back of his neck was pale and vulnerable. She touched his warm skin and almost yanked her hands away at the scorching heat.

He flinched as if he too felt the fire. "You don't have to do that. I'll be fine."

"It's my fault you're sore. If I'd been paying attention, you wouldn't have had to run into the street and save me from that SUV." She flexed her fingers and rubbed, massaging the hard knot of muscle.

"You don't owe me anything. I did what any decent person would."

"Maybe. Maybe not. Let me help. I want to."

"I'd be a fool to turn down that offer. Thanks."

Silence, broken only by the electronic hum of the computer, settled between them as her fingers worked their magic.

The rigid tightness in his shoulders loosened, and he groaned.

An answering wave of heat washed over her. Her fingers stilled.

He swiveled his chair around and faced her.

Her breath hissed out through her teeth. Something hot and visceral zinged in the air, turning her blood molten, and igniting bursts of heady expectation. The desire in his eyes woke butterflies in her stomach. She swallowed, her mouth dry.

His gaze swept over her, settling on her mouth. His eyes darkened, and his nostrils flared.

He's going to kiss me!

Her heart lodged in her throat. Instead of turning away, she held her breath, waiting, longing for the play of his mouth on hers, wondering if... Lost in his heated gaze, her train of thought trailed off.

He set his hands on the indents of her waist above her hips and drew her closer. His hard thighs encased her hips, holding her a willing captive. The warmth of his body seeped through her clothing, igniting her senses. His scent, spicy with a hint of citrus, flooded her.

He tightened his grip on her waist and slid his other hand over her ribs, brushing the swell of her breast, before cupping the back of her head and drawing her face down to his.

Her heart pounded, and her lips parted in anticipation.

His warm breath washed over her, and the soft press of his lips settled on hers.

Desire flared to life as a burst of heat scorched her from her head to her toes, leaving her tingling. When his tongue brushed hers, she tunneled her hands deep in his hair and clung, reveling in his taste.

The kiss deepened.

She sank into his embrace, lost in the wild rush of sensations.

He stiffened and jerked his mouth from hers and dropped his hands from her body.

The meteoric burst of energy and fire vanished, leaving an airless void. A long, taut silence stretched between them.

"Jesus." His eyes shuttered, and his lips barely moved when he spoke. "I'm sorry, I shouldn't have done that."

Her mouth throbbed from his kisses, and blood rushed in a molten stream through her veins. His kiss had shaken her to her core, but she wasn't about to show him the effect he had on her. She tossed back her hair and forced a cool smile to her lips. "No worries. It was just a kiss. No big deal." Now who was lying?

His mouth hardened into a firm, uncompromising line. He grabbed his suit coat jacket and shrugged into it. "Wait here. No one knows about Gramm's place. You'll be safe until I get back."

"Wait. What? You're leaving me here? Alone?" Her heart raced. "What if the people who installed the tracking app on my phone come looking for me?"

"Don't worry. They didn't have enough time to track you before I disabled your phone. I'll be back soon."

She grabbed his arm, stopping him. "Please don't leave me."

"You'll be fine." The tightness in his face softened. "Have a shower and get some rest. I'll be back before you know it. I promise."

"Are you going to tell me where you're going?"

A thin white line rimmed his mouth. "To find some answers."

"From whom?"

"Whatever's going down is pretty elaborate. More than one person is behind this frame job. Secrets are hard to keep. Someone talks. They always do."

Secrets are hard to keep.

Her heart stuttered. She stuffed her hand in her pocket and threaded her fingers through the heavy silver chain. Better for her to tell him about the necklace than for him to find out about it from someone else. Inhaling a deep breath, she inched another step closer. "There's something I have to tell you—"

Even as the words escaped her mouth, he was shaking his head. "You're staying here where I know you're safe." As if his decree settled the issue, he spun around and strode down the hall. His heavy footsteps bounded down the stairs, the front door slammed, and the house was silent.

She waited until the roar of his car faded in the distance and then she hurried downstairs. No matter what he ordered, she refused to hide in this house like a damsel in distress who needed protecting, doing nothing while he risked everything to clear their names.

The anonymous caller had mentioned her uncle by name. That same person had sent her Steven Carmichael's necklace. There had to be a connection. Julio knew more than he admitted. She'd go to his apartment and ask him the hard questions, and she wouldn't leave until he revealed the truth.

First, she had to find a way to get to town. She couldn't call a cab. Not with an arrest warrant hanging over her head. Besides, she didn't have a working cell phone. Not after Scott had removed her phone's battery. Maybe Gramm had a bicycle stored in the shed out back. She smiled at the ridiculousness of cycling to town, but she had to act. She refused to sit there and wait for the rest of her world to implode.

She opened the back door and ran down the steps. The porch light illuminated the weed-infested yard and shed. The unpainted building leaned drunkenly to one side and looked as if a strong wind would blow the whole structure over.

Wrenching the rusted handle, she wrestled with the shed door, but the weathered wood was warped and wouldn't budge. She swiped at the sweat dripping in her eyes. Bracing her feet on the packed dirt, she grabbed the handle with both hands and heaved.

With a protesting squeal, the handle twisted, and the door flew open, nearly toppling her. Using the flashlight she'd found on the kitchen counter, she shone the beam into the dark interior. Dust motes danced in the stream of light. Her nostrils flared at the acrid tang of gasoline and damp rot. An older model car filled the interior of the shed.

She whooped and stamped her feet in a victory dance. "Now *that's* what I'm talkin' about."

A thick layer of dust coated the car's hood, dulling the original vibrant orange to a pale apricot, but the tires were inflated, and the windshield, though spidered with cracks, was intact.

She shone the light through the driver's window and let loose another whoop. "Yes!" A set of keys hung in the ignition, a rabbit's foot key fob dangling. Opening the driver's door, she climbed inside. If this old car had gas in the tank and the motor actually worked, she'd believe in miracles. Rubbing the rabbit's foot for good luck, she turned the key.

The engine caught, sputtered, and died.

She mashed her foot on the gas and twisted the key again. The motor chugged to life, and the car jerked forward. Just as elation filled her, the motor coughed and stalled.

Wiping her damp palms on her pant legs, she twisted the key, and applied a touch of gas. The car rumbled to life, and she shifted the transmission into Drive. Uttering a brief prayer, she flicked on the headlights, applied more gas, and steered the car out of the shed, and along the drive. Flushed with success, she headed down the lane.

The little car's motor settled into a steady thrum as she raced along the highway, and before long, the glow from the lights of the city reflected in the bank of clouds in the distance.

She found a parking space a hundred yards from the front door of Julio's apartment tower. Unlatching her seatbelt, she inhaled a restoring breath and climbed out of the car. Shoulders back, head held high, she marched up to the glass-fronted entrance, yanked open the door, and with a nod, she stepped past one of Julio's big-muscled, armed goons and into the lobby.

Two more guards materialized, crossed their tattooed, bulging arms over their broad chests and glared, blocking the elevator. Another two men watched from their vantage point by the stairs. Was it her imagination, or had the security beefed up since her earlier visit?

She eyed the surveillance cameras and pictured her uncle far above watching her, a smug smile on his bearded face. "I want to see Julio." Her heart raced as she fought to quell her nervousness.

As if on cue, the guards stepped aside and motioned toward the open elevator doors.

The bigger one spoke. "Go on up, Miss Reynolds. He's expecting you."

Chapter 11

The elevator doors swooshed open onto the expansive viewing room. She stepped out of the elevator and into the glamorous but sterile room. Recessed ceiling lights emitted a soft glow that didn't detract from the incredible view of the city revealed through the wall of windows.

A myriad of lights sparkled below, and she could believe she was in the clouds like Zeus and the gods of Olympus. That's why Julio liked living here. He could stand at this window and breathe the rarified air of the super wealthy as he looked down on the common man scrabbling in the dirt and chaos below.

Tiny's giant form appeared in a reflection on the glass.

She wheeled around, all thoughts of the beauty of the sparkling lights forgotten as she remembered why she was in this luxurious penthouse apartment.

He frowned, and the cobra tattoo on his neck seemed to writhe, its mouth gaping, fangs bared, ready to strike. "Mr. DeGrazzi will see you in the study, Miss Reynolds."

She shuddered and followed him down the hall to the same room she'd visited earlier that day. Was it only that morning? So much had happened in the intervening hours.

"Marissa. How very nice to see you again." Julio

beamed, put down his glass, and bustled across the room. He nodded at Tiny. "Leave us."

The armed bodyguard turned and walked on surprisingly silent feet out of the room, closing the door behind him.

"Are you always surrounded by your guards? Even in your own home?" She shook her head. "I couldn't imagine living like that."

"These are dangerous times. A man can't be too careful." He rubbed his hands together. "Now, what would you like to drink? If I remember correctly, white wine is your preference."

"This isn't a social call."

"Really? That's too bad. It was such a treat to see you earlier today. Unfortunately, you were with that tiresome man, and we didn't get a chance to talk. I hoped you'd return so we could catch up." He smiled. "And you did."

Her anger simmered, shoring up her nerves. "I'm here for the truth. Did you murder Flinty McGregor? Did you or one of your goons drug me and take me to that hotel room?"

His eyes narrowed, but instead of anger sparking in the gray depths, she saw something resembling sadness. "You actually believe I'd drug my niece"—he shook his head—"my own *flesh and blood*, and allow you to be blamed for a murder I committed?" Tears shimmered in his eyes. "I knew you were angry with me, Marissa, and that's why you stayed away all these years, but I never for one minute believed you thought so little of me. I thought if I gave you time, you'd forgive me." He shook his head. "I see I was wrong."

She steeled her heart. This was Julio DeGrazzi.

Crime kingpin. He was skilled at artifice. Even if he were involved in what was happening to her, he'd never admit his culpability.

Picking up his glass, he swirled the contents and stared at the amber liquid. "Earlier today I received a phone call. The man who called claimed responsibility for the events at the Condor Hotel last night." The furrows on his face deepened. "He gloated that he drugged you and took you to that hotel room, murdered my man, and arranged for the police to arrive."

He rocked back on his heels, his eyes glacial. "Not that I give a rat's ass about McGregor's demise. The man was prepared to betray me. He deserved to die. No one messes with me, or my family. No one." He smashed his fist on the desk so hard the crystal decanters clattered against each other. "I promise you I'll find this asshole, and when I do, he'll wish he never crossed me."

The venom in his voice chilled, and she wrapped her arms across her chest. "I...I think the same man called me. He had an accent, and he knew I'd been to see you earlier today." She licked her dry lips, wishing she'd accepted the glass of wine. "He...he sent me a package with my wallet and cell phone."

"Why did he have your possessions?"

"I don't know. He must have taken my wallet out of my purse when he drugged me." She swallowed. "The police found my phone in my purse at the crime scene, but my wallet wasn't in it. Somehow this man stole my phone from the police and had the package delivered to my apartment."

"Why would he do that?"

"Scott found a tracking app on my phone."

"A tracking app? Where's the phone now?"

"Scott removed the battery. He said he didn't think they had time to pinpoint my location."

His foot tapped a rapid tattoo on the floor. "Well, I guess Bannister's good for something."

"There's something else you should know. Steven Carmichael's chain was in the coin pouch in my wallet."

"What?" Julio expelled a loud breath. "Are you sure it's the same chain?"

"The pendant was engraved with our initials."

He hefted a crystal decanter and slopped more whiskey into his glass. His hands shook, and liquor splashed onto the antique credenza. He lifted the glass and swallowed half the contents. Not bothering with a handkerchief, he wiped his mouth with the back of his hand. "Do you have the chain with you?"

She dug in her pocket and pulled out the gleaming silver necklace and set it on the table. The engraved, heart-shaped pendant shone in the lamplight.

Silence settled over the room, making the crackle and pop of flames in the fireplace, the resonant tick-tock of the grandfather clock, and the distant rumble of late-night traffic unnaturally loud.

He fondled his beard, his fingers smoothing the grizzled, dark hair. "He sent you the chain to frighten you. That seems obvious."

Her gut twisted. "I knew this wasn't over. I knew one day we'd have to pay for what you did."

"What *I* did? You came to me asking for help. Remember?" He heaved an aggrieved breath. "Carmichael was a menace." He touched her arm, but she flinched and backed away. "He deserved to die, but

I didn't kill him. I would have. I even ordered the hit, but someone beat me to the pleasure."

"Don't lie to me. Not anymore. Tell me the truth for once in your life." She huffed out a breath. This was the reason she hadn't spoken to him in five years. Just seeing him reminded her of her culpability and swamped her with guilt. He'd always denied he was responsible for Steven Carmichael's death, but she didn't believe him. She knew what he was like. Julio would do anything to protect her, even commit murder.

As if reading her mind, he said, "You were terrified. He wouldn't leave you alone. He never would have. I couldn't let a scumbag like that ruin your life. But before Tiny could follow through on my orders, someone popped Carmichael." The light of truth shone from his anguished gray eyes. "Come on, Marissa, you know I'm telling the truth. I didn't kill him."

For five years she'd distanced herself from her notorious uncle, had lived her life in the shadows, but now someone had uncovered her secret. She stared at the chain and crushed a hand to her stomach to still the roiling. "What are we going to do?"

"You're going to stay out of this. I'll find the bastard." His gray eyes sparked with an icy menace, more frightening than outright rage.

"You know who it is, don't you?"

The flickering flames in the fireplace highlighted the deep groove between his brows. For the first time she noticed the fear reflecting in his silver eyes.

Unease settled deep in her stomach. "What aren't you telling me?"

"The man behind this is deadly serious. He's tried for years to destroy me. He'll stop at nothing to achieve his goal." His eyes turned steel gray. "But now he's taken it too far. No one messes with my family." Spittle flew from his mouth as he spat the words. "No one." He threw his glass into the fire where the crystal exploded like a gunshot.

She yelped and backed away.

No one messes with my family.

The ominous phrase rang through her brain like a death knell. He'd uttered the same words five years ago. And look what happened then. "I'm going to the police. I'll tell them everything, explain what happened. I don't care if they arrest me. They'll find the real guilty party, and then I'll—"

Tiny rushed into the room, gun drawn.

"Everything's okay, Tiny." Julio nodded at the broken glass scattered on the tiles before the fire. "I had a little accident, that's all, but I appreciate your vigilance."

Tiny studied Julio and then Marissa. He nodded and jammed his gun back in his shoulder holster. "Okay, Mr. DeGrazzi, if you're sure."

Julio waved him away.

The big man lumbered out of the room.

"You're not going to the police." Julio's stern voice brooked no disagreement. "They didn't help you five years ago, and they won't now." He moved closer and patted her arm. "I'll fix this. Don't you worry, I'll end this once and for all."

"What are you planning to do?"

He stared into the flickering flames, refusing to meet her probing gaze. But it was too late. She'd seen the shadows in his gray depths. His hands bunched into fists, and a pulse ticked furiously in his jaw. "Nothing for you to worry about."

She scooped up the necklace, stuffed it in her front pocket, and turned toward the door. It had been a mistake to come. He wouldn't tell her anything more.

"Where are you going?" His voice reached her across the room. "It's not safe out there."

"Anywhere's better than staying here."

He flinched as if stung by her barb. "You're making a mistake, Marissa. He'll find you. And then what? You'll wish you'd let me help."

She halted and faced him. "*Who* will find me? Who is this person who has you so frightened?"

His mouth tightened, but he remained silent.

She shook her head in disgust.

"Please, Marissa. Let me protect you."

Ignoring his pleas, she lengthened her stride. "Good bye, Uncle Julio."

"If you think Scott Banister can save you, you're making a mistake. He's not your friend. I know the truth about him. He'll do whatever it takes to destroy me. He doesn't care who gets hurt as long as he succeeds."

His taunting words followed her out of the room like the hounds of Hell. She wanted to plug her ears against his vitriol, but his voice penetrated her brain as if shot by a gun.

The elevator doors were open, and she leaped inside and slapped the lobby button on the burnished metal panel. The doors swished closed, and she inhaled her first breath in minutes.

Was Julio right? Was Scott prepared to do anything, go to any length, to destroy her uncle? He hadn't made a secret of how much he hated Julio. Was he using her to destroy her uncle? Even though she and Julio hadn't talked in five years, family was important to him. He'd do anything to protect his family. Scott was smart. He'd figured out she was Julio's Achilles' heel.

Was that why he hustled her away from the police station, and why he'd taken her to his grandmother's house? To isolate her? She flashed back to their torrid kiss. Was that part of his plan? To seduce her so she'd turn against her uncle? Was that all she was to him—a pawn in his scheme to destroy Julio DeGrazzi?

The elevator dinged, and the doors whooshed open onto the lobby.

She rushed out of the elevator and almost sprinted across the lobby past the armed guards and onto the sidewalk. Desperate to distance herself from her uncle and her disturbing memories of the past, she ran down the street to Scott's grandmother's car.

The dirty, old two-door coupe with its cracked windshield was wedged between a gleaming, luxury sedan and a monster-size SUV. She fished the rabbit's foot key fob from her pocket, hurried around to the driver's door, slid the key in the lock, and unlocked the door.

She slid onto the driver's seat and slapped the door lock button. Fumbling with the key, she slipped it in the ignition and started the car. Inching ahead a few inches and then back another few, she maneuvered the car out of the tight space and onto the street.

"What took you so long?"

Her hands slipped on the steering wheel, and the little car swerved into the opposing lane, cutting off a gleaming, dark-blue limo. An angry blast of horn sounded, and she wrenched the wheel and steered back into her lane. She shot a glance in the rearview mirror. "What are you doing in here?"

Scott Bannister grinned. "Waiting for you."

Chapter 12

Scott's gut tightened with guilt. He figured he'd surprise her, but she didn't look happy to see him. In fact, she looked pretty darn frightened.

"How...how did you find me?" Her voice cracked.

"It wasn't hard. When I got back to Gramm's house and you weren't there, I remembered her old car in the shed." He shrugged. "Once I saw the car was gone, it didn't take a genius to figure out where you'd go."

"The car was locked. How did you get in?"

His mouth quirked. "Gramm keeps an extra set of car keys in the kitchen drawer."

They drove along the dark streets for several blocks in strained silence.

Her hands gripped the wheel, her focus on the road. "Where's your car?"

"I sold it." He winced as he said the words, the pain still raw.

"But you loved that car."

He grimaced. She was right. He loved his car, but the vehicle was a liability. The police had his license plate number. Even if he switched plates, the shiny red sports car was far too recognizable. He had to get rid of it, but he couldn't just leave his baby abandoned on the street. Before he was a block away, carjackers would be on the flashy sports car like flies on fish. By morning, his beautiful car would be in a chop shop, sold for parts. The thought alone was enough to bring him to his knees.

If he couldn't have the car, he wanted its next owner to be someone who'd treasure her as much as he had. He had known just the person. From the second he drove the custom-built luxury sports car off the lot, Joe Weatherby, his childhood friend, had lusted after the flashy sports car.

As kids they'd spent Saturdays at Joe's dad's garage, drooling over glossy photographs of high-end sports cars in the stacks of car magazines kept in a dust-covered cardboard box in the back office. Scott's car had been a dream come true.

But even great dreams ended.

He'd never forget the joyous incredulity in Joe's voice when Scott called and offered to sell him the car at a reduced fee. The only caveat was that Joe couldn't register the car yet, and he was to keep it off the streets until this nightmare was resolved one way or another.

At first, Joe had refused Scott's offer, but after Scott explained what was at stake, his friend had jumped at the opportunity. And now the other man was the proud owner of a crimson-red-pearl-metallic luxury sports car with top-of-the-line leather upholstery, eight-speed automatic transmission, and high-performance torque.

Just thinking of the loss of his fantasy car made Scott's gut clench, but he'd done the right thing, the only thing he could do given the dire circumstances. Besides, if he was honest, the car wasn't really him. Oh, he'd liked driving it well enough—got a thrill from the surge of its powerful engine, enjoyed the envious looks from other drivers—but if he were completely honest, he was more of a sedan-type guy. When this was all over, he'd buy a sensible car that got good gas mileage, maybe even a hybrid.

He thrust the thought of his car to the back of his mind and leaned forward, resting his arms on the back of the front seat, breathing in the fresh floral scent of Marissa's silky hair. "So where are we going?"

"I don't know yet." They passed through downtown, and she turned onto Bethesda Boulevard. Apartment buildings, high-priced night clubs, and fancy restaurants gave way to luxury town houses and green spaces filled with tall, leafy shade trees, manicured shrubs, and beds of exotic flowers.

At that time of night, most of the houses in the posh residential neighborhood were dark, and the streets were quiet. Theirs was the only vehicle on the road.

"We should go back to Gramm's house. It's too risky driving around, especially in this old car. If a cop spots us, he'll assume we're casing the houses, and he'll pull us over. Once he recognizes us, we're hooped."

His words of warning had no effect, and she continued her stony silence and kept her foot steady on the gas. He blew out a breath and sank back on the seat. Where could they find refuge? They didn't have a lot of options, but one thing was for certain, they couldn't stay on the streets. And they couldn't go home. The police were probably watching their respective apartments.

They couldn't involve friends in this disaster either. The best option was Gramm's house. No one at work knew about the old house in the country. He'd always kept it as his secret escape from the stress of his job. He never took anyone there. At least, he hadn't until earlier, when he'd driven Marissa to his grandmother's house.

Even though Gramm's house offered their best option, his far-too-small boyhood upstairs bedroom where he'd given in to temptation and kissed Marissa was not a wise choice. If he spent any time alone with her, he'd kiss her again. Hell, he wanted to kiss her now, just one little peck, but he wouldn't stop the next time, wouldn't be able to, not even if a gun was held to his head. Her lips were just that sweet.

He stared out the window at the passing houses, struggling to ignore her tantalizing fragrance. The visceral ache to kiss her, to hold her close and hear her breathy sighs of pleasure, intensified.

He met her gaze in the rearview mirror. Her gray, luminescent eyes were so similar to her uncle's, and an icy blast of reality cooled his ardor. What was wrong with him? Had he forgotten she was Julio DeGrazzi's niece? She could be lying, stringing him along as part of an elaborate plan designed by her uncle. Was she involved in the setup? In spite of telling him she hadn't spoken to her uncle for five years, she'd just come from the man's building.

He glanced up as she turned off Bethesda, swung the car in a tight U-turn, and headed back in the direction they'd come. What was she doing? They couldn't spend the night aimlessly driving around. They were both exhausted and in desperate need of sleep. "Where are you going?"

"The college."

"The college? Why?"

Keeping one hand on the steering wheel, she fished in her sweater pocket and tugged out a set of keys. "I have the keys to the library."

"Doesn't the college employ security guards?"

"I know a back way. No one will see us."

"But what about the cops? They might have a patrol car watching the library."

"The police department is shorthanded. You know that better than anyone. They can't afford to have a patrol car watching the library on the off chance I'll show up in the middle of the night."

He sat back on the seat. She was right. For the past three years, the policing budget for Brunswick had been pared to the bone. The cops couldn't spare personnel to stake out Marissa's place of employment. They'd focus on her apartment.

So, hide out in the library for a few hours. Not a bad idea. Colleges had the latest technology, powerful computers, high-speed Wi-Fi connections, and if there was a God, coffee. He fought back a yawn. It had been a hell of a long day, and this crazy nightmare wasn't over. Not by a long shot.

"Why did you go to see DeGrazzi? What did you two talk about?" The questions had burned like live coals in his gut ever since he'd spotted his grandmother's car parked on the street outside DeGrazzi's high-priced, luxury building. "I thought you hated him."

Her fingers tightened on the steering wheel. "We had some unfinished business to deal with."

He wanted to ask more, to demand answers, but the firm set of her mouth and her rigid posture made clear she wouldn't talk until she was good and ready. Whatever she and DeGrazzi had discussed upset her. Her body was tense, her face pale, and she looked as if she'd gone a round or two in a boxing ring and had her bell rung.

Exhaustion seeped into his cells, and he slumped on the seat. He swiped a hand over his grit-filled eyes and bit back another yawn. His shoulder throbbed, the palms of his hands were scraped raw, and his knees were scabbed and bruised. Worse, his leather jacket was ruined, the back shredded by skidding across a couple of feet of unforgiving pavement.

An unwelcome flood of memories washed over him. He'd only to close his tired eyes, and a vision of his father wearing the worn, black leather jacket rose before him. His dad loved the coat and wore it on weekends when he didn't work at his teaching job at the high school.

Even after all those years, the supple leather smelled like the sweet cherry pipe tobacco his dad had smoked. The silk lining was worn through in places and tattered, the leather on the elbows shiny, but the jacket fit him like a glove.

His father wore the jacket the night he died, the night Scott's comfortable, secure world shattered. The night Julio DeGrazzi and the Russian gunned down his mother and father in a hail of bullets in the parking lot outside the movie theater where they'd gone to watch the latest Johnny Hunt action movie. He rubbed a small, worn hole in the soft leather. A similar hole punctured the sleeve and another rent the material in the shoulder.

The wrong place at the wrong time.

That's how the newspapers described the double

homicide. His parents were innocent passersby caught in the crossfire of two warring gangs. Even though he'd been a young child, Scott recalled the night his world changed as if the tragedy happened yesterday.

The ringing doorbell awakened him, and he'd climbed out of bed and crept to the top of the stairs. He'd lost a tooth, and he couldn't wait to tell his mother and father the exciting news. Visions of a visit by the Tooth Fairy filled his mind.

Instead, another visitor arrived at the front door.

Gramm shuffled to the door, her graying-brown hair in curlers, one hand clutching the neck of her pink, terry cloth robe. She flung open the door. "Did you two forget your key? Oh." She stumbled back a step.

A tall, uniformed policeman stood on the front step. The brim of his uniform cap cast his face in shadow under the glowing porch light. "Evening, Ma'am."

The stern set of the policeman's mouth triggered butterflies in Scott's tummy. He clutched Binky tighter, his small fingers digging into the worn fabric of his beloved stuffed giraffe.

"Can I help you, officer?" Gramm's no-nonsense voice trembled as if she too sensed a looming disaster.

The man removed his cap, revealing the emotion in his dark eyes. "May I come in?"

Scott stood in the shadows at the top of the stairs, jiggling from one foot to the other. He had to pee. He had to pee really, really bad. But he didn't move. His feet were stuck to the floor, and he watched the policeman talk to Gramm. The tone of their voices added to his anxiousness.

Gramm's anguished wail echoed up the stairs.

Warm dampness flooded his pajama bottoms, and

a puddle of pee soaked his bare feet. He wrinkled his nose at the pungent reek, but he still didn't move. Even as the pee turned cold and clammy against his skin, and a chill settled in, he remained hunched at the top of the stairs.

When the policeman left, and Gramm closed the door and shuffled away, Scott crept down the stairs. His tummy was in knots. And he was cold. His teeth chattered as cool air blew against his wet pajama bottoms.

Gramm huddled on the couch. Her hands covered her face, and her shoulders shook. Sobs tore from her throat.

He gripped Binky tighter. "Gramm?"

The awful keening cries continued.

A lump thickened his throat. Tears stung his eyes. "Gramm?" His voice was little more than a whisper, but she heard him this time and lowered her hands.

Her eyes were swollen and puffy, and streaked with red. Her cheeks were wet. She looked as if she'd shrunk. "Oh, Scotty, my little Scotty." She opened her arms. "Come here, baby."

He hesitated. He wasn't a baby. He was a big boy, but suddenly all he wanted was to be in Gramm's arms and held close to her warm body. He ran to her, climbed up on her lap, and wound his thin arms around her neck.

"Scotty, my sweet little boy."

The pain in her strained voice scared him. He tightened his grip and snuggled closer.

He didn't understand what had happened. Not then. In spite of his wet pajama bottoms and the rank stench of urine, his grandmother held him through the night, rocking him back and forth as her tears fell. It wasn't until the next morning when the neighbors arrived he learned what had upset Gramm. His parents were dead, victims of a gang shooting. They were never coming home. They'd never walk through the front door again, never hug him, never—

"Scott?"

He sat up with a start, blinking moisture from his eyes. "What is it? What's wrong?"

"Sorry to wake you, but we're here."

He peered out the window. The stately granite façade of Brunswick City College Library rose before him. Spotlights illuminated the building's classic architecture and the large circular, copper-clad dome that had corroded green from years of exposure to the elements.

She followed a narrow, paved road around to the rear of the library building and drove into a large, deserted parking lot. Old-fashioned street lamps stationed along the edges of the vast lot cast pools of feeble yellow light. Deep, concealing shadows hid the rest of the parking area.

"The lot's empty," he said. "A lone car will stand out and raise concern, especially at this time of night."

"There's a spot over there"—she pointed to the far side of the lot—"by that big oak tree. Kids park there to drink and make out. No one will see this car in the dark." Steering the car across the lot, she parked under the overhanging, leafy branches of the huge oak tree. She turned off the engine but made no move to get out of the car. Light filtering into the small car revealed the suspicion on her pale face. "Where did you go tonight?"

"I'll tell you once we're inside." He opened the car

door and climbed out. "We're too exposed out here."

She didn't move.

A gust of wind blasted him, and he shivered, scanning the empty parking lot, squinting against swirls of dust. He leaned down and peered inside the car. "Aren't you coming?"

"What are you hiding?"

"I'm not hiding anything." He shivered—not from the cold, but his blatant lie. "Come on. Let's go. It's freezing out here."

"The hell you aren't." The words exploded out of her. She ripped the keys from the ignition and stuffed them in her pocket. "We're not going anywhere until you tell me the truth. Where were you tonight?" The stubborn set of her chin and the determined glint in her eyes were visible even in the dim light.

Blowing out a breath, he climbed back in the car and settled on the front passenger seat. He slammed the door, shutting off an icy blast of wind. Releasing another breath, he faced her. "I went to see my assistant, Jonas."

"I thought he couldn't talk to you."

"I tracked him to a bar he frequents, and I convinced him to bring me a copy of the District Attorney's private, updated files on McGregor's murder. Even someone with your skills couldn't hack into those secure files."

"How'd you convince him to help?"

"You don't want to know." He pressed two fingers into his temple and rubbed in a futile effort to ease the unrelenting trip-hammer pounding in his skull. He wasn't proud of the way he'd cornered Jonas in the gay bar. The poor guy didn't know Scott had figured out his assistant was gay months ago.

Not that being a homosexual made any difference to Scott, but Jonas was still in the closet and didn't want his colleagues to know. He was worried how being gay would affect his career. He wasn't any too happy to see his boss walk up to him in the bar and buy him a drink.

Scott shook off his guilt. He'd done what he had to do. He'd make it up to Jonas later. That was, if he wasn't in jail. He grimaced as he recalled how he'd sweated in the shadows outside the District Attorney's offices while Jonas walked into the building, showed his identification card to the security guard, and rode up the elevator to the top floor.

Jonas exited the building fifteen minutes later, slipped Scott a thick file, and hurried off before Scott could thank him.

The episode left a bad taste in Scott's mouth, as if they'd transacted an illicit drug deal. Bad enough he'd broken the law, even worse he'd involved Jonas. He heaved a breath in a futile attempt to dispel his self-loathing. "The important thing is he gave me this." He opened his coat and tugged out a large manila envelope.

"What's in there? Have you read it? Does the District Attorney have new evidence pointing to the person who murdered McGregor? Are we off the hook?" She leaned closer, her eyes bright with hope.

"I haven't had a chance to look. I was too busy tracking you down."

A slight tightening of her mouth was the only sign his jab struck home.

He tugged out a small penlight from his coat pocket. Lifting the flap on the envelope, he shone the narrow beam of light on the reports. He pointed to a paragraph a third of the page down on the top document. "The DA acquired a court order to check your cell phone records."

"*My* phone records?"

"There's evidence you received and made multiple calls to the same unlisted number in the days prior to the murder."

She scrunched her brow. "That doesn't make sense. I didn't make any calls to an unlisted number. Not that I know of anyway."

"The phone number stated in the report is the same as the one on the card DeGrazzi gave me." He squinted in the dim light trying to read her eyes, to gauge her reaction to his revelation. "His *private* cell phone number."

"I don't understand."

Her face remained free of artifice, but phone records didn't lie. "What don't you understand? Seems pretty clear to me. You haven't told the truth. The records show you talked to DeGrazzi on your cell phone before, during, *and* after the time frame the coroner estimates Flinty McGregor was murdered."

She reeled back as if he'd struck her. "I didn't call him. I told you. I haven't talked to Julio for years. I didn't receive any calls from him either." Her gaze turned pleading. "Why would I lie? It doesn't make sense."

Doubt flickered. No way would DeGrazzi be so stupid as to make calls during the commission of a crime that could be traced to his private cell phone number. He blew out a breath. "Whoever's behind this pile of shit wants the police to think you're in cahoots with your uncle, and the two of you planned and executed the murder together."

"Julio said his cell phone number was private, so the DA doesn't know the calls originated from his phone. Right?"

"Not yet, but he'll figure it out, and once he does, the phone calls will be another piece of evidence stacked against you."

She toyed with a strand of hair. "Do the cops know my cell phone was taken from the police evidence locker? Do they know I have my phone?"

He shone the light on the report, rereading the final three paragraphs. "Nothing in here about your cell phone being removed from the evidence locker. Why? What are you thinking?"

The tip of her pink tongue slipped out, and she licked her lip.

He swallowed, remembering kissing those sweet lips.

"Isn't that odd?"

"Odd?" He tore his gaze from her mouth. "What's odd?" Good Lord. He sounded like a moron. *Focus!*

"Don't the police keep evidence from a crime scene locked in a secure location? How could someone just walk into the police station and take my cell phone?" She played with the lock of hair.

"They couldn't."

"Exactly. The person who took my phone is either a cop or someone who works at the police station, someone with access to the evidence locker."

A chill settled deep into his bones. The thought of a bad cop made his stomach heave.

"So now we just have to find this cop."

"How? Someone smart enough to remove a key

piece of evidence from the evidence locker in the heart of the Brunswick Police Department isn't going to be easy to track down."

"Won't there be a record? Wouldn't this person have had to sign into the evidence locker?" Her eyes flashed with excitement. "We can check the records. There's a limited window of time when the phone had to have been taken."

"The log book isn't online. The only way to access it is to look at it in person." He didn't want to dampen her enthusiasm, but what she was suggesting was impossible. "We're wanted felons, remember? We can't show our faces anywhere near the police station."

Some of the fire in her eyes faded, but she soldiered on. "You must know someone in the police department who owes you a favor."

"No way." He refused to involve anyone else in this shady venture. Bad enough he'd compromised Jonas. He was under no illusions what would happen to his assistant if anyone found out he'd helped Scott. Copying secure police files, removing them from the DA's office, to say nothing of handing confidential material over to a suspect, would guarantee Jonas would lose his license to practice law, if not garner a stint in the county jail. They had to find another way.

A germ of an idea dawned, and he twisted in his seat and faced her. "How good are you at breaking into the police department's secure website?"

"I got in once without too much difficulty. As long as they haven't detected the security breach, I should be able to hack in again." Her eyes narrowed. "Why?"

"Surveillance cameras are everywhere inside the stationhouse. All the digital data from those cameras is stored on the police department's computer system. Maybe we can go online and locate the video feeds for that section of the building." His excitement mounted. "There must be a camera in the hall by the evidence locker. Maybe we'll get lucky and get a look at the jerk who took your phone."

She grinned. "That's a great idea." Her smile faded, and she wrinkled her brow. "But before we do that, I have something I should tell you, something I should have told you yesterday."

A flash of approaching headlights lit the interior of the car.

He ducked, pulling her down with him. Her warm breath fanned his face, and he stared at her mouth, unable to look away. For a blissful nanosecond he forgot the approaching vehicle as memories of exploring her soft lips heated his blood.

The sight of her ashen face and fear-filled eyes doused his lust like a bucket of ice water. He peeked out the window and squinted into the glare of high beams.

The car spun in a wide circle and roared out of the parking lot, kicking up a spray of dust in its wake.

He expelled a shaky breath and sat up. "That was close."

"Probably kids looking for privacy."

"They weren't too happy to find their spot occupied." He cleared his throat. "So what were you going to tell me?"

Her hand trembled when she brushed a curl of dark hair off her face. "I went to see my uncle tonight to ask him about this." She dug in her pants pocket and held out her hand. A silver chain glinted on her palm.

He lifted the necklace. Thick links of silver formed a long chain with a dangling, heart-shaped pendant. "What's this?"

"I found the necklace inside the change pouch in my wallet after my wallet was returned. It wasn't in there before."

The cool metal slipped through his fingers. He ran his thumb over the medallion and felt the raised ridges of etching. "What's engraved on here?"

She bit her bottom lip.

"Look, Marissa, like it or not, we're in this nightmare together. If this guy sent you this necklace, it's important. I can't help you if you keep secrets."

Her shoulders sagged, and she slouched in the seat. "That"—she nodded at the necklace clutched in his hand—"belonged to Steven Carmichael."

He nodded, though the name meant nothing. When she didn't say anything more, he prodded, "Who's Steven Carmichael?"

"The man I killed."

Chapter 13

The man I killed.

The shocking statement reverberated through her skull—the first time she'd uttered the incriminating words aloud in five years. And now she'd confessed to Scott, a man whose sworn duty was to prosecute criminals to the fullest extent of the law. Her stomach plummeted as she swallowed the sour taste of regret. She didn't look at Scott, couldn't bear to see the disgust on his handsome face.

"You'd better explain that statement."

She drew her bottom lip through her teeth. No point holding back the truth. Not now. "Five years ago, a man I didn't know, a man I'd never met, decided he loved me. His name was Steven Carmichael. No matter how often I told him I wasn't interested, he kept after me. He called me at all hours, showed up at my home, the gym, the grocery store, even my doctor's office. He came to the library and when I asked him to leave, he waited for me on the street outside. I couldn't go anywhere without running into him."

She twisted her hands together in a painful knot. "Calls came all hours of the day and night. I'd hear the phone ring and hope someone was on the other end, and not just dead silence. I changed my phone number to an unlisted one, but it didn't stop him. He kept calling.

"It…it got so bad I went to the police." Her voice

hitched in her throat as the deluge of frightening memories, sharp as knives, shredded her composure. "They said they couldn't help. He hadn't broken any laws." She shuddered, fighting back tears.

"What did you do?" His voice was a rough husk.

Her nails dug into her palms, scoring the already scraped skin. "I...I thought if I ignored him, he'd lose interest and leave me alone, but the stalking escalated." She studied her clenched hands. "He left me romantic cards, flowers, perfume, even expensive jewelry. I found his gifts on my desk at work, in my home mailbox, even inside my house."

She swallowed, forcing the words out over the boulder-sized lump in her throat. "One day he left a bouquet of flowers on my pillow...on my *bed*...in my *bedroom*." She squeezed her eyes shut, remembering her terror at finding the expensive bouquet of a dozen red roses resting on her pillow. The knowledge he'd been in her house had nearly destroyed her.

"My bedroom reeked of cheap men's cologne. The dresser drawers were open, and I knew he'd pawed through my clothes, fondled my panties and bras, touched my most personal possessions." She swiped a hand over her damp eyes.

"I called the police again." A sob hitched in her throat as she recalled her sense of helplessness, her fear. "They talked to him, but he denied everything."

"Surely the cops didn't believe him."

"They couldn't do anything. There weren't any signs of a break-in." She peered at him through her tangle of hair. "That's what frightened me the most—he had a key to my apartment. He had to. How else did he get in?"

Scott reached for her hand, but she jerked away, terrified that if he touched her, she'd shatter into a thousand pieces. Now she'd ripped the scab off her darkest secret, her anguish spilled out, one condemning syllable after another. "I didn't know what to do, who to turn to. I'd been to the police. They wouldn't help. I...I didn't have a choice. I went to see Uncle Julio.

"He said he'd fix the problem." She met Scott's compassionate gaze. "I thought he'd talk to Steven Carmichael, you know, frighten him so he'd leave me alone. I never thought he'd...he'd..." Tears streamed down her face, and her shoulders shook with sobs.

"It's okay. You don't have to tell me the rest."

She blinked at him through her tears. "This secret's eaten away at me for far too long. It's time the truth came out." She swiped her face with her sleeve. "An...an early morning dog walker found him the next day. He'd been stabbed to death. His body was left behind a dumpster. Cash was taken from his wallet, and his watch was missing. The police said it was a mugging gone wrong, but..." She stopped, unable to form the condemning words.

Wind buffeted the small car. The branches of the oak tree brushed against the roof like claws of a large creature scratching to get inside. She shivered and huddled deeper into her coat.

"DeGrazzi killed him."

She jumped at the rasp of Scott's voice. "He denies he was involved, but I know he's responsible." She turned pleading eyes on him. "You have to believe me. I didn't want Steven Carmichael dead. I wanted him out of my life, but not like...like that. I never thought Uncle Julio would kill him." Even as she uttered the words, she recognized them for the lie that they were. She knew her uncle. Knew what he was capable of. No matter how she played it, she was responsible for Steven Carmichael's death.

"Did the police question you?"

"I...I had an alibi. I was lecturing to a class of first year students on the Dewey Decimal system. A dozen witnesses were there."

He nodded. "DeGrazzi ensured you couldn't be implicated."

"I begged him to confess. I...I went to the police and told them my suspicions, but I didn't have any proof, and they couldn't do anything."

"So that's why you severed contact with your uncle and haven't spoken to him all these years."

The *scritch-scritch* of the tree branch reminded her of the old horror story about the couple in the car and the scratching of the murderer's hook on the car roof. She shuddered.

He brushed her tears with the soft pad of his thumb. "Carmichael's death wasn't your fault. You didn't ask DeGrazzi to kill him." He smoothed a damp curl off her face. Cupping the back of her head in his palm, he drew her closer. "You're not to blame. Do you hear me? It's not your fault." His mouth sealed over hers in a tender kiss.

His soothing words trickled through her like a warm bath, easing her anguish. "Thank you."

He kissed her again.

The kiss began as a gentle tasting, a caress, a reassurance, but she was too hungry, too needy to hold back. She opened her mouth and met his tongue.

A low moan escaped his scalding lips, and he

deepened the kiss. He drew her to him, and his hot breath burned her skin as his lips trailed along her neck, igniting dozens of fiery flames.

The air in the little car thickened.

She gasped, her chest heaving when he slipped his hand under her sweater and molded his palm to her breast. Her nipple tightened to a peak under his warm caress. She shifted closer and closer still until she didn't know where her body ended and his began.

The soft snick of something metallic dropping on the seat and sliding across the vinyl, landing with a small clunk on the mat, drove out all passion.

She tore her lips from his and glanced at the floor. The silver chain glinted in the diffused light. A chill rippled along her spine, and she slid from his embrace. "I'm sorry. I…I can't. Not now."

His eyes were dark with passion. "What's wrong?"

She pointed to the floor where the necklace lay like a coiled snake. Another shudder shook her.

He picked up the chain and cupped it in his palm. "You'd better explain how this necklace is connected to what happened to Carmichael, and why just the sight of it has you shaking."

She inhaled a steadying breath. "Steven Carmichael gave me the chain. He had a heart inscribed on the back of the pendant with our initials inside. He left the gift on the front seat of my car wrapped in a small, jeweler's box and tied in a shiny red bow. He didn't leave a note, but I knew the gift was from him.

"I…I threw the necklace out, but somehow he found it. The day he died, he came to the library. He made a point of showing me the chain. He was upset I'd thrown his gift away." She blinked at him through a fresh sting of tears. "I...I never saw the necklace again until yesterday when I found it in my wallet."

The tree branch scraped the roof. The wind gusted, kicking up swirls of dust and dried leaves that clattered against the car as if someone or something wanted in.

He rubbed the pad of his thumb over the pendant. "Someone's doing their damnedest to rattle you. They knew how seeing this necklace would affect you." The furrow between his brows deepened. "Who else knows about this?"

"I don't know. Julio maybe? Anyone could have seen Steven with the chain. He didn't hide it."

The necklace dangled from his fingers, the silver links twinkling and reflecting the light from the distant parking lot lamps. "We have to find out who sent you this."

"How are we going to do that? I don't know anything about Steven Carmichael. I didn't want to. I just wanted him to leave me alone."

He pointed at the library building. "As long as we're here, we may as well go inside. We'll use the library computers to research Carmichael's murder. Maybe his next of kin is listed in the police reports. His family would know what happened to his personal effects."

For the first time since this nightmare began, the blackness surrounding her lightened. "Okay, let's do this."

"What the hell?" He stiffened. "Get down!"

She whipped around and stared out the rear window. A set of headlights angled into the parking lot. More kids looking for privacy?

He dragged her down beside him.

She huddled on the vinyl seat and held her breath, waiting for the car to turn around like the other one.

But the car didn't turn; instead, its lights illuminated the inside of their vehicle like twin spotlights.

"Who is it? Can you see? Is it the police?" She peeked over the edge of the seat back. The approaching car's high beams were blinding.

"I can't tell."

The vehicle slowed to a stop.

Squinting against the bright lights, she made out a familiar insignia painted on the side of the tan-colored car and the dome of an emergency light on the car's roof. Her breath whooshed out. Not the police, but almost as bad. "It's campus security."

His warm breath fanned her face. "Okay. Don't panic. Get out of the car. Act like nothing's wrong. You're here because you have to work late. That's all. Be cool."

She shook her head. "I...I can't. He'll call the police."

He smoothed a dark curl off her face and tucked the silken strand behind her ear. "Use some of your irresistible charm. Bat your eyelashes, smile your sweet smile. He'll be so enamored he won't be able to think."

Sweet smile? Her stomach fluttered.

The campus security car door opened, and the interior light flared, jerking her back to reality.

A man climbed out of the car and settled a large-brimmed, uniform cap on his balding head. He tightened his security belt around his ample hips, removed a giant-size flashlight, and strode toward their car.

Her heart raced. Her mouth was dry. "Okay. I'll do it."

"Good girl." Scott kissed her, a quick peck on her lips.

Heat shot right to her center. *Oh, my.* She sat up and smoothed a hand over hair tangled by his fingers threading through the strands.

"Let him think you're alone." He slouched lower in the seat.

She nodded, inhaled a deep breath, opened the car door, and climbed out. "Good evening, Martin." She infused as much good cheer as she could muster into her greeting. For good measure, she batted her eyelashes. "I see you're busy keeping us all safe."

A bright light shone in her face, blinding her. She winced and closed her eyes.

"Oh, it's you, Miss Reynolds. I didn't recognize your car." The light swept over Scott's grandmother's old sedan. "What are you doing here at this time of night?"

She forced a wry laugh. "I came in to do some work. You know what the start of semester is like."

Martin kept the mini spotlight trained on the car.

Her heart beat double-time. Had he seen two people inside?

"When did you get the car? It's a lot older than the one you usually drive."

She chuckled, aiming for carefree, but her laugh came out brittle and forced. "My car's in the shop. This is the loaner they gave me. Can you believe it?"

"It's seen better days, that's for sure." He lowered his flashlight, and the beam shone on the ground. A gust of wind blasted across the parking lot, flattening his gray uniform trousers against his sturdy legs. "You shouldn't park so far from the entrance. It's dark in this lot." He motioned to the large tree. "I didn't see you over here at first."

Again she forced a fake laugh. "I'll be safe. Don't worry about me." *Why the third degree? Why wouldn't he leave so she and Scott could sneak into the library and start following the leads they had?*

His jaw worked as he chewed on a thick wad of gum. "An attractive woman like you has to be careful." He cracked his gum. "I've been off on holidays this past week, so I'm out of the loop, but we've had complaints of lone women being harassed on the campus at night. Some poor woman even got abducted from the faculty parking lot." He frowned. "The boss wants us to be extra vigilant."

"Really?" Her heart threatened to beat out of her chest. "That's horrible."

"A woman has to be smart these days." Loud voices crackled over the radio he wore strapped to his wide leather belt. He unclipped the radio and brought it to his lips. "Martin here. What's up?" More static filled the night, but the blustery wind drowned out the words.

Her heart stuttered. Was he talking to the police and learning about the arrest warrant? Her throat closed tight. *Run. Now. While his back is turned. Get in the car and get the hell out of here.* Before she put thought into action, he swung back.

The lines in his face were carved deeper. "Some fraternity students just streaked the girls' dorm." He shook his head. "Mix youth, alcohol, and drugs, and you get a bunch of young fools doing stupid things." He clipped the radio back on his belt. "I've gotta go, but first, I'll walk you to the door of the library."

"Thanks, Martin, but I'll be fine." She faked a yawn. "On second thought, I don't feel much like working. A good night's sleep at home sounds better."

His radio crackled again, the static-blurred voice on the other end sounding more urgent. His frown deepened. "Okay, then. You have a good night. I'll follow your car out. Make sure that old clunker doesn't break down before you get off campus."

She smiled, her face stiff. Why did she have to run into the last chivalrous man in Brunswick? "Thanks, Martin. That's kind of you."

"Just doin' my job." He beamed, exposing a flash of white teeth and a wadded ball of pink gum. Striding over to his car, he opened the door and settled behind the wheel. The car started but didn't move.

The weight of his gaze drilled into her back as she returned to her car. Opening the door, she squeezed in, using her body to block Martin's view of the car's interior.

Scott was crouched on the floor, his long torso squashed under the dash.

"What do we do now?" she asked through tight lips. "He's waiting for me to leave. I told him I was too tired to work tonight."

"So drive. Let's get out of here."

"But I thought we wanted to use the computers in the library."

"That's out of the question now. That security guard doesn't know you're wanted by the police yet, but he will soon enough."

Her hands shook as she started the car and backed out of the secluded parking spot. The twin beams of

Martin's car's headlights followed close behind as she drove across the empty parking lot and out the exit. She followed the winding, narrow road past the library and across the campus to the main exit. Switching on her turn signal, she waited for the traffic light to change from red to green.

As soon as the light changed, the car behind her tooted its horn, and Martin drove off to deal with a bunch of naked, drunk college students.

Her breath whooshed out, and she focused on negotiating through the sparse evening traffic.

Scott uncurled from his cramped position and sat on the passenger seat, rubbing his knees.

She slid him a glance. "You okay?"

He grimaced and stretched his right shoulder. "I am if you call being squished like a pretzel for the past fifteen minutes okay."

"He wouldn't leave. Not until we left the college grounds."

"Probably just as well. At some point, the police will check the library." He heaved a breath. "But now they'll know what type of car you're driving and the license plate number. Martin looked like a real keener. He'll be sure to spill the beans."

She blew out a shaky breath. "So where do we go?"

"Back to Gramm's."

Chapter 14

Leaning back on the seat, he closed his burning eyes. He was exhausted, but his mind refused to shut off. Marissa wasn't anything like he'd expected. Instead of the spoiled niece of a gang kingpin, she'd turned out to be a woman of surprising integrity. She'd separated herself from her uncle's criminal lifestyle and made a life of her own—a good and decent life.

Revealing her long-held secret hadn't been easy. Her anguish was evident in every strained word she'd uttered. He'd interviewed stalking victims for court appearances. Their stories of being followed and harassed, of losing their privacy as the stalkers invaded their homes, their workplaces, and their lives, were shocking.

He didn't blame Marissa for seeking her uncle's help. What choice did she have? Carmichael was a bomb waiting to explode. The police refused to help. Her uncle was her last recourse. How could she know DeGrazzi would kill Carmichael?

He couldn't condone DeGrazzi's actions, but he understood why he'd murdered Carmichael. DeGrazzi's primary goal was to protect his niece. Scott understood that sort of family loyalty. He would have done anything, committed any number of illegal acts, if his actions could have saved his parents. Instead, he'd devoted his life to finding their killers and bringing them to justice.

"I think we're being followed."

Marissa's frantic whisper broke through his turmoil. He checked the side-view mirror. The headlights of a car, four car lengths behind, shone in the reflective glass. "Are you sure they're following us?"

"The street was empty of traffic until six blocks ago, and then those headlights appeared. They've been behind us ever since."

"Keep your speed steady, and take the next right." He focused on the view of the street behind visible in the side mirror. "Drive around the block and see what he does." If the car followed them around the block, it was a certainty the vehicle was tailing them.

They approached the intersection at a steady speed.

The vehicle behind kept pace.

Marissa steered the car around the corner and continued down the street. She took the next right.

He twisted around and stared out the rear window and cursed as the headlights followed. The distance between the two cars narrowed. "Damn. He's still behind us. Take the next right."

Her face was grim, her mouth set in a thin line, but she nodded. At the next intersection, she spun the wheel, and the car swerved a hard right around the corner.

The tailing car followed.

"Is he still there?" Her hands gripped the steering wheel as she focused on the road ahead.

"No question. He's following us." He sucked in a breath. "Okay. Slow down, not too much, but enough so he catches up. I want to check the make and model of his car. If we're lucky, I'll get his license plate number."

She eased her foot off the gas, and the car slowed to a sedate pace.

He stared out the rear window, peering through the glare of lights at the approaching car.

The driver switched on his high beams, blinding Scott, but he'd seen enough. "Damn. Looks like the same black SUV that tried to run you down. Hit the gas. Let's see what Gramm's old car can do."

She gunned the gas. The motor roared as the car surged ahead, and they rocketed down the street. The gap between the two cars widened.

"Yes!" His breath whooshed out. "Way to go, girl. We're losing them."

No sooner were the words out of his mouth than she gasped. "Something's wrong with the car. A red light's flashing."

He peered at the dashboard. His heart sank. The red, low-oil warning light glowed.

"What should I do?" Her voice was frantic.

"Whatever you do, don't stop." His mind raced. They couldn't pull over. The driver in the SUV meant business. He knew they'd spotted him; yet he kept following. What did he want? To finish what he hadn't when he'd tried to run Marissa down on the street outside her uncle's apartment tower? What if the driver was packing a weapon? What if he wasn't alone, and there were several attackers in the vehicle? Sweat prickled under his arms.

The red light flashed its warning.

"Scott, please tell me what to do."

"Keep driving." Was it his imagination or was the little car slowing?

"The speedometer's dropping." She confirmed his fears.

His blood turned to ice. He'd better do something and do it quick, or they were toast. Common sense demanded they stay on the main routes and mix with other vehicles, but traffic was sparse at that time of night. He scanned the street ahead searching for answers. Where was a police cruiser when you needed one?

They flashed past another intersection.

Redmond Street.

He knew this area. His condo was two streets over. The entrance to an alley was a few blocks ahead. He often cut through the alley when he wanted to avoid traffic congestion on the main street.

He pictured the alley—dark, narrow, and winding. Perfect. Both vehicles would be forced to slow down. At one point, the alley widened where two large metal dumpsters were stored. They were dented, rusted, and filled with trash, but if he remembered correctly, each dumpster had a wheeled base.

If Scott could jump out of the car without the driver behind seeing, he could shove one of the heavy dumpsters in front of the SUV. The dumpster would slow their pursuer down enough that maybe, just maybe, he and Marissa could get away.

A crazy plan—*Crazy? Try insane*—but his plan might work, and right now they were down to a hope and a prayer of making it out of this disaster in one piece.

Another block passed.

A scorched-oil stench burned his eyes.

The red warning light flashed.

He had to make a decision. He wasn't being modest when he'd told Marissa he wasn't much of an athlete. He'd always been the gawky kid. And now he was contemplating a maneuver worthy of one of his movie action heroes.

Marissa would hold up her end. She'd proven she was more than capable of driving the car at high speeds and maneuvering around tight corners, but the narrow alley would be more challenging.

The entrance to the alleyway was ahead on the right, looming closer with every spin of the tires. No time for second-guessing. It was now or never. "Listen to me, Marissa. I want you to do exactly as I say."

She slid a look his way, her eyes wide with fright. "What do you want me to do?"

He pointed at the alley ahead. "See that alleyway?"

She nodded.

"Turn in there, but don't brake. We're looking for the element of surprise." He licked his dry lips. "Once you're in the alley, don't slow down, just keep driving no matter what happens. Okay?"

"What are you planning?"

"Focus on the road and keep driving. Can you do that?"

Her face was ghostly pale, and her mouth trembled. "Okay."

A rush of warmth flooded him at the trust in that single word. She counted on him to get them out of this mess. His chest swelled, and he sat up a little taller. He wouldn't disappoint her. No way. He wouldn't let anyone harm her. He owed her that. After everything he'd done, this was his chance to redeem himself, to step up and be the man he'd always wanted to be before his quest for vengeance took over his life.

The alley entrance loomed ahead...three hundred feet, two hundred...almost there.

"Get ready. Slow down when I tell you, but just for a minute. Then drive as fast as this old rattletrap will go." He unclipped his seatbelt and slid the strap off his shoulder. Unlocking the door, he tensed and drew in a deep breath.

She wrenched the steering wheel, and the little car jerked to the right, tires squealing as it skidded into the alley and raced along the narrow, dark lane. Graffiti-streaked cement walls flashed by in a blur. The car swerved and struck a small metal garbage can. The can bounced off the front fender and flew away into the dark.

"Remember what I said—keep driving. I'll meet you at the end of the alley. If I don't show up in five minutes, get the hell out of there and call the police."

"Scott—"

"I trust you, Marissa. You've got this." He pressed his hand on her thigh and squeezed. "You've got this."

She shot him a glance. A smile trembled on her lips. "I've got this."

"Good girl." He tore his gaze from hers and grabbed the door handle. The garbage canisters were a few yards ahead. "Okay, slow down."

The car slowed.

"See you in five minutes." Inhaling a deep, steadying breath, he wrenched open the door and lunged out of the car. He tucked, and rolled, and tumbled across the pavement, smacking against a cement wall. He lay dazed, the world spinning.

Move!

Pushing to his feet, he wobbled, but held steady and placed one tentative foot in front of the other. Time was ticking. He had to finish this.

The red taillights of his grandmother's car vanished into the dark tunnel of the alley. For a brief moment, all was darkness, but then the glare of approaching headlights reflected off the brick walls.

The large green trash bins were where he remembered. Racing across the alley, he slammed both hands on the rusted metal side of one massive container. This was the weak link in his plan. If the dumpster was too heavy, if the wheels were rusted stuck or locked, he'd be too late. The SUV would race down the alley after Marissa, and she'd face her attacker alone.

Failure wasn't an option.

A greasy sludge rimmed the metal container and now coated his palms in a sticky, noxious residue. He gagged and wiped his hands on his pants. A nauseating stench of rotting food and piss flooded the still air. Holding his breath, he jammed his hands back onto the container and shoved, throwing his weight behind the thrust.

Metal creaked and groaned. The dumpster shifted an inch, and another inch, and another.

The headlights of the oncoming vehicle filled the alley with glaring light, and he uttered a prayer and focused on pushing the metal container one foot at a time.

Almost there.

His chest heaved, and his muscles burned as if they were on fire. Sweat dripped in his eyes. He ignored the sting, ignored the festering reek, ignored the pain, and pushed.

Come on, come on.

The SUV driver slowed as he negotiated the narrow, winding alley.

Scott shoved the dumpster the final few feet and waited for the right moment.

The vehicle was so close its exhaust overpowered the reek of garbage. The roar of its motor echoed off the walls.

Now!

He planted his feet, and with a herculean effort, shoved the dumpster.

The container screeched in protest but trundled ahead another two feet, blocking the alley.

Without waiting to see what happened next, he turned and sprinted down the alley.

The heavy grinding of anti-lock brakes, and a loud, metallic crunch sounded behind him.

He cast a quick look over his shoulder.

The force of the collision thrust the dumpster against the wall of a building with a deafening bang. The container bounced back and blocked the narrow lane.

Yes!

He wanted to fist pump the air, but he couldn't spare the effort. Digging deep, he drove his muscles harder and propelled his legs faster. He pounded down the alley, his breath chugging in and out. He'd told her to leave in five minutes if he didn't show up. It would be close.

The end of the alley loomed ahead. A car passed on the brightly lit cross street.

Almost there.

Lungs burning, he sprinted out of the alley and onto the sidewalk. The little orange car was ten yards away, the engine idling. With a final burst, he ran up to the passenger side of the car. The door opened, and he leaped inside and slammed the door.

"About time you showed up." Marissa gunned the engine, and the car surged ahead.

Panting, drawing much-needed air into his burning lungs, he wiped his damp forehead with his coat sleeve. His body throbbed where he'd smacked the unforgiving pavement when he leaped from the moving car, and his hands stunk like something had died on them, but elation flowed through him.

His plan had been a Hail Mary, but it had worked.

Man, had it worked!

The dumpster halted the pursuing SUV.

Incredible.

****

She tried to focus on driving, but a thousand questions burned through her. The past few minutes had seemed like hours as she'd waited for Scott to appear from the lane. What if he didn't show up? What would she do? Go back and get him?

A rank stench filled the car. "What's that smell?" She slid him a glance.

"Believe me, you don't want to know." His shirt was torn and streaked with dirt, and he dripped sweat, but he was beaming like a boy who'd hit a home run.

She wrinkled her nose and dug out the box of tissues she'd found in the glove compartment and tossed the box on his lap. "Use these."

"Thanks." He grabbed a clump of tissues and wiped his hands.

"What happened back there? Why did you jump out of the car? What—" She sucked in a breath. Smoke stung her eyes, followed by an ominous clunking. The red warning light resumed its frantic flashing. "Damn."

"What is it?"

"The light's on again."

The bright neon lights of a gas station loomed ahead. With a quick glance in the rearview mirror to make sure the black SUV wasn't behind them, she slowed the car to a crawl, and turned into the lot. Steering past the gas pumps, she pulled into a parking spot around the rear of the building where they'd be hidden from the street. Other than a semitrailer truck parked on the far side of the lot, they were alone. She cut the engine.

"What are you doing?" His breathing was under control, but sweat beaded his forehead, and that God-awful stink permeated the car. "We shouldn't stop. We have to get as far away from that alley as we can."

"We need oil if we plan on making it back to your grandmother's house." She plowed her fingers through her hair. "What happened back there?"

A wide grin wreathed his face, revealing a row of even, white teeth. The dimples in his flushed cheeks danced. "We kicked butt."

"What do you mean?" Her resentment faded. Hard to be angry with him when he flashed those devastating dimples. "What did you do?"

"I stopped the SUV."

"I gathered that, but how?"

He grinned sheepishly. "I saw the stunt performed once in the movie *Kicking Butt 3*." He chuckled. "Anyway, I never thought it would work in real life, but it did, it really did."

His boyish enthusiasm was infectious, and she gulped under his high-octane grin and resisted the urge to smooth a lock of his hair that had slipped over his forehead. "What worked? Tell me. What did you do?"

"I moved a dumpster so it blocked the alley. You should have heard the bang when that SUV crashed into that old metal garbage bin." Pride shone in his blue eyes. "His air bag deployed. The driver will probably have a stiff neck, and he sure as hell won't be going anywhere, not anytime soon."

"You pushed a dumpster...on your own?" She studied his well-developed biceps. "Wow. I'm impressed."

"The container was on wheels, but it was so damn heavy, I wasn't sure I could move it." He inhaled a deep breath and grinned. "But as they say...the rest is history."

"Are you okay?" She eyed the scrapes on his arms.

He rubbed his hip and elbow and winced. "These past few days have taken a toll on this old body, that's for sure."

She shook her head, struggling to take in his amazing feat. "What are you—an action hero? I couldn't believe it when you jumped out of the car. It was all I could do to keep driving."

"You were awesome." His dimples flashed again with the same knee-melting impact. "We're the dynamic duo." He lifted his hand to high five her but grimaced at the grime crusted on his skin and grabbed more tissues and scrubbed his palms instead.

"There's a bottle of water on the floor of the backseat. That might help."

"Thanks." He leaned over the seat and fumbled for the plastic water bottle. Twisting off the cap, he poured water over his hands and wiped with the tissues. "You've got game, girl." Admiration sparked in his eyes. "You drove this old car down that alley like you were in a drag race."

He had such pretty eyes...navy-blue irises framed by long, dark eyelashes. How was a girl supposed to protect herself? The air in the tiny car sizzled. Heat flared, and she felt the telltale redness sear her cheeks.

His smile faded, and the gleam in his eyes transformed to smoldering heat.

Her body pulsed in instant response. Nerve endings alerted as a shaft of desire so intense she shivered, struck her.

The click of his seatbelt latch was loud in the confined space. He leaned closer, his hands brushing her thighs, her waist, her chest, as he unlatched her seatbelt and slid the strap over her shoulder.

And just like that, she was on fire. Everywhere his fingers caressed, she burned and yearned for more. A jolt of longing, a desperate desire for this man, arced through her.

His hand cupped the back of her head, and he drew her closer.

Her lips trembled beneath the first soft brush of his mouth. In a nanosecond, the kiss turned hard, hungry, and demanding.

But in the next breath, he tore his mouth from hers and flung open the passenger door. "I need to get oil." He exploded out of the car, slammed the door closed, and jogged across the parking lot to the front of the gas station building.

Heart pounding in her chest, she stared after his fleeing figure. She'd watched her share of action movies. Not once had the hero left the girl hanging, not after he'd saved the day.

Scott had proved his mettle. He'd jumped out of a moving car and shoved a massive garbage container across an alley, effectively destroying their pursuers' vehicle.

Incredibly brave acts.

Yet, he ran like a coward from her kisses.

Chapter 15

Scott returned ten minutes later with a can of motor oil and a funnel. He lifted the hood, removed the cap, and poured oil into the tank. Slamming down the hood with a decisive bang, he tossed the empty oil container in a trash barrel. With a closed look on his face and avoiding her searching gaze, he slid onto the passenger seat. No-trespassing vibes radiated off him in waves.

The tension in the car created an insurmountable wall, and neither spoke until she swung the car into the gravel driveway of his grandmother's house. A dozen unsaid words and unanswered questions hung in the stultifying air.

The second she turned off the engine, he undid his seatbelt and opened the door. "It's late. We're both exhausted. See you in the morning." He jumped out of the car and strode up the sidewalk and onto the porch. Opening the front door, he stepped inside and disappeared into the darkness.

She remained in the car, staring through the cracked windshield as the night deepened, and a sliver of moon rose over the shed. Stars winked awake, twinkling like tiny diamonds on a bed of black velvet.

Why was she attracted to this complicated man? What was it about him that made her toss aside years of caution and restraint? Was it because he'd saved her life when the SUV tried to run her down? He'd saved the day again when he'd jumped out of the car and shoved the dumpster in front of the SUV.

Is that what this was—she had a hero fixation?

Because he *was* a hero—the type of man who made a woman's heart flutter. He'd risked his life to save hers. No wonder he only had to look at her with his compelling navy-blue eyes and she melted, begging him to kiss her.

And look how that had turned out. Three times they'd kissed, and three times he'd cut short their passionate embrace and fled as if she carried the plague. Not good for a girl's ego.

Or her heart.

She studied the small house. The porch light was on, and a single light shone through the gauzy living room drapes. The rest of the house was dark. Earlier, a light in an upstairs window had glowed, and his shadow moved about the room as he prepared for bed.

An image of Scott wearing nothing but a pair of boxers rose before her, his bronzed skin gleaming in the soft glow of a lamp… She cut off the tempting picture. He'd made his feelings more than clear. He didn't want to get involved. Not with her.

He was attracted to her. No question. The heat between them was almost a visible force—the way he kissed her, the hunger in his eyes, his passionate caresses. He definitely wanted her, but something held him back, something more powerful than unbridled attraction.

She fought back a yawn. Her eyes burned, and her eyelids grew heavy. Time for bed. She'd think more clearly after a good night's rest.

****

She awakened a few short hours later in the throes of a nightmare. The sheets were tangled about her legs, the pillow beneath her face damp with tears. As her sobs eased, she struggled to recall the terrifying dream, but the gossamer threads vanished, leaving the acrid taste of fear and her thudding heart.

After Steven Carmichael's murder, she'd often awakened in the middle of the night, heart pounding, tears seeping from her eyes, a heavy cloak of guilt weighing her down. Over time, the nightmares had become less frequent, her sleep undisturbed.

Until now.

The upsetting events of the past two days had amped up her guilt, anger, and frustration. She inhaled a shaky breath. Past experience had taught her the futility of trying to go back to sleep. She might as well get up, get dressed, make coffee, and start the day.

Rubbing her burning eyes, she swung her legs off the bed. A sharp pain shot through the middle of her back as her bruised body protested the sudden movement. Her face-plant on the road had taken its toll. Wriggling into her jeans, she tugged on her T-shirt. She opened the bedroom door and slipped out of her room.

Light spilled from Scott's room at the end of the hall. Curious as to why he was up so late—or was it up so early?—she crept down the hall and peered into the room.

He sat hunched at the desk in front of the computer. The screen's blue-white glow bathed his face in cold light, revealing the sharp ridges of his cheekbones and the dark circles under his eyes. His fingers flew over the keyboard as he focused on the flickering screen.

She turned and headed on silent feet back down the hall. Tiptoeing down the stairs, she winced at a loud, protesting squeak of a loose floorboard. The scuffed hardwood floor was cold on her bare feet, and she scurried into the kitchen and flicked on the overhead lights.

The fluorescent lights blazed to life, blinding her. Searching through the cupboards, she found a canister of coffee. She filled the coffeemaker with water and set the machine to perk. Retrieving two mugs, she placed them on the counter and found a container of sugar and a spoon.

The machine gurgled and hissed, and the comforting aroma of freshly brewed coffee charged the air. While she waited for the coffee, she studied the picture on one of the mugs. A colorful image of a comic book superhero was imprinted on one side of the ceramic cup. Words printed in bright red beneath read, "Not your average superhero." Her lips tugged in a smile. That had to be Scott's mug.

Filling the cups with hot coffee, she added two heaping teaspoons of sugar to each cup and stirred. Before she could change her mind, she carried the steaming mugs up the stairs and down the hall.

He didn't look up when she entered the room and placed the superhero mug on the desk. A thin spiral of coffee-scented steam wafted in the air. He startled and jerked back from the computer. "Marissa?" His short hair was rumpled, his eyes bleary as if he'd been staring at the monitor for hours.

"I thought you could use some coffee. It looks like you've been up most of the night."

He blinked as if trying to focus and rubbed his

eyes. "Thanks. You're a lifesaver." He grabbed the mug of coffee and inhaled a deep breath. "Ahhh." He swallowed a gulp and winced. "You didn't tell me it was hot."

"I just made it." In spite of her bone-deep exhaustion, she laughed at his wounded expression. "Did you get any sleep?"

A sheepish expression crossed his handsome face. "Not really." He jerked his thumb at the flickering screen. "Figured I might as well try and get something done rather than stare at the ceiling and listen to the squirrels scramble around the attic."

She perched on the narrow bed and sipped coffee. The hot liquid warmed her blood, and the sugar-and-caffeine bomb energized her, erasing the last vestiges of her nightmare. "What are you working on?"

He set down his mug and returned his attention to the computer. "The guy who stalked you, the one who was killed, was his full name Steven Boris Carmichael?"

Her heart skipped a beat, and she nodded.

"I found his sister." He met her gaze. "She lives not too far from here, in Ashbury." He stood and rubbed the small of his back, undoubtedly suffering aches and pains from the previous day's adventures. "We should talk to her. She might know what became of her brother's personal effects."

"*If* she'll talk to us."

"Why wouldn't she? She doesn't know who you are, does she?"

"Not unless the police told her he was stalking me."

"I doubt you were the only woman he stalked. Men

185

like Carmichael make a habit of fixating on women who are unreachable. It's a game to them." He grimaced. "I've seen the same scenario play out time and time again. You were lucky he didn't hurt you."

She shivered. "That time in my life was a nightmare. I lived my life in fear, terrified I'd wake up one night and he'd be standing in my bedroom."

"Your uncle did you a favor."

Her breath rushed out in an explosive burst. "I can't believe you said that."

He arched his dark brows. "Why?"

"You're the ADA. You represent law and order in this town. How can you condone vigilante justice?"

"I don't, but stalkers are a different breed, especially the type of stalker Carmichael was. Sooner or later, your rejection of his advances would have made him furious. His anger would have led to violence." He threaded his fingers through his dark-blond hair. "If DeGrazzi hadn't taken out Carmichael, you could have been raped or murdered."

"I...I didn't think of it like that. I just wanted him to go away and leave me alone." She rubbed the goose bumps on her arms.

"Don't worry, if I can prove DeGrazzi had Carmichael killed, no matter my personal feelings, I'll haul him in and charge him with murder." Anger vibrated off him in waves.

She swigged a gulp of coffee and then another, not sure what to say or how to respond.

He cleared his throat. "Are you okay with us talking to Carmichael's sister and finding out if she knows how his necklace ended up in your wallet? Or will seeing her and talking about him be too hard?"

The last thing she wanted to do was remember the man who'd made her life hell, but she'd tried forgetting the incident, and look how that worked out. Finding the chain in her wallet had resurrected the old fear and anxiety. It was as if he stalked her from his grave. Tears burned her eyes.

"I'm sorry." His voice soothed, so different from his harshness of a minute earlier. "I can see how hard this is for you. Forget about talking to his sister. I doubt she knows anything anyway."

"No."

"No?"

"I want to find who sent me the necklace and why. I…I have to if this nightmare is ever going to go away."

He stared at her, his blue eyes assessing. "Are you sure?"

She wasn't, not at all. The idea of confronting Steven Carmichael's sister turned her bowels to water, but she wanted this to end more than she was afraid, and so she forced a smile. "I'm sure."

"Good girl." He grinned, rewarding her with a flash of dimples. "If we can find out what happened to the necklace, we may be able to find who sent it to you and who's behind framing us for McGregor's murder. This is all connected somehow."

Her throat tightened. What was it about men with dimples that weakened her knees and turned her blood to liquid fire?

"As soon as it's light, we'll pay Carmichael's sister a visit. I have a good feeling about this." His blue eyes locked with hers. He stepped closer, took her mug from her boneless fingers, and set the cup on the desk. Hands on her waist, he tugged her flush against him. His mouth found hers, and he kissed her.

Her stomach tightened at the enticing crush of his muscular chest against her breasts. Unable to stop herself, she moaned into his mouth.

He slipped his hand beneath her shirt and slid his fingers over her ribcage and tugged her closer. His hand was broad and warm and faintly abrasive, unmistakably male. Her delicate bra was no barrier as his warm palm covered her breast.

Her nipple tingled and hardened. Her blood turned to steam.

"I want you," he growled in her ear.

Chapter 16

The scent of her skin, warm from sleep, was like a taste inside his mouth. He ignored the alarm bells clanging through him. This time he wouldn't stop kissing her. Hell, he couldn't stop, not even if the entire Brunswick Police Force, guns drawn, burst into the house.

He caressed her silken skin, touching, tasting, and groaned deep in his throat. "Marissa." Her name spilled from his lips like the sweetest nectar. "Marissa." He kissed her again, his tongue twining with hers. Fire razed through his veins as he cupped her breasts, molding the soft flesh to his palms, rubbing his thumbs over her responsive nipples.

"Scott? Are you sure? Is this what you want?" Her luminous gray eyes glowed like pearls, reflecting the light from the bedside lamp.

Her breathless voice reached through his haze, and his hands stilled. *Was he sure? Hell, yes.* He'd never been more certain of anything in his life. He wanted her like a drug addict needed a fix. He swallowed over the boulder-size lump in his throat. "Are *you* sure?"

A slow smile played on her full red lips, swollen from his kisses.

He wanted to kiss her again, to taste her sweetness, but he held back. He had to know she wanted this as much as he did. He had to be certain she wouldn't have any regrets. Inhaling a deep breath, he stared into her passion-glazed eyes. "I asked you a question."

"Yes, Scott. I want this. I want *you*."

His heart soared. *Yes*! He wanted to shout from the rooftop, to pound his chest, to whoop with joy. Instead, he did what any sane man would, the only thing he could. He captured her mouth with his and showed her just how much he desired her.

A sliver of sanity wheedled its way into his passion-fogged brain, and he drew back and met her glazed eyes. His hand shook as he brushed a lock of hair off her face. "It feels like I've waited forever for this, but not here. Not like this. You deserve better."

She frowned, her smooth forehead wrinkling.

He clasped her hand and led her out of the room and down the hall to her bedroom. Holding tight, half afraid if he let go of her hand she'd leave, he led her to the double bed.

He lifted her shirt, tugging the soft fabric over her head and tossed the shirt on the floor. Her sheer, white lace bra revealed the dark circles of her aroused nipples. His mouth dried as he unsnapped her jeans and slid them over her slim hips and down her long legs to the floor, where they spilled in a pool at her feet.

She stepped out of her pants and stood before him, wearing only her bra and a scrap of white lace panties.

He gulped. A *burning question answered—she sure as hell didn't wear granny panties.* The single lamp shining on the bedside table painted her skin the color of fine ivory. He ached to touch her, to once again caress her fragrant softness.

Her mouth curved in a sensuous smile, and she nodded at his shirt. "Your turn."

He kept his gaze fixed on her as with clumsy fingers he peeled off his shirt, unsnapped the button on his jeans, and ripped down the zipper. He shoved his pants down his legs and kicked them away. His underwear and socks were next.

Her heavy-lidded gaze roamed over his shoulders, his chest, his abdomen, and lower.

He trembled with the need to touch her, but held still, allowing her to look her fill, to see how she affected him, providing her the chance to change her mind.

An eternity passed before she crooked her finger and beckoned. "Come here."

His legs turned to jelly, and he gathered all his strength and clasped her in his arms and drew her close. He almost lost control when her soft belly rubbed against him, but he was made of sterner stuff, and so he recited the periodic table and held on to his male pride.

Right or wrong, consequences be damned, he craved her. To hell with who her uncle was, to hell with her past, to hell with the whole bloody world. The only thing that mattered was right there, right then, and the incredible, desirable, and willing woman in his arms.

He buried his face in the crook of her neck and breathed in her scent. Trailing kisses along the smooth column of her neck, her shoulders, her breasts, he scooped her in his arms and carried her to the bed. Laying her on the rumpled sheets that smelled of her, he paused a moment.

"What?" Her voice was a breathless whisper.

"Just enjoying the view." He barely managed to get the words past the tightness in his throat.

A red flush blazed across her face and chest. She

crossed her arms over her breasts, shielding them from his view.

"Don't be embarrassed. Please. You're beautiful." He climbed onto the bed and lay beside her, his shoulder brushing hers, his hair-roughened leg nudging her silken thigh.

Her body was a furnace, radiating waves of scorching heat.

He clasped her hand in his, and they lay together for a heartbeat, until with a groan, he rolled over and kissed her.

Her mouth opened, and they melded as one.

He touched her…everywhere, discovering her secrets, learning which spots made her tremble, and which places on her soft skin had her gasping and begging for more. His lips followed the path of his hands. But then a sliver of rational thought pushed past the sensations rioting through him and he stilled. Chest heaving, he pushed away from her heat. "Hold that thought." Stretching above her, he leaned over the side of the bed and grabbed his pants.

"Don't stop. Not now. Please." Her breath gusted in and out in rapid pants.

His hands trembled as he fished in the back pocket of his pants. Where was the damn thing? "Yes!" He held up a small foil pouch and grinned. "Gotta be safe. Right?"

She blinked. "Yeah, sure. Good idea. I…I should have thought of that."

He'd been so wrapped up in the incredible sensations her kisses evoked, he hadn't thought of protection. But Gramm had instilled a strong moral code. He tore open the package with his teeth and slipped the thin sheath over his hardness. Leaning over her, he smoothed her damp hair from her brow and grinned. "Now, where were we?"

"Right here." She lifted her head and kissed him. As the kiss deepened, she arched beneath him, moaning his name.

He'd never heard anything sexier that his name on her lips. His desire ramped up until he thought he'd explode if he didn't have her right now, right this very second. But this wasn't just about him. He paused at her throbbing entrance and met her gaze. "Are we good?"

She moaned his name again.

"Marissa?" He had to hear her say it. He had to know for sure.

"Yes, damn it. Yes."

In the next breath, he slid inside her moist heat, thrusting, plunging deeper and deeper. His breath rushed in and out in furious puffs, but he wanted more, much more.

She clung, her arms locked around his neck, her legs wrapped around his hips. Tensing, her body arched, and she gasped a long, sensual expulsion of air.

The sound of her release was like a match to a can of gas. His body exploded. His heart thundered, and he struggled for breath. One thought paramount—if he died right this second, he'd die a happy man.

****

She collapsed and rested her head on the pillow. Her chest heaved, sweat dampened her skin, and her heart thudded. Body pulsing with rolling waves of pleasure, she closed her eyes and reveled in the sensations rippling through her.

"You okay?"

His husky voice reached through her lethargy, and she pried open her eyes.

He leaned over her, his concerned gaze fixed on hers, his blue eyes dark, almost black.

She nodded. "You?"

The corners of his mouth twitched, and his dimples peeked out. "Good. Really good." He grinned, and his mouth settled over hers.

The kiss deepened, and another rush of desire flooded her. Fireworks blasted behind her closed lids, and the all-consuming heat returned, along with the desperate need.

He trailed a torrid path of kisses across her cheek, down her neck, and along her shoulder. "You're sure you're okay?"

"Mmmmm." Her voice was a purr of pure contentment. A deep, satiated lassitude overcame her, and she relaxed for the first time in two days and allowed sleep to overtake her.

She awoke to the pungent smell of freshly brewed coffee. Sun streamed in through the window, painting the old hardwood floor in bright stripes. Rubbing her eyes, she sat up, shoving a tangle of hair off her forehead.

Scott held out a steaming cup, a grin wreathing his handsome face. "Good morning, sleepyhead."

Her breath hitched at the dimples dancing in his beard-roughened cheeks and the enticing creases crinkling the corners of his eyes. "What time is it?"

He handed her the cup. "Almost noon."

"Noon?"

"I let you sleep. I figured you needed the rest." He smoothed his hand over his cap of golden curls. "These past few days have been pretty wild."

She searched his face as she sipped the delicious coffee. Tiny red lines marred the whites of his eyes and dark circles underscored them. "You didn't sleep."

He shook his head. "I couldn't." His shirtsleeves were rolled to his elbows, his hands shoved deep in his pockets. A haze of dark-blond whiskers shadowed his lean cheeks.

"Why not?" She stared, mesmerized at the play of sunshine on his forearms. The thin white line of a scar stretched across the skin above his wrist. Her mouth dried as she recalled running the tip of her tongue along that fine line, the slight saltiness of his skin, his sharp intake of breath.

"I couldn't stop thinking about you. Last night was"—he smiled—"pretty stupendous."

"It was, wasn't it?"

His lazy grin melted her bones. "I made breakfast, if you're hungry."

"I'm starving, but let me have a shower first." She tossed back the sheets and leaped out of bed.

His eyes transformed from dark blue to obsidian as his gaze smoldered.

Heat rose along her neck and flooded her face. She snatched at the sheet in a futile attempt to cover her nakedness, but he was too quick and grabbed a corner of the sheet, holding it out of reach.

"Please don't." He caressed her shoulder, his fingers trailing a line of fire along her arm. "You're so beautiful."

Beautiful? Her? Her hips were too wide, her thighs not toned, and she had that annoying pouch in her stomach no amount of spinning classes or yoga fixed.

The admiration shining in his eyes was real.

Caught and held captive under his torrid gaze, she licked her suddenly dry lips, and stood a little straighter.

His hand slid down the curve of her back and settled on her hip. "Let me wash your back." He grinned, releasing those devastating dimples.

Powerless under his spell, she nodded and let him take her hand and lead her out of the bedroom, and down the narrow hall to the tiny, upstairs bathroom. Her chest heaved as her breath rushed in and out in anticipation of what was to come.

Breathing became even more of a challenge when he unsnapped the snap on his jeans and shoved them off his narrow hips.

Oh, my.

Chapter 17

She shoved her empty plate away and pushed her chair back from the table. "That was delicious. Where did you learn to cook like that?"

He stood and picked up their plates. "Gramm taught me." His mouth twisted in a wry grin. "Guess she figured no woman would take me on, so I'd better learn to fend for myself." He rinsed the plates under the tap and set them in the drainer to dry.

She gathered their napkins. Gramm was dead wrong. Scott was the total package—handsome, smart, kind, and a considerate lover, all rolled in with a good sense of humor. To say nothing of his solid six-pack and bulging biceps.

The corners of his eyes crinkled as if he knew what she was thinking. "Are you going to sit in that chair all day? Come on. We have work to do." His eyes darkened. "But first…" He tugged her to her feet and drew her close.

The air between them crackled.

She stared into his eyes. The midnight-blue irises were sprinkled with glints of silver like stars twinkling in a velvety night sky. Her knees wobbled. Blood, hot and heavy, pooled low in her belly.

He skimmed his palm over her damp hair and cupped her chin with two fingers, tilting her face to his. Never taking his gaze off her, he lowered his head and kissed her.

She mewed in pleasure and would have fallen if he hadn't held her locked in his embrace.

A phone rang. The shrill clanging cut through her rising passion like a hot knife through butter.

Cursing, he released her and dug his cell phone out of his hip pocket. "Bannister."

She sagged and gripped the back of a chair for support, fighting to regain her shaky breath. Her mouth tingled from the heat of his lips as if he'd branded her.

A vee formed between his dark-blond brows. "Thanks, man. I owe you one." He punched the off button and stuffed the phone back in his pocket.

"Who was that?"

"I asked Jonas if he'd look into the cold case file on Steven Carmichael's murder."

"What"—she swallowed—"did he find?"

He rubbed his beard-shadowed chin. "The officers who investigated the case wrote it off as a robbery gone wrong. The victim's empty wallet was found in the nearby dumpster, and his watch was missing."

"Did they find a silver necklace?"

"A necklace wasn't mentioned in the report. Maybe the chain was stolen as well. Or he wasn't wearing it when he was attacked."

"Are there any suspects?" Her voice was a whisper, laced with fear. Was she listed as a suspect in Steven Carmichael's murder? Had she been under suspicion by the police for the past five years? Was that why they were so easily convinced she was involved in Flinty McGregor's murder?

"No suspects are mentioned. The case is still open." He blew out a breath. "Jonas wanted to know why I was interested in a five-year-old homicide."

She swallowed. "What did you say?"

"Nothing. The less he knows the better. I'm not sure how much I trust him. The DA has him running scared. Jonas will do anything to save his ass and his job."

"If he's so frightened, why is he helping you?"

"For the moment, he's more afraid of me than he is of the DA." A sheepish grin flitted across his mouth. "I might have instilled the fear of God in him when I confronted him last night."

She chewed on the inside of her cheek. "What do we do now?"

"We go to Ashbury and talk to Carmichael's sister like we planned. Maybe she knows something about the silver chain."

He kissed her, a quick peck on the lips, but her toes curled. After the previous night, and again that morning in the shower, she finally understood the meaning of swooning. The heroines in those Gothic romances she'd read when she was a teenager knew what they were talking about.

He clasped her hand in his warm one. "Come with me. There's something you should see."

****

He led her upstairs to his childhood bedroom and yanked out the chair in front of the thrumming computer and motioned for her to sit. "Take a look at this."

She perched on the chair and stared at the screen. A blurry image of a beige-colored, narrow corridor flickered. "What am I looking at?"

He sat beside her, his knee rubbing hers. His clean,

masculine smell washed over her making it hard to focus. "I hacked into the police in-house website and downloaded the feeds from the station house surveillance cameras."

"You did that?" She was impressed. He definitely possessed some serious geek skills. Computer camp had paid off. "There must be dozens of cameras at the police station. Finding the right one would be like finding the proverbial needle in a haystack. How long did it take you?"

"Most of the night. Fortunately, the surveillance camera feeds are digitized and stored online like I thought. I think I found the feed we want." He leaned closer and used the mouse. His arm brushed hers.

And just like that, her skin tingled. She stared at his arm—the soft blond hairs covering the ridge of solid muscle. A flash of heat thundered through her.

She wanted him.

Again.

The scene on the monitor blurred as he fast-forwarded the sequence. "Okay." He pointed to the time indicated by flashing green numbers on the bottom right corner of the image. "This is the beginning of the time frame when I'm assuming your phone was stolen from the locker. The theft had to have occurred after the crime scene investigators bagged and tagged your phone and sent it to the lab for testing."

She leaned closer and studied the screen. "How long would that take?"

He shrugged. "Depends. They'd examine the phone for fingerprints and swab for DNA. The court order to check your call and text records was in the DA's file. The order wasn't approved until hours later.

Until that time, they could only look at what showed on your home screen. They aren't allowed to examine your call history. Not until the court order was approved."

He sat back and rubbed his jaw. "My guess is once the order was approved, the cops removed the phone from the locker and downloaded your call and text history and found those calls to your uncle's cell phone. After that, they replaced the phone in the evidence room."

"Wait. Slow down." She pointed at the screen. A uniformed police officer appeared in the grainy image. He strode down the corridor. "Looks like he's carrying something…a box maybe?"

"That could be your phone. It would be stored in a secure container that blocked Wi-Fi signals so the phone couldn't receive or send notifications." He shifted the mouse, and the image changed.

The officer walked down the corridor and stopped before a closed door. He punched a series of buttons on a keypad beside the door. A green light flashed, and he opened the door and stepped inside. The door closed behind him.

"Is that the evidence locker?"

He nodded.

"Is anyone inside the room? A clerk?"

He shook his head. "Budget cuts. The officer is supposed to sign in and record the item he's dropping off, the time, case designation, his badge number, and his name on the log sheet."

"Real secure." She couldn't keep the sarcasm out of her voice. "Please tell me there's a surveillance camera inside the storage room."

"I guess the cops figure the camera in the hall is

enough."

After several minutes of empty corridor, the door swung open, the uniformed officer stepped out, and he retraced his steps down the hall. His hands were empty.

Scott hit fast-forward. "No one enters or leaves the room for the next two hours. But then, this happens." He slowed the flow of blurred images to a crawl.

Another figure appeared on the screen.

She leaned closer, staring at the fuzzy image of a man. "You'd think with today's technology, the police department would install better surveillance cameras with high definition." Before he could respond, she added. "I know…budget cuts."

He shot her a grin and returned to studying the screen.

Those damn dimples.

A warm flush settled over her, but she forced her attention to the image on the monitor. Judging by the broad shoulders and the way the person moved, she guessed the figure was a man, but that was all she could determine.

He wore a dark business suit, and a cap covered his head. Keeping his head down, he avoided the camera lens and walked with a confident stride to the door. He punched in a series of numbers on the keypad. The red light switched to green, and he opened the door and slipped inside.

She held her breath and waited for him to reappear. Could this be the person who took her cell phone and mailed it to her along with her wallet and the necklace? Was this the man behind the elaborate setup?

A few minutes later, the door opened, and the man exited the evidence room carrying an object like a small, metal canister. Averting his face from the camera, he strode down the corridor and out of view.

She blew out the breath she'd been holding. "Could you make out his face? Did you recognize him?"

"The hat hid his face, but his hair brushed the back of his collar, so he doesn't have a regulation police cut."

"You don't think he's a cop?"

"No, but I was hoping you recognized him."

"Why would you think I know him?"

"Maybe he's one of your uncle's minions?" He arched his brows.

"The only bodyguard of Julio's I know is Tiny. I'm pretty sure that's not him."

"Didn't think so." He slouched in his chair, looking defeated.

"Should we let the police know someone stole my phone from the evidence locker?"

"I called Detective Sandhu last night and filled him in."

"What"—she swallowed—"did he say?"

"He knows we're together, but he doesn't know where we are. He wants us to turn ourselves in." His eyes were bleak. "Your campus security guy was on the ball. He reported us right after we left the college grounds. The only good thing is he didn't get our license plate number, so they can't connect us to my grandmother. This house is still safe."

She placed her hand on his. "I'm sorry."

"For what? This isn't your fault." He raised her hand to his mouth and pressed a light kiss on her scraped palm.

Her knees turned to jelly at the brush of his warm

lips. "Really? Do you really believe that? Because I don't. This whole mess centers around Steven Carmichael's murder." She blinked back the sting of tears. "How else would you explain his chain in my wallet?"

"Carmichael's murder is part of this, but his death doesn't explain why I'm involved. I was still in law school five years ago." He stood and tugged her to her feet. "Look, we'll figure this out. Don't forget, your uncle's working on this, and he has connections we don't. We'll find who's behind this nightmare." He brushed a lock of hair off her forehead. "Believe me, we will."

She stared in his eyes, unable to look away, drawn into the navy depths. The world shifted beneath her feet, the stars realigned, and something deep inside her flowered to life. Warmth rushed through her bloodstream, bringing hope and happiness in spite of the disaster of her life.

Clearing his throat, he reached for his ragged leather coat on the back of the chair. "We should get going."

"Why are you still wearing that ripped coat? It's ruined."

And just like that, the lines in his face hardened, and his eyes shuttered. "I like this coat. It belonged to my dad." He zipped up the jacket and strode out of the room. "Come on."

She shuddered. Even his voice was cold.

Chapter 18

After Scott switched the license plates on his grandmother's car with ones he *borrowed* from a car parked in a driveway a mile down the gravel road where a stack of old newspapers and piles of dried leaves indicated the homeowners were away, they followed the Interstate highway through the mountains to the town of Ashbury.

The stink of sulfur and sour cabbage hit them as they approached the city limits. According to the Internet search she'd conducted, Ashbury was a small city of ten thousand people, most of who were employed by the local pulp and paper mill. Plumes of gray smoke billowed from tall smokestacks. The main road through the bustling town was crowded with long, semitruck trailers loaded with logs or wood chips destined for the mill.

Steven Carmichael's sister lived in a suburb that backed onto a busy, heavy industrial site. They parked before a small, cedar-sided rancher and climbed out of the car. Clouds of dust filled the air along with the roar of machinery and diesel engines. A tattered *Beware of Dog* sign nailed to a wooden stake stuck in the patchy grass flapped in the wind.

Marissa shuddered and pointed to the sign. "Looks like they have a dog."

"People put up those signs to frighten burglars. She

probably doesn't own a dog, or of she does, it's a little ankle biter."

She rubbed her chin, her finger tracing the ridge of old scar tissue. When she was a child, a neighbor's dog bit her. Ever since, dogs made her nervous.

"Don't worry. I'll protect you." He came around the front of the car, grasped her elbow, and guided her up the cracked and broken sidewalk. His grip tightened as they stepped over a huge pile of dog poop and climbed the steps to the tiny porch.

He jabbed the doorbell, and a peal of discordant chimes sounded within the tiny house. Furious barking erupted, followed by a loud thunk as if a large beast struck the door.

Marissa broke free of Scott's grasp and stumbled back, her hand pressed to her throat.

Scott shot her a wry look. "Guess I was wrong about the sign."

She blew out a shaky breath. "You think?"

"Do you want to wait in the car?"

Did she? You bet. But she'd come this far, and she wanted answers. She pasted a brave smile on her face and lied. "I'm good."

His warm breath brushed her face as he leaned close and smoothed a lock of hair behind her ear. "That's my girl."

She bit her bottom lip to stop the trembling, but his words lent her courage. *My girl. She was* his *girl.*

His thumb caressed her cheek.

Another thump, and the door shuddered.

"Down, Brutus. Down." A woman hollered from inside the house.

Brutus's barking ramped up, and once again the

beast threw his body at the door.

"Down!"

A loud yelp sounded, followed by a series of plaintive whines.

The door opened, and a tall, thin woman with startling blue eyes and bleached-blonde hair scraped back from her face in a tight ponytail glared at them. "What the hell do you want?"

A massive black-and-tan monster of a dog, hackles raised, sharp teeth bared, sat on the floor at her side.

Marissa backed up another step.

Scott smiled at the woman. "Afternoon, ma'am. Are you Loretta Carmichael?"

She nodded, her ponytail bouncing.

"We'd like to talk to you about your brother, Steven."

The woman's blue eyes narrowed and filled with suspicion. "My brother's been dead a long time."

Scott didn't seem fazed by her blatant animosity. "I'm sorry for your loss, ma'am, but if we could ask you a few questions, we'd sure appreciate your time."

The dog growled, deep and low in his throat.

The woman patted the dog's head. Her nails were bitten to the quick, blood speckling the torn skin around the edges of her fingers. Her thin lips twisted in a bitter smile. "No one cared about him five years ago when he was murdered, so why do you care now? The damn police didn't even find his killer."

Scott fished in his pocket and tugged out his wallet. He flashed her his identification.

She studied the ID, her lips moving as she silently read each word. "You're from the District Attorney's office in Brunswick?"

"Like I said, ma'am, we have a few questions."

Her hard-eyed gaze flicked over Marissa, and she scowled. "Who's she?"

"My assistant."

She cackled. "Is that what they call them these days?" Sniffling, she swiped her runny nose with the sleeve of her sweater. "Y'all better come on in." Still chuckling, she opened the door wider.

Scott stepped inside, edging around the dog, but Marissa hesitated.

The dog's intense dark gaze fixed on her, and the black hairs on the back of his neck and along his spine bristled.

She shuddered. No way was she entering the house with that animal blocking the door.

"Come in if you're comin'. I ain't got all day." The woman grinned as if she enjoyed Marissa's fear.

"Is…is the dog okay?" Marissa's voice squeaked. *Okay?* The beast looked like it was ready to tear her apart with its razor-sharp fangs.

The woman's smirk widened, exposing stained and crooked teeth. "Don't worry about Brutus. He's a baby. He's more bark than bite." Her eyes narrowed and filled with malice. "Unless he decides he doesn't like you. Then he's a mean son of a bitch."

Heart pounding, knees wobbling, Marissa stepped onto the porch and edged around the big beast, keeping her hands jammed in the pockets of her jeans and her back pressed to the wall.

The dog's thick rope of a tail thumped the floor in an excited frenzy, and his fierce gaze tracked her every move, but he stayed where he was.

She followed Scott and the woman into a small,

dreary living room. Ragged chunks of brown plastic flaked from the battered, pleather-covered couch. Strips of curling, silver duct tape covered the cracks on the cushions.

Canned laughter and high-pitched squeals of excitement emanated from a television tuned to a game show. An empty wine bottle and three, crushed beer cans lay on the worn carpet. Plates covered with dried husks of unrecognizable food were stacked on the stained coffee table. The room smelled like a brewery, with heavy doses of cigarette smoke and sour body odor tossed into the heady mix.

Their hostess plopped on a wooden rocking chair and crossed one bony knee over the other. She rolled up her sleeve, checked her wristwatch, and fixed them with a sharp look. "I don't got all day. My shift starts in an hour."

Nails scrabbled along the laminate floor in the hall, and Brutus bounded into the room. He galloped over to Marissa and perched on his haunches before her, tail wagging. His long, red tongue lolled out. Gobbets of drool dripped on the floor, just missing her shoe.

Her heart skipped a beat, and she scrunched back in her seat, inching her foot away.

Scott cleared his throat. "Miss Carmichael, from what I understand, you took possession of your brother's personal effects after his unfortunate demise."

Her lip curled in a sneer. "Unfortunate demise, my ass. He was murdered in cold blood. Some lowlife stabbed him in the back and stole his money." Her thin hands shook as she picked up a pack of cigarettes from the table beside her and shook out a cigarette. Using the flame from a disposable plastic lighter, she lit the end of the cigarette. Lips pursing, she inhaled deeply, and then exhaled a thin spiral of smoke and sat back. Her hooded gaze settled on Scott. "Did you figure out who killed Steven? Is that why you're here?"

Scott shook his head. "Unfortunately no, but new information has come to light. Do you remember what personal possessions your brother had with him the night he was murdered?"

Her brow furrowed as she puffed on her cigarette.

Marissa's heart thudded. Would Steven's sister remember the necklace? Was this the break they were hoping for?

As if sensing her mounting tension, Brutus whined and laid his massive head on her lap. His big brown eyes watched her adoringly. His tongue dangled, and a trickle of drool soaked her pants.

Her hand shook as she patted his head, surprised at the velvety softness. "Good...good boy."

The dog's tail thumped the floor like a bass drum.

"The creep took his cash, his credit cards, and his watch." Loretta's lip curled. "Not that the watch was worth anything. It was a piece of crap. Stevie didn't have a pot to piss in."

"You don't recall any other jewelry?" Scott's voice was calm and low as if the answer to his question wasn't of any importance.

"Nope." Loretta stamped out her cigarette in a small, metal ashtray piled high with a tower of butts. She slid another cigarette out of the pack and lit the end with the lighter. "He was up to something, though. Those last few days he strutted around with a shit-eating grin on his face and was as happy as a dog with two dicks."

Marissa winced at the woman's crude language and the images it evoked.

"He called me the night he died. He was all excited about some gal. Told me they loved each other and were going to run away together." She swiped at a tear. "Poor sap, but that was Stevie's life. Just when things were going good, life shit on him."

Marissa bit back a gasp. Did this woman know Marissa was the person her brother thought he loved?

Scott shot her a look and gave a subtle shake of his head, warning her not to say anything. "He didn't have a silver chain with him the night he was killed?" He tugged out his phone and thumbed the button for his photos, then showed her the picture he'd taken of the chain. "One like this?"

Loretta squinted at the image. "I don't got my glasses, but it looks familiar. I remember that necklace. Stevie showed it to me. He said he was going to give it to his girl." She looked up at Scott. "Where'd you get that picture?"

"The necklace wasn't in the personal effects the police returned?"

"Maybe. I don't know. What the hell difference does it make now? My brother's dead." She stubbed out her cigarette and studied her watch. "Look, I gotta get to work." She stood and headed toward the front door, making it clear the interview was over.

Using two hands to lift Brutus's massive head from her lap, Marissa rose to her feet. She wiped the damp spot on her thigh. A flurry of short, coarse, dark hairs sifted to the floor as she followed Scott down the hall to the front door.

"Thank you for your time, ma'am." Scott nodded

at the woman and walked out the door and along the path to the car.

Marissa moved to follow but halted when Loretta grabbed her arm.

The blonde woman leaned closer, and her cigarette breath, hot and rank, blasted Marissa. "I know who you are."

Marissa gasped and reeled back, ripping her arm from the woman's claw-like grip. "Wha...what?"

Loretta cackled and waggled her over-plucked eyebrows. "That's right, honey. That's not all. I know lots of things."

"What...what do you know?" Her heart pounded in her ears like a marching band. She shot a glance at Scott. He was standing by the car, his gaze fixed on her.

"That necklace"—Loretta jerked her chin in Scott's direction—"the one you and your boyfriend are so interested in?" She smirked. "I sold it to that man."

"Man?" Marissa's voice was a thin thread of sound. "What man?"

"The one who came by the other day lookin' for Stevie's chain. He offered good money for that tarnished piece of crap."

Marissa swallowed, her mouth impossibly dry. She wanted to run from Loretta's ferret-like face, from the hatred oozing off her in palpable waves, but she took a deep breath, gathered her courage, and asked, "To whom did you sell the necklace? Please. It's important."

"*Whom*?" Loretta's thin upper lip curled "Well, aren't you all hoity-toity? I heard you was a librarian." She nodded at Scott waiting by the car. "Be careful, honey, men don't take to bookworms."

The woman knew who she was! The knowledge rocked Marissa, but she strove for a façade of calm. "Who bought the necklace, Loretta?"

Loretta shrugged. "I don't know...some big dude, dark hair, silver streaks. Kinda cute if you like them all dignified and snobbish. All I know is his money was good." She stepped back inside the house. "I'm late."

"Please, tell me what you know." Marissa jammed her foot in the door, stopping it from closing. "Please."

"Everything all right, Marissa?" Scott called from the curb.

Marissa shot him a quick look. "Everything's fine. Just give me a minute."

Loretta's eyes narrowed. "Did you care about my brother? Did you love him? Or were you just using him?"

"I hardly knew him. 'He'"—she swallowed, unsure how much to reveal, how much Loretta already knew— "he was stalking me."

The woman studied Marissa for several long breaths. "I knew something was up when he went to meet you that night, the night he died. I warned him he shouldn't go, but he wouldn't listen."

"He never met me. I didn't see him that night."

"So you say."

"I didn't. I swear."

"That's not what that man said. He told me your uncle killed Stevie."

Marissa's knees buckled, and she staggered. "My uncle? How do you know my uncle?"

Loretta sneered. "Lady, I know all about the DeGrazzis." She spit a stream of phlegm on the floor beside Marissa's foot. Wiping her mouth with the back of her hand, she turned away. "I don't have time to deal with this shit. I gotta go to work."

Reeling from Loretta's shocking revelation, Marissa clung to the reason they were there. This was too important. She needed answers. "Wait. Tell me more about the man who bought Steven's necklace."

Loretta's gaze was calculating. "What's in it for me?"

"Please, just tell me who bought Steven's necklace. Maybe then we can catch his murderer."

Loretta's eyed her for a dozen heartbeats. "Like I said, he was a big'un. All dressed up in a fancy suit with one of those striped ties. That's how I knew he was good for the money. That suit must have set him back a pretty penny."

Marissa placed her hand on Loretta's arm. "I'm sorry about your brother. I never understood why he thought I loved him or why he wouldn't leave me alone, but he didn't deserve to die the way he did."

Loretta ran her gaze over Marissa and nodded as if she'd reached some sort of decision. "The guy who bought the chain had a dark-colored car. He parked under that streetlight over yonder." She nodded her pointy chin toward the street. "Some sort of official seal was on the door. I couldn't see real well on account of I wasn't wearing my glasses."

"Wait a minute. A seal? Like an emblem?" Marissa's breath caught in her throat. "Was he driving a police car?"

Loretta shrugged. "That's all I know. Goodbye. Don't come back. Brutus won't be so welcoming the next time." She closed the door with a decisive clunk. The deadbolt slid into place.

Chapter 19

Mind whirling, Marissa stumbled in a daze to the car and climbed into the front passenger seat.

"You okay?" Scott started the motor and steered the car away from the curb and down the street.

She nodded.

"You two seemed to be having a pretty intense conversation. I didn't want to interfere. Learn anything?"

"Give me a minute, okay?"

His questioning gaze threatened to burn a hole in her, but he nodded and turned back to navigating Ashbury's busy streets through the downtown core and onto the highway.

As they passed acres of verdant forest, zoomed across a long, narrow bridge over a clear, fast-flowing river, and climbed a winding road into the mountains, she struggled with what she'd learned. How had Loretta known who she was? How did she know Julio DeGrazzi was her uncle? More importantly, who was the man who bought the silver chain?

"Marissa?" Scott's deep voice broke into her tumult.

The car was stopped. They were in a rest area beside the busy highway. A cement outhouse and a large metal garbage container were set back from the road. Two wooden picnic tables were in the shade under the leafy canopy of a small copse of trees. "Why are we stopped?"

"Let's go for a walk. You look like you could do with some fresh air." He opened his door and slid out from behind the steering wheel.

A walk? After what she'd learned from Steven Carmichael's sister, he wanted to go for a walk?

He opened her door, letting in a burst of sweet-smelling, brisk air, and motioned for her to get out.

She clasped his hand and allowed him to help her from her seat. The warmth of his large hand offered welcome comfort.

He led her across the parking area and along a narrow, gravel path into the trees. A meandering stream sparkled in the late afternoon sunshine. The surrounding forest muted the nearby rush of traffic, and the air was filled with the musical twittering of birds flitting through the branches of the tall trees. A battered picnic table—names, dates, and hearts carved into the weathered wood surface—was set amidst a stand of towering coniferous trees.

He released her hand and leaned against the table and crossed his arms over his chest.

Silence quivered between them.

A fly landed on her arm.

She brushed off the pesky insect.

The seconds ticked by.

A crow cawed from somewhere deep in the trees.

She swatted at another fly that swooped in and buzzed her face.

"Are you going to tell me what she said?"

She swallowed, avoiding his razor-sharp gaze. "She knew who I was."

"She knew your name?"

"I don't know, but she knew I was the woman her brother was stalking, and she knows I'm a librarian." She licked her dry lips. "Worse, she knows I'm Julio DeGrazzi's niece. She also said a man came by her house the other day and asked about the chain. He bought it from her."

"What the hell?" He shot up from the table and gripped her arms, forcing her to look at him. "Do you know what this means? The man who bought the necklace has to be the same person who put it in your wallet." His eyes flashed fire. "This is the guy who set us up, the jerk behind everything." He tugged her close and hugged her. "This is great. We finally have a break in the case. Who is he? Who bought the necklace?"

She shook her head, hating to dampen his enthusiasm. "She doesn't know his name. He was a big guy with dark, graying hair, and he wore an expensive suit and had a striped tie. That's all she'd tell me."

"Great. Just great." He released her and threw his hands up in the air. "There have to be a million guys who fit that description."

"His car had an official seal on the door."

"A cop car?"

"I don't know. She wouldn't say anything more."

"Could a cop be behind this?" He shook his head. "No. No way." He picked up a rock and tossed it in the stream. The pebbled landed with a loud splash. "There are hundreds of county, state, and city vehicles, and most have some sort of insignia. For all we know the guy could be the local dog catcher."

His cell phone rang, and he snatched it out of his pants pocket without looking at the call display.

"Yeah?" He stilled, his muscles tensing, his face transforming to stone. "What do you want, DeGrazzi?" He listened, his mouth tightening, and then handed her the phone. "He wants to speak to you."

Her hand shook as she held the phone to her ear. "Julio?" Rock and roll music pulsed in the background along with the clink of glasses, raucous laughter, and loud conversations. It sounded like he was at a party or in a bar.

"Marissa?" Julio's gruff voice blasted from the phone. "Look, I've been looking into this mess, and it's bad...worse than I thought."

She sucked in her breath. "What do you mean? What's going on?"

The noise in the background dimmed as if he'd moved into another room. "I know who sent you the necklace. I know who's behind this."

"You do?" A drip of sweat snaked down her spine beneath her shirt. "Who...who is it?"

"The less you know, the better. This man is dangerous. He'll stop at nothing to destroy me. Promise me you'll be careful."

"What are you going to do?"

"He's been gunning for me for years, but it's time to end this once and for all." His voice softened. "Be careful, Marissa. You're all the family I have."

A lump thickened her throat, and tears stung her eyes. No matter what crimes Julio had committed or how often he'd lied, he was family, her only family. Memories from the distant past of how he'd taken her to the petting zoo to feed the animals, paid for her tap dance lessons, and treated her on Sundays to a strawberry ice cream cone, teasing her about the rainbow candy sprinkles she liked scattered across the top, flooded her.

The line crackled and a woman's voice in the background called his name.

"Look, I gotta go. Don't trust anyone, you hear me, no one, especially that ADA boyfriend of yours. I've heard rumors that someone with connections deep inside the District Attorney's office is involved. Sounds to me like Scott Bannister's a prime candidate."

"What?" Her heart hammered, making it hard to hear.

"Think about it. Your phone went missing from the police evidence locker. Who better to slip into police headquarters unnoticed than the ADA? And who was Johnny-on-the-spot at the crime scene? Who's been with you every step of the way, watching you, leading you on, feeding you information?"

She fought to breathe over the tightness in her chest. *Scott?* She shot him a look.

He stood, arms crossed over his broad chest, staring out over the creek.

She edged a few steps away, turned her back, and lowered her voice. "You're wrong. He isn't involved."

"I'm just warning you to watch your back. Bannister's up to something. I can feel it. If you're any relation of mine, you sense it too."

"But—"

"Look, I gotta go."

"Wait!"

The line went dead.

Was Julio right? Was Scott behind this nightmare? Her heart shuddered as if a hand wrapped around it and squeezed. The phone dropped from her nerveless fingers and landed with a clatter on the gravel.

****

"Marissa?"

She rolled frightened eyes toward him.

"Are you okay?" Stupid question. She was anything but okay. "What the hell did that bastard say?"

"Nothing." Her reply had a definite edge, and she wouldn't meet his gaze.

A wave of apprehension flooded his gut. Had DeGrazzi figured out the truth? Did he know Scott was using the man's niece to find his own parents' murderers? "You seem upset." *Upset*? Hell, she looked like a strong wind would blow her over.

"My uncle wants us to be close like we used to." Her brittle laugh didn't reach her eyes. "He sounded like he had too much to drink." Suspicion radiated off her in palpable waves.

His gut tightened at her all-too-obvious lie. DeGrazzi had told her something all right…something about Scott. The pain in his stomach shifted to his chest, and his breath caught in his throat as if she'd struck him. He shouldn't be shocked. He'd known the truth would come out. He'd just hoped he'd have a chance to explain before she hated him.

Affecting an air of nonchalance, he bent down and retrieved his cell phone. He tugged the car keys from his front pocket. "Huh. Guess he can't handle his liquor. Why am I not surprised? We should get going."

Her face was closed, her expression unreadable, as they retraced their steps along the gravel path to the parking area and to the car. She kept her body tight, her hands glued to her sides as if afraid he'd touch her.

He settled behind the steering wheel and started the

car. His head throbbed, and he felt like he'd been kicked in the gut.

After his third attempt to break through her icy reserve failed, he gave up, and the drive to Gramm's house was made in stilted silence.

With each mile, his anger grew. After what they'd been through, the secrets they'd shared, their lovemaking...everything...she was lying to him. The hypocrisy that he was doing the same to her wasn't lost on him, but her betrayal was different. He was avenging his parents' deaths. She was siding with a cold-blooded murderer.

By the time they pulled before Gramm's house, his anger had hit the boiling point, and he itched for a fight. He held off until they were in the house, giving her one last chance to come clean.

As soon as he closed the front door, she mumbled something about wanting a shower and skulked past him and fled up the stairs.

Fuming, his gut roiling, he stomped into the kitchen, flicked on the overhead light, and yanked open the fridge door. He snagged a bottle of beer, twisted off the cap, tossed it in the sink, and lifted the icy bottle to his lips. The first sip was heaven, the second even better. By the time he drained the bottle, his anger was raging.

He set the empty on the counter and reached into the fridge for another. The frosty beer slid down his throat like silk.

The old water pipes clanked and thumped overhead.

A vision of Marissa standing naked in the shower rose before him...hot water sliding over her lithe body, soap bubbling on her creamy breasts, gilding her skin...

He cursed and guzzled more beer.

By the time he was halfway through his third beer, the room was spinning. Slamming the bottle on the counter, he wheeled around and marched out of the kitchen and into the front hall. He took the stairs two at a time, stumbling on the top step.

A voice in the back of his mind warned he'd had too much to drink, and he wasn't thinking clearly. This wasn't the time to confront her. He swiped a hand over his mouth, tasting the sweet, fruity hops and shut out the annoying voice.

No one lied to him, especially not someone he trusted, and not someone he cared for. A deep, almost visceral pain ripped through him, and he grabbed his stomach and hunched, fighting through the agony.

She'd betrayed him.

The insidious thought raged, unassailable and haunting, slicing deep.

The shower stopped.

He straightened and sucked in a ragged breath.

****

By the time she stepped out of the shower, the water was cold, and thick curls of steam filled the small, antiquated bathroom. The pelting hot water on her tender skin had helped. Her brimming tears were under control, leaving her with a fierce determination to ignore her aching heart and get on with what had to be done to survive this nightmare.

Don't trust anyone, especially the ADA.

Julio's words of warning rang through her like a death knell. Her uncle was right. She wasn't a fool. Scott wasn't telling her everything. She knew he had a secret, had known it from the beginning. How many times had he shut her out or changed the subject when her questions about his past became too personal?

The man had secrets all right, but she never imagined he'd betray her. Not like Julio insinuated. Not after they'd made such tender love. She blinked back the sting of tears. She'd trusted Scott with her heart. Snugging a fluffy, pink bath towel between her breasts, she opened the bathroom door, and froze.

Scott stood in the hall, arms crossed over his chest, a fierce expression on his handsome face.

"What do you want?" She wished she weren't standing before him dressed in nothing but a towel, but he blocked her escape.

"Why are you lying?"

"What are you talking about? I'm not lying about anything."

His lip curled in a sneer. "You forget. I'm a lawyer, and a pretty damn good one at that. I can spot a liar a mile away." He staggered and grabbed the wall for support. "Why won't you tell me what you and DeGrazzi discussed on the phone?"

Realization dawned…his glazed eyes, flushed face, the strong, yeasty smell. "You're drunk."

He laughed, but any hint of humor was lacking. "Lady, I'm not near drunk enough." He scrubbed a hand over his chin, the rasp of whiskers loud in the confined hallway. "Is this the way you want to play it?" He nodded. "Okay. I've been holding out on you, too."

His words confirmed her worst fear, and she shivered, desperate to flee, or at the very least cover her ears. She didn't want to hear his confession, to find out Julio was right, and the man she was falling in love with was using her.

"You have to understand that when this nightmare started, I had no idea"—he cleared his throat—"I had no idea how much I'd come to care for you, how much you'd mean to me. I didn't know—"

"So you lied." Her voice was hard and brittle. "You wouldn't be the first man to lie to a woman to get her in the sack."

"No. This isn't about that. Making love to you is the best thing that's ever happened to me. I never knew"—he waved his hands as if trying to grab something elusive—"I never knew..." His voice trailed off.

The guilt and misery she read in his eyes twisted something deep inside. In spite of her hurt and outrage, her heart softened. So he hadn't told her the complete truth. They could get past this. She focused on his next words, hoping his deception was something small like he'd parked in a handicap zone, or cheated on his taxes. But deep inside, doubt slithered like a viper. She shivered with the certainty his next words would crush her heart.

"As long as I can remember, I've wanted one thing, and one thing only—to destroy Julio DeGrazzi." He smoothed an unsteady hand over his hair.

"You've made no secret you despise my uncle." Where was this confession headed? His single-minded goal to put Julio behind bars and shut down his criminal organization was common knowledge.

"When I found you in that hotel room, I knew it was a setup. I could have walked away right then and avoided all the mess, but I didn't."

She stared at him, trying to determine what he

wasn't saying, what was so hard for him to say. "Why didn't you?"

"At first, I figured you were a hooker DeGrazzi had hired, and you looked like you might need medical assistance, but then"—he swallowed, his Adam's apple bobbing in his throat—"then I recognized you."

"You knew who I was? How?"

A pulse ticked in his strong jaw. "I've spent years studying DeGrazzi, read every file and newspaper article, questioned his known associates, and talked to anyone I could get my hands on." He shrugged. "I probably know more about Julio DeGrazzi than you."

"Okay, so you figured out I was his niece." She tightened her grip on the damp towel.

His eyes were haunted hollows, almost as if he suffered physical pain. "Once I knew who you were, I came up with a plan."

A cool draft wafted along the hall. Goose bumps riddled her arms. She shivered, her teeth beginning to chatter.

"You're freezing. I'm sorry." He shifted aside, clearing the way for escape. "Get dressed. We'll finish this conversation later."

She shook her head. "I want to hear what you have to say…all of it."

His brow gleamed under the hall light, and he swiped his forehead with the back of his hand. "Are you sure?"

Darkness settled over her soul. "What did you do?"

"I figured I could use your connection to your uncle to gain access to him. I wanted him to be so worried about you, that he'd let his guard down and make a mistake, so I could take him down."

Her heart felt like it was in a vise. The grim expression on his face warned her this was only the beginning. "Go on."

"I admit I haven't been completely honest, but when I realized you were DeGrazzi's niece, I figured you were as bad as him. It didn't matter that I was using you. Besides, I had my reasons."

She swore she heard the crack of her heart breaking. "You used me. You didn't give a damn about me. You still don't. It was all about your vendetta against my uncle." She stumbled back a step as darkness threatened to engulf her. "Was everything a lie? Did you have a good laugh about how you bamboozled Julio DeGrazzi's poor little niece into your bed?"

His silence spoke volumes.

"So it was all lies? I was just a pawn in your goal to destroy my uncle." Rage replaced her shocked numbness. "What the hell, Scott? I thought...I thought..." Her voice trailed off, her anger too hot, too visceral to contain. She rushed at him and slapped him across the face.

The crack echoed in the narrow hall, and she stared in horror as a red mark in the shape of her hand bloomed across his cheek.

He didn't flinch, just stared at her with damp, reddened eyes. "I'm sorry. I'm so sorry, but—"

She slammed her hands over her ears, refusing to listen to any more excuses. The knot of cloth between her breasts loosened, and in the next breath the towel slipped to the floor. Ignoring her nudity, she shoved past him and stormed down the hall.

He stumbled and fell to his knees, hitting the floor

with a loud thud. "Marissa, wait. You don't understand. Your uncle…he…my parents…"

In spite of her determination not to, she glanced back.

He knelt on the floor, tears streaming down his rugged cheeks. "Marissa, please, listen to me." He struggled to his feet and stumbled toward her.

Once again, her heart shattered, but she shut her ears to his pleas, and slammed the bedroom door shut.

Chapter 20

The sun was sinking behind the hills, and the shadows lengthening when she sat up and tossed the blankets on the floor. She tugged on her dirty, overripe clothing and threaded her fingers through her tangled hair.

In the mirror above the bureau, she caught a glimpse of a woman she barely recognized. Her eyes were swollen and puffy, her skin blotchy, her hair a wild tangle of dark curls. She had to get out of the house and away from Scott. She had to find answers.

She crossed to the window and peered through the dingy glass at the weed-choked yard. Grasping the bottom of the double window, she heaved, tugging the sash, until with a protesting screech, the window slid up.

She leaned out the opening and studied the sloping roof. The shingles were old, the edges curled, some missing. Thick clumps of moss covered the roof. Leaning out farther, she gulped. The hard-packed ground was a long way down.

Scott's muffled voice reached her through the closed bedroom door.

Why didn't he go away? He'd already shredded her heart. Nothing he said could repair the damage. She swiped her hand over her damp eyes and studied the roof. Okay. She could do this. Her knees shook as she climbed through the open window and stepped onto the roof.

She clutched the window frame and held tight. Her fingers cramped, and her heart pounded. The distance to the old wooden trellis was further than she'd thought. What was she doing out there? Was she so desperate to escape Scott, she'd risk her life?

Yes.

The blatant truth lent her courage. She released her grip on the window and shuffled forward. One step and then another.

Don't look down.

A loose shingle slipped from beneath her foot, skidded down the steep roof, and slid over the rusted metal gutter. A heartbeat later, a plunk reached her ears.

Crouching on all fours, her fingers digging into the rough shingles, she scuttled on her hands and knees to the trellis. Her hands were scraped raw and her knees throbbing by the time she crossed the twenty feet of roof to where the dilapidated, old framework extended a few inches above the gutter and overhung the back porch.

She grabbed the rickety frame and swung her body around and set her foot on the top rung. The old wood creaked and groaned as she eased her other foot onto the next rung. Praying to a God she hadn't believed in for years, she descended the swaying structure, rung by rung.

Once on solid ground, she sagged against the house, fighting to catch her breath. Ignoring her wobbly legs, she pushed away from the wall and stumbled across the overgrown lawn to the car.

Mouthing a prayer, she opened the driver's door

and almost smiled.

Scott had left the car unlocked and the keys in the ignition. For a man who thought nothing of deceiving others, he was awfully trusting.

****

Scott's head pounded as if a drill blasted inside his skull. His mouth tasted like a garbage dump, his tongue thick and coated with fur. Had he really told her the truth? He touched his stinging cheek.

Yep, he had.

What a fool! The beer had been talking. He should have kept his mouth shut, at least until he was sober. Truth was, his betrayal had gnawed at his gut like a cancer, festering until he couldn't stand the guilt. It was a relief when the words spilled out, one condemning syllable after another.

He stared at the closed bedroom door. Was she ever going to come out? He glanced at his watch. She'd been in there three hours. When she'd stormed off, in all her naked glory, her beautiful face a thundercloud, her eyes snapping fire, he'd clambered up from the floor and staggered after her, only to be met by the door slamming in his face. He'd barely avoided a broken nose.

Now, after countless cups of strong coffee and stone-cold sober, he stood outside the door, waiting for her to calm down and come out so he could explain. He grimaced. As if any explanation excused his actions.

All was silent. He'd called to her—many times—but she hadn't answered. Had she fallen asleep? He wasn't leaving until he explained to her why he'd acted the way he had, no matter how long he had to stand there.

So he'd waited, and waited, and waited.

He rubbed his aching head and studied his watch. Another minute had inched past since the last time he checked.

He'd betrayed her. It was as simple and as complicated as that. In his zeal to make DeGrazzi pay for murdering his parents, he'd gone against his principles. He'd lied. Worse, he'd used her. No wonder she hated him. He pretty much hated himself. He shook his head and winced as his hangover headache revved up a notch.

Once he'd realized who she was, his anger and frustration reached a head. This was his chance to destroy his enemy. And so he'd made an inexcusable choice. What he hadn't counted on, what he'd never expected, was she would come to mean so much.

She'd crept under his skin, and he couldn't stop thinking of her every minute of every day. He wanted to be with her, to listen to her innermost thoughts and dreams, and hear the rich sound of her laughter. He sucked in a shaky breath. He'd messed up big time.

From the moment she ended the call with her uncle, her body had stiffened, and she watched him with wary eyes. Hell, every time he'd tried to touch her, she flinched as if he were going to strike her.

He dug in the front pocket of his jeans and yanked out a crumpled card. Staring at DeGrazzi's private cell phone number, he chewed the inside of his cheek. Part of him wanted to call the bastard and demand answers. Another part, a saner part, wanted Marissa to be honest with him and tell him why she was so frightened.

He had to fix this. Somehow, he had to make this right.

Rustling sounds and a loud thump emanated through the thick wood. He thrust back his shoulders and knocked on the door. "Marissa?" He waited, his mouth dry.

Nothing.

"Marissa?" His gut knotted, and he twisted the doorknob.

Locked.

His spidey senses fired on all thrusters. Something wasn't right. Tearing down the hall, he leaped the stairs two at a time to the landing and raced to the kitchen. Tugging open the utility drawer where Gramm kept a jumble of spare screws, nails, twist ties, and elastics, he rummaged through the assorted junk until he found a nail.

He retraced his steps and called once again through the door. "Marissa, are you okay?"

Silence.

Inhaling a deep breath, he said, "I'm coming in." Jamming the nail in the tiny hole in the door lock, he wiggled the nail until a click sounded. He turned the handle, and the door swung open.

The room was empty. Sheets and blankets were tossed on the floor in a rumpled heap. A cold breeze fluttered the frilly, white lace curtains covering the single window. The sash was up, the window open.

He rushed to the window and leaned out. The shingles below the open window were scuffed, the moss coating the curling tiles rubbed bare. A faint trail of footprints led across the sloping roof.

Cursing, he slammed his fist on the window ledge. What was she thinking? The roof was steep, the old shingles loose and slippery. One slip and she risked falling and breaking her neck. His gut twisted at the thought of what she'd risked in her desperation to escape.

A rumble of a car engine filled the afternoon quiet.

Whirling around, he tore out of the room and raced down the stairs. He flung open the front door.

Gramm's faded orange car, with a grim-faced Marissa behind the wheel, sped down the gravel drive, spraying a cloud of dust in the car's wake.

****

She squeezed the car into an open space between a yellow convertible and a luxury sedan and switched off the motor. Removing the keys from the ignition, she stuffed them in her pocket, and mopped the tears from her face with a wad of tissue. She hadn't stopped crying since Scott's drunken confession.

Sure, she was Julio DeGrazzi's niece, but that didn't give Scott the right to toy with her, to use her. He'd rambled on, offering up a dozen excuses for his actions, but she'd shut her ears and fled to her room before she shattered into a million jagged pieces and collapsed on the bed in a torrent of tears.

Tossing the paper hankie on the passenger seat where it joined a pile of sodden tissues, she inhaled a deep breath, thrust open the car door, and stepped onto the street. The luxury apartment building towered over her. She shouldn't be there, but she was tired of being used, fed up with being a pawn. She wanted answers, and Julio knew more than he'd revealed.

With determined strides, she marched toward the glass doors and peered inside. The lobby was deserted. Where were the security guards? The previous times she'd been at Julio's building, at least two hulking, armed brutes guarded the front entrance.

She yanked open the door. Unlocked. What the heck? She stepped inside and glanced up at the security cameras. Maybe the guards had the night off, and the surveillance cameras were enough protection from unwanted intruders.

Maybe.

Heart pounding, she crossed the lobby to the elevator and pushed the call button. She chewed her bottom lip as she waited. Butterflies danced in her stomach. She hadn't talked to Julio for five long years, but in the past few days, she'd been to see him twice.

And there she was again.

She chewed harder on her lip, tasting blood. A similar scenario had played out five years ago, when frightened and upset, she'd run to her uncle, begging him for help. Her visit then had resulted in a man's violent death. So what was she doing?

Turn around and leave. Now.

The elevator pinged its arrival, and the doors swished open.

Too late.

With leaden feet, she stepped inside. What choice did she have? She had nowhere else to go. No one else would help her. Her uncle was her last hope, her only option. Pressing the button for the penthouse, she leaned against the burnished metal as the doors slid closed.

The elevator began its smooth ascent. Classical music filtered through the sound system, and the relaxing scent of lavender wafted in the air. The soothing music and perfumed air were supposed to be calming, but her nerves were too raw, her heart too wounded to relax.

The doors slid open onto the viewing room. The sun was sinking below the distant, forested mountains, and the immense room was filled with shadows. A strange, almost metallic smell permeated the air.

The hairs on the back of her neck prickled, and the pounding of her heart revved to hyper speed. "Hello?" Her quavering voice disappeared into the vastness. She swallowed. "Uncle Julio?"

The unpleasant smell was stronger, and her stomach roiled. She plugged her nose and breathed through her mouth. "Anyone here?"

An unsettling groan echoed through the viewing room, emanating from the darkness beyond.

She wiped her damp palms on her pants.

Something was wrong. Something was very wrong.

The primal warning screamed through her brain. Instead of fleeing back into the elevator as every cell in her body demanded, she shuffled across the room and down the hall.

The hall was unlit and covered in concealing shadows, but a sliver of light glowed from under the closed door to Julio's study. She grasped the doorknob, but hesitated. The foul odor was overpowering. Her gut spasmed, and bile rose in her throat. Her legs twitched, and she fought the urge to whirl around and run out of the penthouse.

Again a low moan sounded, as if an animal were in pain.

Hand shaking, she twisted the handle and opened the door. A single lamp on the desk glowed revealing a scene from Hell. The room wavered, the light pulsating. The rasp of her breathing was muted as if she were underwater.

A man lay sprawled on his back. Dark-red blood soaked the front of his tight, white T-shirt and pooled on the carpet. His shaved head gleamed in the dim light. His face was frozen, his skin waxy, eyes open and vacant. Beneath the elaborate mustache, his mouth hung open. A small hole in his forehead oozed congealing blood that dripped onto the tattooed snake coiled on his thick neck.

Tiny!

She jammed her fist in her mouth, stopping the scream threatening to burst free. Her knees turned to water, and she sagged against the doorframe. The room swam as more horror was revealed.

The second body was propped against the wall like a rag doll. His head drooped over his broad chest. A mat of blood spread like a bib beneath his chin. More blood spattered the walls and streaked the light gray carpet.

Dead.

The unbelievable word pulsed with the frantic beat of her heart. Both bodyguards were dead. She didn't have to check their pulses to know they no longer breathed. Death hung in the air like a miasma. Her fingers curled into fists, her nails digging into her palms.

Run!

The single command rang through her.

Run!

But her muscles wouldn't obey, and she stood frozen, her gaze fixed on the nightmare before her.

An anguished moan broke through her paralysis.

Her heart lurched. They were alive! But even as the

astounding thought flashed through her mind, she knew neither of the two men lived.

Another moan, low and deep, filled with endless pain, resonated from behind the oversized, leather couch.

She stumbled into the room on wooden legs. Heart in her throat, she peered over the back of the couch.

A blood-spattered man lay huddled on the floor.

"Julio!" His name exploded on a breath of air. She tore around the couch and crouched beside him. Her heart thundered in her ears, and her hands trembled. She touched his arm.

His skin was warm. His eyes were swollen, and his bottom lip was mangled as if someone had punched him. Bloody spit drooled from his slack mouth. His nose was bent at an odd angle and caked in dried blood.

"Julio." Her cry was louder, more urgent.

He moaned, and his eyes flickered open. "Marissa?"

"My God, Uncle Julio, what happened? Who did this? Who hurt you?"

He blinked as if trying to focus. "Marissa?"

Her tears dripped off her chin onto his blood-encrusted, white linen shirt. "I'm here, Uncle Julio, I'm here."

"No. It's not safe. You have to leave." His bloodless lips barely moved.

She lurched to her feet. "Where's your phone? I need to call 911."

He clutched her leg, his fingers like talons digging into her flesh. "Do…do you have the necklace?"

Necklace? Really? He was worried about the necklace? Now? "You're bleeding. Let me call for help." She tugged, but his grip was strong, his eyes fierce.

"Give it to me."

She frowned but dug the necklace out of her pocket and handed it to him.

His fingers curled around the silver chain in a tight fist, and he released his hold on her leg. "Now go. Leave me. He might still be here." His face blanched. The grooves beside his mouth carved deep.

His wild-eyed fear amped up her own terror. "Who are you talking about? Who did this to you, Julio?" She sank back on her knees. "Tell me. Who hurt you?"

"The Russian...he..." His breathing grew more labored. "Danger..." Tears of frustration streamed down his face, mixing with the blood and drool, darkening his salt-and-pepper beard as he struggled to force out the words.

The Russian? What was he talking about?

"Well, well, well. Isn't this sweet."

She jerked around.

A short, stocky, white-haired man stood framed in the doorway, a mocking grin on his plump face. His black coat strained over a round belly, and his neck bulged over his shirt's top button. With his bushy, white eyebrows and full, white beard he resembled a storybook Santa Claus—except for the icy menace in his blue eyes and the gun dangling from his hand. "Too bad I have to break up this touching family moment." His voice was thick with a heavy accent. "Ivan." He snapped his fingers.

A tall, dark-haired, bearded man with bulging muscles stepped into the room. His face was steel, his eyes hard, his bearing military.

"Run, Marissa. Save…save yourself." Julio's hoarse croak broke through her stunned disbelief. "Run!" His face was a ghostly mask under the dried blood. His gray eyes pleaded with her through puffy, discolored lids.

"I…I can't leave you. I won't." For years she'd despised him, done everything in her power to distance herself, but none of that mattered anymore. He was her uncle, and he needed help. She wouldn't desert him.

"Go! Be safe." He grimaced through ravaged lips. "It's…it's what I want, what I've always wanted."

Tears flooded her eyes.

"Aww. I am getting all emotional."

The chubby man's cruel voice cut through her tears. She glared. "Who are you? Why did you do this? Why did you kill the guards and hurt my uncle?"

"Marissa, save yourself," Julio gasped. "Run….please…run."

"Too late, DeGrazzi." The white-haired man chuckled. He motioned to his partner. "Grab her."

The muscle-bound goon grinned, exposing crooked teeth, and lunged.

A surge of adrenaline fueled through her, and she lurched to her feet.

Too late.

He grabbed her arms, clamping her biceps, his thick fingers digging deep into her tender flesh.

The man with the white beard raised his gun and pointed the barrel at Julio. "I have been looking forward to this for a long time, old *friend*."

"No!" She struggled, kicking and shoving, but the hulk didn't budge. Panting, tears streaming down her face, but refusing to give up, she wrenched her body, twisting and jerking, clawing to break free.

He tightened his hold, trapping her arms and pinioning her against his solid bulk.

Her stomach heaved at the stench of garlic and stale cigarette smoke. A wisp of memory slammed into her like a tidal wave. This was the man who'd abducted her from the faculty parking lot. He'd drugged her and taken her to the hotel.

A gunshot, as loud as a clap of thunder, cracked the air.

Julio jerked. His body jackknifed, slamming back down on the floor. A red stain bloomed across his chest. He shuddered once, twice, and stilled.

"No," she wailed. Her captor released her, and she collapsed to her knees, her shoulders heaving. "No."

A shrieking alarm pierced the air as if the demons from Hell had escaped.

"Time to get out of here." The white-haired man lowered the gun and limped out of the room. "Bring her."

The muscle-bound hulk tightened his talon-like grip on her arm and propelled her out of the blood-spattered room, down the hall, across the expanse of the viewing room, and into the waiting elevator.

When they reached the main floor, he shoved her through the glass lobby doors and onto the sidewalk. Unfazed by her frantic kicking and struggling, he dragged her over to a large, black town car idling at the curb.

She screamed, but the tape covering her mouth muted her cries for help.

He wrenched open the door and shoved her onto the backseat.

She landed with a thump that drove the air out of her lungs. Spots flashed before her eyes as she fought to breathe through her nose.

Her captor slid in beside her, his hard-muscled body crowding hers.

The older man with the cold blue, terrifying eyes, climbed onto the front passenger seat. "Let's go," he ordered.

The driver punched the gas. The car sped away from the curb and merged with the light, evening traffic.

The goon beside her slammed his hand on the back of her head and shoved, mashing her face into the expensive leather seat.

She sucked in small bursts of air through her nose. Sounds were muffled, but she sensed the motion of the car as the vehicle swerved around corners and stopped, idling at traffic lights. After what felt like an hour, but was probably more like fifteen minutes, the car slowed, the tires thumped over a series of bumps, and the vehicle rolled to a stop. A loud, grinding, metallic sound resonated from somewhere outside the car.

The brute lifted his hand, and the pressure on the back of her head eased. Before she sucked in a full breath, he grabbed her hair, yanked her head up, and ripped the tape from her mouth.

A scream burst free, and tears of pain stung her eyes. Sucking in gulps of air, she thrust back her tangled, sweaty hair. The inside of the car was dark. No ambient light from streetlights or passing cars eased the heavy darkness. They were in a building. A garage? Underground parking?

The front door cracked open, and she blinked in the

sudden glare of the dome light.

The white-haired man heaved himself out of the car.

Her captor shoved open the back door. He gripped her arm and dragged her across the seat and out of the car.

The door slammed shut and once again she was immersed in darkness.

Pinning her to his side, he snarled into her ear, "Shut up! Don't make me hurt you." His sour, coffee-and-tobacco-laced breath blasted her.

She flinched at the deadly menace in his voice and bit her lip, stopping a scream.

A beam of light flared, and the white-haired man drew near in a halo of brightness. "Take her to the storage room." He waved the flashlight, and the beam strobed into the darkness. "We will deal with her later." He handed the flashlight to the man holding her.

The big man jerked her arm, and shining the light ahead, propelled her across the room.

Her rubber-soled shoes slapped hollowly on the bare cement floor. The strong odors of gasoline and motor oil stung her nostrils. Her suspicion she was in a garage was confirmed when they passed a car, hood up, elevated on joists. A shiny red car fender leaned against a wooden workbench piled high with tools and dirty rags. Tires were piled on the floor.

He opened a door set into the cement wall, and without a word of warning, flung her into the darkness beyond.

She screamed, arms flailing. Her hip struck something solid, and she yelped and fell, landing with a bone-jarring thud on her knees on the unforgiving cement floor.

The door slammed shut, followed by the chilling sound of a bolt sliding into place.

Collapsing on her side, she curled into a tight ball. Tears of pain and fear stung her eyes. Who were these men? What did they want with her? Were they going to kill her like they'd shot Julio and his guards? Was that why they'd brought her here?

In the stygian darkness, she lost track of time. Bone-chilling cold leached from the damp floor and seeped through her clothes. Shivers wracked her body.

Get up!

The command fired through her in an urgent litany.

Get up!

Finally, the words penetrated her disabling grief and terror. She uncurled her stiff joints and pushed to her knees and then to her feet. Swiping the tears from her damp face, she rubbed her throbbing hip. The darkness was absolute, as if she were buried deep underground. A sob hiccupped in her throat. There had to be a way out of there. There had to.

She held her hands out in front as she shuffled across the room. Her foot stubbed into a hard object, probably what she'd crashed into when she was tossed in there. From the shape and feel, it was a small wood table. A folding metal chair was beside the table. A few steps more revealed what had to be a narrow cot. A pillow and rough woolen blanket lay on top of a thin, lumpy mattress.

Exhaustion overwhelmed her, and she sank onto the cot and lay down, drawing the scratchy, musty-smelling blanket to her chin. Numb from the horrors she'd witnessed, her heavy lids closed.

Chapter 21

Scott opened the door to the police station and stepped inside. As he'd expected, the lobby was crowded.

Six o'clock was shift change. The day-shift officers were finishing their reports, and the night-duty cops were grabbing final cups of watered-down coffee before roll call and heading out on the streets for their twelve-hour shifts.

A heavy silence descended over the busy room as all heads swiveled in his direction.

Sweat popped out under his arms and trickled down his sides under the weight of so many condemning pairs of eyes. He'd expected the censure, had known his appearance at the police station would not go unnoticed. Every cop in town would have heard about the debacle at the Condor Hotel. They'd know he'd been placed on involuntary leave, know about the arrest warrant.

Keeping his gaze fixed straight ahead, he placed one foot in front of the other and crossed the acre of open floor past the dispatch desk and down the long hall to the detective division. Talk about a walk of shame. Each step required a conscious effort. He was a man, career destroyed, reputation in shambles, walking to his execution.

He had no one to blame but himself. In his zeal to

punish his parents' murderers, he'd gone against a lifetime of moral values. He'd made a backhanded deal with DeGrazzi, and if that weren't despicable enough, he'd used Marissa. He'd lied to the woman he loved. His stomach dropped to his toes, and he stumbled to a stop, ignoring the gaping stares.

The woman I love?

He didn't love Marissa. Sure, he felt bad. Using her for his personal agenda was not cool. He deserved her anger and derision. An image of her wounded, gray eyes rose before him, and he flinched.

Okay, so he was a piece of shit. Now he was even lying to himself. He did love her. Too bad it had taken him so long to recognize the truth. He loved her, and now he'd destroyed that love.

She hated him. Who could blame her?

Yes, indeed, he was a piece of shit.

But before she tossed him to the sharks, he had to fix this mess. He had to clear her name. He'd confess to interfering in an active police investigation and abusing his position of authority for personal gain. He'd fess up to how he'd used Marissa's presence at the Condor Hotel in his quest to destroy her uncle.

Once the DA learned the sordid truth, Scott's career would be in the tank, but Marissa would be cleared. The charges against her would be dropped. She could go on with her life. Without him. He squelched the twist of pain in his gut and thrust open the door to the detective bullpen.

To a person, the swarm of busy detectives halted what they were doing and stared.

Ignoring the shocked silence and the burn of a dozen sets of condemning eyes, he strode across the room and knocked on Detective Sandhu's door. He opened the door without waiting for permission to enter.

The detective sat at his desk. When Scott entered, he looked up, his eyes widened, and a frown carved between his dark brows. "Scott?"

Scott faltered, shocked at the changes in his friend. It was as if the man had aged a decade since Scott had seen him last. His eyes were sunken hollows, his skin sallow, his shirt wrinkled and stained as if he'd slept in it.

He opened his mouth to ask what was wrong but stopped. This wasn't a social call. He crossed the small office and sank onto the chair facing the detective's desk.

Ardash stared at him for an eternity, his gaze delving deep. "Are you turning yourself in?"

Scott wiped his damp palms on his pants. "I have a lot to tell you. After I'm finished, you can arrest me, but hear me out first."

The detective's eyebrows shot to his hairline, but he sat back in his chair, linked his fingers, and rested his hands on his flat stomach. "I'm listening."

Scott licked his lips. He'd thought confessing his sins would be difficult, but in his rush to clear Marissa's name, the words poured out. "Marissa Reynolds is innocent. She had nothing to do with what happened at the Condor Hotel. She's an innocent victim, but because of my actions she's caught up in this nightmare, and someone is trying to kill her."

The lines between Ardash's brows deepened. "You'd better start at the beginning."

"I'll tell you everything, but I want your promise

that the charges against Marissa will be dropped, and you'll assign a team of officers to protect her."

"You're that certain she's innocent?"

Scott nodded. "Will you promise to protect her?" He held his breath. Nothing was more important than the detective's next words.

"You have my word. If what you're telling me is the truth, I'll ensure she has protection until we catch whoever's after her." The earnest gleam in the detective's dark eyes proved his sincerity.

For the first time since Marissa had walked out on him, Scott relaxed. A calm acceptance of his fate settled over him. Without further delay, he related the events that had happened from the moment he received the phone call from Flinty McGregor, until that afternoon when Marissa had given him the slip. By the time he finished, his throat was raw, and his shirt was damp. His heart pounded like he'd run a marathon.

Ardash stood and strode over to the door and opened it. Leaning his head into the bullpen, he called, "Jenkins, bring us a couple of coffees, will you? Both black." He returned to his chair, sat down, and stared at Scott, his gaze assessing.

A sharp rap sounded on the door, and it opened. The furious bustle of conversation, ringing phones, and laughter spilled into the tiny office. A tall, thin man entered, carrying two foam cups. He placed one before the lead detective. Shooting Scott a suspicious glower, he slammed the other cup on the desk and left the room, closing the door behind him with a decisive thud.

The aromatic smell of strong coffee wafted over the small office.

Scott picked up his cup and gulped, uncaring the

hot liquid burned his tongue. He'd never needed a jolt of caffeine more.

"You haven't told me everything." Ardash's piercing gaze fixed on Scott.

Scott's arm jerked, and he cursed as hot coffee spilled on his hand. "What are you talking about? I've confessed to interfering with a criminal investigation, manipulating facts for my own agenda, aiding and abetting a wanted fugitive, among other offenses. You have me dead to rights. My culpability's clear." His lip curled. "Arrest me, and lay any number of charges against me. You'll be a hero in tomorrow's papers. Hell, by next week, you'll be promoted to captain."

Ardash's impenetrable dark eyes studied him. "Why are you so determined to take Julio DeGrazzi down? There are plenty of criminals in Brunswick. You can't turn over a rock without finding at least two. Why your single-minded focus on DeGrazzi? You've destroyed your career, but for what? To save DeGrazzi's niece?"

Scott slammed his cup on the desk. Unable to bear the confines of the hard chair a second more, he lurched to his feet. He needed to move, to burn off the nervous energy zinging through his muscles like electrical charges. "Do you remember a double homicide outside Shermann's Theater twenty-nine years ago?" His voice was hoarse, the words coated in grief. Starting this conversation was like ripping a scab off an old wound.

"The shooting was before my time, but I remember reading about the tragedy. The murders were all over the news media." Ardash's brow wrinkled. "A man and a woman, right? Shot in the parking lot outside the theater. A gang war, wasn't it? Far as I remember, the police never found the perps."

Scott nodded as the familiar pain descended like a dark shroud. "The victims were my parents."

Ardash's eyes widened. "Your parents?"

"They'd gone to a movie." His mouth twisted in a bitter smile. "Date night. They never made it home."

"And you were how old?"

"Five. My grandmother was looking after me. I'll never forget when the cop came to the house to tell her of the shooting."

"Jeez, Scott, I'm sorry. I didn't know. That's terrible."

"DeGrazzi was one of the men responsible."

"How do you know? He would have just been a punk then."

Scott braced his hands on the back of his chair. "I've made it my mission to find the people who murdered my parents. I've spent years studying the files, interviewing witnesses—"

"And that's why you sought the position of Assistant District Attorney."

Scott nodded. "Once I was the ADA, I had access to the cold case files. I could investigate and ask questions that I couldn't as a private citizen."

"Why did you zero in on DeGrazzi?"

"In those days, DeGrazzi was a thug working for the Morrisey gang, delivering drugs, collecting overdue loan payments, providing muscle, that sort of thing. He was small potatoes, but he was smart, and he had ambition. He also had a temper.

"When the rivalry between the Morrisey gang and the Russians reached an impasse, DeGrazzi took matters into his own hands. He set up a kill on a high-ranking lieutenant in the Russian mob. He hid in the shadows and waited outside the movie theater. When Slavadad Marischenko walked out, he started firing."

He rubbed his forehead with the pads of his fingers, digging deep to staunch the piercing pain. "Marischenko fired back. Police records indicate twenty-three shots were fired that night. Rumor has it that Marischenko was wounded, but both he and DeGrazzi got away. My parents weren't so fortunate."

Ardash tapped his fingers on the desktop. "Why did DeGrazzi target Marischenko? What was he hoping to accomplish?"

Scott grabbed his cup and drained the lukewarm coffee. "Marischenko was second-in-command of the Russians. After the shooting, a war between the two gangs broke out. Bodies piled up. When the dust settled, the Morrissey and Russian gangs were destroyed, their networks in upheaval. The way was clear for DeGrazzi to step in and take over. Over the years he built up his gang of hoodlums until he became the leader of the most powerful criminal organization in this city."

The drumming stopped. Ardash leaned over his desk. "What happened to this Marischenko guy?"

Scott shrugged. "He's around town somewhere lurking in the shadows. I've picked up rumors from my informants that he's still pulling strings. Last intel I received indicated he's out for revenge and planning a takeover of DeGrazzi's empire. That could explain why Flinty McGregor was killed."

"You think Marischenko is after Marissa Reynolds because she's DeGrazzi's niece?"

"Her death would be a big hit against DeGrazzi.

She's the only family he has."

Silence settled over the office. Loud, masculine voices in the bullpen filtered through the thick glass. The fluorescent lights seared into Scott's pupils, adding to the pounding in his head.

The door burst open and Detective Barbour, his red hair wild, his face grim, stepped into the office. "Something big's going down, Detective Sandhu. Thought you'd want to know."

Ardash jumped to his feet. "What is it?"

Barbour shot a look at Scott.

"Don't worry about him."

"We got a call from one of Julio DeGrazzi's neighbors. Says she heard shots fired in the penthouse. An alarm's going off. Patrol cars are on scene, and the building's being evacuated."

Ardash rounded his desk and tugged a suit coat from the hook by the door and shrugged into it. "Let's roll."

Scott stepped forward blocking his way. "Let me go with you."

"No way." The detective shook his head. "That's DeGrazzi's place. You're too involved. I can't let you anywhere near him."

"Please, Ardash. Marissa Reynolds might be in that penthouse apartment. I've hurt her so much. I couldn't bear it if something bad happened to her. You have to let me help."

Ardash chewed on his bottom lip. "I know I'm going to regret this, but okay. Don't touch a damn thing, and keep your mouth shut. You may have destroyed your career; I want to keep mine."

Yes! Scott rushed out the door after the detectives,

not giving his friend a chance to change his mind.

****

The unmarked cruiser skidded to a stop in front of DeGrazzi's tony high-rise building in a blaze of flashing red and blue lights and screaming sirens. Four other cop cars were parked at the curb. An ambulance raced down the street, sirens blaring. Another followed. A crowd of reporters and lookie-loos jostled behind the yellow police tape, cell phones raised to record the action.

Detective Sandhu jumped out of the car.

Detective Barbour climbed out of his seat and wrenched open the back door.

Scott charged out. Cameras flashed, blinding him as he raced behind the detectives to the lobby doors. They hustled through the doors and past a phalanx of uniformed police officers keeping out the curious. The elevator doors were open, and they rushed across the lobby and piled into the elevator.

No one spoke as the lift ascended and soft music played.

Fear iced Scott's heart. It was all he could do not to gnash his teeth. If he was right and Marissa had gone to DeGrazzi's penthouse apartment seeking answers, she was in trouble. And it was his fault. If he'd come clean with her sooner, explained his actions better, or better still, never lied to her in the first place, none of this would have happened.

If she was hurt, he'd never forgive himself. He loved her, had loved her from the moment she walked into the middle of the street and became a target for the speeding SUV.

He was under no illusions. This wasn't the movies.

There was no happy ever after. Not for him and Marissa. Whatever spark had existed between them was over. His lies and deceit had destroyed something pure and beautiful.

A resonant ding sounded, and the elevator doors slid open. The stench of a butcher shop displaced the lavender-scented air and punched him with the all-too-distinctive reek of death.

Ardash's face settled into hard lines. He reached for his gun and stepped out of the elevator.

A detective Scott didn't recognize strode toward them. "Glad you're here, Detective Sandhu. We can do with the help. The bodies are in the other room."

"Bodies?" Scott ignored Ardash's frown. "What bodies?"

"It's a meat market. One of DeGrazzi's bodyguards was shot in the head. The other had his throat slashed. DeGrazzi was hit with a bullet to the chest."

"DeGrazzi's dead?"

The detective nodded.

"Anyone else hurt?" Scott held his breath as the world threatened to vaporize. "Any...any civilians?"

"Just gangbangers."

Scott's breath rushed out, and he sagged and would have fallen if Ardash hadn't grabbed his arm and held him up.

"Okay," Ardash said. "Let's have a look." He shot Scott a hard look. "Get hold of yourself. Don't make me regret including you." He didn't wait for Scott's acknowledgement before he turned and charged after the other detective.

Scott's mind whirled as he fought to assimilate what the detective had reported. DeGrazzi was dead. He should be thrilled, should be reveling in satisfaction, vindication…something. But all he could think about was Marissa. Was she safe? The detective had said no civilians were injured. If she wasn't there, where the hell was she?

Only one way to find out. He followed the detectives to the crime scene.

The medical examiner and his team of crime scene investigators had already arrived, and the small room was crowded with technicians photographing the victims and blood spatter, swabbing surfaces for fingerprints, and examining the bodies. The reek of death hung heavy in the air.

"What the hell happened?" Ardash demanded. "The room looks like a goddamn slaughterhouse."

Dr. Stevenson, the top forensic specialist in the department, rose from where he was kneeling by one of the bloody bodies. "Evening, detectives." He nodded at Ardash and Detective Barbour. His eyes widened when he spotted Scott, but he didn't comment. "From what we can determine so far, it looks like DeGrazzi and his guards were surprised by an unknown number of assailants." He nodded at two bloody bodies sprawled in the middle of the room. "The guards were taken out first…head shot for one. Death was instantaneous. The other guy's throat was slit. He bled out in minutes.

"Mr. DeGrazzi wasn't so fortunate." He pointed to the far side of the room. The couch had been shoved aside, revealing another blood-soaked body crumpled on the floor.

Scott sucked in a breath. In death, DeGrazzi seemed to have shrunk. His beaten and bloody corpse resembled a rag doll. Tearing his gaze from DeGrazzi's body, he focused as Dr. Stevenson continued his report.

"From the severe contusions, and the beginnings of bruising on his face, I'd say he was tortured before his killer finished him off with a single bullet to the heart."

Tortured? Scott's mind raced. What information did DeGrazzi possess that someone wanted bad enough he killed three people?

"How many shooters are we looking at?" Ardash asked.

Dr. Stevenson chewed on his bottom lip. "Not sure yet, but at least two. I'll know more after I run the autopsies and we study the forensics."

Ardash grabbed a pair of disposable booties from the cardboard box inside the door, tugged them on over his shoes, and stepped into the room. "Anything else stand out?"

The pathologist lifted a sealed evidence bag from a table and handed the bag to him. "One of my team found this clutched in DeGrazzi's hand."

Ardash held the clear plastic bag up to the light. "What is it? Some kind of necklace?"

Scott's heart stilled, and he snatched the evidence bag out of the detective's hand. A silver chain lay inside, a shiny, heart-shaped pendant visible. "Did"— he swallowed, though his mouth was desert dry—"did you say you found *this* in DeGrazzi's hand?"

"Yeah, why? Have you seen the necklace before?"

Had he seen the necklace before? Last time he'd set eyes on the silver chain, Marissa had been holding it. After she'd shown him the necklace, she'd stuffed it back in her pocket.

He stared at the necklace coiled like a silver snake in the plastic bag. Was this proof Marissa had been there? His heart jolted. Had she witnessed the murders? Was she hurt? Hiding somewhere? The room reeled, but he clung to his sanity and spun to Ardash. "I need to look at the closed-circuit surveillance feeds."

Ardash's dark eyebrows arched, but he turned to Detective Barbour. "See if you can round those up."

The young detective took off down the hall at a lope.

"What are you thinking, Scott? What are we going to find on those surveillance feeds?"

Scott spoke through numb lips. "There aren't any cameras in this room, but they're situated all over the apartment, in the hallways, the elevators, and the lobby. More are located on the exterior of the building." He held up the evidence bag. "The last time I saw this chain, Marissa Reynolds had it."

Ardash's eyes widened. "I'm not going to ask how you know so much about the video surveillance setup in DeGrazzi's building, but you'd better explain what you know about that necklace."

Scott filled his friend in on Steven Carmichael and his stalking of Marissa, and how Carmichael had given her the necklace as a sign of his love. He explained about the package delivered to her apartment with her cell phone and wallet inside with the chain zipped in her coin pouch.

By the time he finished, Ardash's eyes were wide, and furrows lined his usually smooth brow. "So that's why you suggested I check the secure evidence room reference log to see if anything was missing from the McGregor homicide investigation." He scratched the back of his neck. "You think whoever murdered McGregor removed the cell phone." He scratched again. "And the same person murdered this Carmichael character five years ago?" He huffed out a breath. "Come on, Scott. What are the odds of the two events being connected?"

"There had to be a reason why the chain was sent to Marissa. If this chain was found in DeGrazzi's hand, the only way it got there was if Marissa was here, and she gave it to him."

"If that's true, where is she? Do the killers have her? Did they take her?"

Hearing his fears spoken aloud shattered Scott, but he inhaled a deep breath and held on to his sanity. "I don't know, but this necklace is proof Marissa was here."

Detective Barbour hurried toward him. "I found the room with the surveillance camera feeds. Come with me, and I'll show you."

Scott bolted after him and into a small room at the end of the hall.

The room blazed under a row of incandescent ceiling lights situated above a single metal desk. Two padded, white leather desk chairs faced a wall of flat-screen computer monitors. The screens were gray, but Detective Barbour tapped a series of buttons, and the monitors flickered to life.

One monitor showed the building lobby with the police personnel blocking the door to the street. Another screen provided a view of the interior of the penthouse elevator. Several smaller images were inset along the sides of another screen, showing the deserted hallways of each floor in the building.

"How many cameras are there?" Ardash asked.

Detective Barbour shrugged. "A lot. So far, I've

located twelve different video feeds, and I'd bet my pension there are a dozen more. The images cycle through on a preset timer." He blew out a breath. "Do you have any idea how much a system like this costs? DeGrazzi must have been plenty worried about his security to fork out that much dough. And look where his fancy equipment got him"—he grimaced—"gunned down in his study. Just goes to show—"

The pounding in Scott's head mushroomed, and he broke into the detective's long-winded diatribe. "Do any of the video feeds show if Marissa Reynolds was here? Did the killers take her?"

The red-haired detective clicked keys, and a clear picture of the viewing room in DeGrazzi's apartment appeared on the center monitor. "The cameras in the lobby, penthouse elevator, halls, and most of DeGrazzi's apartment were disabled, but the two in the viewing room worked just fine. Looks like someone sent us a message. The perps wanted us to see these images." He shot a look over his shoulder. "Prepare yourself. It's not pretty."

The killers had left them a message.

The terrifying thought strobed through Scott's mind. He studied the unfolding scene on the monitor. A grim-faced man, built like a brick shithouse, stepped off the elevator. His dark-brown hair was razored close to his bony head, and he sported a thick, black beard. He clutched a large handgun in his meaty hand.

A second man followed. His white hair and bushy white beard indicated he was middle-aged. His movements were stiff and jerky as he limped across the room. A black, puffy coat strained over a sizeable paunch. If it weren't for the icy expression on his face and the deadly gun in his hand, he'd have resembled Santa Claus. But this was no jolly old elf.

The hairs on the back of Scott's neck prickled. He recognized the face beneath the white beard. He hadn't seen a photograph of the man for years, but there was no mistake.

Slavadad Marischenko.

Chapter 22

"Do you recognize those men?" Ardash eyed Scott.

Scott waved off his question as he focused on the disturbing screen images. Sweat beaded his brow and dampened his shirt. That was the third time he'd watched. With each viewing, his gut clenched tighter.

The two attackers, guns drawn, strode through the camera's range and disappeared from view. The video played on, but the scene remained unchanged.

Forty minutes after they entered the apartment, the men reappeared. The tall, dark-haired, bearded man had his arms wrapped around a struggling woman as he hauled her across the room to the elevator.

Scott's breath whooshed out like he'd been slammed in the gut. Under the high-definition digital feed, he could almost smell Marissa's fear. Her face was pale, her eyes wide. A strip of silver tape covered her mouth.

Aching to reach through the lens and punch the shit out of the man, his hands tightened, his fingernails digging into his palms. Breathing deep, he forced himself to calm down, to study the images and glean as much information as he could about the attackers.

The man holding Marissa dragged her into the elevator and vanished from view.

The white-haired man faced the camera, grinned, and wiggled his fingers in a cheeky wave. He stepped inside the waiting elevator. The doors slid closed, and once again the cameras recorded the unchanging, empty viewing room.

"Play it again." Even though watching Marissa being manhandled by the brute was agonizing, he wanted to study the video sequence again. He had to be sure. The gloating face of the smirking white-haired man filled the screen. "Pause it."

Detective Barbour did as requested.

Scott studied the face. His bowels turned to water. Take away the bushy white beard, the white hair, the extra forty pounds of weight, and three decades of living, and no question, he knew the guy. "That's him. That's Slavadad Marischenko."

Ardash jerked forward. "What? You're kidding, right?"

Scott turned to Detective Barbour. "Can you zero in on his hand that's holding the gun?"

"Sure"

The scene narrowed and zoomed in on Marischenko's hand and the small black pistol.

"He's packing a Russian-made knock-off. It seems every punk on the street's carrying one these days," said Ardash.

Scott peered at the screen. With this much zoom, the picture was grainy. "Can you make it any clearer?"

Detective Barbour frowned. "That's as good as you're gonna get. Even with this pricey equipment, the pixels are too big for a clear image at this zoom-in range."

"What's that on the back of his hand? Is it a tattoo?" Ardash asked.

A chilling cold flooded Scott's veins. "No question

it's Marischenko. He has a tattoo of a wolf's head on the back of his right hand. It's his signature mark."

Ardash blew out a noisy breath. "So you were right, Scott. The Russian is behind this hit. He must be planning to take over DeGrazzi's organization." He smoothed his fingers over his mustache. "But why now? Why didn't he try to take DeGrazzi down years ago?"

Exactly the question Scott had been asking himself. "He and DeGrazzi go back a long way. Sources tell me there were bad feelings between the two of them before they had that shoot-out in the movie theater parking lot." He scrubbed his hands over his face. "Maybe he's held a grudge all these years and finally got his revenge."

"But why take DeGrazzi's niece? How is she involved?" Ardash asked.

"He wanted to get back at DeGrazzi."

Ardash shook his head. "DeGrazzi's already dead. Abducting his niece is pointless."

Scott's mind whirled. Ardash was right. Abducting Marissa wasn't to get back at DeGrazzi. He rubbed his throbbing temples. Something else was at play. But what?

"Zoom out a bit," Ardash ordered, his gaze focused on the screen. "Move ahead, but stop just before Marischenko enters the elevator."

Detective Barbour zoomed out until Marischenko's husky body filled the screen.

The Russian grinned and waved, turned and limped into the elevator.

The image froze.

"There." Ardash leaned closer to the screen and

pointed. "Behind his back. What's he holding?"

"It looks like a large envelope." Scott rubbed his jaw. "He didn't have the envelope when he entered the penthouse. We would have seen it. He must have found it here. Maybe he tortured DeGrazzi for whatever's in that envelope."

A light flickered on in his brain, and with sinking clarity, he understood why Marissa had been kidnapped. She hadn't been taken to get back at DeGrazzi. Her abduction was all for him. The devious Russian knew Scott would be at the murder scene, knew he'd watch the tapes, and had counted on Scott recognizing him. The bastard had staged everything as a warning to Scott to back off.

He checked the time stamp on the monitor. His gut twisted. Two hours had passed since she was taken.

Two hours!

He bolted to his feet, slammed the chair out of the way, and lunged toward the door.

"Where do you think you're going?" Ardash asked.

"To find Marissa."

"I can't let you do that. I have an arrest warrant in your name sitting on my desk."

Scott shot him a look over his shoulder. "Well, then, you'll have to shoot me, because nothing but a bullet will stop me."

Ardash scowled, but didn't move.

Detective Barbour drew his weapon, but Ardash shook his head and pushed the detective's arm down. "I know I'm going to regret this." He threaded his fingers through his dark hair and looked at Scott with an anguished gaze. "Find her," he said. "Find her and then we'll deal with this."

Scott nodded and raced down the hallway and across the viewing room. The light above the elevator indicated the car was in use. He bolted to the emergency exit, shoved open the door, and raced down the stairs, taking them two at a time.

Find her!

The urgent demand repeated in time to his pounding footsteps.

Find her.

****

She awoke with a start and sat up, blinking in the blinding light.

"Wakey, wakey! Time to talk."

Reality snapped back with a sickening lurch.

The white-haired man who'd shot Julio sat on the metal folding chair watching her.

She rubbed the red welts on her wrist where his partner had grabbed her and checked the room. The big hulk was nowhere in sight. Her relief vanished at the icy menace in the old man's blue eyes. "Who…who are you?"

"You don't know? Your uncle didn't tell you?" He puffed out a breath. "I'm disappointed." Comb streaks showed in his wispy, white hair. His bushy white beard covered the lower half of his chubby, florid face. He grinned, exposing a row of tobacco-stained teeth. "My name is Slavadad Marischenko. People call me the Russian."

The Russian!

Her heart raced. Julio had warned her about the Russian with his dying words. She'd never seen the man before that night, but his heavily accented voice was familiar. He'd called her on her cell phone and taunted her after she received the package. He was the one who'd sent her wallet and cell phone. He'd also sent her the necklace. "What…what do you want with me?"

He unbuttoned his sleeves and rolled his cotton shirt over his hairy forearms. "Your uncle and I have"—he smirked—"or rather, *had* a long and complicated relationship." He smoothed his age-spotted hand over his wiry beard. The bright overhead light shone on a tattoo of a snarling wolf's head on the back of his hand. "We were adversaries, combatants, if you will."

His face flushed, and his eyes flashed. "Did you know he tried to kill me? Years ago. The coward ambushed me outside a movie theater. One of his bullets struck me." He patted his left hip and winced. "Took me months to recover, and I have limped ever since." His bushy, white eyebrows furrowed in a vee over his snub nose. "I have been trying to repay him the favor for years, but the bastard had the luck of the Devil." His lips curled in a cold smile. "Until tonight."

She tugged the blanket to her chest as if the thin wool would protect her from his venom. "That's why you killed him? Because of something that happened years ago?"

"I might have forgiven him if that was all there was." He shrugged. "We are in a harsh business. Alliances come and go like the wind." His mouth tightened. "DeGrazzi's sin was far worse."

"Worse than attempted murder?" *Keep him talking. Distract him until you come up with a plan.* The high-rise lobby had been deserted, and the street outside empty of passing cars or pedestrians. No one had witnessed her abduction. No one knew where she was. No knight in shining armor was riding to her rescue. If she hoped to get out of there alive, she was on her own.

Like she had always been.

An image of Scott's wide smile, dimples dancing in his lean cheeks, and his sparkling navy eyes, flashed before her, but she squashed the fantasy. He was no knight. He may have saved her life, but he'd deceived her. She couldn't count on him. He'd proven that.

A fresh spate of tears thickened her throat, but she swallowed them down. This wasn't the time to wallow in her broken heart. If she hoped to get out of there alive, she had to focus.

She glared at Marischenko, instilling as much bravado as she could. "What do you want with me? My uncle's dead, so if this"—she pointed to him and then to herself—"is about revenge, you've wasted your time."

He lifted a large brown envelope from the table. "Do you know what's in here?"

She shook her head.

"I took this from DeGrazzi's apartment. The file was in a safe in his bedroom closet." He smirked. "Good thing Ivan knows how to open safes."

She stared at the envelope and shivered. He'd killed three people to get that envelope. What was in it that was so important?

"DeGrazzi was blackmailing me, had been for years." He slapped the envelope on his thigh. "This is the evidence he held over my head." He smirked, his thick red lips pursing. "Now he is dead, and I have the papers." His feral grin widened. "I am free of that murderous tyrant." The smile dropped from his fleshy face, and he pinned her with a chilling gaze. "That bastard is the reason my beloved Stepan is dead."

"Stepan?" The blanket dropped to her lap. "Do you mean Steven? Steven Carmichael?"

He nodded. "My nephew."

"Steven Carmichael was your nephew?" She swore the room spun with his stunning revelation.

"I loved that boy. The hardest thing I have ever done was issue the order to execute him." His eyes watered. "I did not have a choice. He had a simple job. He was supposed to follow you, get in your face, frighten you, kill you if necessary. I hoped your fear would draw DeGrazzi out into the open where my men could kill him."

He heaved a sigh. "Stepan fell in love with you, and he refused to do as I ordered. He threatened to tell you the truth." His eyes hardened. "I could not allow that disrespect. Not from anyone, not even family."

"You killed him? Your own nephew?" A strained silence sucked the air out of the room. "It was you, wasn't it? You murdered Flinty McGregor, and you, or Ivan, drove that SUV. You tried to run me down. You sent me Steven's chain, and you took my cell phone from the police evidence locker." The accusations fired fast and furious. "You're a monster!"

He beamed and puffed out his chest as if she'd paid him a compliment.

"How did you steal the cell phone? That wasn't you in the surveillance videos. Was it Ivan?"

"Ivan is most useful, but he is not smart enough to pull off something so challenging." He smirked and shrugged. "I called a friend who owed me a favor."

"You took my phone so you could install a tracking

app. You wanted to find me. Why? What were you planning to do? Kidnap me? Hold me ransom until Julio gave you that envelope?"

"A good plan until your boyfriend disabled the tracking app. Ivan was most upset."

"Why did you send me Steven's chain?"

"I wanted to frighten you and let DeGrazzi know I was coming for him." He fingered his beard, smoothing the unruly mass. "He called me, you know, right after your little visit. He demanded I back down." He snorted. "As if I would listen. I was thrilled he was worried about your safety. I wanted him on the defensive. I wanted him dead." His eyes narrowed, all trace of humor vanished. "And now I have you."

A dozen scenarios raced through her brain, each more terrifying than the one before. She clutched her stomach. He blamed her for his nephew's death. And now he was going to kill her. Just like he'd killed Julio. Resignation settled over her like a heavy weight, but before he murdered her, she had to find out the truth. She had to know. "Is…is Scott Bannister working with you?" She held her breath. "Is he in on this too?"

"Bannister?" He snorted. "Not likely."

The breath she'd been holding whooshed out, and something resembling joy filled her. Julio was wrong. Scott wasn't behind the setup.

"You do not know, do you? He has not told you."

Trepidation fluttered in her belly. "Know what?"

"Your boyfriend's parents were killed the night of the shoot-out."

"Scott's parents?" She rubbed her temples, struggling to assimilate what he was saying. "You killed Scott's parents?"

"Who knows?" He shrugged. "Could have been my bullets, or DeGrazzi's."

The pounding in her head made thinking almost impossible. How had she not known? Scott said his parents had died, but he shut down whenever she'd tried to probe further. Who could blame him? Losing two parents in one night would devastate anyone, let alone a young child.

Marischenko's revelation explained so much. No wonder Scott was so determined to destroy Julio. He wanted her uncle to pay for killing his parents, and he was willing to do anything to make that happen. For the first time since Scott had confessed to using her, a glimmer of forgiveness warmed the layer of ice coating her heart.

"Enough chitchat." Marischenko rose to his feet, his knees cracking. "For now, you will be my guest, at least until I figure out what to do with you." His gaze roamed over her, and his upper lip curled. "I had thought to sell you to one of my pimps, but you are over the age of thirteen. Mind you, some men favor a bit of maturity in a woman."

She couldn't hold back a gasp.

He chuckled and limped toward the door. "Until later, my dear." He rapped on the dented metal. "Ivan will be right outside, so do not get any foolish ideas of trying to escape." He hobbled through the doorway, past the grim-faced Ivan.

Ivan glared at her and closed the door with a heavy thunk. The lock slid into place.

She stared at the closed door, her mind whirling. Marischenko had revealed so many shocking truths, she could barely take them all in. He was Steven

Carmichael's uncle, and he'd set Steven up to stalk her. What sort of man murdered his own nephew?

An insane one.

The certainty she was right chilled her, and she shuddered. Marischenko had been planning his revenge against Julio for years. Everything that had happened the past days circled back to that night years ago when Julio plotted to kill the Russian gangster outside the movie theater.

Who had retrieved her cell phone from the evidence locker? Who was Marischenko's friend in the DA's office? Scott? She shook her head. He may have betrayed her, but she refused to believe he was involved with a cold-blooded killer like Marischenko. Besides, the Russian had denied Scott's involvement.

Scrubbing the tears from her eyes, she shot to her feet. She had to escape and get away from Marischenko before he tired of toying with her.

But how?

The room wasn't much larger than a walk-in closet. No window. One solid-looking metal door, bolted, and guarded by Ivan. The floor was smooth concrete, and the walls brick. She looked up. No vents, no handy, removable ceiling tiles, nothing but solid wood.

She sank back on the cot as fresh tears blurred her vision. The room was escape proof. She was stuck there until Marischenko sold her as a sex slave or killed her. She thumped her fists on the mattress in frustration, raising a fetid cloud.

A metal clang resounded.

She froze. And pounded again.

Another clang.

Chapter 23

Scott raced through the lobby and skidded to a halt.

Two uniformed police officers guarded the door, blocking the entrance.

"Move," he ordered. "Get out of my way." Time was passing, critical minutes while Marissa was in Marischenko's clutches.

The taller cop frowned and shook his head. "No way, Bannister. There's an arrest warrant out for you. You're not going anywhere."

Scott moved toward them, his muscles tense, ready to fight his way through if that's what it took.

The bigger cop drew out his gun. "I wouldn't do that if I were you."

The elevator pinged, and the doors swooshed open. Ardash stepped into the lobby. "Let him go."

The policemen didn't back down, but the one holding the gun lowered it to his side.

"Are you sure, Detective Sandhu? You know who he is, right?"

"I said, let him go."

They shrugged and moved aside.

Scott shot Ardash a thankful look and shoved open the door to the street.

The scene outside was chaos. Three ambulances, lights flashing, were parked in front of the luxury high-rise. A half-dozen police cruisers lined the street. The crowd of curious onlookers had swelled, and they jostled against the yellow police tape roping off the entrance to the building.

Miracles of miracles, the milling throng of reporters didn't spot him. He slipped into the crowd and shouldered through the mass of people, dodging emergency vehicles and media vans, and hurried down the street, searching for a passing taxi. One thought drove him—find Marissa before Marischenko harmed her.

Under the bright glow of a streetlight, he spotted the little orange car wedged between a glossy, foreign sports car and a four-by-four pickup truck. His heart lurched, and he stumbled to a stop. The car's presence provided further proof she'd been there.

Fishing in his pocket for the spare key, he sprinted toward the car, unlocked the door, and flung it open. Sliding inside, he settled behind the steering wheel and started the motor. The engine revved to life, and he inched out of the tight parking space and joined the line of traffic.

Once he hit the outskirts of town, he floored the gas, relieved the engine warning light didn't come on. The oil he'd added the night before must have done the trick.

Traffic was light on the highway, and he made good time. An hour later, he crossed the narrow, one-lane bridge. The *Welcome to Ashbury* sign was lit by a single spotlight. He drove through town and parked on the street in front of Loretta Carmichael's house.

The porch light wasn't on, but a battered, late-model car was parked in the driveway, and a sliver of light leaked through a gap in the curtains covering the living room window. He stared at the house, planning how best to approach Loretta. She wouldn't like him showing up at her door, especially not after he told her the reason he'd come.

He was acting on gut instinct. When he'd seen the tattoo of a wolf's head on the back of Marischenko's hand, not only had the tattoo confirmed the identity of the Russian kidnapper, but it triggered a buzzing in Scott's gut. He'd seen the same image of a wolf, not on the back of a hand, but on Loretta Carmichael's right ankle.

The identical tattoo on two different people could be a coincidence. Hell, maybe they'd gone to the same tattoo artist, or just liked wolves. But he didn't think so. His gut told him the tattoos were important.

He opened the car door, pocketed his keys, inhaled a steadying breath, and loped up the sidewalk to the front door. The distant roar of machinery, and the faint tang of sour cabbage filled the cool night air. The lumberyard was a twenty-four/seven operation. *Nice.* He pounded on the front door. Flakes of paint floated to the warped wooden porch.

Loud barking echoed from within the tiny house.

He thumped again with more force. If she didn't open the door in the next minute, he'd kick the damn thing down.

The furious barking intensified mixed with the scratching of nails skidding on the laminate floor of the small foyer.

The door opened a crack, and a single, red-streaked blue eye peeked out. "What the hell do you want?" Loretta's displeasure with her late-night visitor was plain. "I told you not to come back."

"Too bad. I'm here." He placed both hands on the door and shoved.

She screeched as the door flew back, and she stumbled against the wall.

Brutus's barking blasted into the night. The big black and tan dog lunged at Scott, fangs bared.

"Stop!" Scott ordered.

The dog screeched to a halt in mid leap, nails skidding on the floor.

Scott's breath whooshed out. "Sit."

Brutus sank on his back haunches and stared up at him with adoring eyes. His tail thumped, and his tongue lolled out of his gaping mouth. A long string of saliva dripped on the floor.

Scott barged into the house and petted the dog's head. "Good boy."

"Damn dog." Loretta scowled. "What the hell do you want now?"

"Answers." He didn't have time to make nice. He had to persuade her to tell him what, if anything, she knew.

"I don't have any answers, not to anything you're asking." The dilation of her pupils proved her bravado was false. She was frightened.

Good. Fear would make her talk. "Let's go in the other room. I'm sure you don't want your neighbors knowing your business." He nodded at the open door.

She heaved a loud sigh and pushed past him to the living room.

By the time he'd closed the door and followed, she was seated in the same rocking chair she'd sat in the day before. A cigarette smoldered between her lips. Her tight, multi-colored yoga pants molded to her thin legs and revealed the edge of a tattoo on her right ankle.

His heart rate bumped up a notch, and he pointed at her ankle. "Interesting tattoo."

Her face paled, and she choked on a lungful of smoke. "My…my tattoo?"

"I noticed it the last time I was here. What's that about?"

She tugged the cuff of her pants lower. "None of your damn business."

"Let's say it is my business. A Russian gangster by the name of Slavadad Marischenko has the same tattoo."

She inhaled a sharp breath.

"What's your connection to Marischenko?"

"I…I don't know what you're talking about."

Brutus padded into the room and plopped with a grunt on the floor at Scott's feet.

His years of working in the courtroom confronting defendants had taught him the signs of deceit.

She wouldn't meet his gaze, and a tiny muscle below her right eye twitched. Classic.

"Don't bullshit me! I know you're lying." He glared at her. "I want"—he paused and moistened his lips—"no, I *need* to know about your connection to Marischenko, and I need to know now."

She puffed on her cigarette. Smoke swirled around her in a noxious cloud. "I told you, I don't know any Marischenko."

"You're lying! Where is he?"

Her hand shook as she stubbed out her cigarette and immediately lit another. "Why…why do you want to know?"

He shot to his feet and paced across the room,

stepping over Brutus's sleeping form. "He kidnapped the woman I love. I want her back."

The woman he loved.

Damn straight. He loved Marissa.

"The woman you were with yesterday? You're in love with her?" She laughed, a throaty cackle that turned into a phlegmy smoker's cough.

"What's so damn funny?" He strained the words through his clenched teeth. He didn't have time for a verbal jousting match. Every second Marissa remained with Marischenko, the greater her risk.

"You wanna know what's funny? She's Julio DeGrazzi's niece, that's what's funny." She peered at him through the haze of smoke. "You don't know, do you? You really don't know."

"I know Marischenko murdered DeGrazzi and two of his bodyguards tonight. I know he took Marissa Reynolds from DeGrazzi's apartment, and he's holding her against her will. And I know you know where I can find him."

Silence hung heavy in the smoke-filled room. A sly smile flickered at the corners of her thin lips. "You'll never find him." She crowed. "This woman you love is as lost to you as my brother is to me."

The cruel sound sent chills rippling down the back of his neck. Was he too late? Was Marissa already dead? No, he refused to think that. He fixed Loretta with a steely-eyed glare. "Where. Is. Marischenko?" He imbued each word with deadly menace.

"I told you, I don't know. I don't know anything." Her gaze slid to a pine cabinet against the far wall. "I want you to leave." Her nervousness had amped up to a new level, and she kept shooting glances at the cabinet.

He charged across the room and threw open the cabinet door. Stacks of papers jammed the small space. A small black book lay on top. He snatched the book and studied it. The letters S and M were inscribed on the cover in gold lettering. He thumbed through the pages. Each page was filled with neatly printed letters and symbols in what looked like Russian. The Cyrillic script was impossible to decipher.

"What are you doing? Get out of there. That's my stuff." She lurched to her feet and grabbed his arm.

Her fingernails dug into his skin, but he shook her off. Had Marischenko written down his crimes? Was he that foolish? Or was his ego just that big? He stumbled over to the couch and sank onto its cracked vinyl surface. "This is Marischenko's journal, isn't it?"

She jammed her fist over her mouth, her eyes wide and frightened. "Please don't tell him. Don't tell anyone."

His breath caught in his throat. He'd hit the jackpot. He'd spent most of his life searching for proof that Marischenko and DeGrazzi were the men with the guns that night of the shooting outside the movie theater. He tightened his grip on the book. The answers might be in here. This was why he'd risked everything…his job, his happiness, his life. He looked at her. "Why do you have Marischenko's journal?"

She collapsed back on the chair. All her earlier fight had fled. "Slavadad Marischenko is my uncle, but he's not like your normal American uncle. He…he has a short fuse if you cross him. He demands obedience." She wiped the back of her hand across her mouth. "I…I took the journal from the den in his house after your last visit. I thought I might need it for protection." She blew out a puff of smoke. "Looks like I was right."

Her revelation exploded like a bomb. "Your *uncle*?"

"My real name is Ludmilla Katarina Marischenko. My family immigrated to this country when I was a child. My parents changed our name to Carmichael." She shrugged. "Marischenko was too difficult for American tongues to pronounce. I switched to Loretta when I was a teenager. My uncle chose to keep his name."

Scott set the book on the cushion and stuffed his hands in the front pockets of his jeans to hide their shaking. "Let me get this straight. Steven Carmichael was Marischenko's nephew?"

She nodded.

Wheels turned at her shocking revelations, but he couldn't put all the pieces together. Not yet. "Why did he abduct Marissa Reynolds?"

"You really don't know anything, do you?" Lighting another cigarette, she stuffed it in the corner of her mouth. Speaking around the cigarette, she said, "Marischenko and DeGrazzi hate each other. They have for years. Something about a shooting that happened a long time ago."

She blew a perfect smoke ring. "DeGrazzi destroyed my uncle's organization." Ash fell from her cigarette onto the scuffed floor, joining a scattering of old ashes. "DeGrazzi had some damning information on my uncle that he used to blackmail him. Marischenko wanted it back."

He heard only her first words. Whatever else she said was lost in a roar of tumultuous sound. She'd as good as admitted DeGrazzi and Marischenko were responsible for killing his parents. He grabbed the journal, shot to his feet, and swung toward the door.

"Where are you going? You can't take that book. I have to return it before my uncle notices it's missing." She jumped to her feet and ran after him.

Brutus followed, barking and skidding on the slippery floor.

Scott held Marischenko's journal out of her reach. "What's written in this book could confirm that Marischenko and DeGrazzi killed my parents. Once the DA sees this, he'll—" The sour taste of disgust coated his tongue. What sort of man was he? Marissa was in danger, and all he thought of was his single-minded quest to find his parents' murderers.

Brutus's barking reached a crescendo, adding to the tumult roaring through Scott's head. All the years of loss burst free, and he grasped her arm and shouted over the dog's furious barking. "Marischenko murdered my parents. He killed two innocent people and left a five-year-old child an orphan." He sneered. "Nice uncle, isn't he? Now he's planning on killing another innocent victim, and you won't help me."

"Please, don't take the book." Tears flooded her eyes. "You don't know what he's like. If my uncle finds out I took his journal, he'll—" Her voice broke as sobs shook her thin body.

"You're afraid of him, aren't you? You're afraid he'll hurt you." He swore he heard the click of a light bulb as the shocking truth hit him. "That's it, isn't it? The uncle you're so devoted to murdered your brother." If he was right, and Marischenko killed his own nephew and blamed the murder on DeGrazzi, it explained so much.

Her eyes widened, and she cowered against the wall. The cigarette slipped from her slack mouth and fell to the floor. "No, that's not true. DeGrazzi killed Steven. Uncle Slavadad told me."

"Come on, Loretta. You don't believe that. You know what really happened." He spat the words in her face. "That bastard murdered your brother"—he held up the journal—"and I'll bet he wrote about it in this book." He sneered at the sniveling woman. "How can you defend him? He's a monster."

Her face paled, and she deflated like a balloon, all her earlier bravado vanishing in the face of her fear.

He cursed and released her and stepped back. What the hell was he doing? He wasn't any better than her uncle. Wheeling around, he tossed the journal on the floor and flung open the door. "Keep your damn secrets, lady. I'll find some other way to destroy Marischenko, but you should watch your back. Good old Uncle Slavadad will be gunning for you next."

His tread was heavy as he plodded across the porch and down the steps. Now what? How would he find Marissa? Loretta was his only hope.

"Wait."

He shot a glance over his shoulder.

She stood in the doorway, one thin arm crossed over her sagging breasts, the other clutching Brutus's spiked collar. "Are you telling me the truth? Did my uncle kill Steven?"

"Think about it. If DeGrazzi didn't kill him, and I'm sure he didn't, the killer has to be Marischenko. It's the only thing that makes sense. You know what he's capable of."

Tears glinted in her reddened eyes. "He owns a

garage on Wilson Street. Johnson's Garage." Her hand shook as she smoothed a loose strand of hair back from her stricken face. "If he took her, that's where she'll be."

Adrenaline surged, powering his muscles, sharpening his brain, focusing his thoughts. He had a location, but he had to be sure she was telling the truth. He pinned her with a sharp look. "Why are you telling me this? Why now?"

She wiped her wet face with the back of her arm. "Stevie was my brother. He was a loser, but I loved him. He didn't deserve to die like that."

He nodded. "Thank you." He sprinted to the car, leaped behind the wheel, jammed the keys in the ignition, and floored the gas pedal. The little car squealed away from the curb and sped down the street.

The motor screamed as he pushed the car to its limits as they sped along the highway leading back to Brunswick. The low-oil warning light flashed red, but he didn't slow. He had to save Marissa even if he burned the motor out of the old car. He tightened his grip on the steering wheel and swung the car onto the off-ramp and onto a secondary road.

A voice of reason rose above the cacophony roaring through his head.

Call the cops.

If Loretta had told the truth and Marischenko was hiding out in his garage, he'd have at least one muscle-bound goon with him, probably more. What hope did he—unathletic, geeky Scott Bannister—have to take on a group of hardened killers and free Marissa? As much as he'd always dreamed of being one, he wasn't an action hero, and he didn't possess superhero powers.

Not even close.

What if Loretta had lied? If he called the police, they'd race to the garage. If Marissa wasn't there, he'd have wasted their time. Time where they could be searching for her, saving her. This was a wild goose chase, a one-in-a-thousand chance she'd be at the garage. He'd suss out the situation first and then see about calling for help.

His cell phone rang, but he ignored the persistent ringing. The pealing stopped, but started again, each piercing ring sounding more insistent.

What if the call was about Marissa? What if the police had found her? He fished in his coat pocket for his phone. Keeping one hand on the wheel and his gaze fixed on the road, he jammed the phone against his ear. "What?"

"Scott, it's Jonas."

"Jonas? What's this about? I—"

"Where are you? I heard Julio DeGrazzi was murdered tonight, and Slavadad Marischenko has Marissa Reynolds."

The tires squealed as Scott swerved around a corner, cutting off a motorcycle.

The leather-clad rider scowled and shot him the finger.

Another red warning light flashed on the dashboard panel. Steam billowed from under the hood and streamed in a ghost-like cloud across the cracked windshield. A wisp of acrid smoke stung his nostrils.

"Scott, are you listening? Where are you? Come on. I'm trying to help."

He refocused on Jonas's tinny voice. "Why do you want to help me after what I did?"

A few beats of static-filled silence. "Detective Sandhu told me everything. I understand why you're so determined to take DeGrazzi down. I should never have doubted you."

Scott raced through a red traffic light, narrowly avoiding striking a delivery van. An angry blast of horn followed him down the street.

"Scott, there's something you should know, something I suspect. I—"

The phone slipped from his damp fingers and fell, landing with a thud on the floor by his feet. *Damn.* He fumbled for the phone, fighting to keep the car on the road while his fingers clasped the slippery plastic case. He raised the phone to his ear. Wilson Street was just ahead. If the GPS on his phone was right, Marischenko's garage should be on the next block. "Look, Jonas, I gotta go."

"Wait." Jonas's frantic cry echoed down the line. "Don't hang up. You know where she is, don't you? You know where Marischenko's holding her."

"Maybe."

"You can't take on the Russian on your own. He'll kill you. Tell me where you are, and I'll call the cops." A pause while the line crackled. "Come on, Scott, let the police do their job."

Jonas was right. He should call 911. In minutes, squad cars filled with armed police personnel would be en route to Marischenko's garage. The cops had the manpower and firepower to storm the building.

How could he stand up to armed killers? Was he willing to risk Marissa's life for the sake of his ego? Was he that selfish? "Okay. Make the call." He blew out a ragged breath. "Marischenko has a garage on

Wilson Street. I'm hoping that's where he's holding Marissa." He read out the address.

"Don't do anything foolish, Scott. Wait for the cops."

"Goodbye, Jonas." He severed the call and tossed the phone on the passenger seat. Peering through the dusty, cracked windshield, he eased his foot off the gas and steered the car down the deserted, dark street.

At that time of night, the buildings looked unoccupied. A few had security lights shining inside, but the street was empty of vehicles, and the businesses were closed. Old, yellowed newspapers, plastic bags, and broken shards of glass littered the gutters.

He cruised by a pawnshop, a plumbing outfit, a secondhand clothing store, and then he saw it— Johnson's Garage—down the street on the left. He slowed as he drove past the garage. The big bay door was shut tight, the front door blocked with a heavy steel gate. A faint light shone through the grimy, barred window of the attached office, but there weren't any vehicles parked in the two parking spots lining the front of the building.

Doubt's icy fingers trailed along his spine. Had Loretta told the truth? Was Marissa inside the garage? Every cell in his body thrummed. She was there. He knew it.

Continuing down the block, he turned the corner and headed up the back alley. He switched off his headlights and slowed to a crawl. Steam billowed from under the hood. An ominous clanking resonated from somewhere beneath his feet. The car stuttered to a halt, coughed, and died.

Damn.

The rear of the garage was unlit. A battered, overflowing, green dumpster was jammed against the wall. A haphazard stack of old tires teetered. Rusted mufflers formed another pile.

A dark shape separated from the darker shadows behind the dumpster, and a scrawny black cat darted out and raced across the alley, disappearing into a patch of overgrown, scraggly weeds.

The dented metal door looked solid, but unlike the front door, it wasn't barred or covered by a security gate. Could he jimmy the lock and open the door? He frowned. *Jimmy the lock*? Was he high on something? The only thing he knew about picking a lock was what he'd watched in movies.

Wait for the cops.

The cautionary words ran through him in an unceasing refrain.

Wait for the cops.

Rubbing the knot in the back of his neck, he squeezed his eyes shut. When he opened them a heartbeat later, he'd made a decision. Rummaging in the glove compartment, he found what he wanted. He unscrewed the dome light bulb, opened the door, slipped out of the car, and jogged toward the garage.

Chapter 24

Sitting back on her heels, Marissa stretched the throbbing muscles in her lower back. Blood leaked from where she'd sliced her palm on the sharp metal spring. She inhaled a deep breath and lay back down on the cold cement floor and slithered under the cot. Grasping the coiled metal spring, she tugged.

"Ouch!" She jerked her hand back and sucked at the fresh cut on her thumb. Blinking back sweat, refusing to quit, she gripped the spring, and yanked and twisted with all her strength.

A wrenching squeal resounded.

She froze, holding her breath, staring at the door.

When the door remained closed, she released her breath and grabbed the spring again and tugged. There was another screeching clank as the welding weakened, and the spring sheared off. She fell back on the floor, the spring clutched in her hand. Elation eased the throbbing pain in her hand.

She shimmied out from under the cot and sat on her bottom, her back against the cot, and studied the metal coil. It wasn't much bigger than a large corkscrew, but the end narrowed to a sharp point. If she could get close enough to Marischenko or Ivan, she could use the spring as a weapon.

If.

The single word brought a splash of icy reality. A

dozen ifs had to happen before she'd be free of this prison, but she refused to give up. She wouldn't make this easy for Marischenko. No. Damn. Way.

Pushing to her feet, she slipped the spring under the lumpy mattress and lay on the cot. Now came the hard part—waiting for one of her captors to make an appearance. Earlier, she'd pounded on the door and yelled and screamed until her hands throbbed and her throat was raw. She'd even smashed the metal folding chair against the door.

No response.

Either Marischenko had lied and Ivan wasn't standing guard outside the door, or the big brute didn't care what she did in here. She shivered and dragged the blanket up to her chin. A sob hitched in her throat. They weren't going to let her go. How could they? She'd seen both of her captors' faces. She knew their names. They'd kill her or sell her to a sex slave trader who'd keep her under lock and key until she died. Either way she was doomed. She wiped the back of her blood-and-grease-stained hand over her eyes, smearing tears and grime.

As always, her thoughts turned to Scott. He'd spent his life seeking vengeance on the people behind his parents' senseless deaths. Now, one of the murderers was dead, and the other held her captive and was determined to kill her. She dug her knuckle into her left temple, hoping to ease the stabbing pain. Everything that had happened the past few days was tangled together like a nest of serpents in a Medusa knot.

All those years, she'd blamed Julio for killing Steven Carmichael. Now she knew the truth. He hadn't murdered Steven, but he had gunned down two innocent people.

This whole nightmare circled back to the Russian. Marischenko had planned everything in his relentless quest for revenge. He'd murdered Flinty McGregor and framed her and Scott for the murder. He'd tried to kill her by running her down on the street. All in a ploy to weaken her uncle's defenses and draw him out into the open so he could destroy him.

The metallic clunk of the bolt sliding back in the lock on the door broke into her dark thoughts and jolted her back to the present. A rush of adrenaline fired through her muscles.

Showtime.

She slipped her hand under the edge of the mattress and grasped the spring.

The door opened and Marischenko stood framed in the opening, holding a gun. His pale blue eyes studied her as he limped into the room. "Get up." The gun barrel pointed at her chest.

She tore her gaze from the menacing gun and stared past him at the open door. No Ivan. Marischenko was alone. A seed of hope unfurled deep in her belly. Tightening her fingers around the coiled metal spring, she inched her hand from under the mattress. Her heart pounded so loud she was certain he heard. Sweat popped out on her brow.

His pudgy lips tightened, and he gestured with the gun. "I said, get up." His hand was steady as he gripped the deadly weapon.

The blue-black barrel gleamed under the bright light. A wisp of cordite stung her nostrils. She froze, her muscles paralyzed. All too clearly, she recalled the deafening blast of the bullet exploding out of the gun when he'd shot Julio. "Wha...what are you going to do?" Fighting through her paralysis, she slid the spring another inch closer.

"We are leaving. Now."

"You're letting me go?" Hope fired in her heart, only to be dashed a heartbeat later when he shook his head.

"Not a chance. You are going on a trip." His lips curled in a cruel smile. "A *long* trip."

Chills rippled along her spine. He was going to kill her. The terrifying truth was in his glacial eyes. "I'm...I'm not going anywhere with you."

"You do not have a choice." He grasped her arm and yanked her off the cot.

Ivan lumbered into the room, a scowl on his brutish face. "You need some help, Mr. Marischenko?"

"I am good." Marischenko's pudgy fingers dug into her arm like talons. "Open the garage bay door and get the car ready. I got the word. Trouble is on the way. We must go."

Ivan nodded, wheeled around, and strode out of the room.

"Where are you taking me?" Her throat was tight, impossible to keep the squeak of terror out of her voice. Clutching the spring, she angled the razor-sharp tip so the point jutted between her fingers. Hand behind her back, she waited for the right moment to strike.

"My inside source has warned me the cops are on their way." He jerked her arm and dragged her behind him. His chest heaved with the effort, and his stale breath gagged her as he huffed and puffed.

The police were coming!

Relief spilled through her, instantly tempered by

doubt. What if they arrived too late? What if Marischenko and Ivan escaped with her in tow before the cops came? What if the Russian killed her first?

She had to follow through with her plan. She had to stop him or slow him down until the police arrived. Inhaling a deep breath, she tightened her grip on the spring, and with an animal-like yell, thrust her arm in an upward arc, driving the tip of the spring deep into his chest.

He grunted, stumbled, and the gun clattered to the floor. A bloom of red appeared on his shirt around the quivering spring. "You bitch! What the hell did you do?" He jerked the spring free. His face paled, and he staggered into the table, pressing his hand over the oozing wound.

Run!

The command roared through her, but her legs didn't obey, and she stared frozen at the blood staining his shirt.

He cursed and lunged.

Her paralysis vanished, and she dodged, avoiding his grasp. She raced toward the open door.

His heavy, staggering footsteps pounded after her.

****

Keeping to the shadows in the alley, Scott slunk to the dented metal door and tried the handle. Locked. Of course it was locked. Had he expected to just open the door and waltz right in? He wanted to kick the door down, but that would alert Marischenko. He had to find another way to get inside.

A heavy, metallic grating sound broke the stillness of the night.

He ducked behind the dumpster, kneeling in a

puddle of oily water. The stench of rotting food was overpowering, but he forced down bile and fixed his gaze on the garage.

The garage bay door slowly slid up....six inches...a foot...two feet...all the way. The grinding screech halted. A yawning darkness loomed into the interior of the garage.

Nothing happened for a minute, but then he heard the slap of boots on cement.

The goon from the penthouse security tapes stepped through the opening and peered up and down the alley.

Fire raged in Scott's belly, and his hands clenched into fists. This was the monster who'd manhandled Marissa. He shot to his feet, prepared to charge into the garage and attack the bastard, but a grain of common sense prevailed, and he ducked back down.

The man was a cold-blooded killer. He outweighed Scott by a good fifty pounds. And he was armed. Scott wasn't. Fists against firepower? Not a chance in Hell. He wouldn't do Marissa a lick of good if he got killed before he rescued her.

The light of the rising moon reflected off the gun in the big lug's hand. He nodded, as if satisfied, and disappeared back inside the garage.

Scott breathed a sigh of relief that Gramm's tiny car was hidden by the dark shadows cast by the dumpster. What should he do? He had to do something. He couldn't stand there cowering behind the dumpster while the murderers escaped.

He hadn't been there to save his parents, but he was here now. He didn't have a weapon, but he had fierce determination, and he was on the side of the righteous. If this were the movies, he'd win the coming battle and free his love. He and Marissa would ride off into the sunset and live happily ever after. But this wasn't a movie, and he sure as hell wasn't a hero.

He stared at the dark opening.

Time for action.

Heart thudding, he crept toward the open door. The darkness within loomed like a cavern to Hell, but he didn't hesitate as he placed one foot in front of the other. His muscles tensed, ready for the big, bearded dude to appear and the battle to begin.

A hand grabbed his biceps and hauled him back behind the dumpster.

He spun around, a shout of protest on the tip of his tongue. The words died in an explosion of air. "What the hell are you doing?"

Detective Ardash Sandhu glared. "Stopping you from doing something stupid. Were you planning to take on Marischenko and his goon on your own?" He studied the flashlight in Scott's hand and sneered. "With a flashlight? What were you going to do—beat them over their heads until they begged for mercy?"

Scott's cheeks burned. That was exactly what he'd planned.

"Looks like we got here just in time." Ardash tightened the strap on his bulletproof vest and drew a gun from a holster at his waist. "Now step aside and let the professionals finish this."

For the first time, Scott noticed the small army of armed cops standing in the shadows behind Ardash. Dressed in bulletproof vests and helmets, each man carried an arsenal of deadly weaponry. Their expressions were grim, their hard eyes filled with determination.

Disappointment blasted him. He wanted to be the one to take down Marischenko and free Marissa. One final time he wanted to shine, to be a hero in her eyes.

As if reading his thoughts, Ardash patted him on the shoulder. "You've done well, man. If it weren't for you, we wouldn't know where Marischenko was keeping Marissa. Now stay here, out of the way, and let us do our job." He motioned to his men. Bringing his gun up level, he stepped from behind the dumpster, and ran on silent feet toward the open garage door.

The other cops followed, their dark uniforms blending into the gloom.

Scott stared after them. A mixture of relief and regret filled him. He stuffed his hand into his front pocket and shuffled from one foot to another. His body twitched, aching for action.

Since the SWAT team had entered the garage, no sounds had emerged. It was as if they'd stepped off the face of the Earth into a dark void. What was going on in there? Had they caught Marischenko? Taken down his bodyguard? Or had the Russian mobster seen the police coming and laid a trap? Were the cops tossing down their weapons even now as Marischenko trained a gun on them?

To hell with it.

He wasn't waiting here like a mouse while Marischenko escaped. Inhaling a deep breath, he tightened his grip on the flashlight and ran after Ardash and the other cops.

The garage was dark, and he flicked on the flashlight and cupped his hand around the head, narrowing the beam of light to a pinpoint. He hadn't covered more than ten steps when he came across three cops holding the big, bearded guy in handcuffs.

They wrestled him out of the garage into the alley.

Scott sped past them. His single-minded goal—find Marissa. Not wanting to warn Marischenko of his presence, he doused his flashlight. A menacing silence hung over the garage. A team of cops was in here somewhere, but they weren't making any noise.

The garage was vast, inky dark, and silent. He couldn't see anything other than vague shapes. Where were Ardash and the other cops? Had they rescued Marissa? Was she safe? Was the nightmare over?

Placing one foot in front of the other, he kept his hands in front to ward off any hard objects. Something solid and warm crashed into him, and he reeled back, stunned, and dropped the flashlight. It clattered on the floor.

Her scent hit him first—a subtle floral mixed with cinnamon. Familiar soft curves pressed against him. "Marissa?" Her name escaped in a breath of air. Was this a dream? Was she real? He wrapped his arms around her, holding her close, feeling the rapid pounding of her heart.

She fought him, struggling to break free, but he held her tight. "Easy. It's okay. You're safe." His words seemed to soothe her, because she ceased fighting and burrowed into his embrace.

Shuddering sobs shook her body. "Scott?"

He tightened his hold and pressed her closer, never wanting to let her go. *She was safe. Marissa was safe.* The words rang through him like the sweetest symphony.

But was she? Could the all-encompassing darkness

be hiding an injury? Loosening his embrace, he bent down and retrieved the flashlight. Flicking on the light, he shone it on the woman in his arms.

She blinked at him through swollen, red eyes. Her dark hair was a riot of curls around her tearstained, dirt-streaked face. "Scott."

Never had she looked more beautiful. His fingers trembled as he smoothed away the tears from the satiny skin on her cheeks.

Her luminous eyes softened to a pearly gray. "You're here. You're really here."

"I'm here."

"But I thought—"

He set the flashlight on a workbench and captured her face between his hands and pressed his lips against hers, cutting off her words. The taste of her rocketed through him, igniting a rush of roaring flames. He deepened the kiss, imbuing his fear, his worry, his apology, his love, in the single, searing kiss.

A crash sounded from the depths of the dark garage.

Reality set in like a splash of ice water, and he broke off the kiss and released her. "Where's Marischenko?"

She pointed into the darkness. "I...I hurt him." She grabbed his hand. "Come on. We have to go. He has a gun. He...he wants to kill me." Fear riddled her voice.

"It's okay. The police are here. They have Marischenko's bodyguard in custody." He tugged his hand free and pointed in the direction of the open garage door. "Go on. Get out of here. I'll handle Marischenko." He gulped at his brave words, but he was determined to finish this.

"I'm not leaving you. Marischenko's furious. He'll kill you."

The shuffling footsteps and harsh breathing grew louder.

"I'll be fine." He nudged her toward the door. "Go. Get out of here." Marischenko would appear any second. She wasn't safe yet. He had to make her understand, had to convince her to run to safety. Cupping the back of her head in his palm, he fixed her with a steady gaze. "You have to go. I'll be fine." He swallowed and fought the urge to kiss her again. "This is something I have to do."

"Why? Let the cops handle Marischenko."

"I want"—he gulped—"no, I have to."

"You don't have to prove anything to me. I know why you did what you did." Tears shimmered in her eyes and dampened her lashes into spikes. "I understand."

His brain shut down, and his heart rate shot off the charts. He couldn't breathe. He swore to God he heard angels singing. *I understand.* They were the sweetest words he'd ever heard.

A loud curse boomed out of the dark.

Damn. "Look, we'll talk when this is over, but right now you have to get out of here."

She studied him for one heartbeat and then another and nodded. "I'll be waiting. Be safe." She turned, and with a last soul-searching look, ran into the dark.

He waited until the scrape of her footsteps faded before he grasped the flashlight and pointed the beam in the direction of the lumbering footsteps.

Marischenko stumbled into view. His white hair hung about his face in thin, greasy strands. Blood soaked the front of his shirt. His eyes were wild, his mouth twisted in a snarl. A gun dangled from his hand. He squinted into the blinding light. "Ivan, get that damn light out of my eyes. The bitch stabbed me. She got away. We must find her before she escapes."

Scott cleared his throat. "Ivan's a little busy right now." He kept the beam of light trained on the other man's face, blinding him.

The furrows between Marischenko's bushy white eyebrows deepened, and he squinted and peered through the glare. "You! What the hell are you doing here?"

Marischenko seemed to have forgotten he held a gun, and Scott wanted to keep it that way. "Your niece…Ludmilla… Remember her? She told me about your little hideaway."

The Russian swore and spat on the floor. "Never trust a damn woman, not even if she is family." He pressed a hand to his chest and grimaced. "Do not think of stopping me. No two-bit ADA is getting in my way." He aimed the gun at Scott.

Sweat broke out on Scott's forehead and under his arms. He'd never had a gun pointed at him. The sight was terrifying. He was under no illusions. Marischenko was desperate. He knew he was cornered, and he wouldn't hesitate to shoot. Scott had witnessed the man's carnage in DeGrazzi's study.

Every instinct urged him to run and hide, but he had to distract the Russian until Marissa reached safety and help arrived. The man wasn't getting past him, but he had to stall until the cops found him. "I'm not going to stop you."

"You are smarter than you look." Keeping the gun

trained on Scott, Marischenko hobbled closer. "I do not have time to end this now, but you had better watch your back, *Mr. ADA*. I do not forget people who fuck with me. You never know when a bullet will find you, and you die just like your parents."

Scott gulped at the venom in the man's eyes, but he moved, blocking his escape.

The killer's eyes hardened. His finger settled on the trigger. "I do not have time for this." He leveled the weapon, the barrel pointing at Scott's chest. "I did not want to do this here, but you give me no choice."

This is it!

Marischenko wouldn't miss from this distance. The terrifying certainty of imminent death reared before Scott like an epiphany. One consolation—he'd die knowing Marissa was safe from this monster. The sound of a gunshot would draw the police, and they'd take the Russian down.

"Police! Drop your weapon." Ardash and four uniformed cops, guns drawn and trained on Marischenko, stepped into the pool of light.

Scott blew out a shaky breath. The cavalry had arrived. In the nick of time. Just like in the movies.

Marischenko uttered a long string of Russian profanity. The gun dropped to the floor with a loud clatter.

A cop rushed forward and cuffed Marischenko's hands behind his back.

Another retrieved the gun.

Scott's knees wobbled. He staggered a few steps but managed not to embarrass himself and remained upright. "Took you guys long enough." His throat was tight, and he prayed they didn't hear the fear lacing his voice. He set the flashlight on a workbench and stuffed his hands in the front pockets of his pants to hide their trembling.

A bank of fluorescent lights flickered on, and the big garage lit up like an operating theater. He blinked in the searing brightness.

Police, wearing bulletproof vests and armed to the teeth, swarmed the cavernous room.

Ardash strode over to Scott. "You did good today, Scott."

"Marissa…is she okay?"

"She's fine. Thanks to you."

"Detective Sandhu, you should take a look at this." A cop beckoned from the rear of the garage where an open door was visible.

Without another word, the detective hustled over.

Scott stayed where he was and watched two burly policemen haul a glowering Marischenko away. The nightmare of the past days was finally over. Marissa was safe. A bone-deep exhaustion coursed through him, and he sagged against the bench.

Chapter 25

"Scott?" His name echoed hollowly in the silent garage.

He blinked and rubbed his eyes. *Marissa?* Was his imagination playing tricks? With infinite slowness, he twisted around, afraid she was a fantasy. But there she was....looking more gorgeous than ever. He sucked in a breath.

Her full, red lips curved in a soft smile. "Hey."

"What...what are you doing here? I thought you left." *Don't just stand and gape like an idiot.* The command blazed through him, but his feet seemed stuck to the floor, and his tongue didn't want to work.

She moved closer.

He breathed in her feminine scent as if he were inhaling the essence of life.

"Detective Sandhu told me I have you to thank for saving my life."

"He...he said that?"

She inched another step closer. "You figured out where Marischenko was holding me prisoner, and you led the police here. If it weren't for you, I'd never have escaped." Her voice hitched on the last words, and tears shone in her gray eyes, turning them silver.

"Is that why you came back? To thank me?"

Kiss the girl!

The command blazed, but there was a disconnect

between his mind and his body, and he couldn't move.

"That's not why I'm here." Another step.

Two inches of space separated them. Two inches of heated, buzzing air.

He cleared his throat. "I…I'm sorry about lying to you. I shouldn't have"—he gulped—"I didn't know…" What was the point? Nothing he said excused his actions. He'd messed up. Big time. He'd lied to her and used her. His endless fixation on finding his parents' killers had destroyed the one good thing in his life. He'd ruined any chance he had with Marissa, any hope of love.

"Are you going to stand there all night, or are you going to kiss me?"

"Kiss you?" *Oh, man.* "You…want me to…to kiss you?" A crust of the ice encasing his heart chipped off, and a swirl of warmth and hope filled his soul.

Neither of them said anything for so long, the silence began to hum.

The glistening depths of her silver eyes drew him like a magnet. His heart soared, his paralysis vanished, and he enfolded her in his arms and kissed her. Her lips tasted even sweeter than he remembered.

The kiss began as a tender caress but transformed into a passionate melding of mouths and tongues. The cold, damp garage, the agonizing nightmare of the past days, his unforgivable betrayal, disappeared as he focused on the incredible woman in his arms and the wonder of kissing her.

"Okay, you two lovebirds, time to break it up." Ardash's South Asian lilt pierced Scott's erotic haze like a saber. "Scott, you need to come with me to the station."

Scott's gaze sought Marissa's, and he bit back a groan.

Her pupils were huge, her expressive eyes dark with passion. Her lips were swollen and moist from the kiss, her cheeks flushed, her hair tangled from where he'd threaded his fingers through the silken strands.

Employing superhuman strength, he backed away, inhaled a deep breath, and faced Ardash. A chill rippled through him at the handcuffs in the detective's hands. "You're arresting me, Ardash? Is that what this is?"

"I'm sorry, Scott, but I have my orders." He frowned, his discomfort with the situation all too obvious. "I have to take you in." He stepped forward, and with practiced ease, slipped the cuffs over Scott's wrists. They closed with an ominous, metallic snap.

"What's going on?" Marissa demanded. "Why are you arresting him?"

"I'm sorry, but I can't afford to lose my job," Ardash said.

"But he had his reasons." She smoothed back a stray curl. "You know that, right? You know about his parents." Marissa's eyes flashed, the irises sparking.

Twin patches of red bloomed on Ardash's cheeks. "I have my orders."

"Your *orders*?" She jammed her hands on her slim hips. "Why aren't you arresting *me*? I'm a suspect in Flinty McGregor's murder. Last I checked, you had an arrest warrant for me." She held out her hands. "Here. Cuff me. Take me in."

"The charges against you were dropped."

"Dropped?"

Ardash's gaze shifted to Scott. "Scott explained everything. You were framed."

She looked pointedly at Scott. "And you're okay with this? You're just going to let him arrest you?"

"Let Detective Sandhu do his job." He kept his voice calm, hoping to ease her concern, though in a perverse way, her worry warmed his heart.

Ardash gripped his upper arm and urged Scott forward. "Come on. Let's get this over with."

"Detective Sandhu, please don't do this." Tears filmed her eyes. "Please."

Scott's muscles twitched with the desperate need to hold her, to ease her fear and worry. He tugged against the restraints.

Ardash's grip on his arm tightened. "Don't make this any harder than it is, Scott."

A cold dose of reality washed over him. An arrest warrant had been issued, and no matter what Ardash personally believed, he was duty bound to take Scott in. He stopped tugging on the cuffs. "It'll be all right, Marissa. Get some rest. I'll see you in the morning." Forcing a smile to his stiff lips, he allowed Ardash to escort him out of the garage.

"Detective Sandhu," she called after them. "Who gave you the order to arrest Scott? Will you at least tell me that?"

Ardash stopped and looked back at Marissa. "The arrest order came right from the top. District Attorney Johnson signed the paperwork himself."

Her gasp mixed with Scott's loud explosion of air. Before he could say anything, Ardash propelled him out of the garage to where a police cruiser, motor idling, lights flashing, waited.

****

Marissa paced her small apartment, completing lap

after lap, through the living room, down the hall to her bedroom, back down the short hall to the kitchen, and on to the living room. Her heart pounded in time with her rapid steps. She'd been pacing for hours and had no intention of stopping until she came up with a plan to secure Scott's release.

The past few days had been a nightmare. She rubbed her throbbing temples. Her heart had shattered into a million tiny pieces when Scott revealed his shocking betrayal. As she had five years ago, she'd run to Julio for help, but instead she'd discovered a scene from a horror movie.

Somehow Scott had found her in that garage and saved the day. If it weren't for him and his heroics she'd be dead. She didn't doubt that for a second.

After Scott had been driven away in handcuffs in a police cruiser, Detective Sandhu drove her to the police station in his unmarked police sedan. On the drive to the station, he'd explained how Scott recognized Slavadad Marischenko on Julio's penthouse security feeds. Scott had also figured out the connection between Loretta Carmichael and Marischenko. Something about matching wolf tattoos. Somehow he'd convinced the bitter, angry Loretta to reveal where the Russian had taken Marissa.

When Marissa stabbed Marischenko with the metal spring and fled her cell, she'd been running blind, terrified she'd encounter Ivan. Instead, she'd crashed into Scott's strong body. Heat flared up her neck and swamped her face as she recalled how she'd begged him to kiss her. Blame her ardor on the adrenaline coursing through her bloodstream and her relief at being rescued.

But then Detective Sandhu handcuffed Scott, who was now in police custody facing serious charges. His life was ruined, his career over. She had to do something, had to somehow convince the police to release him.

She hurried to the door, unlocked the deadbolt, and unlatched the security chain. Flinging open the door, she stepped across the hall and knocked on Mike's apartment door. Mike had been a cop for more than thirty years. He knew how the system worked. Maybe he had an idea that would help her free Scott.

He grinned when he saw her. "Marissa." Opening the door wider, he swept his hand in a welcoming gesture. "Perfect timing, I just put on a pot of coffee. Come on in."

She entered his small, cluttered apartment and followed him into the kitchen. The fragrant tang of Mike's special dark roast coffee hovered in the air. She perched on a chair at the table and cleared a space by shoving a plate covered with dried egg and toast crumbs and a cup with an inch of greasy-looking coffee dregs out of the way. A newspaper folded to the sports section followed.

He bustled about the tiny kitchen, filling cups with coffee and adding two teaspoons of sugar to one cup and creamer to the other. Setting the sweetened brew before her, he swung back to a cupboard and retrieved an open package of store-bought chocolate chip cookies and plunked the bag on the table. Satisfied he'd done his part as host, he settled on the facing chair. "So, are you going to tell me what's bothering you?"

"I thought you would have heard." Even though Mike was retired from the police force, he maintained connections to his old buddies. He bowled in the police league, played poker, and enjoyed happy hour at the bar across from the precinct.

"If you're talking about what went down in that garage on Wilson Street last night, I did." He patted her arm. "I was planning on coming over this morning to see if you were okay. You must have been terrified. Good thing the SWAT team got there in time."

A lump filled her throat at the concern in his eyes. "It was pretty frightening, but I'm okay. Or, I will be."

"So why the hangdog expression?" He slurped coffee. "Slavadad Marischenko's in jail, and I hear the DA's dropped the charges against you."

"You knew about that?"

He shrugged. "Of course."

She blew on the steaming liquid in her cup. "I guess you also know Julio DeGrazzi was my uncle."

He nodded. "I've known for years."

"Why didn't you say anything?"

Again he shrugged. "It wasn't any of my business. I like you. You're a nice person. What was the point in bringing up your criminal uncle?"

She chewed on her bottom lip. "Scott Bannister is being held in police custody. He's facing serious charges."

Mike's lip curled in a sneer. "That's why you're upset? Not your uncle's death, or your kidnapping, but that young ADA fellow?" He slammed his hand on the table so hard the cups rattled and coffee slopped onto the scarred wood. "Come on, Marissa. He's a punk. Look what he did. He used you. It's because of him that your life was in danger. The man deserves what he gets."

"He had his reasons." With shaking hands, she raised her cup to her mouth and sipped, hoping the bitter brew would give her strength. She folded her freezing hands around her mug and told him about Scott's parents and their untimely deaths, and his life-long search for their killers. By the time she was finished, her coffee was cold.

"I feel for the guy, but no matter the extenuating circumstances, his career's in the tank." Mike slurped coffee. "We can't have an ADA who's willing to take the law into his own hands and bend the rules whenever he sees fit." He fished in the bag and tugged out a cookie, sniffed the stale-looking biscuit, wrinkled his nose in disgust, and tossed the cookie on the table. "So why do you care what happens to Scott Bannister?"

She studied the coffee dregs in the bottom of her cup. When that didn't help, she stared out the window. A tiny yellow bird flitted amongst the green, leafy branches of a tall oak tree. No help there either. Looking up, she met Mike's penetrating gaze. "I love him."

His eyes widened. "You *love* him?"

"I do."

He jerked to his feet, grabbed the coffee pot, and refilled their cups. Pushing the sugar dish toward her, he plunked down a spoon, poured creamer into his cup, and stirred. The clinking of the metal spoon against the ceramic cup was loud in the cozy kitchen. He sat down and stared at her. "Okay, then. How can I help?"

"Just like that?"

"Just like that." He smiled, and the creases beside his eyes deepened. "You're like a daughter to me. If you say you love this guy, he must be worth your devotion. Maybe I read him wrong. So, I'll say it again—how can I help?" His rugged cheeks flushed red, and his eyes glistened with what looked suspiciously like the gleam of tears.

"Thank you, Mike. You're pretty special to me too." She resisted the urge to jump up and hug him, knowing how uncomfortable her embrace would make the crusty, retired cop.

Wiping her own damp eyes, she leaned forward, elbows on the table. "Something Marischenko said has been bothering me. Last night"—she swallowed the bitter, lingering taste of fear—"when…when I was in that awful room, he admitted he arranged for someone to steal my cell phone from the crime scene evidence locker at the precinct. He sent my phone to me because he wanted to track me. I…I think he was planning on killing me to get back at Uncle Julio."

Mike rubbed the back of his neck. "You're thinking the person who removed the phone from the locker was a cop?"

"Either that or someone who has access to the station, someone no one would question if they saw him hanging around the evidence locker." She sipped coffee. Her muscles twitched with the caffeine jolt, and her brain synapses were firing on all thrusters. For the first time in days she was clearheaded. "Scott and I watched the surveillance footage from the police station cameras. We saw the guy who took my phone, but we couldn't identify him. Scott's pretty sure he wasn't a cop, but—"

"How the hell did you two yahoos break through secure police firewalls and access the station surveillance camera feeds?" He held up his hand.

"Never mind. I don't want to know." He stretched out his long legs. "Okay, here's what I'll do. I'll ask my old cronies who are still on the force if they've heard anything suspicious. If there's a crooked cop, they'll know. You can take that to the bank."

"There's something else."

He narrowed his eyes. "Might as well spit it out."

"I think the same man who took my phone placed Steven Carmichael's chain in my wallet. Loretta Carmichael told me a man showed up at her house last week and bought her brother's silver chain. Her description of the man was vague, but she said he drove some sort of official car. A logo was on the door. Does that help?"

"Maybe. Anything else?"

"Marischenko knew the police were on their way to the garage. Someone warned him. That's why he was so anxious to leave."

The lines in Mike's face carved deeper, and a cold light lit his blue eyes. He shoved his chair back and stood, knees cracking. "I'll see what I can find out."

"Thanks, Mike. I knew I could count on you."

His face softened. "Always, gal. Now, go find that man of yours and get him a good lawyer. He's going to need one."

Chapter 26

Scott stared at Ardash. "Are you kidding me? The DA's office is going ahead with these baseless charges?" He blew out a blast of air. "Any fool can see I was set up. I mean, what about Marischenko's confession? He admitted to everything. He—"

Ardash cut through his rant. "Look, Scott. I don't know what's going on, but the DA himself is pressuring me to charge you, and he won't let this go."

"Charge me? For what? Doing my job? If it weren't for me, Slavadad Marischenko would be walking the streets committing any number of vile offenses. To say nothing of the cold cases I solved. We now know who murdered Steven Carmichael and my parents."

"Calm down. This isn't helping." Ardash jerked his thumb at the glass window separating his office from the detective bullpen.

A dozen sets of curious eyes watched the action in the lead detective's office.

Scott slumped on the visitor chair and scrubbed his hands over his scruffy cheeks. How long had it been since he'd shaved. Or slept? Even a shower was a distant memory. The stabbing pain in his head persisted in spite of the painkillers he'd ingested. "Tell me again what Marischenko said in his statement. Maybe there's something in there that will help."

Ardash lifted a paper from the thick pile on his desk. "Basically, he admits to his involvement in the shooting at the movie theater where your parents were killed, but he swears he was only defending himself from DeGrazzi's attack, and it wasn't him who shot them." His gaze slid to Scott. "If it's any consolation, he's real sorry your parents were killed, but"—his gaze returned to the paper in his hand—"and I quote, 'shit happens'." He grimaced. "Gotta love the man's empathy."

Scott's gasp filled the room. Marischenko's callous words struck home like a bullet to the heart.

Ardash continued. "He blames Julio DeGrazzi for all his troubles. Apparently, Degrazzi tracked down an eyewitness to the movie theater shootings and recorded his statement." He lifted another paper. "The so-called witness says Marischenko started the firefight. It says right here on this transcript"—he tapped the page— "that he saw everything clear as day, even though it was night and the parking lot was poorly lit. Marischenko's bullets killed your parents.

"DeGrazzi, being the standup guy he was, used this damning evidence to blackmail Marischenko." He arched his dark brows. "Not that this statement is worth the paper it's printed on, but Marischenko believed if it came to light, he'd be convicted on two murder charges."

Scott clamped a hand on his gut and pressed hard in a futile effort to still the roiling. What Ardash was telling him explained so much but was almost too painful to hear. Two useless hoodlums playing games with guns while his parents paid the ultimate price. He forced his attention back to the police detective who was still speaking.

"That's why Marischenko laid low all these years, all the while bearing a grudge against DeGrazzi and planning revenge. A few years ago, he learned DeGrazzi had a niece, and he decided to use her to destroy DeGrazzi." Ardash tapped his fingers on the stack of papers. "He sent his nephew, Steven Carmichael, after her. I think his plan was for Carmichael to kill her, but he didn't count on Carmichael falling in love with her, so he ordered the hit on his own nephew." His face flushed with anger. "No one disobeys the Russian's orders. Not even family."

Scott's mind was still on his parents' murders. "Why didn't this eyewitness go to the police? My grandparents offered a reward for information that led to a conviction in the shootings."

"DeGrazzi had him by the short hairs. If he went to the cops, he was a dead man. Besides, I'm sure DeGrazzi paid him well for his silence."

"Who is this so-called witness? Have you talked to him?"

Ardash thrust the document at Scott. "See for yourself."

Scott's gut heaved as he read the gruesome details of that terrible night outside Schumann's Theater....the last minutes of his parents' lives. His eyes widened at the signature at the bottom. "Flinty McGregor? What the hell?" His gaze met Ardash's. "McGregor was the witness? But he was deep in DeGrazzi's pockets. Surely Marischenko knew that. Why would he be afraid of anything one of DeGrazzi's henchmen said?"

"Crazy, isn't it?"

Scott scrubbed his hands over his face. "Everything in this damn case is connected like interlocking links in a chain."

Ardash laced his fingers behind his neck. "Here's something even more bizarre. Loretta Carmichael came in this morning. She'd heard about Marischenko's arrest, and she handed over his journal. She's pretty pissed. I guess she read the journal and found out her uncle ordered the hit on her brother.

"I sent the book to a Russian translator at the college." The corners of his mouth curled. "Marischenko isn't the brightest bulb on the shelf, or he's an arrogant son of a bitch." He shook his head. "He documented everything—Steven Carmichael's murder, how he ordered the hit on McGregor, and his plans to frame Marissa Reynolds and you for McGregor's murder, and eliminate DeGrazzi. His eventual goal was to take over DeGrazzi's criminal organization."

"Are you kidding me? He recorded everything?" Scott plopped back down on his chair. Finding Marischenko's journal in that cupboard at Loretta Carmichael's house was like finding the pot of gold at the end of the rainbow. The proof he'd spent so many years searching for was now out in the open. His parents' killers were finally revealed.

"I told you he's crazy." Ardash grimaced and rubbed the back of his neck. "And deadly." A dark look settled over his face.

"Why would he confess to everything? Why write his crimes down?"

Ardash shrugged. "Maybe he was planning on writing a book. You know, a memoir. People make a shitload of money writing those tell-all books. Hell, some Hollywood producer will probably make Marischenko's sordid life into a movie of the week."

A rap on the door and Detective Barbour opened the door. "There's someone to see you, sir. She says it's important." He stepped aside, revealing a woman standing behind him.

Scott's breath gusted out.

Marissa brushed past the young, red-haired detective and strode into the room. Nodding at Detective Sandhu, she crossed to the other visitor chair, sat, and crossed her long, shapely legs.

Scott drank her in like a man dying of thirst, and she was a glass of pure spring water. He breathed in her scent...roses and fresh spring air.

Her face was pale, but two bright spots of red flamed in her cheeks. Her silver eyes flashed, and her fall of long, dark hair gleamed under the bright fluorescent lights. She wore a prim wool skirt that caressed her knees and a white blouse with a matching wool blazer, looking every inch a college librarian.

"What...what are you doing here?" His voice cracked like an adolescent's.

"I'm here to help."

"Help? *Me*?" A burst of warmth like sunlight on the beach on a hot summer day struck him. "Why?"

"I told you. I care about you."

His mouth dropped open. If there were any flies in Ardash's office, his mouth would be full of the buzzing insects. He managed to shut his mouth and force his addled brain into gear. "You have no idea how much your support means to me, Marissa, but you shouldn't be here. You're free of all charges." He rubbed his temple, desperate to ease the jab of pain lancing through his eyeball. "I can handle this."

"I talked to Mike, my neighbor from across the hall. He's going to see if anyone knows of a cop who's on Marischenko's payroll." She uncrossed her legs and stood.

His gaze strayed to her long, tanned legs, and he gulped.

Ardash choked, and his face paled. "It's not one of my people. I can vouch for each and every one of them."

A phone rang, its strident tone piercing the tension-filled air. Marissa rummaged in her coat pocket and tugged out a cell phone. She shot Scott a glance. "I bought a new phone this morning. This will be Mike." She jammed the phone to her ear. "What did you find out?"

Scott watched her expressive face as she listened to the caller. He couldn't believe she was here, that this beautiful, strong woman wanted to help him. Even after everything he'd done.

Lying awake on the lumpy cot in his cell last night, he'd finally put the pieces together and figured out Marischenko's reason for destroying Scott's career. Somehow the Russian learned Scott was investigating his parents' murders. He'd also discovered that along with Julio DeGrazzi, he was a prime suspect. Now that Scott was the ADA, the pressure against Marischenko mounted. With Scott out of the picture and DeGrazzi dead, the heat would be off him. Marischenko could reclaim his criminal empire.

The irony was, the man didn't have to waste his efforts discrediting Scott. Scott had done the heavy lifting for him. He'd been so driven to find his parents' killers he'd abused the powers of his office and interfered in a criminal investigation. Scott would be lucky to get off with parole.

"Yes!" Marissa's slim body bristled with excitement. "I know who the inside man is." She slipped the phone in her pocket and clapped her hands together and bounced on the toes of her black, leather pumps.

****

Both men stared at her, their faces blank.

"Did you hear me? I know who's been working with Marischenko." She paused, expecting a drumroll. Their expressions remained unchanged, and they seemed underwhelmed. "It's Redford Johnson, the District Attorney."

Scott scratched his beard-roughened chin.

Detective Sandhu drummed his fingers on his desk. He cleared his throat. "Look, Marissa, I know you want to help Scott, but you can't go around pointing the finger of blame at just anyone."

She shook her head with such vehemence the long strands of her hair whipped her face. "You don't understand. Mike says this information is solid. Johnson's our man."

"We can't accuse the District Attorney of leaking confidential police information to a criminal and interfering in a homicide investigation without solid proof," Scott said.

"Mike found a witness. Someone who swears they overheard Johnson talking to Marischenko on his office phone, warning him the police were on the way to raid his garage."

The restless tapping stopped, and Detective Sandhu straightened. "Who is this witness? Is he credible?"

"Mike's meeting us at the DA's office. The witness will be with him. We'll confront Johnson together."

The two men exchanged glances.

"This is crazy, but what if it's true? What if Johnson is involved?" Excitement laced Scott's deep voice. "It would explain why he's so determined to press charges against me."

"I don't believe it," Detective Sandhu said. "Johnson's been the DA in this city for years. He may be a pompous ass, and he's made too many budget cuts, but there's been no hint of impropriety."

"What are you waiting for?" Marissa headed toward the door. "Let's go. Let's find out the truth." When the men still didn't move, she leveled a scathing gaze at Scott. "You're afraid. That's it, isn't it? You're afraid you'll find out I'm right, and you've been played for a fool."

A pulse beat a rapid tattoo in Scott's strong jaw. Finally, he nodded. "Okay. Let's see if this neighbor of yours knows what he's talking about." He shoved to his feet, clasped her hand in his, and squeezed. "Let's do this."

"Wait a minute, Scott. You're under arrest. You can't just walk out of here," Detective Sandhu said.

Both Scott and Marissa halted in their rush to the door.

"Come on, Ardash," Scott said. "Just one more favor before you lock me in a cell and throw away the key."

Detective Sandhu studied Scott for several beats. He huffed out an aggrieved breath and shot to his feet.

"I hope for your sake, I don't end up regretting this." He strode around his desk and grabbed his coat off the hook. "I'm coming with you."

The three of them raced out of the detective's office, wove their way through the tangle of desks in the bullpen, and hurried down the hall to the front door of the police station.

Detective Sandhu commandeered an unmarked police sedan and settled behind the wheel.

Marissa leaped in the front passenger seat, and Scott climbed in the back.

The ride to Number One Police Plaza took fifteen agonizing minutes. Fifteen minutes of silence so thick it could be sliced with a knife.

She glanced back at Scott, but his face was closed, his gaze fixed on the passing buildings. She could only imagine the thoughts running through his head. If Mike's lead was true, Scott's boss was involved in the nightmare of the past few days. Redford Johnson had colluded with a known murderer. He was Marischenko's inside man.

"We're here." Detective Sandhu's voice broke into her thoughts.

She rubbed her damp palms on her skirt, released her seatbelt latch, and climbed out of the car.

The detective took the lead, and she and Scott followed him up the steps and into the large brick building. The lobby was crowded as lawyers and their assistants, arms loaded with files, rushed past. Uniformed police officers flipped through tattered magazines as they waited on hard-backed metal chairs set along the lobby walls. Witnesses and defendants milled about the room. Everyone seemed to be talking at once, the jabber of voices loud.

Mike waved them down, and they made their way to a tiny alcove separated from the busy lobby by a half wall and a row of limp-looking potted ferns.

"You guys took your sweet time," Mike said.

"We're here now," Scott said. "Where's this witness?"

A thin, dark-haired man stepped from behind Mike's broad frame. "Hey, Boss."

"Jonas? What are you doing here?" Scott's eyes widened, and he rocked back on his heels. "Wait a minute. *You're* the witness?"

The young lawyer's face flushed red, and he nodded.

"*You* overheard DA Redford Johnson warning Slavadad Marischenko of the police raid on the garage last night?"

Again Jonas nodded.

"Why didn't you tell me?"

Jonas removed his thick glasses and wiped the lenses with his shirttail. "I tried to tell you last night when I called, but you cut me off. I've had my suspicions for awhile, but I didn't have any proof, and I didn't want to lose my job. This is the only career I've ever wanted. I didn't want to ruin that." He looked at Scott with pleading eyes. "I'm sorry."

Detective Sandhu cleared his throat. "You're positive what you heard? You'll testify to this in a court of law?"

Jonas's throat worked, his Adam's apple bobbing. "Yes."

The detective wiped his gleaming brow. "Okay." He nodded at Jonas, Mike, and Marissa. "You wait here." His gaze shifted to Scott. "Let's do this. Let's confront the bastard."

"I'm coming with you." She planted her hands on her hips and jutted out her lower lip. She'd come this far. Damned if she'd miss the grand finale.

Detective Sandhu must have seen the steel in her eyes, because he blew out a ragged breath and nodded. "Just stay out of the way."

Chapter 27

They stepped off the elevator in a single pack, but Scott took the lead. He ignored the heads that turned, the sly looks, the whispered comments, the raised eyebrows, as he stormed along the corridor to Johnson's office. He threw open the door and burst into the DA's outer office.

Johnson's long-time executive assistant, Margaret Lopez, looked up from her computer. Her matronly face paled. "Scott! What are you doing here? I thought—"

"Is he in?"

She hesitated. "Do you have an appointment?" Her gaze flickered between Ardash, Marissa, and back to Scott.

"Don't need one." Propelled by an inner fury that threatened to rage out of control, he strode across the room and thrust open the door to Johnson's inner sanctum. The door slammed against the back wall with a loud bang.

He marched into the office, Marissa right behind him, followed by Ardash.

The door swung shut.

Johnson looked up and frowned. "What are *you* doing here?" His gaze switched to Ardash, and the furrow between his carefully trimmed eyebrows deepened. "What the hell is he doing here, Detective Sandhu? Why isn't this man under arrest? I gave explicit orders that he was to be held in police custody."

Ardash shuffled his feet but didn't respond.

"We have to talk, Johnson." Scott kept his voice calm and level, though anger blazed through him like an out-of-control wildfire. If Jonas was telling the truth, this man had betrayed not just him, but the entire police department, the sacred oath of his office, and the people of the city of Brunswick. The sour taste of disgust filled his mouth. "We know."

"Know what?" Johnson's expression was one of mild curiosity mixed with irritation, but shadows lurked in his pale eyes.

"Don't bother to deny it," Scott said. "We have an eyewitness who's willing to testify in court that he heard you warning Slavadad Marischenko of the police raid on his garage last night."

The DA's lip curled. "An eyewitness? Really? And who is this so-called eyewitness?" He spit out a breath. "Someone you paid to lie to further your insane claims?" He pinned Ardash with a hot gaze and sneered. "Tell me you're not buying this malarkey. Not after all the laws Bannister has broken." He pointed toward the door. "Now get the hell out of here and do your damn job. Arrest his ass. I have important work to do."

No one budged.

The tension in the opulent office thickened. The muted clicking of keys on a keyboard, the distant ringing of a phone, and the rough purr of a laser printer emanated from the outer office.

"You're something. Do you know that?" Scott said, breaking the silence. "The worst part is I respected you. I really did. I wanted to be just like you."

Ardash stepped forward. "We have you, Johnson. No point denying your involvement. You're done."

The DA slid open his top desk drawer and jerked out a gun. His mouth curled in a cold smile, his eyes shards of ice. He pointed the dull, silver-colored weapon at the group arrayed in front of his expansive desk. "I think not."

Marissa's gasp filled the electrified air.

Scott's heart raced at the deadly intent in Johnson's eyes. He placed a steadying hand on Marissa's arm, edging her behind his body, out of the direct line of fire. Sweat beaded his brow. This was the second time in two days he'd faced a gun. Repetition didn't lessen the mind-numbing horror. "What…what do you think you're doing?"

"Looking out for number one." Johnson smirked. "Just like I've always done."

Scott slid a glance at Ardash.

The detective stood unmoving, his swarthy face ashen, his hands balled into fists at his sides. He made no attempt to unsnap the holster at his hip and draw out his service revolver.

Scott frowned. Why didn't he do something? He had a gun. Why didn't he use it?

Johnson rose, and gun pointed at Scott, he strolled around his desk.

The weapon seemed to grow in size, the barrel looming like a dark tunnel to Hell. "Ardash?" Scott's voice was a husky rasp. His heart hammered in his chest. "Do something."

His friend remained frozen as if under a spell, but his gaze flicked around the room as if he were searching for escape.

Marissa whimpered and shrank behind Scott, pressing her trembling body against his back.

He ached to hold her, to ease her fears, but he gritted his teeth and held steady. If he touched her, if he glimpsed the terror in her luminous eyes, he'd shatter into a million pieces. He slid another frantic glance at Ardash.

The detective had shut down. He stood still and silent, a mute witness to the ongoing nightmare.

Scott stared at the police issue service revolver holstered to the detective's belt. Three feet of space separated him and Ardash. Thirty-six inches. He swallowed. If he charged Ardash, he could grab the gun and— He shut the thought down.

Too many variables were at play. If he made a mistake, misjudged one step, Marissa could get shot. He had to convince Johnson to release her. Once she was safe, he could perform any number of crazy stunts and save the day.

Maybe.

He cleared his throat. "Let her go, Johnson. She's not part of this."

The DA's laughter was chilling. "Are you kidding?" The gun in his hand didn't waver. "She's Julio DeGrazzi's niece. She should die just because she shares that bastard's DNA."

Scott pointed at the closed door. The buzz of voices filtered from the offices beyond. "If you shoot us, where are you going to run? This place is swarming with cops. You kill us, and I guarantee you won't make it ten feet before some nervous, trigger-happy, rookie cop shoots you down."

Johnson's complacent smile didn't falter. "You're

the criminal, remember? There's an arrest warrant out for you. I know. I signed it." He smirked. "Your single-minded quest to find your parents' killers has deranged you. You're discredited, ruined, your career in the toilet. Now you're spinning out of control. A psychotic break, I think they call it."

He moved another step closer, the infernal smug smile plastered on his patrician face. "You burst into my office with your wild accusations and"—he shrugged—"what choice did I have? You threatened me. I was terrified. No one will blame me for defending myself."

"What the hell are you talking about?" Scott snapped. Was the man insane? Did he really think his half-baked plan would work? "I'm unarmed. You're the one with the gun. Besides, I'm not here alone. There are witnesses."

"Ahhh, yes, your friends." Johnson's derisive gaze swept Marissa and Ardash. "The niece of the biggest crime kingpin in this city and a tainted cop."

"Shut up, Johnson!" The DA's words seemed to free Ardash from his paralysis. He unsnapped the holster cover and tugged his gun free. "Just shut the fuck up."

Johnson's smile didn't fade. "What? They don't know?"

"Know what?" Scott swung on his friend. "What's he talking about, Ardash? Why's he calling you a tainted cop?"

Ardash swiped at a drip of sweat on his chin. "Don't listen to him. You can't believe a word he says." The detective's face gleamed with sweat, and his body twitched with nerves. The hand holding the gun shook like he had a bad case of palsy. He looked everywhere but at Scott.

Scott's unease multiplied a thousand fold. A sinking sensation flooded his gut as he recognized the signs. His friend was lying.

"Come on, Detective Sandhu, the jig's up, as they say," Johnson taunted. "Tell him of your involvement with Slavadad Marischenko's criminal empire. Tell them how you murdered Flinty McGregor and staged the crime scene so the finger of blame would point at Marissa Reynolds. Tell them that during this entire investigation you did your damnedest to convince the public of our ADA's involvement."

"What?" Marissa burst out.

Scott had heard enough. Johnson was spouting lies, trying to confuse them so he could— Could what? Get away? Escape? He couldn't walk out of there, not without killing three people in cold blood. "Look, Johnson, you don't want to hurt anyone. Put the gun down and surrender peacefully. You've got the cash to hire a good lawyer. He'll work out a plea bargain. You'll serve minimum time in a country club jail and be out on parole before your prison tattoos dry." He ignored the sweat stinging his eyes. "Just put the gun down, and we'll all walk out of here like—"

Johnson lunged, grabbed Marissa's arm, and yanked her from behind Scott.

She screamed, but the sound came out more like a squeak as the bastard wrapped his arm around her neck, dragging her against his body, cutting off her air.

"What the hell?" Scott leaped toward her but froze when Johnson jammed the gun barrel hard against her cheekbone.

"Don't even think of it, Bannister," Johnson said.

Marissa's eyes were wide, her pupils dilated with fear, her face ghostly white.

Scott's muscles twitched, aching to do something…anything to save her, but if he made the slightest wrong move, he had no doubt Johnson would follow through on his threat. He held his hands up, palms out. He licked his dry lips. "I'll do whatever you want, just don't hurt her."

Johnson nodded with satisfaction. "Always figured you for a coward." His feral gaze shifted to Ardash. "Go on, Detective. Tell them. Don't be shy. Tell them how you ran with the Russian mob."

Ardash kept his head down and refused to meet Scott's probing gaze.

A shiver trailed along Scott's spine, raising goose bumps. "Why are you letting him spout these lies, Ardash? Why aren't you defending yourself?"

Ardash coughed and cleared his throat. "They're not lies."

His voice was so quiet, Scott wasn't sure he heard correctly. "What? Are you saying you work for Marischenko? You killed McGregor?"

Ardash looked at Scott with pleading eyes. "McGregor was a punk. I was doing the world a favor by getting rid of him." Tears filmed his eyes. "You don't understand. I didn't have a choice. I…I was just a kid. I didn't know what I was getting into. I was the only South Asian kid in my neighborhood. No one wanted to hang around with me. But the Russians wanted me. They didn't care that I had brown skin."

A shiny trail of snot leaked from his nose onto his clipped mustache. "At first, it was no big deal. We'd jack a car, filch a TV, sell a few joints to some kids." He sniffed. "But then I decided I wanted to be a cop, and I wanted out." He shook his head. "But there's no getting out. Once you join the Russians, you're in for life."

"What the hell, Ardash? You're a member of Marischenko's gang? All this time you've been helping him?" Scott scrubbed his cheeks as if that would help make Ardash's shocking confession any more believable. "You're a cop. A good one. What happened?"

Ardash shook his head. "Not such a good cop, I'm afraid." He raised his gun and pointed the deadly weapon at Scott. "Look, I'm sorry, but I don't have a choice."

"You're taking orders from Marischenko?" Scott didn't bother to keep the scorn out of his voice. "What are you going to do? Shoot two unarmed people? In cold blood?"

"He'll do exactly as he's ordered." Johnson tapped the gun against Marissa's cheek, emphasizing each word.

She winced and mewed in terror.

Scott's breathing stopped, his whole world narrowing to Johnson, the gun, and the terrified woman in the traitor's arms. *Do something!* The frantic order pierced his heart like a lance.

Do something!

As if reading his mind, Marissa lifted her foot and stomped on Johnson's shoe.

He grunted in pain and raised his arm and struck her on the side of the head with the barrel of the gun.

She screamed and fell, crashing into the sofa and

collapsing on the floor.

"Marissa!"

"Don't move, Scott." Johnson's cold voice stopped him dead. His gun was trained on him, his murderous intent clear.

Marissa huddled on the floor, her body wracked by quiet sobs. A line of blood leaked from a cut on her forehead.

The hardest thing Scott ever did was stand there and watch while the woman he loved cowered on the floor before a madman.

Do something before he kills her!

"Okay, Sandhu, this is how we're going to do this." Johnson's authoritative voice cut through Scott's panic. The DA tugged a cloth handkerchief from his coat pocket and wiped the gun in his hand, removing his fingerprints from the grip and barrel. "ADA Bannister and this woman stormed in here. They were crazed and high on drugs. He had a gun. He accused me of killing his parents."

He shrugged. "I couldn't reason with him. Good thing you were here, Detective Sandhu. You tried to stop him, but he wouldn't listen. You were forced to shoot him before he killed me." He tsked. "Sad. So very sad. Our once-shiny-new ADA, a crazed killer. Shows you what drugs will do."

Scott's breath quickened. "You can't expect that story to fly. A skilled investigator will shoot holes all over it."

Johnson's self-satisfied smile didn't fade. "I'm the District Attorney of Brunswick." He nodded at Ardash. "Detective Sandhu here is a decorated police detective with more than twenty years experience." He set the cleaned gun on the desk and tucked his handkerchief back in his pocket. "I'm confident our story will be taken at face value."

"You're insane." Marissa's voice was tight with anger. She pushed to her knees, her gray eyes shooting darts. A thin red line of blood blazed a trail down her cheek and dripped off her chin. "You'll never get away with this."

A chill settled over Scott. Marissa was wrong. Johnson's crazed plan could work. Scott was under arrest. Marissa was the niece of the infamous Julio DeGrazzi. If Ardash killed them, no one would be the wiser. He and the DA would be hailed as heroes. Marissa and Scott relegated to infamy.

He held on to a single thread of hope. If he and Marissa didn't return to the lobby soon, Mike and Jonas would raise the alarm. All he had to do was keep Johnson talking. How hard could that be? He was a lawyer. He'd been trained to talk. "Your plan won't work. We're not on drugs. An autopsy will prove that."

Johnson reached in his pocket and pulled out a small, plastic vial. He held up the pill bottle, unscrewed the lid, and poured a handful of tiny green pills on the desk. "From what I understand, these little babies pack quite a punch." He nodded at Marissa. "Ask your girlfriend. She seemed to enjoy the experience."

Marissa gasped. "Those are roofies? That's the drug you gave me before?"

"Well, technically, *I* didn't give them to you. Ivan did, but these are the same pills. I removed them from the police evidence locker."

"We won't take them," Scott said. "There's no way."

Johnson tutted loudly. "You seem to be under the impression you have some control over this situation." He pointed at Ardash. "My helper here will do what he must."

The gun in the detective's hand was steady, the barrel pointed at Marissa. His eyes were haunted hollows, his mouth a grim line.

"Now, you'll take these pills, or Detective Sandhu will shoot your girlfriend."

Scott's blood turned to ice at the deadly intent in Johnson's eyes. From his earlier research, he'd learned that the effect of roofies was instantaneous. Once under the drug's influence, they'd be helpless. Ardash and Johnson could do what they wanted with them.

His mind flew, jumping from one impossible scenario to the next, each one crazier than the other. He'd watched hundreds of action movies. In each and every one, the hero performed some wild stunt and took down the bad guys and saved the day.

But this was real life.

In real life, people died.

Chapter 28

"Take these." Ardash pointed his gun at Marissa with one hand and held four green pills cupped in the palm of his other hand.

"No way." Scott backed away. "I'm not doing your dirty work for you. If you want me to take those pills, you're going to have to stuff them down my throat."

"Do you think I want to do this?" Ardash's eyes watered. "If I had any other choice, I wouldn't, but—"

Scott cut him off. "So why the hell are you?"

"They...they have my family. They have Jasinder and my wife." He swiped his runny nose with his sleeve. "You don't know what the Russian gang is like. These people don't make empty threats. If"—his voice cracked—"if I don't do this, they'll kill them." A sob shook his body. "They'll kill my boy."

Scott stared at the anguish scoring deep grooves between Ardash's dark brows. In spite of the dire circumstances, his heart bled for his friend's torment. He knew how much Ardash loved his wife and son. Still...to kill innocent people to save his family. Murder was wrong no matter how you justified it.

But was Scott any better? He'd been all too willing to use Marissa, lie to her, bend the rules—whatever it took to avenge his family. He understood what drove Ardash, but he wasn't about to lie down and play dead. He had to do something, make some sort of move. If

Johnson and Ardash thought he'd given up and accepted his fate, maybe, just maybe he could catch them off guard.

And then what?

He shook off the niggling doubt. Blowing out a ragged breath, he slumped his shoulders, and hung his head. "Okay, Ardash. You win. I won't fight you anymore." He scooped the pills from Ardash's palm.

"No." Marissa's shouted protest split the air. She shot to her feet and slapped his arm. The pills flew out of his hand and scattered across the floor.

In the nanosecond of stunned disbelief that followed, Scott exploded into action. Years of training took over, and his tae kwon do skills surfaced. Whirling, he spun on the balls of his feet and lashed out. His booted foot connected with Ardash's wrist.

The crack of bone snapping rent the air.

Ardash screamed. The gun fell from his hand and dropped to the floor.

Marissa was on the weapon in a flash. She clasped it in both hands, and stood, legs braced, pointing the gun at the injured detective.

Scott spun toward Johnson, his body arced, muscles taut, leg raised, his blood crying for vengeance.

Johnson reeled back, his hands raised in the air. "No, don't. I surrender. I give up." All his fight and bluster fled. He collapsed on the couch as if he were a puppet and someone had cut his strings. His broad shoulders sagged, and his big body seemed to shrink.

The door burst open, and two uniformed cops, guns drawn, charged into the room. They pointed both barrels at Marissa. "Drop your weapon. Now."

Scott gulped. "Easy, boys. She's not the bad guy

here." Sweat dampened his upper lip. He prayed they believed him, but why would they? There was an arrest warrant out in his name. In the cops' eyes, he was a wanted felon. "Please, listen. Miss Reynolds and I are innocent. I can prove it. Just hold your fire and give me a chance to explain."

Marissa released her grip on the gun, and careful not to make any sudden moves, set the pistol on the floor and stepped away, her hands raised.

He released a shaky breath.

Johnson huddled on the couch, his face buried in his hands.

Ardash cupped his injured arm. Tears streaked his ravaged face.

Uniformed cops and plainclothes detectives crowded the doorway.

For a minute, no one moved.

Mike and Jonas pushed past the cops and rushed into the room. "Scott? Marissa? Are you guys all right?"

"We are now that you're here," Scott said, relief washing through him.

"When you didn't return, we figured something was up." Jonas tugged off his glasses and wiped the smeared lenses. "Good thing we called the cops."

"How did you know we needed help?" Scott asked.

"Yeah. I'd like to know that too," said one of the armed police officers.

Mike looked at Jonas. "Go ahead. You tell him. You're the one who made the connection."

"After you guys left to confront Johnson, I got to thinking." Jonas puffed out his narrow chest. "Johnson couldn't have done everything on his own. Even though he's the DA, he didn't have access to the police files, not all of them. He wouldn't have known about the cell phone in the police evidence locker. Someone with insider knowledge had to have told him." He beamed like he'd won an Olympic gold medal. "That left Detective Sandhu."

Scott puckered his brow. "A lot of cops knew that information. Why did you think Sandhu was our dirty cop?"

"Jonas had the idea to send a couple of cops to Detective Sandhu's home to check out the situation." Mike nodded approvingly. "Only took the attending officers a minute to figure out Sandhu's wife and son were being threatened. And that's when we called in the cavalry." He blew out a breath. "Our only worry was we might be too late."

Scott patted his assistant on the shoulder. "Smart thinking, Jonas. Thank you."

Jonas's cheeks flamed red.

A collective burst of air filled the room, and then a whirlwind of activity ensued.

One of the first cops on the scene lowered his weapon, slipped on latex gloves, and confiscated the gun on the floor and the one on Johnson's desk.

Another cop tugged out a pair of handcuffs and snapped them around Johnson's wrists.

Still another officer cuffed Sandhu, ignoring his protests about his injured arm.

Adrenaline pumped through Scott, firing his muscles. His body twitched. He strode over to Marissa. "You okay?" Inspecting the bleeding wound on her forehead, he winced. The gash was deep and probably required stitches.

A wan smile flickered across her pale face. "I...I think so." She brushed a lock of hair off her forehead. "Where...where did you learn moves like that?" She pointed at Ardash. "That was like something in a movie."

Scott couldn't hold back his grin. "That's what eighteen years of tae kwon do lessons will do."

Marissa's smile widened, and it was as if the sun came out in all its stunning glory. "You really are a hero, aren't you?"

He grinned back. "Couldn't have done it without my trusty sidekick."

A police officer grasped Johnson's arms and lifted his unresisting body off the couch and guided him across the office to the door.

"Officer, wait," Scott said. "I'd like to ask him a few questions."

The cop hesitated, but then he nodded. "Go ahead."

"Why?" Scott demanded. "Why did you do it?"

At first, Johnson didn't seem to hear him, but then he raised his head and met Scott's gaze. "I was a young lawyer like you, just out of law school, and I wanted to be the District Attorney. Marischenko and I have been friends since we were kids. He had connections, and he agreed to help me win the election." He licked his cracked lips. "I owed him."

"You tried to run Marissa down, didn't you? And you followed us that night." Scott's heart rate ramped up as the final pieces fell into place. "You have a black SUV. I've seen it. You brought the vehicle to work once."

Now the wheels were spinning. "You drove an official car to Ashbury and bought Scott Carmichael's necklace from his sister." He spun to Jonas. "Check the vehicle requisition logs. You'll find ADA Johnson signed out a department vehicle the day Loretta Carmichael had her mysterious visitor. The mileage log should confirm that."

Johnson's gelled hair stuck up in spikes around his ravaged face. No longer did he resemble the powerful, arrogant District Attorney of Brunswick.

"Why did you buy Carmichael's chain?" Scott asked. "You were in Marischenko's pocket. Why didn't Loretta just give you the chain?"

He stared at Scott with bloodshot eyes. "Marischenko wanted the necklace, but he didn't trust Loretta. He suspected she'd stolen his personal journal, and he didn't want her to know he was involved in her brother's murder."

"You took my phone from the police evidence locker." Marissa planted her hands on her hips, anger flashing in her eyes. "You're the one on the surveillance tape, aren't you?"

He nodded. "It was almost too easy. No one thought a thing of the DA accessing the evidence locker."

Marissa shook her head, disgust vivid on her face.

Ardash strained against the grip of the officer holding him and shot Johnson a look of pure loathing. "You're a piece of shit, Johnson, and an embarrassment to everything the DA's office stands for. You and your Russian *friend* threatened my family. If a single hair on my wife's or son's head is damaged, I'll come after you, you bastard."

"Easy, Ardash," Scott said. "You heard Jonas. Your family's safe. They're being held in protective custody."

Tears filled the detective's eyes and he turned to Jonas. "Thank you for saving my family." He shifted back to Scott, his gaze pleading. "I...I don't know what to say. I'm sorry, I—"

"You stepped over the line...way over the line." Scott understood why his friend had done what he did, but he couldn't condone his actions, and he didn't forgive him. If events had gone differently, both he and Marissa would be dead. He nodded to the officer holding Ardash and stood back and watched as he and Johnson were led away.

The large office was crowded with uniformed officers and plainclothes detectives, everyone talking at once.

He searched for Marissa amidst the chaos.

She slumped on the couch. Dark circles underscored her eyes, and splotches of dried blood stained her pale cheeks. An officer was asking her questions while a medic tended to the wound on her forehead.

The surge of adrenaline that had fired his blood dissipated, and reality set in. He staggered back as if he'd been punched. He'd come so close to losing her. And it was his fault. If he hadn't interfered and convinced her to take him to see her uncle, none of the frightening events of the past days would have happened.

His fault.

The walls crowded in, the air sucked out of the room.

His fault.

He couldn't breathe. Wheeling around, he lurched

out of the office, past the dumbfounded secretary, the throng of police officers, and along the corridor, past groups of gaping employees to the fire exit. He thrust the door open and leaped down the stairs two at a time. At the lobby floor, he pushed open the door and strode through the vast space onto the busy street.

****

Marissa steered the small rental car down the bumpy, gravel lane and drew to a stop before the old house. Turning off the motor, she studied the rundown, white clapboard bungalow. The house was dark, and the driveway was empty, but she knew he was there, sensed his presence deep inside her heart.

A week had passed since the showdown in Johnson's office, a week since Scott had walked out of the building and disappeared into the night.

Seven long and lonely days and nights of silence.

Even though she'd called his cell phone repeatedly, he didn't answer. Jonas had informed her Scott was busy dealing with the fallout from the events of the past weeks.

She'd been questioned by the police and had endured endless hours of intense interrogation. In their scramble to point the finger of blame, Johnson and Marischenko had sung like the proverbial birds. The authorities had more than enough evidence to convict them of a dozen crimes. Both men were looking at spending the rest of their natural lives in prison.

From what she'd heard, Detective Sandhu's charges would be reduced due to the extenuating circumstances. He'd serve jail time, but his family had survived the threat from the Russian mob. They were lucky. Other people affected by the actions of Johnson and Marischenko weren't so fortunate. Some were dead.

She blinked back the sting of tears. So many lives destroyed, so much sadness, and all because of retribution and revenge. She swallowed over the lump in her throat. Time to put the past behind and move on.

She opened the car door and slid out. Tugging down her sweater, she inhaled the sweet scents of clover and damp earth. The sun cast long shadows across the overgrown yard. Crickets chirped in the tall grass. The rhythmic creak of metal sounded loud in the quiet evening.

She followed the creaking to the back of the house.

Scott sprawled on a wooden porch swing, swinging back and forth in slow, steady motions.

"Hello, Scott."

He stilled, and the creaking stopped. "You shouldn't have come." His voice was rough, as if he had the beginnings of a cold.

She crossed the lawn to the steps. "I had to."

"Why?"

"The charges against you were dropped."

"I know. Jonas called me."

"So it's just *my* phone calls you're not taking." She stepped on the bottom step and climbed until she reached the porch.

"Look, I don't know why you're here, but you shouldn't be."

"Why is that?"

He grimaced. "You know why."

She sat on the seat beside him. Inches separated them, but the void might as well have been a mile. "No, I don't. You'll have to explain."

He threaded his fingers through his blond hair, and for the first time, he looked at her. He leaned closer. His warm fingers brushed her cheek, sliding over her skin. Grasping her chin, he tilted her face to the fading light and studied the healing wound on her forehead. "After everything I've done, I'm surprised you want anything to do with me." He released her and fell back on the seat.

Her heart stuttered at the guilt and misery on his haggard face. He looked like he hadn't slept in days. "None of this was your fault." She clasped his hand between hers. "You know that, right?"

He tensed and sucked in a sharp breath but didn't tug his hand free. "You know that's not true. I lied to you." He blinked, and even in the fading evening light, the gleam of tears shone bright. "And if that weren't bad enough, I used you for my own ends."

Crickets chirped in the deepening dusk. A ray of golden light illuminated an old cement birdbath in the middle of the yard. A bird flapped and splashed in the water.

"Tell me one thing." She inhaled the sweet scent of rising sap. "Was everything a lie?"

"No! Never." He wiped the back of his hand over his mouth. "My feelings were real, the kisses, making love to you…it was all real, but—"

She tightened her grip on his hand and cut him off. "You saved my life."

His eyes were deep pools, hidden in the shadows. "I'm not your hero, Marissa. I'm nobody's hero. Far from it. The best thing for you to do is walk, no, *run*, back to your car and get the hell out of here. I'm toxic. Don't you get that? People around me end up hurt." He jerked his hand free. "Look, you'd better leave. I—"

Placing two fingers over his mouth, she silenced him. "Not all heroes wear capes, Scott. You know that, right?"

Their gazes met and held.

A night bird sang a sweet melody from the old, scabbed apple tree overhanging the porch. An owl hooted, its haunting cry echoing over the darkening yard.

The silence between them buzzed as if alive.

She was afraid he was going to kiss her. Terrified he wasn't.

His gaze focused on her mouth.

She swallowed.

He leaned closer and pressed his mouth to hers.

Rockets blasted, her heart soared, and the heavens realigned, but all too soon, he jerked away, tearing his lips free.

He cupped her chin in the palm of his hand and traced her jawline with his thumb. "You're everything I've ever wanted, every dream I've ever had, but…"

A fist closed over her heart. "But what?"

"I can't ask you to spend your life with a disgraced man."

"Disgraced? You mean the ADA job?"

"That and the fact everyone in town thinks I've betrayed them." His mouth twisted. "They'd be right."

"You're a good man. If people talk, that's their problem. You helped this city. You brought down Marischenko and Johnson." Her chest heaved, her breath rasping in and out as if she'd run a marathon. This was too important to quit now. She had to fight, to convince him of the truth. Her heart was at stake.

"Jonas told me you still have your job. You're the ADA of Brunswick. You should be happy. You have what you've always wanted. The men who murdered your parents are dead or in jail, and you can continue to serve the people of Brunswick."

"I'm not the ADA, not anymore."

"But Jonas said—"

"I resigned this afternoon. I contacted a local legal firm. I'll be working pro bono, helping people who can't afford high-priced lawyers, those in need of justice. It's my way of making amends." He smoothed the palms of his hands on his thighs. "So, you see, I'm moving on."

His words sat like stones in her heart. Countless times over the past seven days, she'd imagined this moment. In every version, once she confessed her love, he'd taken her in his arms and sworn his undying love. But now he was sending her away.

A cold, yawning distance separated them. "That's great." She forced a smile. "This city needs lawyers like you." She stood, her heart heavy. "Well, take care. I guess I'll see you around." With leaden steps, she plodded down the stairs. Tears blurred her vision as she stumbled across the weed-infested lawn to her car.

"Wait, Marissa. You're leaving? Just like that?" He pounded down the steps.

Blinking back tears, she didn't slow her pace.

He grasped her by the shoulders, stopping her. "Marissa, wait. Please. I know you can't ever forgive me, but I want you to stay. Don't you get it? That's what I've been trying to tell you, but I'm afraid, terrified you won't want me. I mean, how could you after the terrible things I've done?" His voice was raw and thick. "I...I love you. I want you to stay with me...forever."

I love you.

She resisted the urge to fall into his embrace. This was too important. She had to be sure. "What are you saying, Scott?"

He threaded his fingers through his hair. "Don't leave, please. I...I don't know what I'd do without you in my life." He released his grip on her shoulders and scrubbed his hands over his face. "I...I need you." His voice thickened, and tears filmed his navy eyes. "I love you, Marissa Reynolds. You, and only you."

His words rang through her heart like a healing balm. With a squeal of joy, she stepped into his embrace and burrowed into his familiar strength.

He drew her closer until their bodies meshed, and their hearts beat as one. His mouth claimed hers, and the final barriers around her heart dissolved.

All too soon, he pulled back and stared into her eyes. "So does this mean you'll stay?"

She struggled to force the words past the thick lump clogging her throat. "You're my hero, Scott Bannister, and you know that the hero always gets the girl." Her mouth trembled with a grin. "Besides, every hero needs a sidekick."

He chuckled. "How about if I'm *your* sidekick? What do you say? We'd make a great team."

She looped her hands around his neck and drew him closer. "Shut up and kiss me."

His eyes sparkled, and his grin widened. "That I can definitely do."

He claimed her mouth in a passionate kiss that made her toes curl. For the first time in years, peace settled over her soul. She'd found her real-life hero. He'd made mistakes, big mistakes, but he was the bravest man she knew, and most importantly, she loved him more than her next breath.

The night bird's melody trilled, mimicking the song in her heart.

A word about the author...

C. B. Clark has always loved reading, especially romances, but it wasn't until she lost her voice for a year that she considered writing her own romantic suspense stories.

She grew up in Canada's Northwest Territories and Yukon. Graduating with a degree in Anthropology and Archaeology, she has worked as an archaeologist and an educator.

She enjoys hiking, canoeing, and snowshoeing with her husband and dog near her home in the wilderness of central British Columbia.

Thank you for purchasing
this publication of The Wild Rose Press, Inc.

For questions or more information
contact us at
info@thewildrosepress.com.

The Wild Rose Press, Inc.
www.thewildrosepress.com

To visit with authors of
The Wild Rose Press, Inc.
join our yahoo loop at
http://groups.yahoo.com/group/thewildrosepress/